A PLACE
FOR THE MIGHTY

Also by Henry Denker:

The Director

The Kingmaker

HENRY DENKER

A PLACE
FOR
THE MIGHTY

A NOVEL ABOUT THE SUPERLAWYERS

DAVID McKAY COMPANY, INC.
New York

A Place for the Mighty

LIBRARY OF CONGRESS CATALOG CARD NUMBER: 73–76561

MANUFACTURED IN THE UNITED STATES OF AMERICA

TO EDITH, MY WIFE

•◦❦ PART ONE ❦◦•

THE
ASSASSINATION

I

He stood on the broad steps studying the words engraved in the faultless marble of the Supreme Court architrave:

EQUAL JUSTICE UNDER LAW

The bright October sun reflecting off the white stone made him blink. He lowered his eyes, letting them travel slowly down the tall milky columns which supported the architrave and guarded the portico of the High Court. Must not move swiftly, must not create suspicion, he cautioned himself. Not if he intended to carry out his purpose here today.

Suddenly from behind him a long line of noisy school children clambered up the marble steps pursued by the warnings of two frantic teachers bringing up the rear. In this instant of surprise he reached involuntarily into his coat. The weapon was still there, strapped to his side. Hard, warm from his tense overheated body, it fit his grip easily. Then, withdrawing his hand he straightened his new tan topcoat and continued up the steps.

Once into the shady area under the portico, he paused to let his eyes adjust. With determination he passed between the parted doors and climbed the few stairs leading into the main rotunda where everything sounded as hushed and quiet as a museum, a hospital. He stared up at the richly colored cof-

3

fered ceiling. He had watched tourists do this on his previous visits when he had come here to observe and to plan. As much as possible, until it was done, he had to seem like any ordinary tourist. So he stared upward and moved slowly toward the area where visitors awaited admission to the courtroom.

As he took his place in line, a voice arrested him. Despite his determination not to, he spun around, tense and fearful, to confront a tall black court attendant, neatly dressed in a dark business suit, simple white shirt, plain blue tie.

"No one is allowed to carry anything into the courtroom," he admonished respectfully.

Did the attendant suspect? Would they search him? He stared, unmoving.

"Your coat," the attendant reminded gently. "All coats, parcels and cameras have to be checked. The checkroom is back down the steps and to your left."

"Oh," the tense visitor responded, realizing now that on his previous visits the weather had been warmer so he had not worn a coat. "Sorry."

"If you'd like photographs of the courtroom or the Justices on the bench you can buy them at the souvenir shop near the exit as you leave."

"Yes. Thanks," the visitor said in a whisper. He wondered whether the attendant would remember him later when undoubtedly he would be questioned. Then, turning, he crossed the corridor, his rubber-soled shoes making a whispering sound against the marble.

He had removed all labels and emptied the pockets of his coat, so he confidently handed it to the attendant, waited for his check, and started back up the few steps in time to see the tourist line beginning to move into the courtroom. He had to force himself not to hurry. Instead he pretended to seem casually interested, staring up at the high ceiling, at the large medallions displaying graven faces of ancient Greek and

Roman gods and goddesses, all of them white. Whiter even than white people ever are.

He took his place in the line as it shuffled forward. In front of him a woman, nasal, Midwestern, was reading to her husband from a guide book:

"Among the faces on the frieze are the goddess Juno, the god Zeus, and the lawgivers Moses and Solon."

Her husband kept staring as he half-listened. He muttered, in an irritated whisper, "Christ! This must have cost millions —billions, maybe!"

"Not billions. Nine million seven hundred thousand. The big thing was the marble. Three million dollars' worth."

"From Italy, I bet. Or some other foreign country."

"It says from Vermont and two other states."

" 'It says.' You believe everything it says?"

Like a shepherd counting sheep, the tall black attendant presided over the line as it passed into the courtroom. Most tourists were surprised at first, expecting to see the enormous courtroom instantly. Instead they were confronted by maroon velvet drapes that reached from the floor to the extremely high ceiling. Only after they passed between the parted drapes was the august courtroom revealed to them. All the while, the attendant kept repeating in a reverent whisper, "Please take seats on the benches to the left. Right side for schoolchildren only. Left side, please."

The visitor again hastily felt for his gun just to be certain, then moved forward, searching for a seat directly on the center aisle. That would place him as close as possible to his target, and more important, in an aisle seat he would have only the person on his left to contend with. When the proper moment came, his right hand and arm would be free to act unhindered. If the person on his left were a woman, so much the better.

Ahead, in the aisle seat of the second row, sat a middle-aged white woman. Perfect. He knew that as soon as he

5

began to sit down she would draw away and give him plenty of room. He was black enough to count on that.

The small, plump woman did pull back. He slipped into the aisle seat to wait. He knew the procedure. At precisely one o'clock, the lunch recess would be over and Court would reconvene. The Marshal would make the announcement, the Justices would file in, and court would be in session. But only for a very short time on this particular afternoon.

Now he sensed the woman studying him. Resuming his tourist guise as he had practiced it every day before the mirror in his small room, he stared ahead at the huge mahogany bench and the maroon velvet drape behind it. He gaped up at the clock high over the bench, then at the pillars of veined rosy marble, richer, warmer than the pure, obstinate white of the exterior.

Around him, all voices were hushed. Before him and beyond the mahogany railing, attorneys in frock coats, waiting to argue their cases, were studying papers or talking gravely, unheard, performing like marionettes to whom voices had not yet been assigned. Two minutes to one. Any moment now the Marshal of the Court would receive the signal.

The woman beside him was staring again. Deliberately he faced her, engaged her eyes. She looked away at once, in any direction but his. That was good. He wouldn't want her to be able to give an accurate description of him later.

"A small, dark-skinned Negro. With one of those Afro haircuts, except not so high. And young. I'm sure he was young. And I think he had on a plain suit."

That was about all she would be able to give them, a description that fit thousands of young black men in Washington.

A voice called for order. An immediate and respectful silence fell.

He held his breath, for he knew the Justices would begin to

6

appear from behind the huge maroon drape. Nine men in imposing judicial robes. Eight white faces, one black. But not too black. Just dark enough to show how liberal the power structure was.

They took places, each standing before his own high-backed swivel chair. "Oyez, oyez, oyez!" the voice of the Marshal of the Court rang out. "All persons having business before the Honorable, the Supreme Court of the United States, are admonished to draw near and give their attention, for the Court is now sitting. God save the United States and this Honorable Court!"

The nine grave men slipped into their black leather chairs behind the awesome mahogany bench. On a signal from the Chief Justice, the Clerk announced:

"Stockholders' Committee versus The Delaware and Great Southern Railroad."

A lawyer, white-haired and frock-coated, took up a handful of papers from the desk and moved to the lectern. He cleared his throat, adjusted the microphone before him. "May it please this august Court . . ."

The visitor wasn't listening. He was too busy seeking out his target; the judge sitting one in from the extreme right, a man who looked fairly young but only in contrast to his colleagues. Otherwise he was nondescript, totally lacking in distinguishing characteristics. His was not the sort of noble face one admired in friezes or statues of famous lawgivers.

He had seen Justice Miller before. Several times. He had studied his habits. The way he wore his glasses, and took them off to polish them. The way he shuffled the papers before him, glancing down at them and then up at the pleading attorneys. The habit he had of leaning forward from time to time to reach for his water glass. When Miller did that, he was lower down in his chair and much less visible.

So it would have to be done immediately after he had had his drink of water. Then he would be sitting up straight in his high-back chair, presenting the best possible target. In a way, the very next time he put down his glass, Justice Harvey Miller would be giving the signal for his own execution.

Miller was reaching for the glass now.

The visitor slid his hand inside his jacket. His fingers curved around the snub-nosed gun. It felt hot. He gripped it tightly, knowing that from this moment on things must work precisely as he had practiced them. Draw and rise in the same single motion. Aim and fire without hesitation—and without any foolish attempt to shout brave defiant slogans for the media to seize on. Do the job right! And to hell with empty gestures!

Justice Harvey Miller picked up his glass, sipped from it, put it down. Finally he leaned back in his large chair, his head pressed against the rich black leather.

The visitor rose, not fully drawing the pistol until he was on his feet. He pointed it at Miller and pulled the trigger three times in rapid succession.

Even before the explosions echoed, he had leaped from his place, raced up the aisle. The same attendant who minutes ago had requested him to check his coat, now intercepted him. They struggled for a moment until he forced his way past the startled man. Still clutching his revolver, he raced between the maroon curtains, out the high, wide door, and across the corridor. But there, ahead of him at the door, stood a uniformed officer.

He knew at once he had to try the graceful oval staircase. If he could make it to the top of the five floors, there was an escape door there, his only chance.

He reached the elegant white marble stairs, seized the shining carved bronze rail, vaulted over the heavy polished chain which kept the public out. He started circling up the stairs, two and three at a time. Below him, a contingent of Court police in uniform, guns drawn, raced to the foot of the stairs. Two started up after him. The others scattered in different directions.

Amid the hysterical cries of women and children, they were shouting at him to halt, threatening to fire. He glanced back in time to see one of the pursuing policemen raise his pistol. A shot rang out as he flattened himself against the marble steps. He turned, fired down twice, started climbing again. It was two more flights at the most. Two more. Another shot rang out. He felt the slug burn by him, heard it crash against the marble, stone splinters stinging his cheek. He pushed himself on, forcing to the back of his mind that he felt winded, and that there was a pain in his chest. Only one more floor, and he could make it to the exit, to freedom.

But as he rounded the final level and raised his head, there at the top step were two police officers, guns cocked and ready. He stopped dead.

"Drop that gun!" one of them shouted.

He hesitated only an instant. Then he flung the gun hard over the carved bronze railing, sending it crashing loudly onto the marble floor far below.

"Stand!" the policeman ordered. "Clasp your hands on your head! Now turn around!" He obeyed each command mechanically. With his back to them now, he heard their steps coming close, then their tense breathing. Now two powerful hands seized him, searched him swiftly. The cold metal cuffs snapped around his wrists.

Chief of Court Police John F. Edwards was in his basement office speaking into the phone when the prisoner was led in by six policemen.

"In that case, we'd better get the M. P. Medical Examiner over here right away!" He hung up the phone, glared at the prisoner and the two men who held him by the arms. "That's right, the Medical Examiner! Death was instantaneous." He studied the prisoner, who stared back dully, betraying no feeling.

Edwards lifted his phone again. "Get me the Metropolitan

Police. Better get the FBI, too. This comes under Section 1114. A Justice is a Federal officer."

Edwards hung up the phone, turned to his men. "Adamski and Frisch, remain here with the prisoner! The rest of you get up there to help with the crowd. And to assist the FBI and the police when they get here."

Adamski and Frisch retained their hold on the prisoner, but as the other four left, Frisch called out, "The weapon's somewhere in the stairwell of the right staircase."

"No statements!" Edwards ordered. "I don't want any statements made about the case in front of the suspect! This is going to be handled right, strictly by the book. This isn't Dallas. We don't want any Lee Harvey Oswalds here!"

The four men retreated, holstering their pistols. Adamski asked, "Shall we lock him in the cell, sir?"

"No need. Homicide'll be here in a few minutes. Hold him here till then. Don't question him! Don't touch him! And don't let *him* touch anything! I don't want him to have contact with anything till the FBI technicians get through with him." Chief Edwards rose, glared at the suspect, and left to take the elevator to the main floor.

By this time the alarm had gone out to all security forces in the District of Columbia. For there was concern that the assassination of Justice Miller might prove to be only the first move in a coordinated effort to disrupt and overthrow the Government of the United States.

In the White House, the President was interrupted at a meeting of the National Security Council and rushed to the safety of an upper floor.

Over Indiana, aboard Air Force Two whose passengers included the Vice President, the pilot received radio instructions to remain aloft and take alternate route C prescribed in his flight plan. He was not to land until notified.

At the State Department, the Secretary was rushed to a

10

sealed room in the basement to remain there under strict security.

At the Senate and House office buildings and in both Chambers and cloakrooms, uniformed and plainclothes security men appeared suddenly and in large numbers.

In minutes the entire Capitol and the Government were secured, holding tight until it became clear whether this was an isolated, shocking crime, or the first act of an organized conspiracy.

In the main rotunda of the Courthouse, Chief of Police Edwards found the schoolchildren lined up on one side. They had been terrorized into a hush, except for two little girls and one boy who were weeping hysterically. Their teachers kept up a continual flow of reassuring talk while embracing the children to comfort them.

All other visitors had been herded to the opposite side of the rotunda. They stood mute and frightened, except for an occasional indistinct whisper. One tourist approached a policeman in the center of the floor. "Please, officer," he asked, timidly, "my wife has a kidney condition. She has to go to the bathroom."

Chief Edwards, who was passing close by, stepped in. "Let her go," he said, "but get some identification first. And keep everybody else here until Homicide releases them. Everybody in that courtroom is a potential eyewitness!"

Even as he spoke, members of the Homicide Division of the District of Columbia Metropolitan Police were racing up the wide marble steps of the Supreme Court of the United States.

In the courtroom, the Metropolitan Police Medical Examiner, the FBI technician, and the Court doctor worked separately and silently, each man making his own observations and notes. While one examined and photographed the Jus-

11

tice's bullet-damaged chair, the other examined the position of the body.

Someone had thrown a cloth across it so that only the black shoes and the hem of the Justice's robe protruded. The FBI technician knelt down and pulled back the cloth to study the victim's head. The eyes were still open, the head twisted at an odd angle. On the right side of the face was a large wound where blood had begun to cake. At the top and back of the left side of the head a large jagged hole brutally revealed where one bullet had exited.

The FBI man turned to the Court doctor. "How soon afterward did you get here?"

"Three minutes, four at the most," Dr. Victor Blaine said.

"Head wound like that, penetration of skull and brain, death must have been instantaneous."

"Had to be."

"Any other wounds?"

The doctor pulled the sheet down further to reveal two other wounds, one in the right side of the chest, one through the left shoulder.

"But it was the head wound that did it," Dr. Blaine said.

The M.P. pathologist interrupted them, "Doctor . . ." He pointed to several white and reddish specks stuck to the maroon velvet backdrop. Blaine examined the area closely, the FBI man peering over his shoulder.

"Bits of bone. And there, that looks like brain tissue," Blaine decided.

"Yes," the pathologist agreed. Using sterile forceps he carefully removed the bits of bone and tissue, placing them in small, sterile, transparent plastic boxes.

"We'll take those, if you want," the FBI man volunteered.

"You'll get them eventually, I know. But in a case as important as this one, I want to check the protocol," the M.P. pathologist said. He turned away to make his first official note on the form.

Victim . . . adult, male, Caucasian, tentatively identified as

12

Harvey B. Miller. Occupation, Justice of the Supreme Court of the United States. Apparent cause of death, gunshot.

At that moment a courtroom attendant entered quickly from the Justices' chambers to gesture Blaine aside. He whispered something to the doctor. They both left hurriedly.

In his chambers, Supreme Court Justice Benjamin Robertson lay on his tufted leather couch, his secretary hovering nervously over him. The Justice, a man in his middle seventies with short, unruly white hair, was still in his black robe, and he was breathing more deeply than a comfortable man would have need to. He inhaled so determinedly that he caused himself to wheeze at the deepest point of each breath. It was this sound which had alarmed his secretary and caused her to send for help.

Followed by the Marshal of the Court, Dr. Blaine approached Robertson's chambers. Acting less concerned than he actually was, the doctor entered casually, passed through the outer office into the study where he pretended to discover the Justice by accident.

But Robertson rasped, "I'm all right! I don't need you. My heart's perfectly fine. I was just trying to resolve the tension by some deep breathing." He turned on his secretary. "Did you call this medical vulture?" Robertson said it gruffly but without hostility, for Blaine had nursed him through some bad afternoons when his heart had acted up. And Blaine had been the one who discovered that the Justice needed heart surgery, saving him from a serious attack or worse. After that, self-conscious with anyone who knew the real imminence of his mortality, Justice Robertson always made it a point to joke about Blaine. But he always submitted himself to examination whenever the doctor suggested it.

"Do you mind, sir?" Blaine asked.

"Does it matter if I mind?" Robertson grumbled. Grudgingly, he turned toward the doctor.

Blaine pushed aside the black robe, pulled open the string

tie the Justice always wore, and unbuttoned the shirt. He slipped in the flat cold disk of his stethoscope. As Blaine moved the instrument from spot to spot, Robertson used the silent moments to ask, "He *is* dead, isn't he?"

Blaine nodded.

"Tragic. Young man. Bright liberal young man. With a young family, too." Robertson was silent for a moment. "I didn't even see it. I had just looked down to consult my papers because something the attorney was saying didn't square with my memory of his brief. Between the time I looked down and the time I heard the shots, only an instant later, a young man had been killed. Killed!"

"They've caught him," the Marshal of the Court started to say.

Robertson interrupted, "I don't want to know anything about it! Or about him! In the event we have occasion to rule on it later."

The Marshal nodded, accepting the order of silence.

Blaine had finished his examination. As the Justice was buttoning his shirt, he said, "I don't suppose you'd take a sedative if I prescribed one."

Without looking up, Robertson answered, "I think that today . . . yes . . . today, I would take one."

"I'll have it sent up from the infirmary at once. Then I suggest you go home. Spend the rest of the day in bed. Maybe the next two days."

"What did you find?" Robertson challenged, suspecting that his condition was worse than the doctor had indicated.

"What I found," Blaine began, speculating on how frank to be, "was a patient who was suffering from considerable tension after witnessing a murder. Under normal conditions I would give such a patient a generous shot of Valium and put him to bed for several days. But since this patient is both irascible and stubborn, I am prescribing only a mild sedative by mouth and one day's rest."

Robertson finally relented, forcing a small smile. "I'll out-

14

live you, you young quack." But more soberly, he asked, "I have a lecture scheduled for tomorrow night at the law school . . ."

"I would cancel it," Blaine advised softly.

"Well, I'll see."

Robertson's phone rang once and then stopped. In a few moments, his secretary entered the room.

"Doctor, if you're finished here, they want you to take another look at that woman."

"What woman?" Robertson asked instinctively. "Was there a woman involved in this too?"

"Only an eyewitness. She was sitting alongside the . . ." But Blaine interrupted himself, remembering that the old man had forbid any discussion of the crime. Robertson nodded, approving the doctor's silence.

Blaine turned to the secretary. "I'll send up a sedative. Make sure he takes two pills. And see that he gets home. Not *starts* home. *Gets* home!"

"Yes, Doctor."

In the infirmary of the Courthouse, Mrs. Evalyn Huffman, a short, plump woman in her middle fifties, was lying atop the stark hospital bed. The nurse had removed her shoes so her short, stubby, stockinged feet rested comfortably on the tight white sheet. Mrs. Huffman was breathing easily but shallowly. Behind her rimless glasses her eyes tended to close as if she might doze off. Just outside the door, Captain Kaska of Metropolitan Homicide waited.

When Dr. Blaine arrived, Kaska took him aside. "Let me know if she can face the suspect. We want an identification as soon as possible in this case."

"I put her under sedation. She was almost hysterical."

"I know," Chief Kaska said, "that's why I sent for you. Take a look at her."

They entered together. While Blaine examined Mrs. Huffman, Kaska elicited from her that she was from Cam-

15

den, New Jersey, that she had come to Washington with her husband, an attorney. While he was conferring on a matter on behalf of his client at the Federal Trade Commission, Mrs. Huffman had decided to visit the Supreme Court, which she had never seen before. They were planning to drive home again this evening. She hoped that they would be allowed to go. Would they?

The captain avoided answering by confronting the doctor, "Well?"

"I think Mrs. Huffman is in condition to face the suspect," Blaine said.

"I'd rather talk to my husband first," she protested.

"We have to do this as soon as possible," Kaska said, "or else legally it might not be a satisfactory identification. Before we could locate your husband and get him here, too much time would have elapsed. You *can* identify him, can't you?"

"Oh, I'd know him anywhere," Mrs. Huffman protested. "I was this close to him," she said, reaching out to touch the nurse who stood beside the bed. "This close!"

"Good," Captain Kaska said. "Shall we go?"

In the office of the Chief of Court Police, the suspect was no longer manacled. He was standing alongside the Chief's desk, where the FBI technician, transparent plastic gloves covering his own hands, was treating the suspect's black hand with a thick white liquid. After dipping the nylon brush into a dish of melted paraffin, he meticulously painted the suspect's right hand, covering the thumb, forefinger and most of the top of the hand up to the wrist. The technician was especially careful with the connecting webbed area between the thumb and the base of the forefinger.

Captain Kaska of Homicide had Mrs. Huffman wait at the door and he went in alone. The FBI man very carefully lifted the hardened paraffin from the suspect's hand and placed it in a clean plastic bag, which his assistant labeled. He called

16

for a fresh basin of warm paraffin to process the suspect's left hand, and then turned his attention to the captain.

"I want a face-to-face," Kaska said. "Will we be in your way? Time is important."

"I know. Okay. Do it while I'm taking his left hand," the FBI man said. His assistant was already bringing the dish of fresh paraffin.

Kaska went to the door, gently ushered Mrs. Huffman into the room, let her stare at the suspect who looked down at the floor. She was about to say something, but Kaska interrupted. "Wait for the tape recorder. Case as important as this one, I don't want any slip-ups."

"Yes sir," she said. "Only I wish Harry was here."

The tape recorder was brought in, set up swiftly, as the FBI man painted the suspect's left hand with fresh warm wax. Once the assisting detective from Homicide gave the signal, Kaska referred to his notes and asked, "Are you Evalyn Huffman of 138 Converse Street, Camden, New Jersey?"

"Yes."

"I want you to look at this suspect, unnamed. I ask if you ever saw him before?"

"Yes. I sat next to him in the courtroom when he fired the shots and killed that judge."

"You are sure this is the man who sat beside you, whom you saw stand up, draw a pistol, and fire those shots?"

"I'm sure," she said, but not too firmly. "If you want me to be positive let me see the side of his face. After all, it was the side of his face I saw mostly."

"Stand erect!" Kaska ordered. "Turn your head!"

The suspect straightened up, raised his head and turned, all without looking at Mrs. Huffman.

"That's the man, no question. The Afro hair, but not so bushy. The profile. The same color gray suit. I'd know him anywhere."

"Thank you, Mrs. Huffman," Kaska said, indicating to his assistant that he turn off the recorder. "Take Mrs. Huffman

17

back to the infirmary. I think she might need another sedative. And find her husband!"

Kaska waited as the FBI investigator finished the second paraffin lift. The new topcoat lying on a chair provoked him, and he picked it up. The FBI man explained, "Only coat left in the checkroom when all the others were let go."

"His?"

"Pretty sure."

"How?"

"Size is right. And all the labels have been cut out."

"To conceal his identity. Premeditation. Murder One," Kaska stated.

"Right," the FBI technician said, "and I have a hunch we can corroborate that when we finish with the gun."

"They find it yet?"

"Yeah. Funny how far from the stairwell it was. Must have hit the floor, bounced, struck a wall and slid along the marble floor about forty feet."

"Damaged?"

"Not enough to bother the lab," the FBI man said, as he transferred the freshly lifted paraffin cast into the second sterile plastic bag. He tied that bag and labeled it himself.

Just then there appeared in the doorway the tall, neatly dressed courtroom attendant who earlier had instructed the assassin to check his coat. He glanced at the suspect with obvious hostility, "I'd know that black sonofabitch anywhere!"

"Hold it!" Captain Kaska said. "I want it on tape." He signaled his assistant to start the machine again. Once it was rolling, he asked, "Your name, address and occupation?"

"Harley Bevans, 1227 Madison Street, Northwest. Attendant in the courtroom here."

"Where is here?"

"Why, the Supreme Court, sir."

"Okay. Now take a good look at the suspect."

"Yes, sir."

"Have you seen him before?"

18

"Yes, sir."

"Where and under what circumstances?" Kaska asked.

"In the visitors' line just outside the courtroom. I asked him to go check his coat. He went away, came back without his coat and got in line. When he entered the courtroom I noticed him again."

"You saw him enter the courtroom, you're sure?"

"Yes, sir. Sure. I saw him start running out, too."

"Describe that."

"When I heard the shots, I ran inside and down the aisle. He came toward me. We struggled a moment. He shoved me aside and ran out."

"And you're sure this is the man you saw all three times?"

"Yes, sir. As I said, I'd know him anywhere."

"Thank you."

Captain Kaska turned to the FBI man. "If you're done with him, we'll take him over to Headquarters and book him."

"Carefully, I hope," the FBI man said.

"Don't worry, we're not going to risk any Miranda violations in this one. Everything according to the book!"

"Only two identification witnesses?" the FBI man asked.

"We've got a hundred more, if we need them. But on a face-to-face I wanted only the best two," Captain Kaska said.

"Right!" the FBI man agreed.

For purposes of safety and secrecy, they did not take the prisoner down the wide front steps of the Courthouse. Instead they chose a private side entrance and took him out unseen.

In the Washington office of *The New York Times* Fred Anthony, Bureau Chief, was searching for a lead. He ran the eighth piece of paper into his typewriter.

"Extremism in the cause of freedom is no vice. . . ." Thus spoke a one-time candidate for the high office of the Presidency of this country. How those words echo through the hallowed halls of the Supreme Court of the United States on this day when an as yet unidentified right-wing extremist fired three shots that struck down one of the few young liberal voices on our highest Court and brought this Nation to a new threshold of shame and disaster. Have we reached a time in our national life when the Supreme Court of this nation can itself be overruled by an assassin's bullet? When the voices of liberalism, few as they are becoming, can be stilled by a madman?

For the first time since he had tackled the piece almost an hour ago, Anthony's column was going along well. Suddenly, against all the instructions he had given the switchboard, the phone on his desk rang.

"Sonofabitch!" he exploded and lifted the phone. "I'm busy!"

Before he could hang up, he recognized the voice of one of his legmen. "I just got word from one of my sources in the Court. No identification yet. But the assassin is black!"

"Black?" Anthony was stunned. "Are you sure?"

"Black!" the legman repeated.

"I don't believe it! Why would a black man kill a liberal judge like Miller?"

"This source is never wrong. Black!"

"Let me know when they make a positive identification," Anthony said, still doubting the accuracy of the source. Then he hung up. Turning back to his typewriter, he ripped out the half page of copy, pondered it for a time, and finally set it aside. He lit a new cigarette, poured himself a fresh cup of strong coffee from the electric pot on the table next to his desk, and settled down to begin again. By the time he had finished his coffee, he was ready to start typing.

The bloody history of this nation in the past decade, abroad and at home, leads every responsible citizen to ask himself what we have done to this precious system of ours to create a climate of such futility that otherwise decent men are driven to

20

acts of violence and terror because they feel they have no redress even in our highest Court. The very protectors of our freedoms and our Constitutional rights have become the targets of those whom our inequities have driven to such extremes.

The new day that dawned in Brown vs The Board of Education and came to an untimely end when Richard Nixon ruthlessly persisted in inflicting his Southern strategy on the Supreme Court of these United States has today reaped its bloody harvest. Whoever this new murderer turns out to be, and whatever his insane delusion is, the guilt lies also with us who have permitted, aided and abetted this vile frustration, caused it to accumulate and boil over in senseless killing. By our own iniquities we may have created a new Nat Turner.

Yes, Anthony felt, now he was under way, really under way.

At Metropolitan Police Headquarters, his hands again manacled behind him, with a Homicide detective holding him by each arm, the prisoner was hauled before the booking sergeant who began to fill out the required Form PD 111.

"Name?"

The prisoner did not answer. The sergeant repeated the question, not once but several times. The prisoner remained silent. He was not hostile or defiant, only absent and remote.

"Search him!" the sergeant commanded.

But after he was thoroughly searched, turned this way and that, his pockets emptied, they still had found no identification. No wallet, no railroad, bus or airline ticket, only some money amounting to fourteen dollars and seventy-three cents.

The sergeant tried once more, "Name? Age? Draft status?" But this time he did not expect answers, and when none came, he shook his head and wrote in the proper places on the 111: "Refuses name. Refuses age. Refuses." Further down, where the form provided for it, he wrote in, "Prisoner, black adult male, held on charge of homicide with gun, com-

21

mitted on this date on premises of Supreme Court Building against adult male Caucasian, identified as Harvey B. Miller."

Then the sergeant looked across at the prisoner and said to the detectives, "Okay, mug him, print him. And read him the warning!"

When the prisoner had been photographed and finger-printed, he was led to the small bare interrogation room where Victor Kaska, Captain of Homicide, waited. Once the prisoner was seated, Kaska signaled his tape-recorder operator to turn on the machine. Meticulously, Kaska read from a form he held out far enough so that he didn't require his glasses.

> You are under arrest. Before we ask you any questions you must understand what your rights are. You have the right to remain silent, you are not required to say anything to us at any time or to answer any questions. Anything you say can be used against you in court. You have a right to talk to a lawyer for advice before we question you and to have him with you during the questioning. If you cannot afford a lawyer and want one, a lawyer will be appointed for you. If you want to answer questions now without a lawyer present, you will still have the right to stop answering at any time. You also have a right to stop answering at any time until you talk to a lawyer.

Then Kaska waited for a reaction. None came. After a longer time than was usual, he presented a form to the prisoner.

"You sign this. Here."

The prisoner neither looked at the form nor raised his eyes toward Kaska. The captain went on to explain, "It's a form that simply says that I read you the instruction that I just read you. It doesn't incriminate you in any way. It simply says, I read it, you heard it. That's all. Here, see for yourself."

Kaska turned the form toward the prisoner.

"You *can* read, can't you?"

The prisoner did not respond.

22

One of Kaska's assistants leaned over and whispered to his captain, "I think he's on the nod. We ought to test him."

"Uh, uh!" Kaska countermanded. "We don't want to take any chances on defective self-incrimination. Not with this one. Everything has to be airtight. We don't want another Dallas here."

Kaska turned back to the prisoner. Speaking as if to a child or a foreigner unfamiliar with the language, he asked slowly, *"Did you understand me? Do you want to make a voluntary statement?"*

"No need," the prisoner mumbled, the first words he'd spoken since his capture. "No need. I did it."

"Did what?" Kaska asked, seeking a more specific confession.

"Shot him. I shot him."

Kaska glanced at his assistants. "You men heard that, didn't you? Call a secretary. I want to get a signed statement."

One of the assistants left the room. Then Kaska returned his attention to the prisoner. "Do you have a lawyer? Do you want a lawyer? *Do you want to call a lawyer?"*

The prisoner's lips twitched, though his eyes did not focus or turn toward Kaska. He finally spoke in an almost indistinct mumble, very briefly, no more than a few syllables. But what he said caused Kaska to look up at his assistant in surprise.

"Did you get that?" Kaska asked.

"I think . . . I think he said Lincoln Winkler."

"Winkler? Jesus, not Winkler!" Kaska turned back to the prisoner. "Did you say 'Lincoln Winkler'?"

The prisoner half-nodded and repeated a bit more distinctly this time, "Lincoln . . . Winkler. . . ."

Kaska looked up at his assistant. "Oh, Christ! He turns every case into a circus!" Kaska rose, signaled his assistant to join him outside the door.

"He strike you as a militant?" Kaska asked, his voice low and tense.

"Doesn't have the attitude. Doesn't have the lingo. Unless he's high."

"So where does he come off asking for Linc Winkler?" Then he added with great concern, "One thing, we better get a lawyer over here right away. Get Public Defender Service on the phone!"

PART TWO
THE LAWYERS

Because of the urgency of the situation, Kaska himself made the call to Public Defender Service. But he might have foreseen the result. As always, they were overburdened with more cases than they could handle and no attorney was in the office or free to appear on behalf of the prisoner.

So Kaska quickly called the administrators of the Criminal Justice Act. That office was set up to supply counsel for indigent defendants in criminal cases. They kept a roster of practicing trial attorneys who, barring other commitments, agreed to make themselves available to the undefended poor at the nominal fees the law provided.

Once he discovered the urgent matter on which Kaska was calling, the administrator promised to find an attorney as swiftly as possible. The first two names on his list proved to be attorneys engaged in trials. The third was Scott Ingram, of the firm of Ingram, March, Clark and Valentine. He called at once.

"Ingram, March . . ." the operator began, but the administrator cut in.

"Mr. Ingram, please! Urgent!"

"Which Mr. Ingram?" the operator asked politely.

"Mr. Scott Ingram! And hurry!"

"Which Mr. Scott Ingram?" the operator asked, unhurried.

"Why? Do they come in sets?" the administrator demanded curtly.

"We have two Mr. Ingrams. Mr. Scott Ingram the Second. And Mr. Scott Ingram the Third."

The administrator impatiently explained the nature of his call. "Then you must want Mr. Ingram, the Third," the operator suggested, and she began to put the call through.

Scott Ingram the Third was in his shirtsleeves, working at his desk, trying to eat a late lunch and at the same time listen to the radio to follow the developments in the shocking assassination of Justice Miller. The radio droned on repeating most of what was already known. The Attorney General had issued a statement saying there was no evidence of a plot. The rumor that Justice Benjamin Robertson had suffered a heart attack and was hospitalized had proved to be unfounded. The identity of the assassin was still unknown.

Scott Ingram bit into his sandwich and began to concentrate on the transcript of an examination before trial in an anti-trust suit in which he was assisting one of the senior partners of the firm.

With his mouth full of ham on rye, he had difficulty replying when the administrator demanded, "Scott Ingram the Third?" But by the time he discovered the nature of the call, Scott Ingram had pushed his sandwich away and was sitting up, erect and tense.

"Can you get down to headquarters at once?" the administrator asked.

Scott surveyed the desk covered with testimony and other papers. In that moment of hesitation, the administrator said, "If you're too busy, I'll try someone else. I've got others on the list."

But Scott answered quickly, "I'll get there. Right away!"

"Good," the administrator said wearily. "Ask for Captain Kaska."

On the way to police headquarters, Scott Ingram the Third

28

pondered that conversation. The way the administrator had enunciated "the Third," the swiftness with which he offered to call another attorney, the diffident manner in which he had said, good, when Scott agreed to appear—all of it added up to the same damned burden he had carried from the moment that he had been christened with that name.

It hadn't been so bad in his early years when he was sequestered in fine private schools with boys of his own social group. But once he had gotten into college he had become terribly sensitive. It had almost resulted in his quitting the basketball team when the coach, as a joke, had assigned him the number three. He refused to wear it and a bitter argument had ensued, and though he had gone on to become all-Ivy forward in his senior year, he and the coach were never on the best of terms after that early encounter.

In law school it had been even worse. When the mix of students became more densely Jewish, Italian, Irish and black instead of predominantly WASP, Scott became even more self-conscious. And when cases came up in class in which the appeals to the Supreme Court had been argued by Scott Ingram the Second, then Scott Ingram the Third would have gladly traded places with any other student.

On Law Review, where he was the only non-Jew who had qualified, he was known as the house gentile or the *shabbos goy*. But it was not so bad there because by that time there was great affection mixed in with the joking. At least there he was accepted for what he was—one of the handful of the brightest students in the class.

He wondered sometimes, as right now, whether he had signed on to make himself available under the Criminal Justice Act in order to accomplish a needed public service, or to serve his own need to be more fully accepted by his law school friends.

His father always kidded about that. But then his father had a patronizing attitude toward all the young men who had recently come into the law, and especially into his firm. "Law

29

school liberals" his father called them. They were the young lawyers who would agree to work for his firm and other firms of similar stature only after being permitted a two-year period of service as store-front lawyers or Public Defenders. But if you wanted the best of today's young graduates, he would say, then that was the kind of indulgence you had to agree to.

What irritated Scott most about his father's attitude was his confident expectation that Scott and all his young colleagues were simply playing with the idea of public service. That once they got a taste of the big money they would forget their idealistic notions and settle down to the practice of law as it had always been carried on by firms in the tradition of Ingram, March, Clark and Valentine, serving the nation's leading corporations.

It was partly because of this attitude that Scott had moved out of the family house and taken a modest flat in a middle-class part of Washington. It was the reason Scott insisted on reporting not to his father, but to the head of the litigation department of the firm, and why his name took its place on the firm's letterhead strictly in order of seniority, despite the fact that the name Scott Ingram the Second, was at the head of the list.

One thing he could say for his father, when Scott or any of the young men in the firm took on an assignment to defend an indigent person, all the facilities of the office were made available, as if this were indeed a paying client. But whether that policy was an act of devotion to justice or merely an exercise in vanity, Scott was never quite sure.

But there was one certainty. Scott Ingram the Third had a quite different view of the law than his father. And a different view of life. He would practice in his own way. Live his own life. And until he had settled his own career objectives he would neither marry nor become seriously involved with any one girl. During his last year in law school there had been an intense and painful affair with a beautiful and bright Jewish girl which she ended when they graduated. He would never allow that to happen again.

When Scott Ingram introduced himself at Metropolitan Police headquarters, Captain Kaska led him down a hallway and opened the conference room door. The prisoner, who was handcuffed to the arm of a heavy chair, didn't even turn to see who was entering. Kaska glanced at Scott, and the look said, unenvyingly, There's your client.

"Do you have to keep him manacled?" Scott asked. "I don't like to talk to a client under such circumstances."

"Ordinarily, no. But in this case, yes. We don't want anything to go wrong."

"I understand," Scott said softly, starting into the room. Kaska waited only long enough to close the door behind him.

As Scott approached, the prisoner sat motionless, head down, staring at the floor, still not acknowledging Scott's presence.

"My name is Scott Ingram. I'm your lawyer." The prisoner remained silent, remote. "I've been assigned to represent you. You can trust me because I work for you and only you. Do you understand?"

The accused man gave no response.

"Everything you tell me will be held in complete confidence. I'm like a priest. Or a doctor. Even if you tell me that you're guilty, that it was you who killed Justice Miller, I would keep that in strictest confidence. So you can be completely frank with me. You'll be helping yourself if you tell me the whole truth. Especially if you *are* guilty."

Scott paused, hoping the young, thin black man would turn to him.

"In a short time, they'll be taking you across the street to the Courthouse to plead before a magistrate. I have to know how to proceed, what to say. But unless you talk to me, tell me what happened . . ."

31

It wasn't working, so Scott decided on a different attack. "Then tell me some things *not* connected with the crime. About yourself. Any prior convictions?"

For the first time the prisoner responded, vaguely shaking his head. Scott felt encouraged. "The Captain said you're not a heroin addict. That's true, isn't it?"

The prisoner reluctantly extended his free arm so that Scott could push back the sleeve and examine the inside of the arm. As Kaska had said, no tracks. "But they think you're high from something else," Scott said. "Are you? Let me see your eyes."

The prisoner hesitated, then slowly turned to face Scott who studied not only the accused man's eyes but his entire face. He was about the same age Scott was, in his late twenties. His eyes did not betray any drug-related myopia, nor did they show fear. Instead Scott found a distant look in them, something suggesting shock, a total remoteness which seemed to signify only that he was not aware of the serious degree of his jeopardy.

"I understand you wouldn't tell them your name. Is that true?" Scott asked.

The prisoner nodded and started to turn away.

"Listen to me! No matter what you did, I can help you. But you have to cooperate. Tell me your name. Where you live."

The prisoner averted his eyes.

Scott waited, then said, "At least tell me why you won't answer."

"Winkler. I want Lincoln Winkler," the prisoner blurted out.

"Winkler? You know Winkler? Then I'll find him, no matter where he is, but I have to tell him who asked me to call. I'll need your name."

The prisoner didn't answer.

"Do you know Winkler?" The prisoner shook his head. "Has he ever represented anyone you know, any friend?"

32

Another small, timid, negative gesture. "Then you only know him from what you've read in the papers or seen on TV. Is that right?"

The prisoner nodded.

"Look, Winkler's the busiest civil-rights lawyer in the country. He's got a schedule jammed with cases. I can't promise that if I reach him he'll come, but I'll do my best. I promise you that."

The prisoner looked across at Scott. He seemed reassured, almost thankful. Scott used that moment to ask his name once again, and this time he was successful.

"Midge," the young man said, "Midge Grove."

"Is that your full name?"

"Midgely Grove," the young man amended.

"Is there any family you want me to notify?"

"No family."

"Families are a lot more loyal than you think . . ."

"No family," he said, closing the subject.

A single knock on the door announced Inspector Kaska.

"Counselor, I don't want to break in, but we just got a call from the Federal Attorney's office. They've drawn up their complaint, and they're waiting across the street to plead your client."

"Okay. Just one more minute." After Kaska withdrew, Scott turned to Grove. "Do you want to tell me now? Did you do it?" Grove did not answer. "Then may I give them your name?" Scott asked.

Grove hesitated, finally nodding his head, Yes.

Outside headquarters a police van was backing up, forcing the TV trucks and the reporters to give way. Two Homicide detectives, manacled to a black man, marched grimly out of the door to the back entrance of the van. Reporters crowded in on them, photographers held their cameras high to catch them. As the door slammed shut and the lock clicked, the van pulled away in the direction of the Federal Courthouse.

Reporters followed on foot, and TV trucks pulled away swiftly, their tires leaving black scars on the pavement. At the same time, an unmarked sedan quietly left a side entrance of headquarters. Inside, Scott Ingram and his client rode to the Federal Courthouse two blocks away. There, unnoticed, the prisoner and his lawyer quickly made their way into the building under escort by three detectives from Homicide.

In the courtroom, under tight security, with a very limited number of pool reporters present, the judge ordered Scott and his client to rise. A representative from the U. S. Attorney's office presented the charge against John Doe.

"Counselor?" the judge asked.

Scott answered crisply, "The Defendant pleads not guilty."

"Preliminary hearing is set for two weeks from this day," the judge intoned. "Are there any motions Counsel wishes to make at this time?"

"No, your Honor, except I wish to state that I am authorized by my client to reveal that his name is Midgely Grove."

The courtroom broke into a flurry. "Gentlemen," the judge reprimanded the press, "we will have order! And no one will leave this courtroom until the accused is safely out of here!"

The reporters who had risen and started toward the doors dropped into the nearest empty seats. The judge turned back to Scott. "Will Counsel approach the bench?" The assistant from the U. S. Attorney's office started forward as well, despite the fact that the judge intervened. "Just Counsel for the Defense, please."

When both men were at the bench the judge leaned forward benignly, "Look, son, this is a mighty serious case. The Criminal Justice Act provides that once there's been an indictment, the Defendant must have two lawyers. But maybe it would be a good idea to have two lawyers starting right now. I mean, if you feel at all uneasy, no one would criticize you. In fact it might be looked upon as a very mature move on your part."

"I'm intending to call in additional counsel," Scott said.

"The accused has requested that I call A. Lincoln Winkler."

"Winkler?" the judge responded, unable to conceal his surprise and his distaste. "Is your client an activist?"

"My client asked for him. So I'll do my best to get him," was all that Scott would say.

"Well, if you don't succeed, remember there are plenty of fine lawyers here in the District."

"I know, Your Honor," Scott said.

By the time Scott emerged from the Federal Courthouse the entire press contingent was awaiting him.

"What's the real plea going to be, Counselor?"

"What was that conference about at the bench?"

"Do you know any more about the assassin than just his name?"

"Did he tell you what his motive was?"

"Why would a black man kill a liberal like Justice Miller?"

Questions bombarded him, cameras blocked his view, microphones prevented his escape. Finally Scott raised his hand to demand silence.

"Gentlemen, this case is in its earliest phases. And I do not wish to say anything that will in any way jeopardize my client or his legal position. So for the time being, no comment."

"No comment? About the most important news event in the nation today? Don't you think you owe any obligation to the press and the people of this country?" one enraged reporter called up to him.

"I don't owe anyone anything, except to give my client the best representation I can."

With that, Scott pushed brusquely through the crowd of newsmen and started away.

It was past six when Scott arrived back at his office. In addition to the transcripts, pleadings and law books which had covered his desk when he left, there was now a stack of messages. The top one read, "Don't forget your match today. Mitch."

35

Scott had forgotten. This was the week of the interclub squash tournament and this afternoon was to have been his first match. He'd already defaulted by being late.

But all messages would wait. The main thing now was to reach Lincoln Winkler. He lifted the phone. The dull hum of the dial tone meant the switchboard was closed; he was on a night line. It also meant, as he discovered a few minutes later, that the office of Winkler and Pottish in New York was closed, too.

He would have to locate Winkler through his home. He dialed interoffice to the secretarial pool. Fortunately a handful of girls were working overtime on a rush brief, and he was able to steal one of them to help him find Winkler. Because he had remembered reading once in a magazine piece that Winkler lived in the suburbs of New York, he set her to work calling information in Long Island. And since Winkler most likely had an unlisted number at home, he instructed the girl to get the number of every phone listed in the name of a female Winkler, as well.

Scott himself called some old law school buddies practicing in New York who might know Winkler or someone in his office. He had made a few such calls, all of them futile, when his second line rang. Interrupting his conversation, Scott picked up the second line and asked irritatedly, "Yes? What is it?"

"Scott. . . ." it was the even, controlled voice of his father.

"Can I call you back?" Scott asked hurriedly.

"I would like to see you. At once," his father said, the voice unemotional, the language crisp. "Is that possible?"

"Okay. Sure. But I'm busy as hell."

"So I understand. I'll wait for you," the older Ingram said.

Scott hung up, disengaged himself from his conversation with his friend and started down the long, paneled, carpeted corridor that separated his small junior office from his father's large corner room.

The older man's secretary was a good barometer of his moods. This evening she seemed as cool and aloof as his father had sounded on the phone.

"Go right in, Mr. Ingram," she said.

Engrossed in a brief that he was scheduled to argue before the Supreme Court within the week, his father finished reading the paragraph before he took off his glasses and looked up. He was a mature and handsome man, his graying hair had once been as fair as Scott's was now. If he was an inch shorter than his tall son, the older Ingram was as broad and muscular, and frequent golfing vacations had kept him tan and fairly lean.

"Well, it's been quite a day! I don't even know if the Court will adhere to its calendar or not," he said, referring to the brief he was still holding.

"You know about my appointment, don't you?" Scott said, anxious to get to what he suspected was troubling his father.

"Of course. And if I didn't, I can tell you that a dozen of our clients do." He indicated the messages lying on his desk. "But you know our policy, Scott. When one of our men takes on a case of this kind, the firm stands behind him one thousand percent. All the facilities, all the personnel you need to give this poor devil a proper defense are available to you. As far as we are concerned, he's another client of this office, regardless of how we feel about the crime he's committed."

The words sounded reassuring, almost prescribed in the same way that warnings read to defendants were prescribed by law. Except that in this instance, Scott realized, if this were all his father intended, there would have been no need for this meeting. There must be more.

"I understand you just borrowed one of the girls from the pool," his father continued.

"I know you've got them all working on a rush job," Scott apologized, "but I did need help."

"It's not the girl I'm concerned about. It's what you've got her doing. Is it true she's trying to locate Lincoln Winkler?"

37

"My client asked for him as co-counsel."

His father nodded gravely as he fingered the messages from irate and inquiring clients. "I can explain your involvement in the case, and if any client doesn't like it, he can take his business elsewhere. But Winkler? How do I explain that?"

"I told you, my client requested him."

"Not good enough!" his father said, his anger beginning to show. "I don't mind, and my partners don't mind, giving you young kids your head on a volunteer case every now and then. But we *do* mind having the name of this firm associated with that of A. Lincoln Winkler. Why, half the bar associations in the country are trying to find some way to have that bastard disbarred! So we don't want our firm linked with Winkler. And in view of the fact that your name is Scott Ingram too that can't be avoided. So I would ask you to seek other co-counsel."

"My client asked for Winkler," Scott persisted.

"Your client may not know what's in his own best interest!" his father exploded.

"I'm sorry."

"Scott, I want to make it as clear as I can. If you take on Winkler in this matter, then in fairness to my partners I will have to ask you to take a leave of absence from this firm."

Because his father had lowered his voice and spoken quite slowly, Scott realized not only how serious his father was, but also how much it had pained him to say it.

"I understand," Scott said.

As he turned away, his father called out to him, "Maybe Winkler will be too busy, or he won't want to become involved."

"Then I'll convince him!" Scott shot back, defiantly.

He burst into his own office and slammed the door.

"Sonofabitch!" he said vehemently before he had time to realize that he was not alone.

In a chair near the wall sat a pretty girl with a radiant café au lait complexion and dressed in a miniskirt that revealed her long graceful legs.

Embarrassed, Scott said, "I didn't know anyone was here. Sorry."

"That's all right." She smiled at his embarrassment, her cheeks dimpling slightly. "I'm Marlene Hutch. I do emergency typing for the firm. The girl in secretarial told me you're trying to reach Lincoln Winkler at home."

"I sure am," Scott said.

"There's one woman in Washington who knows his home number, if anybody does," the girl volunteered.

"Who's that?"

"Honey Rosenstone."

"Honey Rosenstone? The woman the columnists call the Jewish Perle Mesta?" Scott was smiling. As if encouraged, the girl smiled again, her black eyes shining.

"Here's her unlisted number. When you tell her why you need Winkler, I'm sure she'll give you his home number." She held out the slip of paper on which she'd typed the number.

Scott reached out, asking, "How do you happen to know this number? It's not my right to ask, I know, but I am curious."

"She supports a number of causes I'm active in," the black girl said, releasing the paper to him after they'd both held it for what seemed like a long time.

"Thanks. Thanks very much."

Scott watched her as she turned toward the door. He couldn't help noticing her graceful pleasing figure, a lovely complement to her lovely face. He called out after her, "What did you say your name was?"

"It's an odd name. Most people think I'm joking. It's Hutch," she said.

"I meant your first name."

"Marlene," she answered as she slipped out, leaving Scott staring at the door she had closed softly behind her.

39

After a few moments, Scott's concentration returned to the problem at hand. He picked up the phone and dialed the number Marlene Hutch had given him.

A crisp voice answered and then abruptly announced that Mrs. Rosenstone was not available.

"This is an emergency," Scott insisted, "Could you interrupt her? I'll hold on."

The open line echoed with the sounds of a party, in all likelihood one of those radical chic soirées for which Honey Rosenstone was so famous.

Finally a woman's voice, deep and sensuous, demanded, "What's the big emergency? Who *is* this?"

"Mrs. Rosenstone? This is Scott Ingram. I'm the attorney assigned to represent the man accused of killing Justice Miller . . ."

"God, yes! Wasn't that awful! What can *I* do?"

"I've been asked by my client to call in Lincoln Winkler."

"Linc Winkler." Cautiousness chased the warmth from her voice. "Well, I don't know . . ."

"I need his home phone number. Will you give it to me, please? It's urgent. This is a crucial stage in this man's defense."

There was a long pause at the other end of the line. "Mrs. Rosenstone, all I want to do is call Winkler. If he doesn't choose to become involved in the case, let *him* make that decision."

Finally she conceded, "All right, Mr. Ingram. Area code 914. 462-3919."

As he scribbled it down on a yellow legal pad, he said, "Thanks! I'll try him right away!"

"Tell Mr. Winkler if he does decide to come down, we expect he'll stay with us."

"Yes, yes, I will," Scott said, but even as he said it he could hear Honey Rosenstone laugh in her throaty way at what must be a private joke.

When Mrs. Winkler answered Scott Ingram's call she was

40

just as protective and secretive as Honey Rosenstone had been. After Scott explained the purpose of his call and its urgency, she relented only enough to say, "He's delivering a speech tonight. Leave your number and I'll have him get back to you."

"Where is he speaking? Maybe I can reach him there," Scott persisted.

"Just give me your number," Mrs. Winkler said firmly.

Scott gave his number and hung up. He had no other choice but to wait.

·•❦ III ❦•·

The small lecture hall at Columbia University was crowded with students so closely packed that, from the speaker's platform, they seemed to form a solidly woven tapestry of human faces, captured in varying expressions of eagerness and anger. Young and dissatisfied with a world of imperfections, they clamored for the kind of leadership and revolutionary change that A. Lincoln Winkler promised every time he spoke.

Winkler was in his typical pose, both hands tightly gripping the lectern, head held high, his glasses shoved back as if to discipline his long, unruly hair and keep it from falling into his eyes. Winkler had the stature of a young man, a defiant young man, and he projected vigor in his voice and in his manner as he leaned forward to emphasize his plea.

Inwardly, Winkler knew he was fooling himself. Three or four years ago, his youthful followers would have filled Columbia's largest auditorium. And they wouldn't have merely debated and talked, they would have *acted*, used their *bodies* to express their convictions. Those kids of the late sixties, those were the kids!

Lately, whenever he got to bed more tired than usual, Winkler would wonder why he continued speaking at colleges. Sure, the kids came, but the response, the frenzy that he once received in such measure was now missing. Tonight fists would be raised, the right words of defiance and protest would be spoken, but tomorrow they would turn back to their classes and their books. What Winkler needed was an issue, a new cause that would really shake them up, give them a new rallying cry.

For the time being, he would just have to do his best.

"Law and order," Winkler cried out. "Law and order they demand of us! Particularly of you who attend the law school. Well, I ask you, *whose* law? *Whose* order?"

"Right on!" shouted one of the young men and a hundred others joined in.

"If injunction and conviction can achieve the same results as the rope and the sword, then judges have become no more than executioners! And due process of law is only what the high and mighty dictate!"

There was an outburst of applause, cheers, and shouts. Winkler overrode the applause before the wave could recede.

"The role of lawyers, especially young lawyers, can no longer be passive. They can no longer remain society's most complacent eunuchs. They must move from passive acceptance to open resistance!"

"Right ons" echoed from all sides of the hall. Winkler knew that now he must finish quickly, or else the tide of their emotion would expend itself. He took a deep breath, then, raising one hand to exact a reasonable degree of quiet from them, he concluded:

"Almost two hundred years ago, a man who was addressing the Virginia Convention, one Patrick Henry by name, demanded, 'Is life so dear or peace so sweet as to be purchased at the price of chains and slavery?' Today's practitioners, today's young lawyers, today's youth, may well ask a different question. Is law so dear or order so sweet as to be purchased at the price of our brothers chained in slavery?"

His ringing challenge delivered, Winkler raised his fist high. The exuberant cheers and outcries that met his gesture were so strong that their vibration ran through his body like

43

a tremor of sexual excitement. Students poured down from the amphitheater and flooded the stage. Young men embraced him, young girls kissed him. He held out his arms to them, embracing each in turn, and with particular enthusiasm he drew close to him the prettier girls, girls with young, firm, unsupported breasts.

Physical contact was an important part of any relationship, Winkler felt. "I can't be honest and open with anyone I can't touch," he would say. "This new, wonderful, free generation of fine young people taught me that!"

But there were times when Winkler went beyond mere embracing and touching. Then, he would be seized by a particularly pure, intense, beautiful face in the audience. He would engage the lovely eyes during his speech, and at the end, when she came up to congratulate and embrace him, he would capture her hand, holding it tight until the fervor and enthusiasm died down, and the rest of the young crowd left them alone, finally and for the night.

It troubled him sometimes that the older he became the more he needed firm young flesh. It inspired him, reassured him, enabled him to pursue his tiring life in court where there was no end of cases, and out of court where there was no end of causes. The energy he gave to the poor and the underprivileged he drew from the young girls who adored him without reservation. People said he had a way of turning on the young. In truth, he was turned on by them.

If it was a weakness, he felt entitled to it. A man who had to be so strong for so many was entitled to a human weakness or two of his own.

Tonight there were two girls in the audience who had caught his eye. But tonight he would go home to Rose. She was aware of his propensities and made no protest, for it was understood that whenever he made a speech anywhere in the metropolitan area he would return home. So tonight no selection, no enticement, no handholding. Just kisses, hugs, and

44

little tempting accidental brushes against the deliciously free, young breasts.

Suddenly out of the crowd broke one woman, holding high a slip of paper as she called out, "Urgent! Mr. Winkler, this is urgent!"

Across the heads of his youthful admirers, Winkler reached out for the slip. Lowering his glasses, he read the name, Scott Ingram and a Washington phone number. Whoever Ingram was, he must be in desperate need. Winkler decided to call him at once.

Linc Winkler had slipped into the chair in the dean's office to place the Washington call. When the number answered he said, "This is Linc Winkler. I understand you want to talk to me."

"Mr. Winkler? I'm Scott Ingram, an attorney in Washington. I've been asked to contact you by my client, Midgley Grove. You must know by now he's being held as the man who killed Justice Miller this afternoon. He expressly wants you to represent him.

"There is a technicality," Scott raced on. "You're probably aware that down here an attorney from outside the jurisdiction can only be admitted to practice in a particular case if he is joined by an attorney regularly admitted to practice in the District. But if you came in to join me as co-counsel there'd be no trouble on that score.

"I know you have a very busy schedule and this case came up suddenly to say the least. But I don't think Grove is going to talk freely to anyone except you. If you could come down here for a brief advisory conference, then we can make the immediate decisions and ask for delays to give you time to meet your other obligations. Mr. Winkler, you must forgive my impatience and perhaps even my impertinence in pursuing you in this manner, but it is vital. Will you do it?"

Winkler smiled, shoved his glasses back up on his head

and said, "Young man, if you would just give me a chance, I'd say yes. Yes. *Yes!!*"

During the silence of surprise that greeted him from the other end, Winkler continued warmly, "What did you say your name was?"

"Ingram—Scott Ingram."

"Okay, Scotty, now you listen to me."

"Yes, Mr. Winkler!"

"Linc! Linc!" Winkler corrected. "I don't like to be associated with anyone who can't call me Linc, or anyone I can't touch. I've got to feel people to know them. Otherwise, life is one big polite standoff."

"Got you . . . Linc."

"What time is it?"

"Quarter of ten," Scott said.

"Tell you what," Linc Winkler said with sudden decision, "I can still make the eleven o'clock shuttle. Pick me up at National Airport at midnight."

"Right on!"

"See you then," Winkler said. "I'll be the one in the trenchcoat with the glasses on top of his head," as though he were not the most photographed attorney in the country.

Scott drove to National Airport with a sense of determination and conviction. He had called Lincoln Winkler, and Winkler had said yes. If that meant Scott had to take a leave from the firm, then to hell with it. Perhaps this was precisely the pretext he needed to make a clean and final break with his father. In practice on his own, or with some other firm, he would feel freer, stronger. He would not have to worry that all conversation among his young peers would cease or become guarded when he entered a room, and the hellos might be less cheery, but they'd probably be more honest. He was thoroughly fed up with being the son of the senior partner and feeling apologetic about it. He had made Law Review on his own, something that his father had never done, and he

46

was as capable as any young lawyer he knew. He would like to be accepted on that basis and no other.

Yes, this break might be a lucky one.

And working with Lincoln Winkler! That was like standing at DeBakey's side when he did heart surgery, or working with Clarence Darrow on the Loeb-Leopold case.

Among all civil-rights lawyers in the country Winkler was the most famous, and the most deft. He had the audacity to challenge the courts and the system. Judges didn't stifle him with threats of contempt. Juries warmed to him. Downtrodden people looked upon him as a savior, and he did not let them down—just as he would not let Midge Grove down. Scott let the words luxuriate in his mind, "For the Defense, A. Lincoln Winkler, Scott Ingram the Third, Co-Counsel." But he immediately corrected that to A. Lincoln Winkler and Scott Ingram. By the time this case was over those hated words, "the Third," would disappear forever. From now on, when men in the law referred to "that Ingram," they would be referring to Scott himself, not his father.

Winkler came bounding down the ramp of the plane, his open trenchcoat flying, his briefcase bulging, his glasses thrust back on his head. Scott couldn't help but admire the energy of the man at midnight, after a day in court and an evening lecturing.

Winkler seemed to have picked him out of the handful of people who were waiting, for he headed straight for Scott.

"Scotty?"

Instead of shaking Scott's extended hand, Winkler embraced him, clapped him on the back.

"Mr. Winkler . . ." Scott began.

But Winkler interrupted, "I told you, call me Linc. Linc!"

"My car's right outside, Linc." Scott reached for his heavy, overstuffed briefcase.

"Good. We can talk on the way to Georgetown."

"Which reminds me," Scott said, "when Mrs. Rosenstone

gave me your number she also said to tell you she expected you'd stay at their place tonight."

"I always stay there when I visit Washington," Winkler said.

On the way to the Rosenstone mansion in old George-town, Scott briefed Winkler on everything of a legal nature that had transpired since he entered the case late that afternoon. When he finished, Winkler asked thoughtfully, "You think Grove flipped out?"

"He's not agitated. He's calm—far too calm for the situation. That fact alone could mean that he's psycho."

"And he said nothing that would give you a clue as to his motive?" Winkler pursued.

"Not a word."

"H'mm!" Winkler said, wondering whether that was a reflection on the prisoner's intransigence or on Scott's ability as a lawyer.

They pulled up in front of the Rosenstone mansion. Suggesting that Winkler might be tired, Scott tried to excuse himself when Winkler invited him in. But Linc only smiled. "To me trouble is adrenalin," he said. "I get my highs on impossible cases, and this sounds like an impossible case. I can stay up all night. Come on in, let's have something to eat and rap a little more."

Scott Ingram had lived all his life in what people referred to as well-to-do surroundings. Still he was enormously impressed by the interior of the Rosenstone mansion. It was an old Federal house, with a graceful winding staircase dominating the entrance foyer, and two huge, magnificently decorated rooms on either side. The sitting room to the left contained rich, ornate damasks and an exquisite and valuable collection of French antiques. The room on the right was, in the English manner, of ancient woods and fine leather, and large enough to serve as the library of many a private club.

It was to this room the butler directed them, as he took

Winkler's trenchcoat and briefcase. They found a fresh fire blazing in the brick fireplace. Winkler went directly to the bar in the corner and mixed himself a drink. But before he could take a sip, someone at the door interrupted, "Don't, darling! You'll spoil your taste. And I have an excellent Margaux opened."

Honey Rosenstone was standing in the doorway. She was a striking woman dressed in a gold brocade hostess gown. It was obvious the name Honey derived from her long blonde hair, braided and coiled around her head and her light creamy complexion, which seemed illuminated from within. Maturity had given her only its advantages, voluptuousness and a sense of herself. Scott thought she was one of the most attractive women he had ever seen.

She moved confidently and gracefully across the luxurious oriental rug to take the whiskey glass from Winkler's hand, at the same time offering her cheek to be kissed. But Winkler pulled her close and kissed her passionately on the lips. Then, as if it were important that the information be delivered to Winkler as soon as possible, Honey Rosenstone explained about her husband.

"I'm sorry Bill isn't here. He's at an ADA meeting out in Los Angeles. There's a fight going on that can wreck the whole party. One thing about California politics, nothing ever stays settled."

"Too bad," Winkler lamented. But if he was truly disturbed, Scott failed to detect it. Winkler turned to him. "Honey, Scott Ingram."

"I spoke to Scott on the phone earlier this evening," she said as she advanced toward Scott and held out her hand. It was soft, strong and warm in his and she released his own hand only when she turned to acknowledge the butler who was wheeling a serving cart into the room. The wine had already been uncorked and decanted so it could breathe. There was nothing left for the butler to do but fill three glasses and leave.

Honey took a plate and generously ladled out Beluga caviar, minced egg and onion, and several slices of melba toast. She selected carefully from among the sliced turkey, cold roast beef and sturgeon until she had assembled all of Winkler's favorites. Then presenting the plate to him, she opened his napkin, spread it across his legs and took his reading glasses off his head, slipping them into the pocket of her gown as she invited, "Please, Scott, you must be famished at this hour, do help yourself!"

Winkler ate quickly, but there was no mistaking that he relished each bit of food and the excellent wine Honey had chosen for him. She sat by him, watching him constantly, obviously pleased by his approval.

"Any more news about Grove on TV tonight?" Winkler asked.

"Not much," Honey said. "Only that the press was steamed about getting fooled when they took the killer over to the arraignment."

"No hard news?"

"Yes, they know the identity of the killer now."

"Scotty told them that," Winkler explained, still eating swiftly, with gusto. "That all?"

"Miller's body is going to lie in state in the rotunda of the Supreme Court for a day and an evening before the burial. And they discovered Grove doesn't have a criminal record, but there *is* a rumor about his mental history. One report said he'd been recently released from a hospital."

"There!" Scott said to Winkler. "My hunch was right. We ought to move for an M.O. at St. Elizabeth's Hospital first thing in the morning."

"Waitwaitwaitwait, let's not move for mental observation so fast," Winkler said. "Let's get all the facts, try to determine how they fit in with the broad view of the case, and then decide about the M.O."

Winkler put aside his plate and his wineglass. He rose slowly to his full height. He rubbed his hands together, as if

50

debating with himself. Finally he turned to Scott, began to talk, and then eventually to pace.

"Look, Scott, you should know a few things about me before you're willing to take me on as your associate. I am not interested in cases solely because of the people immediately involved. This poor, dazed devil Grove sounds enormously pathetic as you describe him. And, of course, I am sympathetic to him. But before I can devote myself to any case it has to have implications far beyond those that apply merely to the defendant. I think what we are faced with here is a nation that is already screaming 'This black bastard is like all black bastards! Vicious! A born criminal! A killer! So rush him off to trial! Convict him and put him away forever! Or better yet, execute him, if the law will let you!' Like it or not, this crime involves the entire black race! And if we don't do something to prevent it, this case will become a vehicle for Establishment racists to prove their own vile, vicious, ethnic slanders."

Scott stared up at Winkler admiringly. He was proving to be the intense involved man Scott had expected.

"Scotty," Winkler continued, "You want to understand me and the way I work? Let me tell you something about my own life. My father was a tailor, had a little shop up in the Bronx. Until the Depression, that shop and my father's hands supported us. We kids went to school. My mother, who was a bit of a religious fanatic, was able to run her house as she wished, which meant celebrating with big dinners on Passover and Rosh Hashannah. But mainly she had her heart set on my becoming *bar mitzvah*. And I was to have the best *bar mitzvah* anybody in that part of the Bronx had ever seen! She started making plans for the big catered affair a year in advance. Whenever my poor father tried to say something about business not being so good anymore, she would say, 'There'll be enough money. God will provide.'

"Well, it seems that God was having troubles of his own that year. He did *not* provide! Who provided was my father.

51

He took on work from department stores and bigger tailoring houses. He would work in his little shop until late at night, and then very early the next morning he would pack up the finished stuff and take it downtown, to return again with another load. I tried to pick up some of those boxes and couldn't even lift them, and I was a big strong kid. Yet he lugged them up and down the subway stairs day after day. Each day my *bar mitzvah* was coming closer, and my mother had to keep nagging him for more and more money, so her little Abe could have his *bar mitzvah* the way she wanted it."

He turned suddenly to Scott. "Abe. That's from Abraham Lincoln Winkler. No Jewish kid gets called up to the Torah by a name like Lincoln. Yes, Abe was going to have his big day and Papa was going to pay for it. He sweated and strained until four days before the big event. Lugging a huge box up the subway stairs at Thirty-fourth Street, he keeled over and was rushed by ambulance across town to Bellevue Hospital. He had had a heart attack, but he did not die. He was in the hospital for eight weeks. And he was *not* in synagogue the day I became *bar mitzvah*. All the while I was saying the required prayers, making the speech they had written for me, I kept thinking about him, and I wanted to cry. But I couldn't spoil the day for my mother.

"That was the day I decided something had to change. Men were not born to live out their lives as dray horses, until they keeled over from hauling loads too heavy for them. *I* was not going to become a cardiac invalid by the time I was forty-nine, like my father.

"But I made my resolve a little broader. I didn't say, 'This is never going to happen to *me*,' I said, 'This is never going to happen to *any* man, if I can help it! No matter what his color or origin, no son is going to have to stand by helpless and watch his father work himself to death if I can prevent it!"

Winkler stopped abruptly, took a gulp of wine as if for energy, and then he went on.

52

"Now everyone talks about change, but they don't mean what I mean. To them, change is slow, planned, virtuous. But the fact is that their kind of change is not only slow, it defeats itself. People say they hate slums, but slums do *not* disappear, because *people* perpetuate them.

"But you take a place like Frankfurt, Germany, where the city was demolished during the war. There are no slums there. A whole city has risen fresh and new and clean. Lesson? Man only does what he *must!* What he is forced to do. So I say, to hell with good and pious intentions! *Make* the society change! *Force* it to change! Sometimes this means destroying certain institutions first. But I believe it's the only way we'll ever accomplish really significant change in this country.

"For that, I have been called everything from a gadfly to a radical to a lunatic sonofabitch! And I love it! Because it means that I *am* having an effect, helping to change things for *all* exploited people. Not as fast as I'd like. But a hell of a lot faster than other people like!

"So I don't want just to defend Grove, to reinforce and sanctify the system by giving the repressors the chance to preen themselves on a 'fair trial,' to advertise their own 'integrity,' to proclaim the 'virtues' of their own system. I want to use this opportunity, this case, to change the entire system of justice. *That's* why I'm here, Scott, that's why!"

After that, Scott felt called on to try to justify his suggestion about moving for a mental observation of Grove.

"Linc," he began, "I thought that with everything they've got on him—eyewitness testimony, the weapon, to say nothing of the emotional climate in the country—insanity was his only chance."

"Maybe," Winkler admitted, then sipped his wine thoughtfully. "The emotional climate, we have to do something about that right away. But first I want to see our client. Then I have to be admitted to the case by the court. After that, I'll decide what steps we take. That's another thing about me, Scott. I listen to my associates. I discuss. But in the end, *I* make the decisions! Pick me up here at nine!"

"Right!" Scott said enthusiastically, and set down his half-empty wineglass.

Honey and Winkler saw him to the front door. "If you and Linc want to use this place as your working quarters during the case, please do," Honey said. "In fact, I insist!"

She smiled invitingly as she said it, and held Winkler's arm tight around her waist. They remained that way until Scott's car pulled away from the front door.

On his way back to his apartment, Scott felt elated. Winkler had justified every hope and impression he had ever had about the man. He was dynamic, dedicated, strong and inspired. Not the proper, cool, reserved types one met at Ingram, March. It would be exciting to work with him, and they *would* be working together. Winkler had said, "First I want to see our client." *Our client.* That sealed it. And if that didn't then surely Honey Rosenstone's invitation to Scott to use her house as their working quarters certainly did.

And a good thing. For he had decided to send his father a letter not asking for a leave of absence but resigning from the firm. If Scott had had any doubts, this first meeting with Winkler had resolved them. He would resign.

IV

Scott pulled his red Mustang into a parking space across from the District jail. Lugging his heavy briefcase, Linc got out first and looked across the top of the car toward the jail entrance where newsmen and TV cameras were waiting. Scott had just slammed shut the door on his side when he heard one of the newsmen call out, "There he is now! That's Winkler!"

All eyes, all cameras swung around to focus on them. Newsmen and mobile news photographers started across the street to greet them, TV cameras zoomed in on the familiar Winkler head, his glasses sitting atop the unruly hair.

Before they were besieged, Linc said softly but urgently, "Let me handle this, Scotty."

"They seemed to know you'd be here."

"I thought it was only fair to tip them off. As I said last night, our toughest job will be turning around public opinion."

They were surrounded now, the profusion of greetings and questions was so overwhelming that for the first few moments no single question stood out clearly enough to demand an answer. But when the initial barrage had subsided, Linc started across the street, grabbing Scott's hand so they would not be separated. As they walked, the questions continued.

55

"Mr. Winkler, when did you first know that you were in this case?"

"First, I am not *in* this case yet. It is up to the Court to admit me to *appear* in this case. Whether I will be granted admission is open to question. Large question!"

Scott tried to interrupt but Linc continued, "However, even before that, I have to assure myself that this is a case in which I have natural sympathies with the defendant. There's an old-fashioned belief that a lawyer must defend anyone in trouble who comes to him. I do not subscribe to that!"

"Isn't that one of the Canons of Ethics all lawyers are bound by?" one reporter asked.

Linc turned on him and responded sharply, "We are living in a time when we have to question all the established values that all our professions are bound by. Defending a man on trial for murder is no easy business. It requires constant devotion that I cannot render unless I believe implicitly in the man, his cause, and his *moral* innocence."

"And *do* you believe in Midge Grove enough to undertake his defense?" another reporter persisted.

They had reached the area where the stationary TV cameras could pick up more intimate coverage. Linc stopped and faced in their direction. "I'll discover that in the next few hours. I'm going in there now to have my first real confrontation with Grove. When I come out I'll let you know. But remember what I said, it's up to the Court to grant me permission to appear. I'm not at all sure I'll get it. Not down here!"

With that, Linc turned and, ushering Scott ahead of him, started for the entrance. At the door all newsmen were barred by District police officers in uniform.

They waited in the rotunda of the jail, a huge high room, not too well lit and filled with what seemed an endless number of small tables surrounded by chairs. Each grouping pretended to be a small conference area of its own, but actually the voices echoed, and there was little feeling of privacy.

56

"Don't they have any private conference rooms?" Linc demanded.

"Not in the District jail," Scott explained.

"Then how do you ever get to talk to your client confidentially?"

"People at the other tables can't really hear much. Besides, in here, everybody's concerned with his own troubles."

"I like a quiet, confidential place," Linc said thoughtfully.

While they waited for Grove to be brought from his cell, Scott took the opportunity to say, "Linc, I wouldn't make such an issue over your being admitted to handle this case. I don't know of a case down here where any accredited attorney has been refused admission, as long as he has Washington co-counsel. Stirring up an issue like that can only antagonize the judge."

Winkler smiled, toyed with the hair of his long sideburn.

"Don't you think I know that? But it's public sympathy I'm after. A case like this, which looks so hopeless from the start, has to be won *outside* the courtroom first, so it can be won *inside* the courtroom later. I'll tell you what, Scotty, I will depend on you implicitly for all legal motions, papers, and procedural advice on practice in this District, provided you depend on me for tactics, the broad plan, the overall strategy. Okay?" Linc asked, smiling warmly, indulgently, as he would have if Scott were his own son.

"Okay," Scott agreed, as they saw Grove being led toward them.

Grove was dressed in prison garb. Since it was stiff and new as well as too large for him, he seemed even more pathetic to Scott than he had the day before. Grove blinked, stared at Scott whom he seemed to recognize finally, then stared at Winkler whom he did not identify at all. Linc waved the guard out of hearing. He took Grove by both shoulders, looked into his face and said, "You sent for me and I'm here!" When the words had no effect, he glanced at

Scott, then turned back to Grove. "Linc Winkler. You asked for Linc Winkler and I'm here!"

At the mention of the name, Grove at last seemed in contact with reality, but he appeared overawed as well, as he whispered, "Linc Winkler . . ."

"That's right," Winkler smiled and gently urged Grove into a straight-backed chair. Seating himself across the table, he leaned toward Grove and said, "First, Midge, let me explain something to you. Mr. Ingram and I are your lawyers. Or we will be, *if* you tell us the truth. You don't have to be afraid of us, because whatever you tell us will remain secret. If you tell us the whole truth, that does not mean that we're going to have to tell the whole truth to save you. We only tell that part of the truth that we think will help. But in order to know what to hold back we have to know it all. Do you understand that?"

"They going to kill me," Grove said, scarcely above a whisper.

"No, Midge," Linc said. "We have a chance to save you, if you tell us everything. Understand?"

Grove nodded but Scott felt he didn't really understand. The blank look in his eyes, his unresponsiveness, all confirmed for Scott his original feeling that Grove was ill, mentally ill.

"Now," Linc continued, "first thing, you did shoot that judge, didn't you?"

Grove hesitated, then nodded.

"Did you *intend* to kill him? I mean did you go to that courthouse, with a gun under your jacket, intending to kill that judge?"

Grove thought an instant, then nodded.

"*Why* did you want to kill him?"

"They . . . he told me to. . . ."

"Who? Who told you? A voice?"

"A doctor," Grove said.

Winkler suppressed surprise as he continued carefully. "A

58

doctor you know told you to go to the courthouse and kill a Justice of the Supreme Court of the United States?"

Grove nodded again. Linc and Scott exchanged looks.

"This doctor, what's his name?" Linc pressed on.

"Randolph."

"Where's his office?"

"St. Elizabeth's."

Scott was astounded and he was more than ever convinced that an insanity plea was their best defense.

Linc proceeded cautiously now, hoping to keep his tenuous contact with Grove. "Now . . . listen to me carefully, Midge. Did Dr. Randolph tell you to go out and kill a Justice of the Supreme Court?"

Grove nodded.

Linc did not choose to pursue the matter further, but made a mental note of Randolph's name. Then he changed the course of his questioning. "Midge, your name has been public for at least twelve hours now, yet no one has stepped forward to speak up for you, or claim you. No relative, no friend. Where's your family?"

"No family."

"No one at all?" Linc asked skeptically. "No mother, no father?" Grove shook his head. "You're an orphan?" Grove nodded. "Since when?"

"Always," Midge Grove said.

"Who brought you up?"

"Nobody."

"Midge, is there anything else you want to tell me about yourself. About any girlfriends, or places you've lived, or people you know? Friends you might like to contact, or who might like to contact you?"

Grove thought for a few moments, then shook his head.

"Is there anything you'd like? Magazines? Books? Paper to write on? Cigarettes?"

"I don't smoke," was Grove's simple reply.

Linc Winkler stood up and moved around to where Grove

59

sat, immobile. Taking him by the shoulders he lifted Grove so they were facing each other, and looked down into Grove's eyes. Grove did not resist, even when Linc spread his eyelids and stared in deeply. Satisfied, Linc patted Grove on the shoulder. "Midge, I want you to think of me as your friend as well as your lawyer. I wouldn't be here if I weren't your friend. Call me Linc. Understand?"

Grove nodded. But Winkler wanted more. "Say it," he insisted. "Call me Linc! Say, 'Okay, I understand, Linc.'"

Grove seemed puzzled, then summoning special effort he said in a low monotone, "Okay, I understand, Linc."

"Good! We'll see you very soon." Linc signaled to the guard, who led Grove away.

Once they were alone, Scott said, "You see? He's completely removed from reality. Especially that part about a doctor telling him to kill a Justice of the Supreme Court. On that alone we could plead insanity and get him off."

"Not so fast, Scotty, not so fast."

"The least we should do is get hold of that Dr. Randolph," Scott persisted.

But Linc didn't answer. Instead he toyed thoughtfully with his glasses, polished them, replaced them on his head, and rubbed his hands together, seeming to decide on their next move.

"Before we see Randolph, or settle on our defenses, let's find out how much of a case the Government actually has. Find out who the U.S. Attorney has assigned to prosecute the case, demand a preliminary hearing so we can get some estimate of their strengths and weaknesses. Then we'll see."

Scott nodded. The plan made sense.

Linc added suddenly, "And request in advance the composition of the grand jury. I want to know precisely how many whites and how many blacks will be sitting at the time of the indictment."

"Won't work," Scott warned.

"What do you mean?"

"By sheer statistical impact, all grand juries down here are predominantly black. We can't plead prejudice," Scott explained.

Linc thought a moment, then he said, "Get me those figures anyhow. And let's hurry things along so that they appoint a judge to sit and you can move to have me admitted. I'll meet you at the house."

When Scott Ingram returned to the Rosenstone house he brought bad news.

"Linc, we won't get a preliminary hearing."

"We have a right! We'll appeal!"

"They've already gone to grand jury, got an indictment. In the District an indictment supersedes a preliminary hearing."

"Of course," Linc agreed angrily. "Bastards! Rushed through an indictment just to keep us from discovering the extent of their case."

"There's nothing irregular about moving for a quick indictment. Not in a case like this," Scott said.

"Were you at least able to get a rundown on the make-up of the grand jury?"

"There were nineteen grand jurors sitting. Sixteen of them black. No loopholes there."

"Maybe not," was all that Linc would admit. "But I still want the make-up of that jury. Name, race, profession, income and whether or not they're civil servants."

"In the District a good percentage of them are always likely to be in civil service."

"Exactly. So in a case like this, where a Government official was the victim of the crime, it's possible their objectivity was, to say the least, clouded."

"A point," Scott conceded. "Not a strong point, but a point."

"*Boychick,*" Linc laughed, "in a case where you have no strong points, you damn well better make the most of your weak ones. Now how do they select trial judges down here?"

"By lot," Scott said.

"Even on a case like this?" Linc asked dubiously.

"On every case."

By that time the butler was wheeling a teacart into the room. Honey followed, dressed in at-home pajamas of a rich Chinese silk.

"Am I too early?" she asked, presenting her cheek to be kissed, first by Linc, then by Scott, who couldn't help noticing the provocative fragrance she wore, and the intriguing fact that the same perfume worn by other women he knew had never seemed so sensual.

"All the serious discussion over?" she asked as she began pouring tea. "Because *I* have a problem."

Linc smiled at Honey. "What can we do for you, my dear?"

"Before all this happened, I'd scheduled a dinner here for next Tuesday," Honey began.

"No problem," Linc said quickly, "just lock us in this room. Scott and I can work all night without disturbing anyone. By then, a secretary from my New York office will be down to work along with us."

Scott broke in, "It might be better to have someone with legal experience in the District. Someone who'd be familiar with all the forms, motions, and practice here."

"You have someone in mind?"

"A girl from my old office. Very bright and involved. Her name is Marlene Hutch."

"Of course," Honey volunteered. "She's been at several cocktail parties here. She's not only bright, she's extremely pretty. And if there's one thing Linc likes, it's having attractive girls around." Honey seemed to be jesting at Linc's expense, but Scott detected a note of jealousy as well.

"Okay, get her here by this afternoon if you can," Linc said to close the subject. Then he turned to Honey, "Now, as for your party, just lock the library door on us, that's all."

"Linc, you don't understand. It's a party to raise funds for C.W.A., Clean World Association. The guest of honor is Ben Robertson."

"Justice Robertson?" Linc asked thoughtfully. "Well, what's the problem?"

"I wondered. Robertson and you in the same place at the same time, would that involve legal ethics or compromise the Justice's position?"

"Not at all!" Linc said. "In fact, if you can find room for me at the table, I'd love to sit in. I've never met Robertson."

"If you think it's proper."

"It's proper, it's proper," Linc assured her quickly.

Then the details of the case reclaimed his attention, and he turned back to Scott. "How long will it take for a trial judge to be appointed so we have to plead?"

"A few days, no more."

"Good, good!"

"That'll also be our first chance to move for an M.O. at St. Elizabeth's," Scott reminded him, "so I think we should see Randolph immediately."

"I don't know," Linc said thoughtfully, "I wouldn't be too sure we can sustain insanity."

Scott was amazed. "Why not?"

"You mean because of what he said about killing on a doctor's orders? It'll take a hell of a lot more than that."

"Take all the pieces together, Linc. His remoteness. His unawareness of the danger he's in. His statement about the doctor. His psychiatric history. And one other fact."

"Which is?" Linc asked.

"It's been bugging me from the beginning. As far as anyone can make out, Grove had no plan for escape. What sane man considers such a crime and doesn't plan an escape?"

"I can't explain that," Linc admitted, "But that's not enough to prove he's insane. As for moving for an M.O., definitely not, for the time being."

63

"There's one definite drawback," Scott conceded. "We'd have to give notice to the Prosecutor. He'd be privy to our findings, too."

"Exactly! And if it turns out Grove isn't legally insane it could hurt our case enormously," Linc said, summing up Scott's line of thought. Then he added pointedly, "There are a few other motions we're going to make when we plead to the indictment. First moment you find out, let me know the name of that judge!"

"Right on!" Scott said.

Linc smiled and turned to Honey who was leaning forward, her ample breasts invitingly exposed as she offered him some small iced cakes with his tea.

V

The huge gold seal of the United States dominated the courtroom. Set against the wall of green marble behind the judge's chair, it seemed to look out as a benign and reassuring eye on all judicial proceedings that took place in these august premises. Counsel for both sides were already seated at their respective tables, parallel to each other and perpendicular to the imposing judge's bench.

At the defense table, Scott Ingram was setting out yellow legal pads for himself and Linc Winkler, who was thumbing through his notes more in an effort to appear busy than from any need to refresh his mind. Now a man entered the well of the courtroom and joined the two men at the Government's counsel table. Unobtrusively, Scott reached across to alert Linc.

"Carroll," Scott whispered, "the U.S. Attorney himself. I don't believe he's ever personally tried a case."

Linc peered over his reading glasses. "Aha!" he said, endowing the fact with great significance.

The two spectator sections were already filled to capacity with accredited members of the press, radio, and television networks, forcing several reporters to stand in the back of the room. Between the tight security and the pressure of the media to be represented in the courtroom, there was no room for the public. Uniformed guards were everywhere, proof of the determination to prevent a repetition of the shattering events of Dallas or Marin County.

Suddenly there was a tense whisper of excitement. One of the doors flanking the judge's bench opened and Midgley Grove, manacled to two Federal Marshals, was escorted into the room. They led him to the counsel table where Linc Winkler and Scott Ingram rose to greet him. Winkler straightened his young client's prison garb, deliberately making Grove appear even more pathetic and inept than he already seemed. Then he pulled out a chair between himself and Scott and gestured Grove to sit down.

The clerk called for attention and announced the arrival of the judge. As the courtroom stood in respect, Judge Alfred W. Beecher entered and climbed to his place on the bench. A lean, thin-lipped man in his early sixties, he seemed more severe than he actually was as he stared out at the courtroom.

He looked down into the pit, first at the Government's counsel table, then at the Defense. Impartial as he was required to be, Judge Beecher experienced a distinct feeling of distaste at having to confirm what had only been a strong rumor until now. A. Lincoln Winkler was indeed present and ready to join Defense Counsel. Beecher was not surprised therefore when even before the indictment was read, Scott Ingram rose and moved to the lectern before the bench.

"If Your Honor please, I would like to move at this time to have a distinguished member of the New York Bar, A. Lincoln Winkler, admitted to this jurisdiction for the limited purpose of acting as co-counsel in this case."

"Your name, Counselor?"

"Scott Ingram, Your Honor."

"And are you duly admitted and authorized to practice in the Federal Courts in this District?"

"Yes, Your Honor."

"In that case, the Court admits Mr. Winkler, *pro hoc vice*." Explaining for the benefit of the press, the judge added, "For the purposes of this one case."

66

Then Beecher proceeded to order the clerk, "Due to the nature and gravity of the charges, you will read the entire indictment aloud!"

Since they had already received a copy of the indictment, Co-Counsel Winkler and Ingram listened gravely but made no notes. The indictment charged Midgley Grove with murder in the first degree by virtue of the premeditated killing of one Harvey Miller. Plus an additional count of murder in the first degree resulting during the commission of a felony, it being a felony to obstruct justice by attacking a Federal judge. Plus, A.P.O., assault on police during the escape by firing shots; A.D.W., assault with a deadly weapon, for using a pistol during his escape. C.D.W., carrying dangerous weapon. Entering a Federal building with the intent to commit a crime. And a number of other charges covering every facet of the crime from planning and carrying out the act to trying to make good his futile escape.

When the indictment was concluded, Judge Beecher himself proceeded with the formality of asking, "How does the Defendant plead?"

Scott Ingram proceeded to the lectern. "Defendant pleads not guilty," he announced.

"Defendant's plea will be so entered," Beecher said ritualistically, "and unless there are any motions at this time, the Court will confer with Counsel and the United States Attorney to set a convenient date for trial in the very near future."

Before Scott could return to the counsel table, Linc Winkler had risen in his place, his shaggy hair more disheveled than usual. He shoved his reading glasses back on his head and let his long frame slip into an easy slouch. Speaking from his place at the table instead of advancing to the counsels' lectern added a note of insolence to his attitude, although his voice seemed quite calm and respectful.

"Your Honor, I would like to request that the Court set reasonable bail at this time."

"Due to the public reaction in this case, for the Defendant's own safety as well as to assure his presence at the trial, Defendant will be held in District jail, without bail!" Beecher ruled briskly, a bit annoyed at Winkler's effrontery. Bail was never granted in cases of murder one where such a calculated violent death occurred.

"May we take exception to that ruling, Your Honor?" Winkler asked softly.

"Under our rules it is not necessary for Counsel to take exception in order to protect his record on appeal," Beecher said, prepared to adjourn the hearing, but Winkler remained standing, his attitude adamant. "Does Counsel have any further statement or request to make?"

"Your Honor, in a case of this gravity it is most essential that counsel and client have the chance to confer in utmost secrecy. Meeting in the rotunda of the District jail precludes that. Therefore I request that Defendant be moved from District jail to the cell block beneath this courthouse where, I understand, private consultation rooms *are* available."

"Defendant will remain in District jail, except that he may be removed to this courthouse under proper guard for occasional private meetings with Counsel. The first such meeting to be arranged for tomorrow at ten o'clock," Beecher ruled.

"May we have a delay, Your Honor? We'll need several days to study the indictment in order to make the most of such severely limited private consultations."

Again Winkler's voice was low, hardly the strong authoritative voice that the media publicized so often.

"Counsel will notify the Court when such a meeting would be most advantageous and, if it is within a reasonable time, the Court will grant it," Beecher concluded, reaching for his gavel to bring the hearing to a close.

But Winkler had not yet moved. Without changing attitude, voice or inflection, he said as what seemed almost an afterthought, "There is one more motion the Defense would like to make, Your Honor."

"Yes?"

"The Defense requests that His Honor recuse himself from presiding in this case."

Winkler delivered that motion in the same low drawl as all the others, but the effect in the courtroom was a sudden shocked silence, followed by a torrent of whispered reactions from the press. Beecher stared down at Winkler.

"I shall ascribe that motion to the fact that Counsel is a stranger to our courts. And I urge Co-Counsel Ingram to instruct his colleague on the general practice here."

Linc's motion had come as an even greater surprise to Scott, who felt his face flush and sweat begin to ooze from his brow. He started to rise to explain, but he felt Linc's hand on his shoulder restraining him. Winkler glared at the judge challengingly.

"Counsel," Beecher continued, "having been indulged in other jurisdictions, has undoubtedly formed some erroneous conclusions, courtroom habits and practices. In this District a motion that a judge recuse himself from sitting in a case is extremely rare. And, when resorted to, Counsel is required to state specific and substantial reasons for such a motion."

"Which Counsel is prepared to do!" Winkler declared in a loud strong voice, intended to reach the last standing newspaperman in the courtroom. "There seems to be a clear pattern here—a conspiracy between this Court and the U.S. Attorney. An indictment is handed down by the Grand Jury in record time, depriving us of a preliminary hearing, keeping us in the dark about the details of the Prosecutor's case. We are rushed to plead to the indictment. And now it seems there is some unwritten agreement to force us to go to trial in a suspiciously short time. Whether this is some political ploy to satisfy the public hunger for revenge, I do not know. But it has all the earmarks of a pre-planned plot to convict this Defendant without a fair chance to present his defense."

"If Counsel were familiar with our practice . . ." Beecher began. But Winkler interrupted.

"Counsel is familiar enough with your practice to know

69

that this is the first time—mark you, the first time—in all his tenure that the United States Attorney himself has appeared to try a case. Why? Because there is political capital to be made here! The Romans are gathered in the arena and they are demanding a spectacle—and a victim. And this poor black boy is that victim!"

Winkler placed his free hand on Grove's shoulder protectively.

"When the Government so lusts for a conviction that even the Court becomes a co-conspirator, then I think we are justified in asking the judge to step down. I reiterate my motion!"

Beecher's face had grown flushed. "The fact that the indictment was handed down so quickly is due to the relative simplicity of the facts involved. The decision of the U.S. Attorney to try this case himself is perfectly within his prerogative. As for myself, I was chosen to preside over this case strictly in accordance with the procedure followed in every criminal case in this District. Not by appointment, not by personal selection, but by lot. There is no plot afoot here. The motion is denied!"

But Winkler did not relent in either his attitude or his attack. "There is another reason, Your Honor. We feel, and strongly, that His Honor, being white, comes to this case with certain innate prejudices which he cannot possibly overcome."

"An erroneous supposition on Counsel's part! If Counsel had experience in the District, or recourse to the facts and figures, he would know that any judge sitting in criminal cases in the District presides mainly over cases involving black defendants. And does so quite fairly and impartially. The question of prejudice is never raised."

"Then maybe it is time it *was* raised!" Winkler countered. Scott Ingram reached out to signal Winkler, but the senior lawyer continued. "I restate my motion. I ask that His Honor withdraw from this case on the ground of prejudice, both unconscious as well as that already exhibited in this case thus far!"

Without raising his voice, Beecher ruled, "Motion is denied."

"We take exception to the ruling!" Winkler said sharply. "And we will appeal forthwith!"

"No exception is necessary," Beecher reiterated. "However, the Court feels obligated to point out that in this District any appeal from denial of a motion to recuse a judge can only be made *after* the trial is concluded. So any hopes Counsel may have of delaying this trial by endless motions will prove vain."

"Then I feel we should inform the Court that a motion for change of venue will be made shortly," Winkler said.

"On more substantial grounds, I hope! Now, since Counsel feels that failure to have a preliminary hearing has been damaging to his preparation, the Court will entertain a motion of discovery."

"We move for such disclosure and discovery."

"Upon presentation of such motion in writing the Court will order the Government to make available to the Defense all scientific tests made by the District Police and the FBI, all statements or confessions by the Defendant, all eyewitness identifications, including the names of all witnesses, as well as all relevant physical evidence such as weapons, expended bullets, clothing or other items germane to the case. Does the Government have any objection?"

Roger Carroll, the U.S. Attorney, half rose from his chair to accede. "No objection, Your Honor."

Beecher turned his severe gaze back upon Winkler and Ingram. "Defense has ten days in which to make any further motions before trial!" He rapped his gavel and started to leave the bench.

Only then did Linc relax his grip on Scott's shoulder. Scott rose and confronted Winker, "Look, Linc, down here . . ."

"Later, Scott! Later!" Linc said. "Now we have to get out

71

front as soon as possible." He turned to Grove, patted him on the shoulder, and released him to the two U.S. Marshals. Then he stalked out of the pit and up the aisle of the courtroom, flanked by eager newspapermen who besieged him with torrents of questions.

Smiling, Winkler said, "Boys, you have your job, I have mine. There is a certain sanctity to the judicial process, especially inside the courtroom. So no questions in here."

The strategy behind his professional decorum became clear to Scott as soon as they appeared outside the courthouse. Waiting there was a contingent of TV cameras, some mounted on the backs of trucks, some hand-held. All zoomed in on Winkler as he appeared. The pursuing mediamen crowded around him, asking questions in profusion. Smiling, sheepish, pleading, Winkler said, "Boys, boys, please! One at a time."

One of the TV men shoved his mike closer, calling out, "Mr. Winkler, do you think you antagonized the judge by asking him to disqualify himself?"

"I'm not a seer or a psychiatrist. I wouldn't venture to guess what goes on in another man's mind. Except . . . I repeat, except . . . as it is reflected by what he actually does and says. Now I think it's pretty obvious what Judge Beecher thinks and feels. You were there. You saw him. It only confirms what I felt about him in the first place. It is perfectly obvious that there is a plot here to railroad my client into a life sentence. In the old days it would have been the chair. And how Beecher would have loved that!"

"You feel that way in the face of known facts?" a less sympathetic newsman asked.

"Facts?" Linc demanded, as he put his arm around Scott's shoulder, drawing him closer into the picture. "We have good reason to believe that the U.S. Attorney doesn't have quite the strong case the public has been led to believe. Or else he wouldn't be in such a rush to get to trial."

72

"Mr. Winkler, are you saying that the Prosecution's case is not as airtight as it seems, considering all the evidence that's already been made public?"

Linc appeared quite pained as he said, "That's the trouble in cases like this. Prosecutors like to try them in public instead of in the courtroom. So they let little bits of evidence leak to the press until there is built up in the public mind a picture of guilt that is almost impossible to eradicate."

"Are you saying Grove won't get a fair trial here?" a TV reporter persisted.

"I am saying it is open to considerable doubt. So we are moving for a change of venue. And that's all I'm going to say!" His arm still around Scott, he started shoving through the crowd of newsmen, who followed, pressed, urged and pleaded until, smiling, Linc said, "Boys, you know I don't like to try my cases on the sidewalk."

Then quickly, he and Scott slid into the first cab that was available, leaving the newsmen behind with enough material to make headlines in the afternoon editions and on the six o'clock news.

Inside the cab, Scott said, "Linc, in the future, if you're going to do anything like that for God's sake let me know first!"

"Like what?" Linc asked, innocently.

"Asking the judge to recuse himself. We don't do that here in the District. And not to a man of such excellent reputation as Beecher."

"Oh, you don't?" Linc replied. "Well, let me ask you just one question. What percentage of the population in the District is white? And what percentage of the judges sitting in the District are white?"

"Population, twenty-three percent white. Judges? I've never figured it out but I'd say, about seventy percent."

"There! Do you need any more proof of prejudice?" Linc challenged.

"Percentages don't mean that Beecher is prejudiced. He happens to be a very fair judge. We'll never sustain a charge of prejudice against him."

"I'm not through with him yet," Linc said, grinning. "Scotty, you listen to the old man. Judges are like bulls. You pick at them, toy with them, torment them until they become helpless and enraged. After that, reversible error flows from them like spring wine in Vienna."

They were silent for the rest of the trip to Georgetown. When they arrived at the Rosenstone house, they found Marlene Hutch waiting for them. Scott introduced them. Linc, as was his habit, ignored Marlene's outstretched hand, embraced her and kissed her lightly on the cheek, explaining, "Can't be comfortable with people I can't touch."

Marlene smiled back, her tan cheeks dimpling, making her even more attractive and appealing. Scott did not suspect that she resented the way Linc's hand brushed her breasts as he released her. As Linc stared into her shining black eyes, he joked, "Scott, we'll have to replace her with a homely girl. Or else I'll never get any work done!"

Scott smiled, hardly aware of the vague feeling of resentment awakened by Linc's familiarity with the girl.

Linc turned to the bar and started to fix himself a drink, speaking rapidly as he worked, "A good day! A real good day!"

"All we'll actually get out of it is the discovery. Which we're entitled to anyhow," Scott said.

"*And,*" Linc reminded him, "a few very important rulings that will help us on appeal. Now, you draw up that discovery motion, and as soon as we get all that material from the Government, I'll want a private meeting with Grove."

"That's another thing. Why a private meeting? There's nothing we have to say to Grove that can't be done in the usual way in the rotunda."

"Mystery, young man, mystery," Linc said, smiling. "Get

74

the press wondering what's so secret that we can't interview our client in the usual way, in the usual place. Create a feeling that we have more of a defense than we actually do. And you'd better get started on that motion for a change of venue."

"On what ground?"

"Inability to get a fair trial here, of course!"

"Linc, where are you going to find a Federal District in the entire country in which Grove can get a better shake than here? The jury'll probably be ninety percent black!" Scott argued.

Winkler seemed extremely thoughtful as he said slowly, "You just start on a rough draft of the motion papers as if we *did* have a case of prejudice here. I'll get you the facts." He started out of the room, calling, "Honey? Honey, you home?"

VI

Benjamin Owen Robertson was the only one of the nine Justices of the Supreme Court of the United States who owned two dinner jackets. Other Justices kept one for those few formal occasions that included White House evenings, law school reunions, club functions and the few dinners given by various bar associations at which they were guest speakers. But Robertson used both his dinner jackets very frequently and for this reason he was considered a rebel in his social life as well as when sitting on the Court. While most of the Justices preferred to live secluded private lives, protecting themselves from exposure to people or situations which might later create embarrassments in the courtroom, Ben Robertson believed, and strongly, that any judge of any court who removed himself from the mainstream of life was not only living in an ivory tower but worse, making law from one.

This evening, as Ben Robertson picked up his crisp white dress shirt, into which his man Oliver had already inserted the gold studs and links, he did so almost as an act of defiance. Defiance against his doctor, who had forbidden all outside activity since Miller's assassination. Defiance, too, against all those men in government and among the press who had cautioned that in view of the assassination the Justices should eschew all outside appearances if possible—not only for personal safety, but because the coming trial was sure to be the main topic of conversation at every gathering in Washington. And there was the chance that one day the Court might be called to rule on some phase of the Grove case.

Another fraud, Robertson said to himself, as he slipped into the cool white shirt. Merely because a Justice does not discuss a public matter doesn't mean that he doesn't think about it—or, in this case, could ever forget that horrible moment of unreality. Even now, the only real thing about it to Robertson was Miller's twisted body, half in his chair and half out, the blood seeping from his terrible head wound, his eyes still open, staring but seeing nothing. It was asking the humanly impossible to expect any man to forget it, or ever put that image out of his mind. So not going out in public to avoid being reminded of the tragic event was a fraud.

What was mandatory, and what Robertson would do as soon as he arrived at the Rosenstone house, was to let it be known that he would not enter into any discussion on the Grove case. But he did not intend to preclude any other guest from talking about it.

If he had wanted to, it would have been simple to use that unfortunate event as a reason for backing out of tonight's dinner party. But the purpose of the occasion was to raise money for the Clean World Association, a cause so dear to him that it superseded other considerations.

As he grew older, Ben Robertson had firmly promised himself two things. To the Court he would leave a legacy of liberalism which would endure. And for the nation he would do all in his power to leave the people with at least an awareness of the need to preserve God's earth, its water, mountains and forests, protecting it from men who invaded and laid waste its natural assets. Tonight's cause was worthy of any embarrassment or criticism which might come to him for making an appearance.

Besides, he liked Honey Rosenstone. He admired her far

more than he admired her husband. Bob was one of those bright men who show promise in their youth, but once they marry into wealth, seem to lose all incentive and desire to advance. Bob Rosenstone might have become an excellent lawyer or a fine public official if he had not decided to play lord of the manor after he married into the Niles money. From that time on he fancied himself a man with a mission, to make the best possible use of the Niles family wealth. And he had indoctrinated Honey into that way of life too.

Still, Honey was a refreshing change from the stiff, cold, ambitious, gentile women around Washington, wives and mistresses of men seeking official favor or advancement. It was a strange distinction to make, since Robertson was himself a Christian, though he was not known to attend church except for funerals of associates, present or past. There was something about Honey, warm, delightful, relaxed and, yes, sensual, that he liked a great deal. She was the kind of woman who in her subtle way made a man feel young and sexually desirable again.

Honey would always arrange to seat him next to an attractive and highly intelligent young woman. And Robertson would take roguish delight in starting off the conversation with some slightly ribald joke. It set the woman at ease, dispelling at once the usual stiffness and solemnity that pervaded all conversations with Supreme Court Justices.

Judges, all judges, are first and foremost human beings. Ben Robertson insisted on that prerogative. So he made no secret that he liked the company of women. Twice since his wife Edna had died, he had almost married again, but in the end decided against it. He loved the bachelor's life to which he had grown accustomed. And going to dinner at Honey's or some of the other homes in Georgetown and Washington offered him enough diversion and enough female company to allow him his little flirtations which he, and everyone else, knew would come to nothing.

Robertson stared into the mirror, trying to straighten the

ends of his black satin bow tie and stealing a look at his own roundish face, his cheeks ruddy despite his heart trouble. Santa Claus cheeks, Honey liked to call them. And they were, especially with his snowy hair for contrast. Some women liked to call him "cute," a word he detested. But there were times, such as right now, when with a glint of anticipation in his blue eyes, he could plead guilty to looking cute.

Oliver was waiting at the door with Robertson's hat, gloves, scarf and evening coat. While he held the coat for the justice to slip into, Robertson took the opportunity to ask, "Oliver, that joke you told me last week . . ."

"Yes, sir?" Oliver asked.

"Could you refresh my recollection, as we are wont to say in the courtroom?"

"The one about the Jewish merchant in the Southern town? And the White Citizens' Council came to get him to join in the fight against busing," Oliver offered.

"That's the one!" Robertson exclaimed.

"Well, they started pressuring him, saying how, if the civil righters had their way on busing, next thing his daughter would not only have to sit next to nigras in school but would associate with them socially. She might even be tempted to go out with one. And who knows what that would lead to? So as a clincher they asked, 'Now, Sol, you wouldn't want your daughter to marry a nigra, would you?' And the little Jew looked up at them and said, 'Gentlemen, to tell you the truth, I wouldn't want she should marry *any* gentile.'"

"Yes, that's the one," Robertson said. But he seemed disappointed. "Somehow, I thought it was a little risqué. But it isn't, is it?"

Sadly Oliver shook his head, unhappy that he had failed the Justice. Then he opened the door, and watched Ben Robertson hurry down the front steps to where the Rosenstone Rolls Royce was waiting.

The other guests were well along with their drinking by the time Justice Robertson arrived. Honey greeted him at the door as usual. He kissed her on the lips, inhaling the sensuous perfume she always wore on such occasions. There was never a time when he kissed Honey that he didn't lament a little, privately, and sometimes openly, that he had not met a woman like her years before. She would have been the ideal wife for him. Better still, the ideal mistress. As he grew older, Ben Robertson discovered there was more and more to regret, and Honey was one of the things he regretted most.

She helped him off with his coat, handed it to the butler, and escorted him into the formal living room. There she introduced him to the guests, all of whom he recognized personally or by reputation. With each handshake and nod, each smile and simple greeting, he did a bit of financial arithmetic. The hands he shook represented wealth mounting into several billions, most of it newly made in the last generation. Honey had rounded up an able group of contributors. He must put forth one of his better efforts tonight. So his smile grew broader and his compliments to the women more effusive.

As Robertson turned away from his last handshake and his final word of greeting, he saw standing in the doorway at the far end of the long room a figure who struck him as eminently familiar. Yet it was someone he had not met tonight or on any other night as far as he could remember. Then suddenly he knew. It was a face he had seen many times in the newspapers and magazines in recent years. It was A. Lincoln Winkler.

Honey hadn't mentioned that Winkler would be here tonight, an unusual oversight on her part. She was always very solicitous about briefing Ben on who the guests would be, in the event that any of them could prove to be an embarrassment to him in court or in the public press. Perhaps, he thought, Winkler appeared at the last moment and she hadn't had time to explain. In any case, he did not resent

80

Winkler's presence. The fellow was colorful and interesting, if a bit extreme and unorthodox in the courtroom. But it was good for the law to be shaken out of its stuffy ways every so often—in practice as well as in substance. Robertson himself had a reputation for doing just that in some of his opinions and decision-making. No, despite his momentary surprise, Ben Robertson felt no reluctance to meet Linc Winkler socially.

Now Honey was approaching, leading not only Winkler but a tall, handsome young man as well.

"Linc is staying with us during the Grove trial," Honey explained. "So it was either have him eat with us or out in the kitchen with the help."

Robertson knew it was Honey's way of apologizing for what might prove an awkward situation. To put her at ease, he said, "A wise choice, my dear. Out there he'd only organize your help and they'd be out on strike before dinner was even served. It's much safer to have him in here with us." He turned to Linc, "Mr. Winkler?" and held out his hand.

A look passed from Winkler to Honey which seemed to say, There, the old man doesn't seem to mind at all. Then Linc introduced Scott Ingram. Justice Robertson knew Scott's father, so the moment passed pleasantly. Except that Scott was forced to wonder, if there *is* a Heaven and a St. Peter at the gate, would he also say, "Oh, yes, of course. Scott Ingram the Third. I know your father."

Since Bob Rosenstone was off on a trip, Justice Robertson sat in the host chair at one end of the long, elegantly set table, facing Honey at the other end. To Robertson's right sat Mrs. Percy Soames, whose husband had made a fortune in electronics for the military during Korea and Vietnam. Recently he had sold out his business and taken up residence in Washington where he was hopeful that he might receive a Cabinet post one day soon. In the meantime the Soameses dedicated their wealth and their time to worthy causes. Mrs.

Soames, Caroline, was a dark young woman, slender, with bright violet eyes and delicate features. She smiled easily and was an outgoing person—exactly the sort of young lady Robertson preferred. Once he had made her laugh heartily at a few of his jokes, Caroline Soames overcame her original surprise and stiffness and proved to be a charming companion.

Midway down the table, Linc Winkler was heard to raise his voice. "You find it not only in the White House but in the Congress as well. Planned repression is what it is! And now the Court! With those new appointments there's no avenue of escape. If there's one last bastion against repression in this country, he is sitting right here at this table tonight!"

By the time Linc had reached that point in his outburst all other voices around the table had ceased. "There are only three edifices in Washington worthy of preservation. The Washington Monument. The Lincoln Memorial. And Justice Benjamin Robertson!"

Only then did he pretend to realize that he alone was speaking. He stopped abruptly, looked about, and finally glanced toward the end of the table.

"I'm sorry if I've embarrassed you, Mr. Justice. But with the new Court, you're our last hope—our only hope against an era of repression that gives one the cold, clammy feeling of a new Dark Age. Still I shouldn't have let my emotions run away with me. Certainly not in your presence. Just in the unlikely event that the Grove case might one day come up before you. I'm terribly sorry."

"Quite all right, Mr. Winkler. Let *me* worry about that," Robertson said.

"It was thoughtless of me to put you in a position where you're forced to worry about it," Linc responded.

"If the shock of witnessing the crime didn't prejudice me, surely I can retain my judicial integrity in the face of something as corrupting as a little flattery," Robertson said, putting Linc and the rest of the company at ease again.

After that, Linc moderated his voice and Robertson turned

his attention back to Mrs. Soames. When dinner was over and coffee had been served, Robertson leaned back in his chair and proceeded to make a short but intense speech which reflected his own fervent feelings about the need for private assistance in ecological research. Since this was really the purpose of the evening, when he was done and before any contributions were solicited, Robertson pleaded the lateness of the hour and his advanced age, made his apologies to Mrs. Soames, thanked her for being such a pleasant companion, and excused himself. Honey saw him to the door, helped him on with his coat, and kissed him warmly, assuring him, "Half a million tonight, Ben. I promise you."

He kissed her back and whispered as he'd done so many times before, "I'd give it all for one night with you when I was young." It was a joke he made often, and yet it always left her a little sad. When he was young he must have been five times the man that Bob Rosenstone was.

By the time Honey returned to the dining room, Percy Soames had taken over the matter of raising the money and was well on his way to pledges in excess of three hundred thousand dollars. Honey's job was merely to increase it enough so that with her own donation of fifty thousand it came to an even half million.

That done, everyone assumed that the evening was over. But Linc Winkler leaned forward to say, quite gravely, "I wonder if you very nice, very decent people have a moment for a kind of pollution that disturbs me. The pollution of the body politic. The pollution of the legal system by which we are all judged, and by which some are judged more severely than others. Because I am confronted with a serious problem in regard to a case that I don't have to mention, I'm sure."

Shoving back his chair and rising to his feet in a way that reminded Scott of his courtroom manner, Linc stood towering over all of them, his graying hair a wild, defiant mane, his eyes intent with his purpose.

"You've heard a hell of a lot about the woes of lawyers

who embrace unpopular causes. I don't intend to play that tune, because frankly, whenever I hear a lawyer bemoan the fate of those who defend unpopular causes, I am tempted to say, 'Then get the hell out! Don't waste your concern on yourself, devote it to your cause, to your client!'

"Now, I know I am not the best-loved lawyer in this country. Tonight I am probably its most hated lawyer, to have undertaken the Grove case, especially after all the others I've handled. But that's the nature of this beast. And I am here without fee. Now I don't want your applause for that. What I *do* want is the money it costs to run a defense like this, money to pay secretaries, phone bills, taxi fares, investigators, doctors' bills, psychiatrists' bills.

"I can only give my time and what little skill I have. Someone else will have to provide the out-of-pocket expenses. Now, mind you, I am not saying that I ask this in the name of an innocent man. I am not saying he should get off. All I'm saying is that it's my duty to do my damnedest to see that Grove gets a fair trial. I'd like your help in that."

Having said that, Winkler turned and walked out, as though to linger might hurt his cause or embarrass Honey's guests. But within fifteen minutes after he had left, Honey had succeeded in collecting pledges adding up to a hundred and ten thousand dollars.

The last sounds of the last guests had long since died away. From below, the discreet noises of the staff cleaning up were finally over. In her bedroom, in the dark, Honey Rosenstone lay naked on her bed, her coverlet thrown aside. Beside her, his face pressed against her fragrant cheek, his hand on her ample breast, Linc Winkler whispered softly, "I told you it would go off all right."

"Ben didn't say anything. But I'm sure he didn't like what happened tonight. He's a fine old man. A great friend. Don't ever ask me to do anything like that again," she said.

"It was an emergency, darling. I had to, you know that. Certainly the other guests didn't mind."

"Just don't ever do that to him again," Honey insisted.

Instead of answering, he drew her close, buried his face between her breasts. When he felt her fingers toy with his bushy hair, then press his head tightly against her, he knew he was forgiven. Now he could begin to enjoy her full and fragrant body.

Honey had reached for a cigarette. Linc was lying on his back staring up at the ceiling. Suddenly he asked, "When is Bob coming back?"

"I don't know. A week, maybe longer."

"Darling, have you ever thought what it would be like if there were no Bob?"

"And no Rose?" she countered, mentioning Linc's wife.

"The kids are grown. It could be managed," he said quite firmly.

"It wouldn't work."

"Why not?" he asked resentfully, turning on his side to face her.

"Bob respects money. So he doesn't interfere in my life. That's why you're here now. But you'd never allow this. You have to dominate, be applauded, lionized, remarked on. If I married you I'd have to live your life, your way. Instead of Rose alone in a house up in Westchester, I'd be Honey, alone in a house in Georgetown. Well, Honey does not sit around waiting for any man."

"If you can say that, you don't really know me," Winkler responded, hurt.

"I've seen it, Linc. The way you've blossomed in the last dozen years, once you found out you could be a personality. Remember in the early days when you were trying to be a writer and a lecturer? Law was just a necessary chore then. You were seeking personal recognition, fame. Then you

85

found you could achieve it through the law. And you're not about to give it up for any woman, not even for me. So I'll take you this way, in short, convenient doses, between those cause-crazy chicks who chase you on every campus. Do those kids really know anything about making love? Or is it all hurry, hurry, hurry, like little long-haired rabbits?"

Linc laughed. "Love it isn't," he said a bit sadly. "But it does wonders for a man. And God, those eighteen- and nineteen-year-olds have the most wonderful, firm, high breasts. If the girls in my day had gone without bras, I never would have graduated from college.

"You know something I think about," he exclaimed suddenly. "The age difference between an eighteen-year-old and me is no greater than the age difference between you and Robertson. Tell me, did he ever make a pass at you? Really?"

"No," Honey said a bit sadly, "but if he ever did I'd say yes."

Linc Winkler laughed.

"Yes, I would!" Honey insisted. "He's a fascinating man. The most interesting man I know, of any age."

"He certainly says the most interesting things," Linc said significantly.

"Meaning?" Honey asked, disturbed by Winkler's tone.

"Just that he says the most interesting and enlightening things, darling. That's all."

As he embraced her, he whispered urgently, "You and me, Honey, I want you to think about that. Seriously. A woman like you deserves better than Bob."

She tried to protest, but he kissed her hard. Then he insisted, "Think about it!"

Her answer was a fierce embrace.

VII

Unencumbered by his bulging briefcase, with his trench-coat open, his glasses shoved back on his head, Linc Winkler stood before forbidding St. Elizabeth's Hospital and looked up at the barred windows of the prison ward where he knew his meeting with Dr. Paul Randolph would take place.

Because Scott Ingram was totally involved in the discovery proceeding at the U.S. Attorney's office and for other reasons of his own, Linc Winkler had chosen this afternoon to meet Randolph alone.

He made his way along the corridor which smelled of strong disinfectant and roach powder. All sounds seemed magnified as they echoed belligerently from the walls of the kitchen and the wards. Voices assailed him, some plaintive, some angry. Metallic grinding noises shrieked from hospital carts whose rubber wheels had worn down too far or were entirely missing.

Winkler finally located Dr. Randolph's office and walked into a small, ill-furnished reception room. It abounded with file folders stacked haphazardly atop cabinets and on both corners of the front desk. No one was in the room, not even the receptionist. After a few minutes, when still no one had appeared Winkler went to the closed door and listened. Hearing sounds, he knocked.

"One moment!" a man's deep voice called out with some

irritation. The door finally opened and Winkler was confronted by a tall black man in a spotless white lab coat. The hostile glance from sharp eyes behind glasses changed to recognition, then relaxation as Randolph put out a huge strong hand.

"Dr. Randolph?" Winkler asked.

"Mr. Winkler, it's a pleasure. And an honor," Randolph said. Winkler reached out with his left hand to grip Randolph's arm in a gesture of friendship and was impressed by the muscularity of it.

"Come in, come in, brother," Randolph said, stepping away from the door so Winkler could enter and then locking it behind him. It was clear Dr. Randolph did not wish to be interrupted for a long time.

The inner room was no more tidy than the outer office. More case histories awaiting filing or review covered the large desk, an old battered armchair and half the treatment couch. And there was another stack of dusty and untidy files on the table where a glass coffee pot was lazily bubbling on a small electric hotplate.

Randolph invited Winkler to sit down in the only fairly new chair in the room, then he poured cups of coffee for himself and Winkler. Randolph spoke with meticulous diction in a deep bass voice, and Winkler formed the conclusion that the black man must be an islander, Jamaican probably.

"I'm delighted that you have been called in on the case, Mr. Winkler . . ."

"Linc," Winkler corrected pleasantly.

"Linc. Because other lawyers might look on this case as an affront to the body politic and hence one to be finished off and put out of sight as quickly and quietly as possible."

Winkler nodded. "An attack like this strikes at more than the life of one Justice of the Supreme Court. It threatens the entire white concept of law, order and government. Naturally most people are very bitter about it, including many black people."

"Don't I know that!" Randolph agreed. "Turn Grove loose among certain blacks and they'd lynch him even faster than a white mob. Group guilt, or the old quarantine psychosis. The criminal is diseased. Separate yourself from him and you won't catch it. Accuse him first, so no one will accuse you. It's part of ghetto mentality."

Randolph's precise enunciation of the t's in ghetto was almost surgical in its effect.

"Now, I think I have enough material here," Randolph gestured toward the single manila folder that occupied the center of his desk, "to make an insanity plea plausible. At least we can put up a good fight."

"Fine," Winkler responded politely, but without any great show of enthusiasm. When Randolph stopped to sip his hot coffee, Winkler asked, "When was the last time you had Grove in here? For how long? And what was the diagnosis?"

Randolph opened the file to Grove's summary sheet. "He went on out-patient status three months ago this coming week. He had been in here for five months before that. And the diagnosis was 'mild psychosis of schizoid type, induced by his early environmental pattern.' The final psychiatric evaluation by the board reads in part, 'It is our conclusion that while suffering from a mildly abnormal mental condition, patient Grove has recovered sufficiently so that, in our opinion, he will not be dangerous to himself or others, within the reasonably foreseeable future.'"

"And yet," Winkler said pointedly, "within three months he went out and committed a most serious crime, one which evidently took great determination!"

"Those things happen, Mr. . . . Linc. We have no way of knowing what might have triggered it, what might have happened to him between the time the board arrived at this conclusion and the time he was impelled to commit this crime."

Not wanting to drive directly at the main purpose of his visit, Winkler smiled. "Doctor, wouldn't it be a little embarrassing to go into court and plead insanity with that opinion

89

on the record? Suppose I put you on the stand to testify as to his mental incapacity now or when he committed the crime. Wouldn't the jury be likely to say, if Randolph and his board were so wrong before, how can we have any faith in his professional opinion now?"

"I understand," Randolph said quickly.

"I'm glad you do," Winkler said. "Some doctors are very touchy about things like that."

"Not I!" Randolph said, rather proudly.

"Good! Because there's one other delicate but important question I have to ask."

"Fire away!" Randolph said, a big, confident smile spreading across his face.

"Were you on good terms with Grove while he was here?"

"Exceedingly good terms. I might say that I was the first real father figure he's had in his entire lifetime. You see, he was an orphan. Deserted, actually. He has no recollection of anyone except one old lady whom he referred to as his grandmother. When she died he was placed in an orphanage, where he lived until he was fourteen.

"As a child he was picked on by the other boys. At first he would fight back, but he's small, so continual beatings led him to become passive, withdrawn, totally amenable to those around him. At fifteen, when he was sent to a reformatory, he allowed himself to be subjected to a number of homosexual experiences, though he was not homosexual by nature. Eventually there evolved an adolescent who had completely throttled the ability to express anger or hatred, even under the most justifiable circumstances. His response to almost any situation was to cower, hide, and do whatever would assure the least notice or response from those in authority.

"He became," Randolph said finally, "almost a non-person. The cleanest, quietest, least offensive boy in his environment."

"Yet he went out and committed an act of murder," Winkler challenged. "Would it surprise you if I told you he said *you* instructed him to do it?"

"No," Randolph answered quite calmly.

"Doesn't that seem strange to you?" Winkler asked, honestly puzzled now.

"With his history, of course not. Even when he committed the sole act of defiance of his entire life against a system that had destroyed him, even then he couldn't take the responsibility. He had to blame someone else. That's precisely the point. When his anger is justified, he can't express it openly. He can't stand up and say, 'I killed that white motherfucker because he has robbed me of my manhood, of my right to life.' He has to say, 'Someone else told me to do it.' Not unusual at all."

Winkler nodded understandingly. "But I was struck by the fact that he doesn't use that kind of language. He's soft-spoken."

"Precisely," Randolph said, "another symptom of his problem."

"I assume you discussed his problem with him?" Winkler asked.

"For hours on end."

"You told him that the root of his trouble was his inability to express his hostility?"

"He would go to work for one employer after another, mainly white. He would be conscientious, gentlemanly, on time, hard-working. I checked out several myself and found that he always did more than he was hired to do. But when it came time for him to assert himself, to ask for a raise or for time off for some personal matter, he could never bring himself to do it. So after a while, he simply didn't go back to work, though in each case that I checked they would have been glad to have him back, glad to give him a raise. When I confronted him with these facts, he was paralyzed. He didn't deny what I said, but he couldn't explain it either. He was

91

terrified of admitting his own hostility and enormously fearful of allowing it to come out. Naturally, as his doctor, it was my job to point that out."

Randolph rose and began to pace, talking with more urgency now, "Whitey thinks he's got a problem when he's confronted by black violence. I tell you the bigger problems are those like Grove. The majority!

"When he was first brought in here, withdrawn, almost catatonic, he couldn't talk at all. I had to put him under sodium amytal I.V.'s the first four sessions to get anything out of him. Then it started to come out, his horrible early life, his fears in the orphanage. If he didn't behave he would have to go hungry. That happened a number of times, until he throttled the impulse to fight back, to hate back, just so he could go on eating. Then later his fear of beatings made it impossible for him to resist bigger boys, so he had to acquiesce in their sexual games. And he was always the female. Today he is sexless for all practical purposes, emotionally castrated, hating homosexuals yet feeling grossly inadequate insofar as women are concerned. His only salvation was to learn how to fight back, how to express hostility. I tried to show him that."

Winkler put down his cup and swung around to face Randolph, listening more and more intently.

"One day, when his treatment was reaching a climax, I tried to goad him into openly declaring his hatred for all white people, but he couldn't. So I tried to get him to call me a black motherfucker in a white coat. I even went so far as to accuse him of deliberately inviting those homosexual acts that he claimed were forced on him. I knew from the amytal interviews that was not true, but I hoped my accusations could enrage him enough to make him explode and give vent to his rage. Yet all he did was sit there and shake his head—little, timid shakes of the head. Those were all the denials, all the anger, all the protest he could express.

"I said to myself that day, I hate every white sonofabitch in this whole world! Because Midgely Grove was not an unintelligent boy. You could see that for yourself. But what intelligence he once had has been ground out of him by a world that destroyed him. A white world, a world that not only hated him but denied him his rightful chance to hate back.

"I told him that day, until the time came when he could express his anger, he would never get well. He had to find some release, some way of acting out. Unless he did, there was no more that I could do for him."

Winkler sat still for a moment, then leaned forward in Randolph's direction. "Did you see him much after that?"

"Very little. Just like his jobs, he just drifted away. He must have taken my challenge as a rejection."

"But that board evaluation?" Winkler asked.

"Some weeks later he came back asking for more official termination. It seemed he would be able to get a job if we gave him clearance. So I presented his case and was authorized to write that report," Randolph said.

Winkler nodded, slowly, thoughtfully.

"If you want me to testify," Randolph said, "I would be only too happy to. I still think there's a chance to sustain a plea of insanity. Of course it's far from the strongest case I've ever seen."

Winkler didn't answer at once for now he was thinking more about Randolph than about Grove. This was the moment he had anticipated. And without Scott Ingram here, he was free to proceed with his plan.

"Randolph, I want a few straight, off-the-record answers from you," Winkler said. "If I were any other white man in the world I wouldn't dare ask this, but I've given a lot to the cause, as you know."

Winkler paused, then added, "One professional man to another, never to be repeated outside this room?"

Tense, his fierce eyes betraying enormous curiosity, Randolph nodded his agreement.

"Suppose we *were* able to sustain insanity, or incapacity to stand trial, suppose Grove was remanded to St. Elizabeth's or some sanitarium for the rest of his life, what would we really have accomplished?" Winkler asked.

Randolph studied Winkler's face, but did not respond.

"From what you told me, psychiatrically he's virtually a lost cause," Winkler continued. "But even if by some miracle you could salvage him, he would only have to stand trial for this murder eventually. So what have we achieved in the long run? We've simply cooperated with the white power structure to eventually carry out their vengeance against a victim they produced in the first place."

Winkler rose, stood eye to eye with Randolph, and said, "On the other hand, tried now this case could become a case of enormous importance in the life of this nation. Midge Grove may have been destined to become part of history, in an unprecedented opportunity to change the entire judicial process. So you have to weigh, as I do, the relative values involved. The fate of Midge Grove against the chance to accomplish something of nationwide, even worldwide importance for the black race. Think about that."

Winkler paused only for a moment. "If Midge Grove goes to trial, then that courtroom is our forum to the world."

"But if all that comes of it is a sanity proceeding which determines he isn't fit to stand trial," Randolph said, "it dies there, hidden from public view?"

"Exactly! Or let me put it another way. Grove has already been destroyed by the system, but he can help reform the system before it does the same to countless other black kids. There's almost a divine justice in that."

Randolph nodded. "Whatever I have to do, I'll do."

"Good!" Winkler said. "Because this trial has two purposes. First, I am going to give that poor boy the most determined defense you or anybody else has ever seen. Everybody else in the world may write him off, say he's guilty, but not I. And not my colleague, Ingram, who I can tell you is a bright young lawyer.

94

"But," Winkler emphasized, "just as important to me is the second purpose. This trial will be our platform—yours and mine—to let the world know about the real injustice involved here. This will be the most thoroughly covered trial in the history of this nation. It's the trial that would have taken place if Jack Ruby hadn't shot Lee Harvey Oswald. We have to make use of that publicity."

Randolph nodded thoughtfully, then smiled in anticipation.

"Now, here's what I want you to do," Winkler continued. "Make no statements, grant no interviews to the press. Instead prepare yourself to throw up a psychiatric smoke screen. I want to establish, for example, that Grove never intended to harm anyone. Maybe he was simply acting out an impulse of great therapeutic value to free himself from his deadly inhibition. We admit there was the need to express hostility, but no premeditation, certainly not the genuine intent to kill."

Randolph nodded thoughtfully. "The episode might have proved just as cathartic if he had fired that pistol and never hit anyone."

"Yes . . ." Winkler agreed, surprised for the instant at the genuine impact of the argument. "Yes! Precisely! Excellent!"

"And Randolph," Winkler continued, "remember while you are on the stand you will be talking to the nation, to the world. Every promise you ever made to yourself, every act of discrimination you ever experienced, you'll finally have the chance to let the whole world know!"

Winkler could sense the anger and the determination he had summoned up in Randolph. The black face grew leaner, harder, and the intense eyes focused more sharply behind his thick glasses.

95

·◦❧ VIII ❧◦·

Scott had just finished reporting to Linc Winkler what he had learned in the discovery examination. Winkler was silent for a moment, twisting the ends of his graying hair in a nervous gesture that Scott had learned to recognize as a sign of frustrated thought.

"All the labels cut out of his coat?" Linc finally asked.

"Only a man contemplating a crime does that. So they've got premeditation," Scott said.

"H'mmm," Linc grunted. "That's for sure."

"And the weapon was a new Saturday night special, purchased just two weeks before the crime. Corroborates premeditation."

"Any value in getting a ballistics expert to work on that gun?" Linc asked.

Scott shook his head. "The FBI did a most careful, precise job of reconstructing the fragments and proving their origin. And they've got his prints on the weapon too."

"They didn't miss a trick," Linc admitted grudgingly. "He struck a blow at the Establishment right where the Establishment lives, and they're not going to let him get away with it!"

"Maybe we *should* reconsider raising the insanity issue," Scott suggested, with growing conviction.

"Christ, Scott, after what I found out this morning I wouldn't be in any hurry to move for an M.O.!"

96

"Randolph was no help?" Scott asked.

"He's a brilliant man. Very helpful and eager to cooperate. But when the chips are down he admits that we'd be in a very weak position trying to make out a case of previous legal incapacity to commit a crime of intent, or of present incapacity sufficient to keep him from standing trial. It could boomerang and destroy our entire case. We'd better forget the M.O."

Scott nodded, reluctantly.

Winkler thought a moment, then said, "Scott, let's prepare motion papers asking for Midge's removal to some hospital facility where a staff of our own specialists can give him a thorough physical. It may take as long as five days. I want it that thorough!"

"What good will a physical do?"

Linc turned and smiled at Scott. "Don't you ever give the old man credit for anything?" And then he quickly changed the subject, "Those face-to-face identifications, go over those again."

"There were two. The woman from Camden, Mrs. Evalyn Huffman, who sat next to Midge in the courtroom before and during the time he fired the shot. And the court attendant, Harley Bevans. Black man."

"I know, first class Civil Service Tom," Winkler said with some irritation. Then suddenly, "Both identifications made immediately after the shooting?"

"Within a half-hour, near as anyone can remember," Scott said.

"Wait until they get to court, they'll remember precisely," Winkler said. Suddenly he declared, "I think we're ready to have that private conference with Grove now. Get permission from Judge Beecher as soon as possible." Linc made it sound so crucial that Scott decided to leave for the courthouse at once. When he reached the library door, he turned. "I still don't see what a physical can do for us."

Linc smiled. "Trust me, Scott. Just trust the old man. Okay?"

97

The private consultation room in the cellblock of the courthouse basement was small, with a single window above viewing height and barred on the outside. A cheap pine table stood in the middle of the floor, a smelly plastic ashtray on top, and four small, straight-backed chairs placed around it. Scott took some yellow pads and a fistful of sharpened pencils from his briefcase, setting them down on the table in two groups, one for himself, one for Linc.

But Linc pushed his aside. "I depend on memory in meetings like this," he said. "Whatever is important I remember. Notes only distract me."

The door opened. Two Federal Marshals ushered Midge Grove into the room. He looked smaller, thinner, even more pathetic than the day he had appeared in court. His hair had grown out more and was now a disheveled afro.

Winkler went to him, embraced him. "How have they been treating you, Midge?"

Grove nodded vaguely as Linc led him to a chair on one side of the table. Scott half rose from his seat, shaking hands with the timid black man. Winkler settled Grove into his chair, and then instead of sitting down himself, he moved behind Grove and gently placed both hands comfortingly on his narrow shoulders.

"Midge, you've got to help us so we can help you. Answer my questions. Tell me everything you remember. What may seem like a detail to you may be extremely important to us. You're not a lawyer. We are. Let us judge what's important. Right?"

"Right," Midge said, in a voice barely audible even in that small room in which Winkler had to moderate his voice to keep it from reverberating off the walls.

"After they apprehended you, tell me exactly what happened."

"I told you . . ."

"I want it all again from the beginning!" Winkler insisted.

Grove's description of events was halting, but it coincided exactly with what Scott had learned at the discovery examination. With a head signal Linc beckoned Scott to join him in the corner. He spoke in angry whispers, "Airtight! Everything according to Miranda! The only loophole they leave us is a possible question on the face-to-face identification. Tell you what, you hotfoot it over to the U.S. Attorney's office and ask to hear those identification tapes, then demand a transcript. I'll finish up with Grove. There's not much more to cover anyhow."

Scott nodded, turned back to the table to gather up his papers swiftly as Linc started on Grove again.

"Now, Midge, I want you to try and remember if they ever said anything at all to you, or in your presence, about making a confession. Anything!"

As Grove concentrated on trying to remember, Scott gestured good-bye to Linc and slipped out of the room.

As soon as the door closed, Winkler commanded, "Midge, forget about the confession and listen to me!"

Winkler rose, began to pace within the tight confines of the bare room. When he had aroused sufficient fear and tension in Grove, he said suddenly, "I asked Scott to leave us because I have something to discuss with you privately."

He paused, until Grove was forced to turn and look up at him.

"Midge, I went to see Dr. Randolph at St. Elizabeth's. We had a long talk about you. Randolph is your friend, you know that. So what he told me about you, he told me for your own good. In strictest confidence. That's why I didn't want even Scott to hear it."

Grove turned away, tense and uneasy. Winkler moved behind him, leaned in toward him to speak softly into his ear.

"Randolph told me everything about you, Midge. Everything. He had to—for your sake. He told me about your difficulty with your hostility. That you had to learn to express it, but never did. He doesn't think that you wanted to kill anyone. You only wanted to express your hostility—in an attempt to regain your manhood."

Winkler stared down at Grove. His ears and cheeks had flushed, and he dared not breathe.

"Yes, and he told me what those boys did to you in the reformatory, too. I understand, Midge. Believe me, I understand. It could have happened to anyone under the same circumstances. And I will keep your secret forever. It will be between you and me and Dr. Randolph."

Grove seemed to relax just a bit until Winkler added, "But if I have to put you on the stand, then I can't guarantee anything. On cross-examination, the Prosecutor might bring all that out in public. But as far as it remains in my control, you don't have to worry about it. Understand?"

Midge nodded, a single, stiff, guarded gesture.

"The only reason I went to see Randolph was to find out if we could make an insanity plea stand up. He said no."

Winkler moved around the table, dropped into his chair. Leaning forward, staring directly into Grove's eyes, he said, "Midge, if it meant getting on the stand to testify about your homosexual experiences, or going to prison for life, which would you choose?"

"I won't talk about that," Grove managed to blurt out.

"I thought so. So our choices are even more limited," Winkler said hopelessly. "Unless . . ."

Grove looked up expectantly.

"Midge, did you ever hear the expression, 'political trial?' Do you know what it means?"

Grove thought for a moment and then shook his head.

"We could proceed on the basis that this was not a premeditated murder, but an act of protest. Not directed at Justice Miller or any one man but directed at society as a whole. It was your way of expressing resentment against a society that did these terrible things to you.

"We'll claim you're not on trial for killing a man, but because of your opinions and your hostility toward the white power structure. And this is the important part, Midge. I won't have to put you on the stand to prove that, so the Prosecutor won't have the chance to cross-examine you to ask you about your experiences in the reformatory. But what I *will* need from you is evidence of your political opinions. I will need it in the courtroom, during the trial, so the whole world can see. All the hostility you've never been able to express before, you can show now. And by doing so, you can save yourself!" Winkler drilled home.

Grove lifted his head and stared, not at Winkler but straight ahead, as if he dared not look at any other human being.

"Did you hear me, Midge, you can save yourself!"

Grove nodded.

"So remember that you did not intend to kill that man, or any man. You wanted to express hostility toward a system that's ground down your people for hundreds of years, that forced you to grow up the way you did, that put you in that reformatory and allowed those terrible things to happen to you. But I can't stand up in front of the court and say these things and expect them to believe me. They won't. You've got to *show* them!"

Suddenly Winkler seized him, turned him about, lifted his chin and stared down into Grove's eyes. Still holding Grove's chin with his left hand, Winkler lifted his own right in a clenched fist salute.

"Do that!"

Grove slowly made a fist, timidly raised it.

"Higher!" Winkler ordered. Grove lifted his fist higher. "Higher!!" Winkler insisted sharply. Grove thrust his hand as high as he could. "Okay," Winkler said, finally satisfied.

"Now you will do that every time you come into the courtroom. You will do it to the judge, and each time you face the jury you will do it. Understand?"

Grove nodded.

"The judge will be angry. He will order you not to do it, but don't be afraid, I'll be protecting you. We'll show the whole world that you *can* express yourself, that you *can* speak out. Midgely Grove is a man! With all the feelings and rights of a man! Understand?"

"Yes, Mr. Winkler," Grove said in a hoarse whisper.

"Linc! Call me Linc! Okay?"

"Linc . . . okay," Grove said tentatively.

"Now sometimes I'll ask you to shout out certain things in court, or do certain things. We'll practice them together in private first, then you'll do them. Understand?" Grove nodded.

"If you do what I tell you, you won't have to testify. And all those things that happened to you in the reformatory can remain our secret forever. But most of all, we might be able to get you off. Free!"

Winkler put both his hands on Grove's thin shoulders. "We'll show them, kid. We'll make them pay for everything they ever did to you. Everything!"

IX

At the same time that Scott Ingram heard the identification tapes, he also got U.S. Attorney Carroll's promise that a physical for Grove would not be opposed. During the five days of tests and examinations, Midgely Grove would be held in the prison ward section of a hospital, not far from the District jail. Prior to exposing Grove to the doctors, Winkler gathered them in a conference room on the ward to instruct them.

"Gentlemen, in addition to the usual professional confidence that prevails between doctor and patient, in this particular instance I will demand an even higher degree of confidentiality. Nothing that comes to light concerning this unfortunate man's medical background is to be allowed to leak. Else it may seriously damage the Defense case. No matter how you feel personally about the Defendant, or the crime of which he is accused, I'm sure you all want to see that he gets a fair trial."

The doctors, grim and as impressed as Winkler had intended they be, nodded soberly.

"I want a complete and thorough series of X-rays of every organ, every bone in his body. I want a complete rundown on his glandular system. When I have your reports in hand I want to know every illness that he's ever had, every injury he's ever suffered, every deprivation—everything that it is possible to learn about a human being. In a phrase, I want an autopsy before death."

Having said that, he turned Midge Grove over to them.

During the period of days the tests would take, Winkler left Washington to fulfill public appearances, some of which had been added to his schedule after Midge Grove became his client. Any questions which came up about the case during Winkler's absence could be handled by Ingram.

Winkler's entrance into the Grove case had sent his popularity surging again. If those who attended his speeches now were not all militant believers, if they came to see a celebrity, still they came. By the time he had finished presenting Midgely Grove as the victim of an oppressive system, the crowds of young people were with him. They answered Winkler fist for fist! They were almost as militant in demanding a fair trial for Midge Grove as he was. He had recaptured some of the old feeling again. It felt good, nostalgic.

And, of course, he had daily coverage in all the media, even though the first shock waves after the killing of Justice Miller had begun to recede. Whenever Linc Winkler was involved in a case, the press, TV, and radio were alert to follow his every word.

Scott, too, found himself beseiged by the press during his trips to and from the District jail and the courthouse. He was also confronted at unlikely places such as restaurants, hamburger stands, and service stations by reporters who expected him to follow Winkler's example and reward them with a nugget of news or some tantalizing hint of future events, material for headlines or the TV evening news. But Scott always brushed them off with a "no comment" or its equivalent, silence. It was not his style to pander to the press.

During Linc's absence, Scott spent most of his days at the law library or at the Rosenstones' where he worked diligently on the motion papers for a change of venue, and going over draft after draft trying to have one finally ready for Winkler when he returned.

Working with Marlene Hutch proved to be somewhat more difficult than Scott had anticipated. At moments when he was pacing to collect his thoughts and phrase them, he would turn suddenly to find her staring at him. Other times, when she was typing he caught himself stealing glances at her—at her fine features, her slightly turned-up nose on which her rose-tinted glasses rested. At times, she might glance up suddenly. Their eyes would meet in self-conscious stares which always ended as suddenly as they had occurred, Marlene looking quickly down at her work, Scott returning to the statistics which were the basis for his motion for a change of venue.

Only the immensity of the work ahead of them kept him from becoming more deeply involved with Marlene. Scott was exhilarated by working with Winkler and the materials that Winkler put at his command, and he spent countless hours perfecting each part of their presentation. The money Winkler had raised the night of the Robertson dinner was being well spent to build their case—a portion of it on the extensive physical examinations Winkler had ordered, and some on obtaining a public opinion poll.

Taken by an independent polling organization of national reputation, the poll revealed that an overwhelming percentage of the registered voters and thus eligible jurors in the District of Columbia were aware who Midge Grove was, and more than seventy-four percent believed him to be guilty. More than fifty percent of those who believed he was guilty were also in favor of giving him the chair, if it were possible. All of which provided Scott with powerful ammunition to urge a change of venue due to prejudice.

Most lawyers would not have thought to undertake such a poll, or so accurately anticipate the results and use them in this way. But Linc Winkler did. Every tool, every resource, even the press and public opinion were his domain.

105

It was exciting to work with a man who did the unconventional things, the things you never learned in law school. Winkler practiced the law as a living experience, not just a theory. He related the law to people, not to old legal principles or cases long decided and growing musty in quiet libraries.

Twice Linc had made tempting hints about wanting Scott to join his law firm after the Grove case was over. In combination with his flair for courtroom action and for unorthodox legal theories, Winkler needed just such a bright, inexhaustible, well-trained mind as Scott possessed. Returning to his father's firm would assure Scott far more money, but Winkler's practice enticed him with the promise of a life of exciting, innovative legal adventures. It was an attractive offer and a flattering one, one deserving serious consideration.

Scott had reached the end of the day's work. He was exhausted from dictating, and Marlene was exhausted from taking down what he said, concentrating on her accuracy even through long stretches of silence when Scott pored over the legal citations he'd assembled and the statistics from the polls. In addition, they both felt worn from the ambivalent tensions of working so closely, being so strongly attracted, and yet so determined to resist.

"It's dark out. I'll drive you home," Scott said as he dropped his papers back on the desk.

"That's all right," Marlene answered, too quickly. "I'll take the bus. It lets me off two blocks from the house."

"It's a long two blocks," he said. "And dark."

"And in a black neighborhood," she said acerbically, "where every second man is a rapist."

"I didn't mean that. But you *are* an attractive girl. And you *do* live on the same street where those two Australian girls were murdered two years ago. I worry about you." He might as well have said, I love you. It would have sounded the same.

It defused her of any further brittleness. She said simply,

106

"I'll be all right. And you've still got a lot of work to do."

"I bet you have a date," Scott said suddenly, surprising himself more than Marlene.

"I'm just going home, make something to eat, bathe, do my hair and go to bed."

"An attractive girl like you . . ." he challenged.

"Unattractive girls settle for a lot less and get a lot more. An attractive girl keeps holding out. What for, I don't know. But holding out seems so important."

She seized her coat quickly, pausing at the door to say, "I'm really not that vain. But my mother, who was a very good laundress at some of the finest homes right here in Georgetown, always used to say to me, 'You got the looks, child, you can marry real good. You should marry light. Don't waste yourself.' The strange thing, she was a much better looking woman than I'll ever be. I always wondered why she didn't 'marry real good.' But I never asked her."

"How long has she been dead?" Scott asked.

"A month after I finished college she caught pneumonia and died. As if my graduating released her from a life she didn't much like anyhow."

With sudden awareness, Scott said, "This is the first time you ever mentioned anyone in your family."

"She was all the family I had," Marlene said softly, and slipped out, closing the door.

Scott stared after her for a moment, and then turned back to the large antique desk on which he had spread statistics, legal citations, and the material which Marlene had typed in the past few days. Slowly, methodically, he started from the beginning to make sure that his draft not only had the proper legal foundations but progressed logically from point to point, that it had the structure his old law school professors used to urge.

He had been at it almost an hour when the door of the library opened softly, and Honey spoke.

107

"I wasn't sure there was anyone here," she said. "I'm sorry if I disturbed you."

She was standing in the doorway not unlike the way Marlene had an hour ago, wearing the same gold hostess gown that she had worn the night she and Scott had met. Her blonde hair was piled on her head in such a casual fashion that Scott knew she was not expecting to be seen by anyone tonight.

"I was almost getting ready to quit," he said.

"Then do you mind if I sit in here for a while? The house is empty. I feel alone. And this is an awfully big place to be alone."

"No, I don't mind."

"Maybe you'd like to have a cold supper with me. On Thursday nights, Aurelia usually prepares a cold supper for us, but with Bob away . . . unless you have a date."

"No, no date," he said, "I'd love to share your dinner."

"Good! Like a drink?"

"I certainly could stand one!"

Scott resumed working while Honey crossed quietly to the bar to make the drinks. Unobtrusively, she put his glass down on the desk. Then she sat down opposite him on the luxurious oriental rug, her back resting against the leather couch, her legs crossed before her and hidden by the gold fabric of her gown.

She could have been an innocent girl of twelve, the way she sat cross-legged. Or a very attractive, mature woman. For there was something extremely open and seductive about her pose—her lovely gown, her lovely figure, the tempting expanse of pink flesh from the top of her bodice to her delicate neck, and her strong face.

She kept sipping her drink, small sips, icy cold and stimulating, as she watched Scott earnestly try to concentrate on his work. Because of her, he was distracted, and secretly Honey enjoyed that. But she gave no sign of it, preferring for the moment to play the twelve-year-old girl.

108

Finally, Scott put down the draft.

"You haven't touched your drink," she reminded.

Scott smiled, picked it up, and held it aloft as in a toast. She returned the gesture, though her glass was almost empty.

"You enjoy working with Linc, don't you?" she asked.

"Yes, I do. His way with the law is exciting, full of surprises! Like these polls for this change of venue."

"Linc's always been full of surprises," Honey smiled.

"You've known him a long time?"

"Since my student days when I first came East. We met at some radical function or other. I've been through so many causes with Linc that I forgot now which was the first one."

Suddenly she changed the subject. "This motion for a change of venue, I hope you don't win it."

Scott looked up at her.

"For your sake, if for no other reason," she added.

"Why?"

"Linc says if there's a change of venue, they can send the case to any Federal District court anywhere in the entire country."

"True," Scott said.

"Linc could move and be admitted anywhere. But then he'd need local counsel. I'd hate to see you lose your chance to work with him."

"I've thought about the same thing," Scott admitted.

"I'd miss you both," Honey said. "Life in this town can be pretty dull, for all the superficial excitement. All the parties are alike—as if they're all done by one big catering service. And the men aren't much different. They're all either fighting their way up or fighting to stay where they are. There isn't one of them who wouldn't leap out of bed just before he's had an orgasm if he got wind of a nomination or a promotion.

"Sex is only a hobby in this town where there's damn little time for hobbies. Well, for me that's not enough. I like to be the main order of business."

She laughed, a small light laugh as if she had been joking. "Fresh drink?" she asked.

"This one's on me," Scott said, picking up her glass on his way to the bar. When he returned with fresh drinks and handed her one, she accepted it with her right hand and with her left she pulled him down to the leather couch.

"Sit right there," she said, resting her head against his legs. "I'm lonely. I need someone near me. Nights like this are rare, thank God. But tonight I need warmth, the presence of another human being, very close."

She reached for his hand.

"I guess I should have had children. Sometimes I ask myself why I didn't. It could have been because I wanted to put an end to the line—no more Nileses. Everyone thinks, give a person all the money she could want and she'll make a great life for herself. A lie! It warps the way you look at life. I know what it did to my father.

"The only one who ever got any fun out of the money was my grandfather. He *made* the money. That's where the fun was. And he was an old whoremaster, had two mistresses as soon as he could afford them, and went to a high-class house at least once a week besides.

"He was the scandal of the family, but no one dared say a word against him because it was old Sigmund Neilander who made the money."

She paused to take a few sips of her drink. Then she tightened her grip on Scott's hand. "I would have liked to be him. Doing, gathering, making, loving, all very aggressively. Instead of only wanting to, just holding on to the money, and loving with only half a heart. There is nothing more disgraceful or debilitating than devoting your life to holding onto money that someone else has made. Or making love in a small select circle where you know and are bored with every possible partner.

"Maybe that's the real reason I never had children—afraid

of incest." Now when she laughed, Scott knew she was joking.

"Make love to me?" she asked suddenly, in a soft, pathetic whisper.

Perhaps she had always tantalized him, or perhaps because tonight his groin was alive and aching for Marlene, Scott slipped down from his place on the couch and embraced her. Her fragrance, and her open, inviting mouth seemed to encompass him. When he reached into her gown, he found that her breasts were as large, as firm, and as welcoming as he had imagined they would be.

Honey was warm and accomplished. She made it all so easy and delightful that Scott soon forgot Marlene or any other girl he'd ever known. Her hands seemed to glory in every strong muscle of his young body. She was hungry to possess him completely.

When she was spent, she lay back on the rich oriental rug and breathed deeply, enormously satisfied. Although her eyes were closed, she was smiling. Then her smile broadened and she whispered into his ear, "It could have been incest. You're almost young enough to be my son." Even though it wasn't true, she laughed, a small laugh that tickled his ear and aroused him again.

It was one o'clock. They had had their late supper. Reluctantly, Honey took him to the front door. She kissed him, innocently, this time. "It's easy for you," she said before she opened the door.

"What?" Scott asked guiltily, expecting the usual female plaint that sex and involvement are always easier, less demanding for men.

"You don't have my problem. I have to decide, am I unfaithful to Bob? Or to Linc?" She was still laughing when he heard the door lock behind him.

X

"These facts, figures, and conclusions, Your Honor, were assembled by one of the leading research organizations in the country, an organization long qualified and expert in determining public attitudes, overt and hidden."

Linc Winkler brandished the volume containing the findings of the polls and surveys he had ordered.

"Among registered voters in the District of Columbia, hence those available for jury duty in this case, 92.8 percent have knowledge of this case and the alleged crime of Midgely Grove from reading about it in the newspapers. A far larger 99.1 percent are familiar with both the crime and the Defendant from having continuously seen and heard the news on television; 92.9 percent are familiar with Grove's face. And, significantly, 76.4 percent have already formed a conclusion as to his guilt or innocence.

"And among those who have, 94.8 percent already believe him to be guilty!" Winkler declared, outraged.

"The conclusion is inescapable, Your Honor. This Defendant cannot obtain a fair and impartial trial in this District. A change of venue would not only be desirable but, under the circumstances, mandatory! Lest this entire procedure mock the justice it purports to pursue!"

Judge Beecher turned his attention to Carroll who rose

112

slowly, selecting some papers from the profusion of notes and memoranda which had been laid out by his assistants.

"Your Honor, Defense Counsel has made a number of points of considerable validity. In fact, on some counts the Government not only does not challenge Counsel's arguments but reaffirms them."

Scott Ingram began to tense slightly. Even Linc Winkler leaned forward in his chair, abandoning his usual disarming slouch.

"For example," Carroll continued, "we accept without reservation the qualifications of the highly reputable organization which Counsel retained to make this very illuminating survey, nor do we quarrel with its findings. This crime and this Defendant are indeed well known in this District.

"But the question before the Court now becomes, is there some other jurisdiction where the Defendant can have greater assurance of securing a fair trial? Zealous in our obligation to protect the Defendant's rights, a duty which falls no less heavily on us than on distinguished Defense Counsel, we proceeded to have our own survey made."

Scott expected Linc to shoot up out of his chair to object. But Winkler remained perfectly still, like a fixed frame in a documentary motion picture.

"In order to do away with all questions of credibility, we did, in fact, retain the very same research organization which Defendant's Counsel retained. And we too have come up with a highly interesting set of statistics. They were just completed last night, which is the reason they are not part of our answer to this motion."

Bullshit! Scott said to himself. He turned to Linc expectantly, but Linc only gripped Scott's thigh, urging patience.

"Now, as for public reaction among registered voters who might be available for jury duty in other Federal districts, we have made studies in four vastly different cities: Minneapolis, Los Angeles, Honolulu, and Denver. These cities provide

113

as great a variety of ethnic mixes, geography, supposed prejudices and lack of prejudices as can be covered in only four cities.

"The results, Your Honor, are quite fascinating and significant. Using Defense Counsel's own breakdown of categories and questions . . ." Carroll turned to Winkler as if in a gesture of respectful deference, before quoting:

"Among registered voters available for jury duty in all four cities, 91.3 percent are familiar with this case and this Defendant by reading the newspapers. As here in the District, a larger percentage of registered voters are aware of all this from watching the news on television.

"As for those who have already formed a conclusion about the Defendant's guilt or innocence, in the District 76.4 percent, but in the four cities—and this is highly significant—78.1 percent! Among those who have formed a conclusion, 94.8 percent in the District believe him to be guilty, whereas in the four-city total 95.7 percent assume him to be guilty. Thus, if one is to rely on the argument that the prejudicial attitude of the community is the basis for a change of venue, it would seem that, if anything, the District is a more, not less, favorable place to hold this trial. And the Government so contends. All these figures will be in the hands of Your Honor and the Defense before the day is out. I regret that they were received too late to be made part of our answer."

Carroll returned to his chair without even glancing at the defense table where Winkler rose quickly.

"Your Honor, we object strenuously to this highly melodramatic bit of business, this last-minute, shabby Marines-to-the-rescue stunt! And I question the ethics of the Government in procuring the services of the same research organization as Defense employed! I insist that His Honor throw these figures out and proceed on the basis of the motion papers and answers now before the Court!"

The judge looked to Carroll.

"Your Honor, if Defense objects to the manner in which

114

these figures were introduced, we are quite agreeable to the Court granting him sufficient time to study and challenge them."

Without rising, Winkler shot back, "We object to the inclusion of these figures in the record now or at any time in the future! This entire strategy stinks of chicanery! One can only suspect that the distinguished U.S. Attorney has resorted to such a tactic in order to prevent this highly publicized case from slipping out of his hands!"

Dryly, Judge Beecher observed, " 'Those who live by the sword must be prepared to die by the sword.' A loose paraphrase perhaps, but apt. Surely if surveys can argue *for* a change of venue then surveys are relevant and admissible to argue against a change of venue. The Court will take all the figures into consideration in ruling on this motion."

From the manner in which Beecher laid aside both sets of papers, it was clear the hearing was over. Carroll rose swiftly.

"Your Honor, as long as both sides are here, may I make a request? Defense requested, and the Government readily agreed to a complete physical examination of the Defendant. Frankly, the relevance of the Defendant's physical condition escapes me. But there is one area of investigation that might prove highly relevant and yet, strangely, continues to go unexplored—Defendant's mental condition!"

Carroll turned to confront Winkler. "For some reason, Defendant's Counsel have failed to avail themselves of this opportunity. In the interest of a fair trial we urge that such observation take place at once. Under the right granted in the District's Rules of Practice, the Government moves for a thorough mental examination of the Defendant!"

The judge looked to Winkler for some reply. Linc leaned toward Scott who explained in a whisper, "Under our rules, the Prosecution does have a right to ask for an M.O."

Linc hesitated only an instant before rising to speak. "If the Court grants the Government such an examination, the Defense will lodge an objection."

115

"The examination is granted," Beecher ruled.

"Objection," Winkler replied, without raising his voice.

"The record will so state."

"Carroll's reacting," Linc said to Scott as they started down the steps. "We've got him going crazy trying to figure out why we avoided an M.O. but asked for a physical. He's determined to find out if we're hiding anything."

"*Are* we?" Scott asked pointedly.

Suddenly Linc remembered that Scott had not been present at his first or any succeeding meetings with Dr. Randolph.

"We are hiding nothing. We haven't got a chance to make an insanity plea stand up, so why pursue it? Let Carroll worry about that."

"And the physical?" Scott persisted.

"We can only judge that when we get the results," Winkler said.

But Scott suspected that Linc already had some rather specific thoughts on the matter and that they would come to light once Linc was ready to reveal them. If Linc's habit kept Scott off-balance, the refreshing innovations of which Linc was capable always made the waiting worthwhile.

Suddenly they were surrounded by newspaper and television reporters eagerly seeking Winkler's reaction to the courtroom events. Mainly they had questions about Carroll's tactic of asking for a mental examination of Midge Grove. And Winkler was ready for them.

"Some lawyers, when they run out of arguments of substance, resort to cheap grandstand plays. You may put Carroll's maneuver down as a phoney. What my young friends on the campuses of this nation would call a fake-out, a ripoff. And you can tell Mr. Carroll that if he thinks he is fooling the people of this country by such tactics, then *he's* the one who needs an M.O.!"

The next morning, Judge Beecher denied the motion for a change of venue.

Secretly, Scott was relieved. Now that the case would continue in the District, he was assured of working with Linc Winkler on it. Of course, an appeal would follow, but Scott's own legal sense told him it would fail.

By mid-afternoon there was a call from Judge Beecher's legal secretary asking if Scott and Linc would appear in his chambers at the end of the court day for an off-the-record meeting of Counsel for both sides.

Divested of his robes, Beecher seemed like a taller man, though less robust. His gray business suit gave him the appearance of a bank vice president or the head of a small public utility.

"All right, gentlemen," he said as if calling together a meeting of the local Chamber of Commerce. Though the court stenographer was recording every word Beecher said, he did not resort to legal language or courtroom etiquette. "Now, I want to set a few things straight. We are conducting an important trial here—historic trial—and I will not allow it to be turned into a circus or a nightly television series.

"If Counsel on either side persists in presiding over his own special court on the steps of this courthouse he will be held in contempt!"

He turned to glare at Winkler who remained unmoved, unresponsive. Then Beecher continued.

"I forbid any outside comments on events transpiring in my courtroom! And I mean to enforce that! Yes, Mr. Winkler, I said enforce! And this time it will be on a day by day basis. Not like in Chicago. I'm not saving up my contempt rulings for the end of the trial!"

Beecher waited for Winkler to acknowledge his reprimand by word or nod, but Winkler was totally aloof, which only irritated Beecher even more.

"Now, there is one other matter I want to cover today. In view of the concern of the Defense for a fair trial and an im-

117

partial jury, it is my judgment that the sooner the matter comes to trial the more likely we are to achieve that result. Therefore, unless I hear some strenuous objection backed up by solid legal support, I am setting trial for sixty days from today's date." Beecher faced Winkler again, and this time he was not disappointed.

"Sixty days is arbitrary and prejudicial!"

"In view of the comparatively simple set of facts in this case, I don't think so."

"*We do!*" Winkler retorted, pronouncing each word distinctly and emphatically.

"Counsel on both sides will be ready to proceed to trial in sixty days!" Beecher said, ending the matter.

Linc sprawled luxuriously in the back seat of the Rosenstone limousine as if everything were going his way. His long legs rested on the jump seat before him, and he had loosened his tie.

"Like spit on a hot stove," he said enigmatically to himself. "Spit on a hot stove."

Linc was silent for a moment, then he turned to Scott and said, "You know, when I was a kid about eight or nine years old, we'd go to visit my grandfather who lived in a cold water tenement out in Brooklyn. He had an old coal stove in his little kitchen that was used for both heating and cooking. In mid-winter it would get white hot from being coaled up so high.

"I would stand as close to it as I dared. And whenever nobody was looking, I'd spit at that stove and watch my spit steam up and disappear. I loved the sizzle it made.

"Right now, if I spit on Judge Beecher I bet he would sizzle the same way. He's that hot under the collar . . . which is fine with me. So he's going to threaten me with contempt during the trial . . ."

"Not threaten," Scott corrected. "He'll *hold* you in contempt each time instead of ruling at the end of the trial, just like he said. He's not bluffing, Linc."

"Fine! It's reversible error for him to do that in front of the jury. So let him hold me!"

Winkler laughed. "Like spitting on a hot stove," he said and laughed again.

XI

"They will tell you, turn your back on your brother! Because he's guilty! Don't sully the movement! But I tell you Midge Grove *is* the movement! I tell you, if you let that little black man down, you are letting yourselves down!" Linc Winkler was reaching the peak of his oration as he stood with arms upraised like a fiery prophet.

Before him, the audience, packed beyond the capacity of the small auditorium of the Negro college, was a solid field of intense faces. Young women as well as young men. Many wore large Afros. Some peered at Winkler through steel-rimmed glasses, some through thick, heavy, black-framed ones, some with naked angry eyes.

"This is no act of contrition we are involved in. It would be easy to abandon a brother and say he has brought shame to the movement. To all of us! But if you do that, who knows when *your* time will come?

"Mind you, all I am asking is that you demand a fair trial for Midge Grove! Let the court and the jury decide whether the facts prove him guilty. But grant that lonely black man the simplest right, the most fundamental right assured to him under our Constitution, the presumption of innocence!"

Winkler could feel the tension of the crowd increasing as he spoke. Shouts of "Right on!" and "Brother for brother!"

were beginning to support him, urge him on, as in a revival meeting.

"Now, I want to level with you! My being here tonight is an affront to all of you. Or should be! Why is Midge Grove being defended by whitey? Yes, that's what I am. Whether I'm on your side or not, I am whitey! My fine and brilliant co-counsel, who is sitting right down there, and whose brilliant efforts on behalf of Midge Grove will put his name in the history books, he, too, is whitey. How long are you black brothers going to have to depend on us for your defense? I'll tell you! Just as long as you allow the legal system to continue as it is. Until you get *black* judges, *black* lawyers, *black* courts!"

His challenge focused the energy of the crowd as it intensified.

"I am not supposed to say this in public. Under an edict from King Alfred, I have been forbidden to say it. His Honor Judge Alfred Beecher, who called me into his chambers only a few days ago, told me that my Constitutional right to freedom of speech was being abridged, throttled, destroyed for the duration of this trial! My co-counsel can attest to that. He was there. I am not permitted to make comment on this case in public—under threat of being held in contempt.

"That will severely limit my ability to present this case fairly to the public. Well, King Alfred is right about one thing. What I feel toward that court *is* contempt!"

They were laughing in sympathy with Winkler now. Derogatory shouts of a highly personal nature about Beecher were called out from parts of the auditorium and echoed by others, until a rhythmic chant of "Fuck King Alfred" was pounding through the room. Winkler, with a half-smile on his face, made a futile gesture indicating that he was forced to give way to their emotion.

When he felt the chant had peaked, he raised his arms, imploring their silence.

121

"All these sentiments are fine. But as long as they are limited to this college and this hall, they mean absolutely nothing. If this is the way you feel, let the world know it! If this is really the way you feel, *do* something! I would like to see a Defend Midge Grove Movement start here in this historic hall and spread across the nation! I would like to hear the voice of concerned, angry, brilliant, beautiful black young America in front of that courthouse every day of this trial! Because trials like these have to be won in the streets!

"*You* are under no court orders! *You* are under no threat from King Alfred! By God, if you don't see to it that Midge Grove gets a fair trial, who will? And if he doesn't get a fair trial, how can you be sure that any one of you, or your brothers, or your sons, will ever get a fair trial? If you need a rallying cry, here it is! *If we don't, who will?*"

They were all on their feet now, cheering, shouting, defiant, angry. Their voices united and echoed rhythmically. "If we don't who will?" Having roused them to such a frenzy, Winkler felt that now he could afford to protect himself without diminishing their fervor.

"Remember one thing. Whatever you do, do it within the law. Collect money. Make public protest. Picket the courthouse. Demonstrate. Sit in. But all within.the law."

But even as he said it, Winkler knew that their youthful passion could never be delimited or contained by such soporific phrases as "within the law." Still it would serve him later, especially since his entire speech was being taped by the college, and, undoubtedly, by FBI plants in the audience as well.

To signify that he was done, Winkler raised his right hand in a proud, belligerent fist. They all responded, starting out of their seats to come streaming down the aisles.

They surged up onto the stage surrounding Linc Winkler, shaking his hand and embracing him. Winkler seemed a hundred hands and arms. He reached out with left hand as well as right to clasp each outstretched black hand for an instant.

122

The fervor and the excitement, the total sense of arousal equaled the best days of a few years ago when campuses were aflame every time he talked—proof that finally he had found his issue.

When the crowd began to thin out, a small core of the most militant remained, begging Winkler to join them for a coffee and rap session. He was so intoxicated by his success tonight that he would have agreed if Honey were not waiting to drive him back to the house. Instead, he hastily found Scott, and arm in arm, they made their way outside.

Scott Ingram had driven down in his own car, so he declined Honey's offer to drop him off at his place. Instead, he left them and crossed the campus toward where he had parked, moving along the walks between the fragrant dewy lawns. Ahead of him he soon noticed a strangely familiar figure, a tall, shapely, graceful girl in a white coat. Only when she passed under the street lamp was he sure. It was Marlene. Alone. Automatically he speeded his pace, until when he drew closer he called out.

"Marlene!"

She stopped and turned. In the full light of a street lamp falling on her face, her white coat complimenting her tan skin, she looked more appealing than ever to him, as she waited for him to catch up.

"I'm surprised to see you," Scott said.

"Bridger, an associate professor in PoliSci, invited me down to hear Winkler."

"Isn't he driving you back to town?"

Marlene smiled. "It seems he didn't figure on my going back to town tonight. When I refused to stay over, he found some excuse. I'll take the bus."

"At this hour? I wouldn't allow it," Scott said. "I'll take you home."

"But it's out of your way," she countered.

"Come on!" Scott took her arm and they walked together to his car.

"Quite a night!" Scott said as soon as they had left the college grounds and turned onto the highway.

"Quite," Marlene agreed, but with not nearly as much enthusiasm.

Scott stole a glance at her, and noticing, Marlene grew shy. They had never been this closely alone before.

"Didn't you find it exciting, tremendous?" Scott continued, hoping to put her at ease. "It's the first time I've heard him speak at a rally. He's great! And those kids love him. That's the only word for it. They *love* him!"

"Oh, they love him all right," Marlene conceded, but she made no secret of her own reservations. "Firing up a crowd of kids and turning them loose, that frightens me."

"He has to. How else are we going to turn public opinion around? It starts with the kids, and then spreads. I think he did fine."

"As long as he doesn't turn out to be a medicine man," Marlene said quietly.

"Medicine man?" Scott asked, puzzled.

"We've had too many. Whites just passing through, using our cause for kicks of their own. Then, they're gone. Like a medicine man the morning after, when his remedy turns out to be a fake."

Scott turned to look at her. She turned away, but not before he'd caught a glimpse of her shining black eyes in their full intensity. She was a girl of deep convictions about her race. And her opinions were clearly her own.

"That's not quite fair to say about a man who came down here, at no fee, and has devoted himself to Grove's case the way Linc has," Scott defended.

"I don't want to see any more black blood shed for slogans," Marlene said simply.

That ended all conversation until she had to direct him to where she lived. When the car came to a stop in front of her building, Marlene got out. Scott was coming round to escort her to her front steps, when she protested, "Don't bother,

Scott. And thanks. Thanks a lot." She turned and ran up the steps of the modest apartment house so swiftly that he knew it would have been awkward to pursue her.

Scott got back into his car and pulled away, fully aware of the tantalizing fragrance Marlene had left behind, and he wondered why he hadn't used the ride back to involve her more. Did he hang back because of his painful memories of Lily, the Jewish girl he had been involved with during their last year in law school? Or was it because she was black?

With conscious determination Scott decided not to get involved—particularly with girls who promised only dead-end romances such as the one he'd already lived through. There had been all kinds of resistance and bitterness in both Lily's family and his own. And when they finally separated, he was so shook he was in danger of failing his bar exams. Besides he had Midge Grove to think of. He would stick to his original resolve, to settle his own future before he became deeply involved again. Affairs, yes. But deep involvements, no.

Suddenly it dawned on him, without a single word having passed between them on the subject, he already assumed that if he and Marlene did become involved it would be deep, intense, and, in the end, painful.

Linc Winkler had decided to delay his meeting with the staff of physicians giving Grove his physical. He wanted to wait until U.S. District Attorney Carroll had received a complete M.O. report on Midge. As he had anticipated, only one psychiatrist on the panel held Grove to be abnormal. The other two, including Dr. Randolph, held him to be of low mental capacity but quite definitely legally sane, regarding both his ability to stand trial and the state of his mind at the time of the crime.

With a copy of that report in hand, Winkler now assembled the internist, pathologist, endocrinologist, and pediatrician who had examined, tested and X-rayed Midgely Grove. They met in the consultation room of the hospital. It was a large room dominated by a long conference table. Around the walls was a continuous line of opaque glass panels, recessed X-ray view boxes. Scott had arranged for the pertinent X-rays to be mounted before the doctors arrived. Copies of their reports were pinned to the cork boards so that in sequence both the reports and the X-rays would reveal in thorough detail as much of the life history of Midge Grove as it was possible to obtain.

All the physicians were white men, this at Winkler's request and for a reason he had shared with no one. When Winkler arrived, accompanied by Scott Ingram and Dr. Paul Randolph, it made Randolph the only black man in the room. Winkler introduced him to the other doctors, then turned the conference over to Dr. Langer.

"Okay, Doctor, let's have it!"

Linc sat in a chair from which he could face all the X-rays, charts and reports, with Dr. Randolph and Scott sitting on either side.

After the overhead lights were extinguished and the view boxes lit up, Langer, the internist and expert in forensic medicine, used the X-rays and the reports to assemble the details of the birth and infancy of Midgely Grove. Then Barsky, the pediatrician stood up to draw conclusions about certain of the significant facts and to offer some strong suppositions as well.

Barsky was a small, chunky man, whose middle-aged bulge overflowed his unpressed trousers. He would have been the first physician to put any patient in a similar condition on a rigid diet at once. He spoke softly but bitterly and pointed with pudgy fingers at various sections of the X-rays and the reports.

Tapping his forefinger against one lit-up X-ray, he was saying, "Winkler, if we didn't know any more than this, we'd know enough. These dense lines along the shafts of the long bones strongly suggest calcified subperiosteal hemorrhage, a

126

usual healing reaction in those who have suffered skeletal trauma."

"Skeletal trauma?" Winkler asked from the darkness.

"Severe injury to the bone structure," Langer interposed.

"How severe?" Winkler pursued.

"Severe!" Barsky said. "As to actual fractures, we find here"—and he moved to the next X-ray—"calcification of old healed fractures. Here. And here."

"Three fractures? At what age?" Winkler asked.

"I would guess very early childhood. You see, it's difficult to pinpoint in this case," Barsky explained.

"Why?"

"Because in addition to the healed fractures we have another serious factor to contend with in this patient. If you will notice here, here, and here, these dense lines? Growth arrest lines. Skeletal evidence of interrupted physical development where growth stopped and started again, due to periodic and painfully insufficient diet."

Winkler joined Barsky at the X-rays, their faces lit only by the light that seeped through the plates.

"At what age?" Winkler asked again.

"Between one and four."

"About the same time he was being injured?" Winkler asked reflectively.

Barsky nodded. "Possibly. But there's more. Take a look at this." He pointed to an X-ray of Grove's skull. "Dr. Langer noticed it when he palpated the patient's head on examination, and the X-ray confirms it. Malformation of the skull which clearly leads to the conclusion that about that same time he had also suffered a fracture of the skull. Not fatal, as we know, but quite serious."

Winkler studied the skull X-ray at length. While he did so, Barsky asked, "Did you notice, Winkler, that when you talk to him he inclines his head somewhat like this?" Barsky cocked his head slightly, favoring Winkler with his right side.

"Yes?" Winkler asked, for he had noticed it, but not ascribed much importance to it.

At that point, Dr. Claire, otolaryngologist who had done the examination on Grove's throat, nose and ears, spoke up from the darkness. "There is traumatic damage to his left eardrum, including an old central perforation. Probably from a blow across the head, or a number of blows. Also possibly in early childhood."

"Any other evidence of damage?"

"A healed fracture of his nose. Not immediately apparent because of his Negroid features. But on internal examination there is clear evidence of traumatic displaced cartilage and bone."

Dr. Langer turned to the most elderly of the doctors in the room. "Dr. Catchings?"

Catchings, who had been peering through the lower half of his bifocals in order to see his notes in the semidarkness, now raised his eyes to stare at Winkler and Scott Ingram.

"I have made a thorough examination of the eyes of this subject and found clear evidence of traumatic cataract formations. There were attempts made to correct this surgically, but they were not altogether successful, leaving him with noticeable impairment of vision," Catchings declared. It seemed painful for him to make his statement, as though in some way he disapproved of the conduct of the entire human race.

Winkler asked, "Dr. Catchings, from your experience in dealing with children with defective sight from whatever cause, have you found that it affects their ability to study, and to learn in general?"

"When a child is born with defective vision and it remains uncorrected it most certainly does affect him in these areas. And as long as that condition remains uncorrected, to my mind, it is tantamount to criminal negligence," Catchings declared.

"And when a child has been born with perfect vision,"

Winkler prodded, "and that vision has been impaired by deliberate blows about the head?"

"I deem that a crime not only against that unfortunate child but against the state and against nature itself. The older I become the more resentful I become of anyone who diminishes or destroys the human body. His own or anyone's else!"

"And I assume you would so testify in court if called upon, Doctor?" Winkler asked.

"Most definitely!" the old man answered.

"Now, gentlemen," Winkler said, "I would like to ask you some questions about the accused which cannot be answered by reference to X-rays or laboratory tests of any kind. I have noticed in my dealings with him that he is a quiet, reserved individual, either so terrified of the situation that confronts him that he seems to have made himself unaware of it or else resigned, in the way that a man who has accomplished a mission is resigned. He has done his work and it is over and he is quite content to disappear forever without a struggle."

Winkler began pacing, adjusting his path so that he never lost eye contact with Randolph. "I find, too, that he rarely answers questions directly. Most times he does not respond at all. Or when he does it is with vague recollections or unrelated information. It is only when you talk of things other than himself that he is most apt to betray extremely revealing information about his past."

Suddenly Winkler addressed Randolph directly. "I believe, Dr. Randolph, that you found this to be true to such a degree that you resorted to sodium amytal in an attempt to evoke any enlightening responses."

Randolph said, "I did indeed."

Winkler turned to the other specialists and asked, "During the course of the examinations you gentlemen performed, did any information come to light that may not have been germane to your own field but which would help us fill in the profile of this shy, introverted young man?"

Each physician lapsed into his own peculiar expression of thoughtfulness. Barsky, the pediatrician, was the first to answer.

"He said one thing which I wasn't able to forget. Mainly because it corroborated a suspicion I had. We physicians have a habit of always remembering those moments when our difficult diagnoses are confirmed for us, especially if we think we have made some extremely brilliant deductions." He smiled a bit self-indulgently.

"I was trying to elicit from him some picture of his early childhood, trying to nail down some statement of fact that would explain the evident traumas of skeletal damage. And as you said, Winkler, either he didn't answer at all, or he responded with unrelated information. Then one time, while he seemed preoccupied with being examined by fluoroscope in a dark room, I ventured a remark that he might have sustained a severe blow across the back, possibly with some hard instrument.

"His answer surprised me. He said, 'Not *me*.' To my ear he was actually saying, 'It didn't happen to me, but it did happen to someone else.' So at a later stage of the examination, I used various examining procedures merely to divert him and I probed a little further.

" 'Who *did* it happen to, Midge? Who *did* get hit?'

" 'Nessa,' was all he would say.

"I continued examining, palpating, whatever I could improvise to keep him in that frame of mind, keep him talking. 'Who was Nessa?' I asked him suddenly.

" 'My sister,' he said.

"I had his history before me as it had been assembled by Dr. Randolph and some of you other gentlemen, so I took the time to flip through it. I had not remembered any reference at all to any sister."

"He never mentioned a sister, even under amytal," Randolph interrupted, "so I would conclude that it was simply a projection. Things too painful for him to remember about himself he displaced onto a fictitious sister. This is not so strange, considering his homosexual experiences in the reformatory, his revulsion, and his inability thereafter to consider himself a man."

Barsky wiped his damp face with his large thick-fingered hand and said, "Dr. Randolph, if you will forgive me, and there is nothing personal about it, but I am getting sick to death of physicians with nice, neat hypotheses. Physicians who pursue theories instead of facts. I get sick of myself at times, because I had formed precisely the same conclusion as you did. It was such a convenient, intelligent, 'scientific' and up-to-date theory for explaining that poor boy's strange story.

"But something kept scratching at my brain. So I figured out what age Grove must have been *when* and *if* this happened. Then I went and checked the vital records in the District.

"And, gentlemen, yes! There is listed among deaths, at about the time Midgely Grove was three and a half, a girl who died at age four and a half. And her name was Vanessa Grove! The cause of death was recorded as injuries sustained in an accidental fall. But as any pediatrician knows, death by 'accident' to a child that age may not be the result of an accident at all, but of child abuse, and where you have a history of 'accidental' death to one child in a family, you will often find another child in the family who bears all the marks of early traumas just as Midge Grove does.

"Gentlemen, what I am saying is this. Bad as was his own suffering, his own deprivation, his own pain, there was the hidden but ever-present threat that what had happened to Nessa might happen to him. So he grew up terrified, mute, afraid to assert himself.

"Who inflicted all this? Was it his mother? His father? I don't know and I wouldn't even guess. Perhaps it was one of numerous 'uncles' that his mother brought into the house. But that is speculation that will do us little good now. And, unfortunately, it will do Midgely Grove little good. I wish I could help him because in the few days I had with him, I came to feel sorry for him, and I came to like him. This . . . this assassin."

Barsky turned to Winkler. "But beyond reporting my findings there's nothing I can do. The crime has been committed and the criminal caught. Of course I will testify in the trial. But by any legal test I know, he is guilty."

Carp, the endocrinologist, spoke up. "My findings, too, fit with what's been said here. He shows marked retarded endocrine development quite typical of socially deprived battered children, which could account for his general sexual shyness, and which could account for the fact that, as far as I could determine, he has had only the most limited contact with women. He is, for all practical purposes, asexual. My assumption would be that this condition preceded his term in the reformatory. It might well have acted as an enticement to the older, larger boys to rape him. But as Dr. Barsky has so eloquently stated, all our theories may be wrong. Only one thing is sure, his present condition. Of course, how that helps Mr. Winkler and Mr. Ingram who are charged with defending this poor soul, I don't know."

Winkler rose, moved to the light switch at the door and snapped on the overhead lights. "Gentlemen, you've been most helpful. And I trust that when we find it necessary for you to testify at Grove's trial I can count on all of you?"

They all gave him assurance by word or sincere nodding of heads.

·◦⧉ XII ⧉◦·

It was late the same evening. Honey and Bob Rosenstone had gone to an opening at the Kennedy Center, leaving Winkler, Scott, Marlene and Randolph with the house to themselves. This was to be the decisive meeting. Linc was determined to arrive at what he termed "the theory of the case."

In order to perform to his utmost, Linc Winkler always required a theory on which to proceed, a theory sometimes legal, sometimes factual, sometimes emotional, but at all times political, and with dimensions extending beyond the single case and the particular courtroom in which it was tried.

"If nothing else," Winkler had once said to Scott, "we need an issue to take the jury's mind off the crime and the criminal and focus it on something else." But the entire afternoon and evening of discussion since the medical conference had produced no theory for the Grove case.

Scott was discouraged by the failure of all the medical statistics to help their case legally, and he was annoyed as well by the fact that since Randolph's arrival this afternoon the handsome black psychiatrist had been making quite a play for Marlene. Though she acted deliberately cool toward him, Randolph had the sexual cockiness and assurance that any tall, handsome, well-built man is justified in having. If he played the game long enough, he was sure he would win. This very smugness irritated Marlene and enraged Scott.

Randolph took a fresh cup of coffee from Marlene, smiling his appreciation, and then he turned to Winkler. "Linc, maybe we should make a stab at establishing insanity after all. With all the new material in that extensive medical history, I could credibly revise the report on the M.O. I think we might just pull it off now."

Winkler kept stirring his coffee. "We could make an issue of it. Even throw up a hell of a smoke screen. But when the chips are down we'd be beaten by the preponderance of expert testimony. Carroll is no genius but he's no shmuck either."

"You're sticking with our original plan, then," Randolph concluded.

Original plan? Suddenly Scott knew that there had been previous conversations and agreements between Winkler and Randolph which had been kept secret from him. Involuntarily his eyes flicked from Randolph to Winkler. But either by design or accident, at that moment Winkler was staring down at his coffee cup, stirring quite intently. When Scott looked past Winkler to Marlene, he found corroboration in her eyes.

If the need for finding a theory for the case hadn't been so urgent, Scott would have demanded an explanation at once. For Winkler to treat as secret from Scott his own evolving thoughts and strategies about the case was bad enough. But to share them with outsiders and not make his co-counsel privy to them was a situation Scott did not intend to endure. That issue would have to be faced, and damned soon, Scott promised himself.

Winkler must have sensed Scott's surprise and resentment, for suddenly he put aside his coffee cup and leaped to his feet. He combed his bushy hair with his fingers, let his glasses fall free to hang from the cord around his neck and exploded with a new burst of energy.

134

"It can't be that tough! First off, this is not merely a murder. It is an assassination, which means that inherently it has political components. After all, what is the essential difference between a murderer and an assassin? Choice of victim. The assassin's victim is a person of importance to the Establishment. Well, the Establishment is what committed all those terrible crimes against Midge Grove. The Establishment is his enemy! And under our system there is nothing wrong in killing your enemy. Our entire national morality is founded on that one concept. And we find nothing reprehensible about it. We even honor the men who do it in time of war and call them heroes. Why, then, should it become reprehensible because a man's enemy happens to be the system as symbolized by someone in public office?"

Instead of pursuing that, Winkler glanced at his watch, turned briskly to flip on the television set. The program that preceded the eleven o'clock news was just coming to an end.

Winkler continued, "Nobody can tell me that what happened to that poor kid during his early days didn't *do* something to him!"

"If it didn't create a condition that we can now legally label insanity, how can it have any bearing on his defense?" Randolph asked.

"Unless . . ." Scott started to say. But Winkler silenced him with a gesture, his concentration already riveted on the television set and the news, which had just begun. There were the usual items and brief interviews concerning the continuing conflict between the president and the Congress, the ever-present threat of further inflation and the demands by numerous groups for extensive and radical programs to improve the ecology while being careful not to increase the national budget. The local coverage reported one fire and two street murders, before it mentioned the impending trial of Midgely Grove. The trial had been mentioned each night during the many weeks since the assassination. Tonight's item concerned a columnist's rumor that fingerprints proved

135

that the gun, alleged to be the weapon Grove used in the killing, had turned out to be the wrong weapon after all, but that the FBI was suppressing that fact.

At which point Winkler observed in half-voice, *"Allevei."* When Scott glanced at him, Winkler explained, "An old Yiddish word meaning, it should only happen."

Winkler concentrated on the news to the very end when, irritated, he turned off the set. "Sonofabitch! They said they'd use that tape of my speech at Howard University tonight. Well, back to work! Scotty, you were saying?"

"This idea may be far out, Linc," Scott said, tentatively.

"What have we got to lose?"

"Well," Scott began, "in a few jurisdictions they still accept irresistible impulse as a legal defense."

Winkler turned to Randolph. "A man who kills under an irresistible emotional impulse can plead it as a defense if the cause of the impulse is acceptable and understandable to the average man. For example, if a man discovered that another man had raped his wife or was sleeping with her . . ."

Suddenly the doors of the library opened. Honey and Bob Rosenstone, both in evening dress, had just returned from the Kennedy Center.

"Hi, dear," Linc said in his most casual way. "How was it?"

"Same as ever. We donate all that money. They build those damned cathedrals to the Drama. And each show is more boring than the last," she said. Yet her eyes shone with their usual sparkle and excitement. It seemed Honey Rosenstone could not even be bored without beaming.

"As the buildings get bigger, the shows get duller," Randolph suggested, smiling at Honey in his confident way.

Scott could sense the beginnings of sexual stirrings between Honey and Randolph. Evidently so could Bob Rosenstone, for he said, "Come, darling, these people have work to do."

"Interesting work, from the little I heard." Honey stared at

Linc. "Go on, Linc, let's hear more . . . about that man whose wife got raped . . ."

"I think we ought to go up," Rosenstone urged in a soft but firm voice.

"Good night, dear. I'll be up in a while." Honey moved into the room, taking a cup from the coffee wagon and pouring for herself. Then she slipped gracefully to the floor, resting her back against the couch. Wearing brocade evening pajamas, she crossed her legs, in what Scott had learned by now was her favorite position. The seductive pose, her golden hair, her soft pink flesh against the red of the low-cut top, stirred feelings in Scott that he knew were shared by Linc and probably by Randolph.

Bob Rosenstone was about to insist once again that she join him, but instead he resigned from the game with a mere, "I'll see you upstairs, love."

Even before he left the room, Honey was saying, "I only heard that part about a man whose wife was raped or who was sleeping with another man . . . how does that apply to the Grove case?"

"Scott was just starting to explain," Winkler said.

"Well, in some jurisdictions in this country there is a legal defense for murder called the Doctrine of Irresistible Impulse. It can be invoked when a man reacts to a particularly emotionally shocking discovery. Such as that his wife has been raped. Or she's having an affair with another man."

"You mean when he catches her *in flagrante delicto?*" Honey said, her eyes sparkling mischievously.

"It doesn't have to be that first-hand," Scott said, blushing. He could see that Honey was enjoying his discomfort.

"Can he just find out about it later and kill her or the man, and get away with it?" Honey asked.

"Not in this jurisdiction, sweetie," Winkler said, smiling.

"Well, that's a relief," Honey laughed.

"Suppose we use that doctrine as a starting point," Scott continued. "The concept of forces being put in motion which

137

make a man's impulse irresistible. Now, let's apply it to Grove's situation. . . ."

Winkler interrupted, "With all the obvious preparation they're going to prove? The labels cut out of his coat. Procurement of the weapon. How could we claim sudden impulse?"

"Suppose," Scott argued back, "relying on the extensive medical history we have, we take the firm position that it *wasn't* sudden. *Grove's entire life* was the preparation for this impulse. This was *not* the sort of impulse that bursts on a man when he discovers his wife *in flagrante delicto*. This is far, far deeper.

"Suppose that all his life, society had been preparing Midgely Grove to turn on it and try to destroy it?"

By that time no one in the room was smiling any longer. Linc Winkler had stopped hand-combing his bushy hair. He lifted his reading glasses to his eyes and reached for a pad and pencil, staring eagerly at Scott, encouraging him to continue.

"Think of Grove as having no will of his own. He was programed to play a particular role in this life. Programed by a society which had let him starve, be beaten, be threatened with death like his tiny sister. Which robbed him of his mental development. Which turned him into an asexual eunuch. Which subjected him to involuntary homosexual abuses. A society which had done to him everything rotten and wrong that could be done to a child and still permit him to survive. And a society which left him only one means of protest.

"I think we could claim that what he did was just as inevitable as an irresistible impulse even if it wasn't sudden. If there's no doctrine to support it, we can establish a new doctrine. *The Doctrine of Social Inevitability!*"

"The Doctrine of Social Inevitability," Winkler repeated in a slow, thoughtful way. "The Doctrine of Social Inevitability." He printed it carefully. Then he underlined it. Finally he put big quotation marks around it. He put the pad aside, got to his feet, moved to Scott and embraced him. Playfully he kissed him on the cheek.

"Tell me, my boy, what right have you got to be so smart? You're not even Jewish!" Winkler joked.

"Then you think it might work?" Scott asked, revealing for the first time his own enormous doubts.

"For our purposes it can work! Damn well!" Winkler declared. " 'Life, liberty, and the pursuit of happiness,' inalienable rights. Of the three they made it possible for him to have only one. Life. And they made a hell out of that! With his medical history we could have a field day with this!"

As the theory took on exciting substance and form in his mind, Winkler began to pace. "A repressive society has no right to expect that any individual shall continue to suffer the effects of repression without taking countersteps. Once, before he dies, each man is entitled to speak out, to protest. When a society has deprived him even of the ability to speak out, as in Grove's case, then it must suffer the consequences of the only remaining voice he has. Action! Destruction! Violence! Even assassination!"

Playing the scene as he might enact it in a courtroom, Winkler turned to Scott, Marlene, and Randolph. "It is time this honorable Court took judicial notice of certain of the real facts of life. The society which *creates* men like Midgely Grove is *responsible* for their actions. The unfortunate individual who is on trial here is as much a victim as your late lamented colleague, Mr. Justice Harvey Miller!"

After a moment of silent thought, Winkler proclaimed, "It will not only work for us during the trial, but if it's necessary, on appeal, too! Robertson would love it! It's his kind of argument. He might even sell it to enough of the rest of them to prevail. Conservatives or not! Yes, Robertson would be our man!"

Honey was beaming warmly in Scott's direction, as if she

139

were his proud mother, or his wife. Marlene seemed equally impressed. Even Randolph was thoughtful, nodding his head as he considered the entire theory and approved of it.

"The Doctrine of Social Inevitability," Winkler repeated, letting it expand as he spoke it slowly, giving it a sense of historic grandeur. "One thing, it'll be an unprecedented legal question, and provided we sell it properly, it should get plenty of attention. On TV, in the press. Yes, it has to be planted very carefully and soon. So that it's set up and ready when the time comes for us to use it."

Still smiling, Winkler said, "A good night's work! Now, let's get some sleep!"

Marlene started to collect the coffee cups but Honey stopped her. "Never mind, dear. I'll do that. You must be tired. All of you."

As Marlene started for the door, Randolph offered, "Can I drive you home?"

"Thanks," Marlene answered quickly, "but Scott's already promised."

Scott glanced at her, surprised, but he went along with it gladly. "Yes, it's on my way," he said to Randolph.

"Of course." Randolph was obviously disappointed as he turned to go. He bid Honey good night, holding her hand a long time. Then he said to Winkler, "I could line up considerable professional support for a theory like that."

"First, I'd like you to help draw up a whole list of questions to ask of all prospective jurors," Winkler said. "I want to string out the selection of the jury as long as we can. Weeks, if possible. So we have time to plant the doctrine."

"I'll help in any way I can," Randolph promised. With another big warm smile to Honey, he departed.

As soon as Scott and Marlene had left, Winkler took Honey in his arms with that familiarity and habit between lovers which made her know that he fully expected to have her tonight. She avoided his embrace deftly, saying, "Uh uh, Linc. Bob's waiting."

140

"Bob!" Winkler disposed of him, disparagingly.

"After all, he does have feelings . . ." Honey said, as Winkler embraced her again. "Though sometimes I'd like to see him become angry over me. Not embarrassed, not hurt—just plain angry. But the money's robbed him of everything."

Winkler pressed against her more urgently, and she could feel him, all of him.

Softly she whispered, "All right, Linc. But don't take all night."

Scott was driving his red Mustang down dark, deserted Columbia Road.

"I'm sorry. I didn't mean to impose," Marlene said. "But I knew he was going to ask."

"That's okay. No problem," Scott said.

"I don't like him," she said suddenly. "He's an uppity nigger." She laughed. "The black revolution has accomplished *one* thing, anyway. *You* can't use the word nigger, but *we* can. It is now our exclusive property.

"But that's what he is. Out of Harlem. I can hear it. That Jamaican accent? Put on. It lapses every once in a while. But being as black as he is, he has to pretend to be a non-American Negro. That gives him class, status—the Harry Belafonte of the psychiatric world.

"And he's so sure he's irresistible to all women, especially black women. We don't usually get the chance at such a prize package. Or, so he thinks. And did you notice the way the sparks flew when he got his first look at Honey? It was hard to tell who was sending signals faster. She's a mantrap, that one."

Scott said nothing, just drove on.

"Anyhow I don't trust that man. He's bad."

"Bad? How?" Scott asked.

"I can't zero in on it. He's educated, got degrees and all, but he's also got to prove how much of a man he is—being

141

wanted and taking advantage of women. A generation ago he could have been one of Midgely Grove's 'uncles.' "

There was no space in front of the house where Marlene lived, so Scott parked down the block. Since it was late and the dark street was deserted, he insisted on walking her to her door.

"Thanks," she said as they reached the top of the front steps. "Sorry I took you out of your way."

"Don't worry about it."

She inserted her key into the lock expecting him to leave. When he didn't she said reassuringly, "It's okay. I'll be fine."

"Sometimes they figure on that. They get into a house and lurk in the hallways. There was a rape on this block only three days ago," Scott warned.

"How did you know that?" Marlene was surprised.

"Read about it in the *Post*. The address stuck in my mind."

"I'll be all right."

"I'd better see you to your door."

Finally relenting, Marlene turned the key and opened the door. A long hall separated the building in two, doors on either side. The worn carpet let the floor boards creak under their cautious steps.

At her own door Marlene found another key on her ring, inserted it in the lock and turned it. She opened the door slowly, with obvious apprehension. Scott realized that she must open her door that way every time, always alert and tense to the possibility that an intruder might have gained entrance to her ground floor flat. The thought that she lived in such constant fear troubled him enormously. Marlene entered the room, going immediately to the two high windows to examine the locks even before she snapped on the lights. By the light of a street lamp outside, Scott could see that both windows were protected by grillwork of sturdy iron bars.

She drew the shades and finally put on the floor lamp at one end of the studio couch.

"There! Everything's fine. You don't have to worry about

me anymore. And thanks again for saving me from the 'Jamaican' wolf." She laughed.

It could have been her laugh that did it. The way it crinkled the skin around her dark eyes and made them sparkle. The way it created that suggestion of a dimple in her right cheek that made her even more beautiful. Or it could have been everything that had happened this night. Her excuse to Randolph. His refusing to leave her at the front door. Their closeness.

No doubt all of it shared in the making of this moment when mutual desire too long delayed would now be shared.

He embraced her. She seemed to relax in his arms, willingly. And when they kissed, her mouth open to his, the last hesitations fled.

He held her close to him, one hand exploring her body, finding it as good to touch as it had promised to be, as he had imagined. Her breasts were firm, high, crested by nipples that were now erect. He caressed her face, covering her cheeks with damp kisses.

"Tasting?" she asked playfully. "To see if black tastes like you expected?"

Scott's reply was a deep, long kiss.

After that, they didn't talk. Together they undressed in some instinctive way. He drew her down to the studio couch, stared into her dark eyes, kissed her lips, held her close. Closing her eyes, she embraced him tightly in return, her nails digging into the muscles of his bare back. Her skin, so smooth on her cheeks, was smoother still on the rest of her body. Her young breasts thrust upward and made access to her nipples inviting and delightful.

Gently, he led her until she reached a high pitch of expectation and desire. She welcomed him into her, embracing him with her graceful arms and legs, enveloping him completely. At the instant of her orgasm he could feel the muscles of her abdomen tighten against his own. She went limp and made a small relieved sound that was almost a whimper. It made him

143

look down. Her pretty face was placid, her eyes closed. She seems so shy, Scott thought.

Without opening her eyes, she accused softly, "You're staring at me."

"At your face, your cheekbones, your lovely smooth skin," Scott replied.

"You've never made love to a black girl before, have you?" She opened her eyes to confirm her suspicion. "Does it make a difference? Be honest with me."

"Would you like me better if I were blonder?" he countered.

"If you were any blonder, you'd be invisible." They both laughed.

Then Marlene became sober again and asked, "I've always wondered. How did you get involved in the rights movement?"

"Next thing you'll be asking, 'What's a nice boy like you doing in a place like this?' "

"Okay. *What?*" she asked quite directly.

"I didn't 'get involved.' I was forced into it."

"Forced?"

"In a way. I entered law school expecting to do my three years, get good grades, make Law Review if I could, and then go into my dad's office. One year we were scheduled to compete in moot court against a black law school in Alabama. We did it mainly to give them the prestige of competing against an Ivy League school.

"I know it sounds like charity work. Maybe it was. After all, we were the best in the East and their team was new. Naturally, we won hands down. And we sure felt virtuous. What we didn't know was that while we were engaging in moot court *inside* the old law building, there was a demonstration going on *outside*.

"The shots were the first we knew. Two shots. Followed by hundreds of others. There were screams. The lights went out.

Someone yelled, 'Nobody leave! Everybody hit the floor. They're coming in shooting!'

"We hit the floor. Girls in the audience started screaming, becoming hysterical. The shots continued. They came closer. Then there was silence. Nobody moved because we didn't trust that quiet. Until a voice, deep, husky, Southern, but obviously white called out from the back of the hall, 'All right, now! You all get up! Nobody makes no sudden moves. File out! Hands clasped on your heads. Girls as well as boys.'

"We made our way toward the light at the door where two state troopers carrying submachine guns stood guard. The sergeant with the deep husky voice was saying, 'Just keep walking, slow and easy. And don't nobody gather outside the building. Or else we are going to have more trouble.'

"When Roger Cohen, who was on our team, and I reached the sergeant, he must have realized we didn't belong to the school because he apologized, 'I didn't mean for you fellows to come out this way.' Then he indicated that we could lower our hands and walk out any way we pleased. I was about to lower mine, but Roger didn't. He glared back at the sergeant, who explained in a hurt tone, 'We didn't have nothing against you. Fact, you being here saved lots of trouble. Otherwise we'd had a shootout. This way nobody got hurt. Just a few wounded.'

"Roger glared at him. I, quite surprising even to me, suddenly said, 'Fuck you, officer! Fuck you!' And we both walked out with our hands still clasped on our heads.

"From that moment on, for me, courts were no longer moot. Students were no longer students. They were participants in a war. A real live shooting war. On the flight back every man on the team promised that when he got out of law school part of his time every year was going to be devoted to rights work.

"The thing that lived longest with me was that sergeant, shooting at blacks, apologizing to whites, and expecting to be

145

thanked for it. If that was the law, something had to be done about it. And someone had to do it.

"That's how," he concluded simply, though he felt indignant all over again merely having to recount the events of that night.

He turned to her, embraced her, lifting her slender body against his own strong, muscular frame. Her moistness and her fragrance began to arouse him. Her breasts pressed against his chest. They kissed, her lips parting to his, and they were hungry for each other again.

Marlene was making coffee. She wore only her thin dressing gown which made the most of her slender figure. Scott was dressed once more, sitting on the couch where they had made love, staring at her. Every move she made enchanted him. Perhaps the gratification of satisfying sex did that to a woman, changed her, made her more graceful, more sure, more proud of being a woman.

She set the coffee tray down on the table in front of the couch. The fragrance was enormously pleasing. He remarked on it.

"My mother never believed in the instant kind. She used to say, 'No matter how short the time, make yourself real coffee. It'll satisfy your soul.' She was a great believer in natural things."

"She'd be just right for today's health food trend," Scott joked.

"She'd have been right for so many things now," Marlene said sadly. "With some education she would have been a great woman. She had ideas and convictions—her own, not someone else's. She was always putting down people who demonstrated. She used to say, 'You don't beg, you do. Demonstrations and protests are only another way of *asking*. You do what you're supposed to do, and you'll get respect. You don't get it by asking.' "

"She must have been right," Scott said softly. "She raised a terrific daughter."

Perhaps the compliment or the talk about her mother had caused her to feel self-conscious, for Marlene suddenly changed the subject.

"That was a brilliant idea of yours, that Doctrine of Social Inevitability."

"We won't know that until the court gets through deciding the case," Scott said, always eager to discuss the trial. "It might turn out to be a big red balloon that'll burst the first time Judge Beecher sticks a pin into it."

"Winkler doesn't seem to think so."

"It gives him his theory for the case. A premise to proceed on beyond the mere contention of his client's innocence."

"And when the client isn't innocent, then he certainly needs a theory," Marlene observed.

"Linc doesn't have any illusions about this case. Neither do I. It's going to be tough to save Midge Grove. Possible, but tough. And we're going to give him the best defense we can. The easy way would have been if he *were* insane. Then they'd have to put him in some institution for treatment for a term of years and that would have been the end of it."

"Why didn't Winkler take the easy way?" Marlene asked.

"Because Grove isn't legally insane," Scott said, defending Winkler.

"And who said he wasn't?" Marlene's words were delivered like a challenge.

"Randolph, first of all. The Government's doctors after that."

"The Government's doctors were *trying* to find him sane. What was Randolph's angle?"

"Who said he had any angle? He knew Midge wasn't insane. In the psychiatric board's opinion, he wasn't dangerous. He was untreatable. So they released him," Scott argued.

147

"The very word 'untreatable' can also mean *hopelessly sick*," she pointed out.

Scott reached over to take her hands so that she had to face him. "What are you trying to say?"

"I could tell by the look on your face tonight. You never suspected that Winkler and Randolph were holding private meetings. Meetings at which *they* had decided not to plead insanity."

"I *didn't* suspect," he confessed. "But Linc and I are going to have it out. Tomorrow."

"Good! Because I think Winkler's less concerned with how he'll do in court than with how he's doing on TV," she said angrily.

"Tonight . . . that was . . ." Scott made a vague gesture diminishing the earlier event.

"He stopped the discussion of what he considered the most important point in this case to see if he was on TV! You can't get around that, darling!"

The word had slipped out. Her tan cheeks turned tan pink, her eyes filled. She had intended never to let him know how deeply she felt about him, or that in her private thoughts, darling was what she called him.

He moved to her, lifted her, held her, tried to kiss her lips, but she turned her face away.

"Tonight has to be the end of it, as well as the beginning," she said, trying to be firm and cool, still looking away from him until finally he released her.

"Your mother 'told' you, I suppose!" he said angrily.

"Yes . . . yes, she did," Marlene responded coolly.

"Was she right about everything?"

"She was right about that!"

"How can you be so sure?" he asked.

"My father was white! And they were happy together until I was born. He could love a black woman, but the pressures got too great when he had a black child, too. He never explained it to her. He just disappeared. And she never had any man again for the rest of her life."

"Are you going to let one bitter experience determine what you do with the rest of your life?" Scott demanded.

She couldn't answer. Her eyes overflowed. Scott took her into his arms compassionately.

"You can't spend the rest of your life trying to make up for the actions of a man who couldn't face his own prejudices."

How many of us know the depth of our own prejudices, or our own fears? Until it's too late? Marlene thought. But it was useless to answer. She took a handkerchief from the pocket of her robe and dried her eyes. "I want you to be careful. About Winkler, I mean. And Randolph."

Scott nodded.

"Now you go on home. And don't worry about me," she instructed, putting on a smiling face for him though her eyes were still damp.

"Okay. I'll go home. And I won't worry about you—except most of the time." He kissed her gently on each eye and then on her dimpled right cheek. He left, but not until he heard her slip all the locks into place.

·◦❧ XIII ❧◦·

Linc Winkler was having his second cup of coffee and poring over the draft of the appeal for a change of venue when Scott Ingram came into the library. He did not look up, pretending he was not aware of Scott's surprised and hurt reaction of last night, hoping Scott would not broach the subject. But he did.

"Linc, there is something we have to discuss. You and Randolph have obviously had meetings at which certain strategies were decided on, strategies on which I was never consulted."

Winkler looked up, shoving his reading glasses back on his head. He reached for his cup, sipped at the coffee, all quite gravely, as though intently waiting to hear what else Scott had to say.

"It's not only the question of keeping our relationship open and honest. It's Grove, and Grove's defense. In fairness to him either we work together or you get someone else to serve as co-counsel. There are plenty of good willing men in the District."

Winkler shook his head, sadly, as if he would be grieved to have to make such a choice.

"Scotty, have I ever doubted your ability or your devotion to this case? Have I?"

"No. But obviously you don't trust me," Scott continued.

"And what about *you* trusting *me?*" Winkler asked, reproaching him gently. "I'd rather not discuss it right now, but if you feel we have to, I will."

"I feel we have to," Scott said firmly.

"Okay, kid, okay." Winkler reluctantly put aside his cup, shoved the papers back on the desk and rose from his chair.

"Scotty, I'm sure I don't have to tell you the Establishment is out to get me. Whether it's the FBI or local police, wherever I go they'd like to catch me in some infraction. My phones are tapped most of the time. My every move is under surveillance. And the bar association! I'm a thorn in their fat regal behinds. They'd *love* to catch me in anything that would give them grounds for disbarment.

"Now, it happens, working with the kind of cases I do, that occasionally I have to prepare a witness. Okay, I'll come right out with it, sometimes I have to tell a witness precisely what to say and how to say it! I have no qualms about doing that, or about admitting it to you now, privately. Not with the legal system stacked the way it is.

"But the fact that *I* am willing to take that risk is no reason why I have to jeopardize the career of a young man like you, whom I consider to be the brightest legal prospect I've come across in years. Don't you understand, Scotty, I am trying to *protect* you."

Winkler paused, stared across at Scott, then continued in a soft but pregnant whisper, "All right! I did conspire with Randolph. Suppose it comes out one day. I want *you* to be able to say under oath in complete honesty, 'I never knew anything about it.' I want *you* to be in the clear. I'm old enough to take risks. You're not. So now, because I was protecting you, you begin to doubt me. That's what I meant by *you* trusting *me.*"

Scott felt abashed and embarrassed. He could find neither the words nor the voice to apologize. But Winkler made that unnecessary.

"At times I need freedom, freedom to improvise and to act

151

on my impulses. Suddenly. Without checking every detail with you. Take last night. I was so excited by your Doctrine of Social Inevitability I couldn't sleep. I spent hours trying to figure out the most impressive way to capitalize on it. So it not only works for *us*, but works for *you*—to *your* best interest.

"Early this morning it hit me! A speech before the National Press Club! What better forum could we find? Should I have called you at five o'clock this morning and asked your permission to address the National Press Club?"

Winkler smiled reproachfully as a father might at a beloved but erring son.

"I am about to make your theory important and famous. And all you can think about is that I didn't tell you about a meeting or two that I had with Paul Randolph!"

"Are you going to call the press club?" Scott asked.

Winkler smiled. "I already have. It's all arranged. I'm going to address their Tuesday lunch."

Scott felt even more self-conscious. Winkler reached over and tousled his hair. "Scotty, since I'm running this defense, I could very well say to you, I'll run it any damn way I please. But I never have. I explain whenever I have the chance, and I try to get your concurrence. But when I don't, believe me it is not because I don't respect you, or trust you. To prove it, I repeat my offer. When this case is over, I want you to work with me. I want you to join our firm. I mean that!" Then Winkler smiled, "That is if you don't mind having the names Winkler and Pottish on the same stationery as Scott Ingram the Third." Scott finally smiled.

Winkler felt relieved. The entire confrontation had gone off more easily than he had anticipated.

It was the most heavily attended luncheon of the National Press Club since the delegate to the United Nations from the People's Republic of China had been the speaker. And be-

152

cause the guest of honor was A. Lincoln Winkler, there was television coverage as well.

Even Fred Anthony, chief of *The New York Times* Washington bureau, had decided to attend. Anthony was known to hold himself aloof from most of the Washington press corps, choosing to use the weight and prestige of his position to secure only exclusive news interviews and opinions from other than the generally available sources. If an official or other important person had a story of great significance to break and desired the best and widest auspices, he sought out Anthony either directly or through a more easily accessible informant.

What compelled Anthony to appear at the Winkler luncheon was the fact that the trial of Midgely Grove was to start on the following Monday, and that he had gotten a call from a friend in the black movement. It seemed that Honey Rosenstone had called that friend to suggest that Anthony might like to hear a speech of nationwide interest and possible history-making legal precedent at the Press Club luncheon for Linc Winkler.

So, curious, and with tomorrow's column safely on the wire to New York, Anthony decided to attend. From the moment he stepped off the elevator to enter the hallowed premises, the word began to spread. Fred Anthony had arrived. Anthony was here today. Drinks were left unfinished as men left the bar to greet him. Among all the veteran reporters who gathered around him, Anthony was by far the youngest. It made his power more awesome since he would endure longest.

Jokes were made about his rare appearances at the club. Still other laughs were shared privately about his fury over a national television broadcast that had criticized him for espousing busing in his column, while, at the same time sending his own children to a segregated private school in Georgetown.

153

Anthony was escorted to a long guest table, accorded a seat just to one side of the lectern and next to the empty chair reserved for Linc Winkler.

When Winkler finally arrived at the main table, Anthony rose to his feet, ready to shake his hand. Winkler smiled warmly, and then almost as an afterthought introduced his co-counsel Scott Ingram, who stood at his side. Anthony only dealt with prime news sources, and so he made no move to shake Scott's hand.

During lunch, though Anthony probed deftly about the trial and about his speech today, Winkler gave evasive answers and spoke only in generalities, until Anthony began to suspect that perhaps his informant had relayed a bit of deliberate misinformation. It seemed Winkler had not come to reveal any secrets. Or he was saving himself for the meeting at large, a fact which only served to irritate Anthony. Or maybe the pushy lawyer was so spoiled by all his TV coverage that he no longer appreciated the nationwide impact of Fred Anthony's column in *The New York Times* and in syndication elsewhere.

The chairman of the meeting called for silence.

"We seem to be living in a time when once again lawyers are taking an active part in the shaping of our world. I need not, I am sure, recall that fact to our more historically minded members. But for the rest of you poor slobs who labor in the sandy vineyards of the press, I remind you that A. Lincoln Winkler's distinguished predecessors include Mahatma Gandhi, Fidel Castro, and Nikolai Lenin. They, too, were lawyers with a social conscience. So I urge those of you who disagree with our guest today to listen quietly, if not out of respect for the present, then out of fear of the future."

There was a good deal of laughter, and then the chairman announced, "A. Lincoln Winkler!"

When the applause died down Winkler chuckled, "Believe me, I would rather be addressing your sons and daughters."

He evoked some laughter with that.

154

Aiming at the television camera, he went on, "The young sustain me. They force me to go on when those times come— yes, they do come—those times when, like you, I feel it can't be done.

"And then those magnificent young people are out front, looking up at me with expectation in their faces. And I know I cannot disappoint them. I cannot answer their desire for freedom from repression by looking back to the past, by saying we must not depart from ancient beliefs, ancient traditions, ancient heroes. For had our forefathers done so, we would still be on our knees to stone idols, primitive tribes instead of nations. We would still be deciding guilt or innocence by drowning. Those, too, were hallowed traditions in their time.

"Just as slavery was a hallowed practice to the very men we hold up as the founding fathers of our own nation. But we are past the time when we can look upon such men as unalloyed heroes. We are living in a time of great change. Those who change with change, survive. History has shown us what happens to those who resist change!"

The atmosphere in the room had grown quite tense. Winkler began to sense a growing resistance in most of his audience. Deliberately, he changed his attitude and attack.

"Now, there are those of you sitting before me who like to pin labels on me. It makes such nice, convenient, lazy reading for your public. Winkler is the 'New Left.' Winkler is a 'rabble-rouser.' Every time he makes a speech a fire breaks out somewhere. You can label me or libel me. You can accuse me or damn me. But the worst you can ever convict me of is seeking progressive change."

Now Winkler laid both hands on the lectern and leaned forward. "People have asked me why I take unpopular cases. Because I am a lawyer, that is my answer. Because the courtroom is my battleground, to alter, change, and if necessary completely overthrow the system of justice as we have endured it for almost two hundred years.

155

"New times demand not only new laws, but new approaches and new institutions. Just as *you* have seen the evolution and emergence of personal journalism, so *we* have seen the emergence of a new breed of lawyer dedicated to the activist practice of the law. I have no icons in the law—be it the court, the judge, or the law itself. Either the law must change, conforming to the realities of the time in which we live, or the law itself cannot be allowed to survive!"

There was applause when he finished but it was polite, reserved. Even the most liberal of the members had the sudden cold feeling that they had encountered the future, and it terrified them. The chairman rose to welcome questions from the floor.

Most of the questions quite naturally concerned the trial of Midgely Grove. In each instance Winkler made a careful disclaimer, explaining that he could not ethically comment on a case about to be tried in the courts. Then he proceeded to comment very freely.

Grove, he said, was entitled to the presumption of innocence. The Government would have to prove its case, and only then would his defense be interposed. Did Winkler have grave doubts that the Government could prove its case beyond a reasonable doubt? Yes, he did indeed. Did he approve of Judge Beecher's conduct to this point? No, or else he would not have made so many objections to Beecher's rulings.

Scott began to feel more and more uneasy, as Winkler began to enter areas of comment that might invoke disciplinary action by Beecher.

"Could you give us some hint as to what your defense will be?" one reporter asked.

Winkler smiled and said, "Cases that can't be won in the courts must be won in other places."

They had time for one last question, the chairman announced.

156

"Mr. Winkler, if you had the power to change the legal system immediately, what changes would you institute?"

"We can no longer be content with a system in which the society judges men. We are living in a time when men must judge the society."

With that, Winkler thanked the press club for inviting him to speak and pleaded that the pressures of the Grove case allowed him no more time. But as the others left, Linc Winkler accepted Fred Anthony's invitation to a private talk.

Fred Anthony, Linc Winkler, and Scott Ingram adjourned to a corner of the club. Seated in worn leather easy chairs and supplied with fresh drinks, Anthony began some skillful probing.

It seemed, if Anthony was correct in his assumption, that Winkler's last statement hinted at a new and unusual line of defense. And if that was so, could he reveal what this new line of defense would be?

Winkler made his usual gesture reflective of deep and troubled thought. His fingers combed through his hair, his brow wrinkled, his face seemed even more deeply creased as he sucked in his cheeks.

Later, writing about it, Anthony would use the word "Darrowesque" to describe Winkler's very convincing performance of a man wrestling with his conscience. Should he or should he not disclose a preciously guarded professional secret? Finally, he leaned closer to Anthony and asked, "Off the record?"

"Off the record." Anthony agreed.

"In that case," Winkler began, "we are proceeding on a totally innovative theory of law. A new doctrine which has not only never been tested before, it has never even been proposed!"

Anthony repeated the phrase he had heard Winkler use in his speech, ". . . we are living in a time when men must judge the society . . ."

157

"Exactly!" Winkler said. He paused and then gave great gravity to his revelation. "We are proceeding on the Doctrine of Social Inevitability."

"Doctrine of Social Inevitability?" It was obvious Anthony was tasting the new phrase, and he liked it.

"Society," Winkler continued, "by its repressive actions makes it inevitable that certain deprived citizens will have no alternative but to resort to criminal conduct. Then it punishes those whom it has made into criminals. We find that not only immoral, but illegal. We are proceeding on the basis that the courts, including the Supreme Court if need be, will hold with us."

"Then you feel the Grove case will go to the Supreme Court?" Anthony asked.

"Either that doctrine will be upheld or we'll go to the Supreme Court!" Winkler declared.

Anthony nodded thoughtfully. "Doctrine of Social Inevitability." His trip to the club had not been in vain. He rose, shook hands with Winkler and started toward the elevators.

As soon as Anthony was out of hearing, Scott asked with concern, "Do you think it was a good idea to tell him, even before we raise the issue formally?"

Winkler waited until Anthony had stepped into the elevator, then he smiled and said, "You're thinking he'll break it in his column before we do? Well, you're right! By tomorrow he will have convinced himself that the Doctrine was his discovery, and by Sunday he'll run his piece on it. The Sunday *Times* goes all over the country and it will be read! By all kinds of people—law professors who'll find food for thought in it, conservatives who'll be shocked by it, liberals who'll conjure with it, and radicals who'll blow their minds over it. But right now, that phrase 'social inevitability' is on its way to becoming part of the language.

"So when the time comes, Scotty, we won't be wild-eyed radicals with an outrageous new doctrine. We'll have had the ground broken for us by that newspaper of record, the august

New York Times, and a lot of others. And Judge Beecher will have to take that into account. And one day maybe even Ben Robertson will!"

Winkler smiled reproachfully. "Scotty, next time I say, trust me, trust me. Okay?"

Scott nodded admiringly. Winkler threw his arm over Scott's shoulder, and they walked together to the elevator.

Linc Winkler was proven right. Despite their off-the-record agreement, the following Sunday Fred Anthony's column ran opposite the editorial page of *The Times* in the fourth section, "The Week in Review." Anthony raised the question of whether the time had come in the evolution of this nation when the law, like all other human institutions, must be moved to basic change, when fundamental values must be rethought, when the question of guilt or innocence must be viewed anew, in the light of societal guilt, not individual guilt.

For the first time in print, Fred Anthony launched the phrase, Doctrine of Social Inevitability.

Linc Winkler clipped that column and had Marlene start a file for their records. During the succeeding weeks she would add to that file every article that appeared in any American publication and repeated the phrase that Scott had created.

Within several weeks *Time* magazine did a small piece on it in its Behavior department. A week thereafter a professor at MIT wrote a lengthy article on the doctrine in *The New York Review of Books*. The phrase began to be mentioned on educational and Sunday afternoon television shows. By the end of several weeks, a committee at Ford Foundation decided to vote a grant to a professor of sociology at Harvard to undertake an intensive study on the question of Social Inevitability. And, at the same time, *Harper's* magazine engaged Arthur Schlesinger to write a comprehensive thinkpiece on the Doctrine of Social Inevitability and its historical perspective.

Thus the phrase metastasized into the language and became an accepted part of the obligatory vocabulary of every intellectual who owned a typewriter or could hold a cocktail glass.

Linc Winkler's collection of articles on Social Inevitability would grow from day to day so that by the time he had used up weeks of court days in jury selection and the actual trial of Midge Grove finally began, he would have accumulated a weighty file which even contained a report from a Presidential Committee on Law Enforcement, touching very lightly and gingerly on the subject, singling it out as a subject to be watched carefully for future development.

Linc sat at the large antique desk in the Rosenstone library. Before him were two lists which Scott had secured from U.S. Attorney Carroll. One was the jury list. The other was the capital list, which included the name of every possible witness that the Government intended to call during the trial. The capital list had only one point of interest as far as Winkler and Ingram were concerned. By listing his witnesses, in effect Carroll was giving them an advance look at his entire case. There could be no surprises from the Prosecution.

Carroll's case seemed almost routine: the witnesses to the shooting, the identification witnesses, the medical examiner, ballistics expert, fingerprint expert, FBI lab technicians, arresting officers, Metropolitan Police Captain on Homicide detail who was witness to Grove's voluntary confession, and the psychiatrists who had done the M.O. on Grove and found him sane. Complete in all details. Airtight.

Winkler could deal with the witnesses later. His first concern was the jury list, for the first earnest battle of Winkler's war would be fought over the composition of that jury. Though he had gone to great expense and made quite a display of emotion in his argument for a change of venue, secretly Winkler had not wanted such a change at all. Wash-

160

ington, D.C., suited him better than any other jurisdiction. It was not only the focus of world news coverage, but a central location that would enable him to flood the streets with demonstrators when the time was right. And it had one other advantage. It was actually the scene of the crime—a fact that would enable him to battle over every possible juror, stalling for as much time as he needed.

Linc had asked Scott to do a random check of the names on the list. Even a cursory investigation revealed that the racial percentage was, if anything, overbalanced in favor of blacks. Whereas blacks were not quite 80 percent of the population, they were 81 percent of this particular jury list. A goodly number were civil servants, and there was a surprising number of black professionals.

"Not much hope here, Linc," Scott concluded as he handed Winkler his report.

"I don't know . . ." Winkler mused. He turned to Marlene and said, "Get me Paul Randolph!"

"A psychiatrist? To work on a jury list?" Scott asked.

"Scott, forget what you learned in law school. Get out of the habit of thinking logically. Leave that to Carroll and his very careful capital list, and his step-by-step case." Linc was smiling. He rose from his desk chair, taking the jury list with him. As he paced the elegant oriental rug he spoke thoughtfully.

"The prosecutor has one job: Present a case, an airtight case, beyond a reasonable doubt. We have another job: Find just one hole, one weakness, and work on it until we develop it into a doubt. A nice, healthy, reasonable doubt. On top of that, if we can find a few raisins, some questions of law on which we can go up on appeal if we need to, and with a little groundswell of public opinion behind us, even an assassin can come out pretty well." He turned back to Marlene. "Randolph!"

Randolph sounded delighted to hear Marlene's voice, but

161

his tone lost a bit of its enthusiasm when he discovered that she was calling at Winkler's behest. Yes, he would be free about three. He would be there about three-thirty.

"Paul," Winkler said, fingering the jury list, "what I have here is a jury list of blacks. Slice it any way I can, the percentages won't help me. So I need your help in framing a list of questions to put to black jurors making them ineligible, or at least questionable, to serve on this jury."

Randolph seemed helpless for a moment, until Winkler added, "They don't necessarily have to be questions the judge will finally allow. Just give me questions that sound scientific enough to put up a fight."

Randolph nodded and smiled. It became a game he seemed eager to play.

"There's a whole list of questions you might ask a group of middle-class blacks that would embarrass them," Randolph began.

"That's the key!" Winkler seized on it. "Middle class! They vote, so they make up the jury roles."

"First, most middle-class blacks are Toms—natural, inevitable Toms. Most of them, if you asked and if they were honest, would say they'd rather be called Negro than black. It sounds more dignified."

"Good question!" Winkler said, turning to Marlene, dictating: "Which word do you prefer to have used to describe your color, black or Negro?"

"Being new to the middle class they are more rigid, more strict with their children, more concerned with what their neighbors think."

"I can't just ask them that. How do we phrase it, dramatize it?"

Randolph thought a moment, then a big smile broke across his black face. He looked at Marlene, but spoke to Winkler, "Why not ask simply, 'Do you approve of your daughter wearing an Afro?' Or, 'Do you approve of your

162

daughter going without a bra?' Most black, middle-class parents *won't* approve."

"A little rephrasing and that could work," Winkler agreed, smiling along with Randolph.

Marlene had caught Randolph's obvious reference to her own Afro and the delightful fact that she never wore a bra. But she ignored him with determination.

Winkler continued to pace, "You once told me that if Grove were turned loose among certain blacks, they'd lynch him faster than a white mob. Can we prove that middle-class blacks would be even *more* hostile than a white jury?"

"That wouldn't be hard to sustain," Scott interjected. "The percentage of convictions of black defendants by predominantly black juries is higher here than in any other jurisdiction."

"Now if we had a nice theory to explain it, we could tie this case up in knots for days!" Winkler exclaimed.

Randolph leaned forward a little. "Has a psychiatrist ever been called in to testify for that purpose?"

"Who cares! If you've got an idea, I'm willing to try it!"

"I did my master's thesis on the psychology of the middle-class black. There's a detailed explanation of the syndrome in there.

"For example," Randolph continued, "a Jew in need will almost always be helped by other Jews. Jews raise millions for almost any cause that affects other Jews. Not so with blacks.

"The successful black likes to get away. He likes to segregate himself with other blacks of the same social and economic status. To him, every black accused of a crime is viewed as a blot on all middle-class blacks. It's the main gap between the young black of today and his parents. The young black has a consciousness of his brother's problem; the middle-aged, middle-class black has no patience with it. No wonder a jury of middle-class blacks is so quick to convict an accused black. They rush to find him guilty, get him out of the way before he contaminates them! Before he threatens the position which they have struggled so hard to achieve!"

"Excellent!" Winkler exploded with delight. Turning to Marlene, he asked, "Did you get it all down?"

"No need. It's practically verbatim from my paper," Randolph said.

"Get me a copy," Winkler ordered, already beginning to formulate additional questions which he could present to Judge Beecher to be asked of prospective jurors during the *voir dire* examination.

Questions flowed in profusion from his active mind, as if Randolph's suggestion had given him new impetus and energy.

He dictated them to Marlene,

"Have you ever witnessed a fatal shooting? Have you ever witnessed any crime of violence? Did you witness, or did anyone you know witness the crime in question in this case?"

Winkler's list was to mount into hundreds of questions, the answer to any one of which might provide him with cause to excuse almost any potential juror.

PART THREE
THE TRIAL

XIV

On the morning of the first day of his trial, Midgely Grove was awakened at dawn. Since this was a special day, he was allowed to shower. Then, wearing his plain prison garb, he breakfasted alone in the large jail mess hall an hour before the other prisoners. When he had eaten what little of the simple meal he wanted, Midgely Grove was turned over to two United States Marshals and driven to the United States Courthouse in a shielded, windowless van. Rumors had spread through Washington that extremist groups might attempt to intercept the van this morning and free Grove before the trial, so he sat between the two Marshals, manacled to each one.

There was no incident on the way. But as the van approached the Federal Courthouse, a solid phalanx of students, white and black and carrying placards, massed in its path to prevent the van's access to the courthouse. WHITE JUSTICE IS NO JUSTICE, END PIG JUSTICE, FAIR TRIAL FOR MIDGE, the placards demanded.

When members of the Metropolitan Police tried to make way for the van, black girls lay down in the street to block the wheels with their bodies. Young men, black and white, stood guard over them and grappled with the police who tried to haul them out of the way. Finally, clubs swinging, the police dragged the girls off. More than fifty were thrown into police cars to be driven to the station to be booked for a variety of offenses. The press, which had been notified, covered the entire conflict in dramatic detail.

The prison van finally arrived at the gate where it released its passenger and his two guards.

Inside the courthouse, Grove was escorted to the small bare room where Linc Winkler, Scott Ingram, and Marlene Hutch waited for him. Laid out on the table were the new clothes which Marlene had bought on Winkler's specific instruction—black jeans, black turtleneck sweater, black leather jacket, smelling new and fresh, their tags and size marks still on. Winkler had Grove strip off his stiff, crude prison outfit. Then, as if he were dressing his son for the first day of school, Winkler helped Grove into the jeans, drew the turtleneck over his head, and slipped the black leather jacket on him, zipping it up only halfway.

Finally, from his own pocket Winkler produced a pair of dark glasses and a black beret, surprising accessories to be sure. Though Scott and Marlene exchanged bewildered and disapproving glances, neither said a word to Winkler until he had placed the glasses on Grove and set the beret on his head. Examining Grove carefully, Winkler seemed quite satisfied with the overall effect. At that point, Scott whispered harshly, "Linc!"

Scott motioned him aside and demanded, "Why make him out to be a Panther? He's the furthest thing in the world from that. Besides, it'll prejudice our case with the jurors."

Winkler nodded smugly, "Which will help us in delaying the selection of a jury, to say nothing of getting us valuable support outside the courtroom from some very influential people."

"Not from the public at large!" Scott insisted.

"Trust me, Scott, just trust me. I know what I'm doing." With that Linc closed off any further discussion, but turned to inspect Grove once more and was satisfied. "Midge," he said quite compassionately, "we'll see you in the courtroom in a little while."

Grove's face which had been immobile, suddenly looked tense, frightened. His eyes darted from Winkler to Scott to Marlene, as if pleading for a way to avoid entering that courtroom where his crime and his life would be the focus of the country and the world. Before panic could take hold, Linc clasped Grove's shoulder to give him strength.

"Do I got to go dressed like this?" Midge asked finally.

"Midge, all your life you've been wanting to run away and hide. But this time we won't let you!" Winkler said. "We can't. You're an important man now. Do you know who's coming to your trial? Bobby Strong, leader of all the Panthers! He's coming down here just to see you—to see that you get a fair trial. Now if you weren't important, he wouldn't be coming here. Because he's got things to do, big things. But *you* are the biggest. Bobby wants to see you at the lunch break today. Would you like to talk to him?"

Grove nodded uncertainly.

"See you upstairs," Winkler said and started out.

Scott and Marlene followed, passing the two marshals who stood guard at the door. As Winkler strode down the hall, Scott and Marlene lagged behind, speaking in whispers.

"You should have told me," Scott reproached her.

"Yes, I knew what he was after when he gave me the list. I should have told you, but then, so should he," she said pointedly.

"He's right about one thing. If there's latent prejudice in the jury this'll bring it out."

"And if there isn't, this'll create it!"

"What's the alternative? To let him go to trial with a formal, uninspired defense, be found guilty and sentenced to life? Life in jail for him, with his history, is worse than a death sentence."

"Bobby Strong!" Marlene exploded. "If he sits through this trial, there's no doubt they'll sentence Midge to life!"

169

"Marlene . . ." Scott called out. But she had gone ahead of him to slip into the elevator just before the doors closed, leaving him to wait for the next car.

When Scott reached the courtroom doors, he found a crowd forming outside. Winkler was there, too, waiting impatiently, hair flowing, bulging briefcase in his left hand, his right hand stroking the dry sides of his mouth as if to wipe away excess saliva.

Scott pushed his way past the group of spectators to peer through the glass inserts in the locked leather doors. Inside the courtroom at least twenty men in uniform were making a careful inspection. Some crawled on their hands and knees through the aisles, staring at the underside of each bench and chair. Others were being hoisted by their colleagues to examine high areas, including the tops of the doorsills. Still other guards tried the doors, standing to one side, opening them gingerly to see if they were booby trapped. They were taking all the precautions that followed a bomb threat.

Scott turned to Winkler.

"Either a nut call—or else the real thing," Winkler informed him.

Now word was passed from inside assuring the crowd that the courtroom was secure. Three men in uniform took places at the door. One announced, "All participants in the case line up here. All spectators and representatives of the press line up on the other side. Every person will have to be searched before he is allowed into the courtroom!"

As the crowd separated into two groups, Winkler started for the door, lugging his bulging briefcase, Scott and Marlene following close behind. He reached for the door handle, but one of the three men stepped into place in front of him.

"Sorry, Counselor, you too." Then he and another man began to frisk Winkler.

"Of all the goddamn foolishness," Winkler muttered, as he lent himself to the procedure. They felt up and down his long legs, patted his hips, chest, and underarms. Then, turning

170

their attention to his briefcase, one of the men held it while the other opened it, eventually finding nothing dangerous, but scattering many of the papers.

Both Scott and Marlene were searched and identified in similar fashion, and then all three were permitted to enter the courtroom.

It was a large room with a high ceiling. Since the courthouse was not very old, the wood furnishings were still shiny and the blue leather upholstery fragrant. The well of the courtroom was dominated by the high judge's bench, unoccupied at the moment. Two long counsel tables parallel to each other and to the jury box were bare. Of shining, light-colored oak, they matched the armchairs that surrounded them.

Across the entire width of the courtroom, separating the well from the rows of spectator seats, a shield of bulletproof plastic had been erected. It rose to a height four feet above the level of the railing, making it impossible for any armed spectator to inflict injury on any of the participants. No precaution had been overlooked by Federal officials. Mindful of that day when a judge had been abducted and slain in Marin County, California, during a trial of some black defendants, they were taking no chances.

Winkler took his place at the head of the table farthest from the jury box, so that he faced the bench. He set down his briefcase and began to unload papers, notes, blank pads and legal memoranda. Scott joined him, taking the seat to Winkler's right so that he would face the jury but would have to angle slightly to see the judge's bench.

From the rear of the courtroom, reporters and spectators were being admitted singly as each was searched and cleared. Carroll and his assistants entered the courtroom from a side door. Winkler smiled sardonically and discreetly gestured to Scott to look up. The U.S. Attorney had brought with him only two assistants. And both young men were black. Carroll glanced cordially toward Winkler and Scott.

171

There was a stir behind the door opposite the jury box. The clerk opened it to investigate, only to discover Midge Grove there, manacled to two Federal Marshals. Winkler crossed the well of the courtroom swiftly and disappeared out the door. When he returned he was leading Midge Grove, who was no longer handcuffed. The two Marshals followed closely behind. As they reached the counsel table, Winkler patted Midge gently on the shoulder and settled him into the chair next to his own. The Marshals took chairs directly behind Grove.

With spectators, counsel and defendant in their places, the clerk sent word for the judge, and in a few moments he ordered all persons to stand as Judge Albert Beecher entered.

Beecher climbed to the bench and stared out at the courtroom. Immediately his eye caught Midge Grove dressed in black jeans, sweater, and jacket. The judge seemed about to make an observation, but he refrained.

Under the table, Winkler quietly slapped Grove on the thigh. Midge rose from his chair, faced the bench and gave a fisted salute. It was a timid gesture, not fully or vigorously executed. Winkler pulled Grove down into his chair. Beecher's expression was now openly disapproving, but he restricted himself to glaring. All the while, Winkler pretended to be engrossed in his notes, as though he were totally unaware of the judge's irritation.

The clerk of the court led a large group of prospective jurors into the room, seating them in the jury box until it was filled. The remainder were directed to the roped-off rows of seats on the left side of the courtroom, ready to replace each man or woman in the jury box who might be disqualified during the *voir dire*.

Judge Beecher looked out at his courtroom. Everything seemed in order, so he finally spoke.

"The case we begin here today is a most important one. To assure the Defendant a fair trial will take the efforts of us all. The Court shall demand decorum from both Prosecution and

172

Defense Counsel. And from the press, both within this court-room and without. Any outburst from spectators will be dealt with peremptorily." Beecher turned to face the jury box. "Every prospective juror is to answer all questions with a simple, truthful answer. Do not volunteer any information. What may seem a matter of importance to you may serve to taint the rest of the panel. So if you have any answer to make beyond the specific question, signify by raising your hand and I will ask you to come to the bench and tell me privately. Is that clearly understood?"

He gave a slight nod to the clerk, who rose and announced, "Criminal Number 2747-73, United States of America versus Midgely Grove."

Carroll rose from the prosecution table and said gravely, "The Government is ready."

Winkler half-rose, as if a prisoner of his voluminous notes, and without looking up at the judge declared, "The Defense is ready."

Beecher returned his attention to the jurors. "I will now introduce to you the participants in this case. If you know any of them personally, please signify at once. The Prosecutor, United States Attorney, Roger Carroll."

Carroll rose, faced the jury box and then the jurors in the spectator seats. No one indicated any familiarity.

Beecher continued, "His associates, Mr. Philip Washington and Mr. Roland Spence." Both black assistants stood until it was certain they were not recognized.

Beecher turned to look at Winkler. "The Counsel for the Defense, A. Lincoln Winkler."

As Winkler rose and faced the jurors, there was a buzz of excitement from some of the jurors.

Beecher observed somewhat tartly, "With Mr. Winkler's frequent and extensive appearances on television, I daresay most of you recognize him. That was not my question. Do any of you have any relationship with him, any personal acquaintance?"

When no prospective juror so signified, Beecher proceeded to introduce Scott Ingram. One black juror raised her hand. Scott stared at the woman but did not know her. The judge summoned both Scott and the woman to the bench.

"You know Mr. Ingram?" Beecher asked.

"Yes, Your Honor," the woman said.

"In what way, may I ask?"

"He was appointed to defend my nephew on a charge of breaking and entering. And he got him off. He's a very good lawyer," the black woman said righteously.

To the woman, Beecher said, "You are excused." To Scott, "So you have a private fan club, too. Smaller than his, but just as loyal it seems."

Beecher continued with the presentation of participants. He introduced the defendant, read the capital list, the names of all the witnesses the U.S. Attorney intended to call, and the very brief list that the Defense had submitted. None of the prospective jurors claimed acquaintanceship with any of the persons named.

"Now ladies and gentlemen, you will respond to specific questions put to you by this Court, by the U.S. Attorney and by Mr. Winkler or his associate, Mr. Ingram. You will answer truthfully without trying to determine for yourself whether your answer will qualify or disqualify you for service on this case. Each side has unlimited opportunities to strike, that is, to excuse a juror for cause. But each side is also allowed a number of what are called peremptory challenges. Challenges for which they do not have to give any cause. The Government is allowed ten. The Defense is allowed twenty. It is not within your province to guess why such challenges are being used, or to attach any significance to them."

Beecher looked down at Winkler, then at Carroll, before he turned back to the jurors.

"Since this may be a case of considerable duration, and this jury will be sequestered, I should like to ask now if there is any prospective juror who, by reason of health or other special personal pressures, feels that he or she cannot serve for as long as the case demands?"

A young black man in the second row of the jury box raised his hand. "My wife is expecting within two weeks," he explained, "and I would like to be free for that time."

The judge smiled. "You may be excused. But I caution the rest of you, do not volunteer reasons in open court. You will have your chance to come to the bench and explain."

After the young man had been replaced in the box, Beecher addressed the remaining jurors. "Ladies and gentlemen, the defendant in this case is accused of having planned on October 14th, 1973, to enter the Supreme Court of this nation and there to kill, with premeditation, a Justice of that court. He is accused of having actually committed that crime on October 14th, 1973. And of having committed other lesser crimes in preparing that crime and attempting to make good his escape. Does any member of the panel have any direct information from whatever source of this alleged incident?"

The entire panel of jurors raised hands.

"I do not mean information gained from the news media. I mean personal, first-hand knowledge by virtue of your presence at the time of the event or from conversations with someone actually involved in or witnessing the event."

All hands came down.

"Now, all potential jurors, listen to me carefully," Beecher cautioned. "From the information you have gained through reading newspapers or magazines, listening to radio, watching television, have any of you formed an opinion as to the Defendant's guilt or innocence? This time do not raise your hands. I will call on each of you personally. Do not give me your conclusions. Simply answer yes or no. Have you formed any conclusion as to guilt or innocence in this case?"

He indicated the first man in the jury who answered by saying simply, "Yes, sir!" The other answers followed: yes, no, no, no, yes, yes, not sure, no, no, yes. Beecher excused all those who answered yes, including the woman who had said

175

not sure. When they were replaced by six new jurors from the spectator seats, Beecher repeated his question. Of these new ones two more had to be excused. And of the two who replaced them, one had to be excused. Finally twelve men and women sat in the jury box, none of whom had formed a conclusion as to Midgely Grove's guilt or innocence.

Before he turned to Counsel, Judge Beecher summoned the clerk to the bench and ordered, "You'd better get another fifty jurors up here at once, the way it's going!"

Beecher addressed both counsel tables. "Now, gentlemen, the Court will entertain any questions you may wish to have asked of the jury." Focusing on Winkler, he said, "It is the practice in our courts, Mr. Winkler, for the presiding judge to ask most of the questions on *voir dire*—unless you have some special objection?"

Winkler untangled his legs, raised his glasses, and looked up from the list of questions he seemed to be reading. He rose slowly. "We have no objection to the *voir dire* being conducted by His Honor. But we do have a list of questions which we insist be asked."

"Counsel will please come to the bench."

Winkler and Scott advanced to the bench, as did Carroll. Winkler handed his list to Beecher, who took a cursory look at the almost two hundred questions. He glanced indignantly at Winkler who stared back, unabashed. Beecher began to read the questions one by one.

At the very first question, he asked in an irritated whisper, "You seriously wish this Court to exclude all white persons from this jury?"

"Yes, we do," Winkler replied.

Beecher did not respond, but went on to the next question. First he read it silently, then aloud but out of hearing of the jury box. *"If a white witness said one thing and a black witness disputed him, which one would you be inclined to believe?"*

The judge glared at Winkler who met him stare for stare.

"If a policeman in uniform testified and if his testimony was

disputed by a civilian witness, which one would you be inclined to believe?'"

"Are you a Federal employee? Do you work in any Federal building? What is the range of your annual earnings? Do you own your own home?"

Beecher asked in a sharp whisper, "Just what do you expect to accomplish by these questions, except possibly to strip this jurisdiction of all eligible jurors? If that's your tactic, Mr. Winkler, you will not succeed!"

"I would suggest, Your Honor . . ."

But Beecher continued, "I am not finished! Due to the fact that we are in the capital of this nation, it is natural that most persons of whatever color will be employed by the numerous government agencies which constitute the main business of this city."

"Exactly, Your Honor," Winkler said, raising his voice. "And whom we deem, for sound and scientific reasons, to be ineligible to fulfill the Constitutional requirement of providing this Defendant with a jury of his peers."

"You will keep your voice down!" Beecher said. "I do not wish to taint this entire panel by having them become parties to this dispute. In fact, I think we had better have a hearing out of court on this entire matter."

"I quite agree!" Winkler said, since a hearing was exactly what he had been aiming for.

"Can you be ready this afternoon?"

"I certainly can!" Winkler responded.

The judge looked at Carroll, who asked with concerned deliberateness, "I would like an explanation first. What form will these 'sound and scientific reasons' take? We want a chance to combat any expert testimony."

"We will introduce psychiatric testimony," Winkler answered.

"Psychiatric testimony? To determine fitness for jury service?" Beecher sounded quite annoyed.

"Yes!" Winkler shot back.

"Then we will need time to gather experts of our own," Carroll said quickly.

"Do so by tomorrow morning! However, we will dispose of this list of questions in chambers today," Beecher ruled.

That afternoon Linc Winkler, Scott Ingram, United States Attorney Carroll, his two black assistants and the court stenographer gathered in Judge Beecher's chambers. In four hours of wrangling, Winkler's list of almost two hundred questions was whittled down by more than two-thirds.

On most of the questions, Winkler gave in after sharp discussion, but on a handful of them he remained adamant.

"Have you ever been the victim of a crime of violence?"

"Have you ever been threatened with violence with a gun?"

"Has any member of your family or any close friend or associate ever been the victim of a crime involving the use of violence?"

"Have you ever witnessed a fatal shooting?"

"Were you in the courtroom, or in the vicinity of the Supreme Court Building, when the crime alleged here was committed?"

Since Carroll had no great objection, these questions became part of the small group which Judge Beecher agreed to put to all prospective jurors. Winkler seemed quite gratified with that victory, minor as it seemed to Carroll and Beecher.

The next morning when Winkler, Scott, and Marlene approached the courthouse, they found that the police had set up barricades to keep all demonstrators at least a hundred feet from the entrance. Today the placards bore new and different legends.

"FREE THE WASHINGTON FIFTY!" some demanded, referring to the young men and women who had been arrested in the violent outbreak of yesterday.

Placards which had demanded a fair trial for Midge Grove had undergone a change, as well. Now they proclaimed SAVE MIDGE GROVE and SAVE MIDGE GROVE

178

FROM PIG JUSTICE. The voices of the pickets were louder today, but there was a noticeable effort to avoid physical force.

Inside the courtroom, all prospective jurors were excluded. The press and spectators filed in to fill the room to capacity as Linc Winkler called his expert witness to the stand.

Dr. Paul Randolph took the oath and then settled back in the witness chair. His voice was moderate in tone and level as, under Winkler's guidance, he recited his background. Public elementary schools until he was awarded a high-school scholarship to Ethical Culture Fieldston School in New York City, a scholarship to the University of Wisconsin, and then a full scholarship to Meharry Medical College. His post-graduate experience included his internship and residency in a New York City hospital and his eventual appointment to his present post at St. Elizabeth's Hospital in the District. Finally Winkler elicited from Randolph a recital of the various papers he had written, submitted, and published in medical journals in the United States and abroad.

Throughout the opening portion of Randolph's testimony the U.S. Attorney took copious notes, his concentration broken only when he leaned back toward his own expert psychiatrist to ask or receive some information.

"Dr. Randolph, are you the author of a paper entitled, 'The Black Middle-Class Mind—A Phenomenon'?" Winkler was asking.

"I am."

"And where was the article published, Doctor?"

"The Journal of the American Psychiatric Society. In the year 1967. March, I believe."

"Dr. Randolph, how long and extensive a study did you engage in before writing that article?"

Randolph leaned forward now. "The phenomenon of the black middle-class mind first interested me when I was a child at the Fieldston School. Even then I was aware of the strange mentality of the middle-class Negroes, as they were called in those days. In fact, I think that that awareness was the deciding factor in choosing psychiatry as my field."

"And precisely what was it about the middle-class Negro mind that intrigued you so?" Winkler asked gravely.

"We had in that school a small number of Negro children who were paying students because their parents could afford it. We had also a small token group of black students who were there on full scholarship."

"Of which you were one?" Winkler interjected.

"I believe I said that before, Mr. Winkler," Randolph replied, the formality in his address intending to mask their close relationship and the detailed planning they had done. "While it took some time and a great deal of personal control to become used to the condescension of the spoiled, white Jewish students in the school who felt they were doing an act of infinite charity to put up with us, I did become adjusted to that."

Here Randolph paused, sipped from the water glass at his side, adjusted the microphone before him. Then he leaned in a bit closer. "How ever much the white students may have condescended, even to the extent of inviting us to their homes, the attitude of the middle-class Negro children was quite different. They avoided us poor blacks as if we were their enemies. We were never invited to their birthday parties or to play at their homes. In a word, they wanted nothing to do with poor scholarship students."

"Despite the fact that you were black, too?" Winkler asked.

"*Because* of that fact," Randolph said. "As a child the reason was not clear to me, but as I went forward with my education, especially when I began to specialize in psychiatry, I devoted myself to finding it out.

"And your article is the result of your long study of that phenomenon?" Winkler asked.

"It is," Randolph said gravely.

"Now to apply the conclusions in your article to this trial: Is it your contention that middle-class black persons are actually more prejudiced against lower-class blacks than white persons might be?"

"It is!"

"In the course of researching your article, did you uncover the reason for that phenomenon?"

"I did!"

"And found it to be?" Winkler prodded.

"The inherent fear that underlies all black people in this country, ingrained by more than three hundred years of slavery, deprivation, third-class citizenship . . ."

"Third-class citizenship?" Winkler interrupted to make the most of the phrase.

"Yes!" Randolph replied sharply. "First class, the white American-born Protestant. Second class, the white Catholic or Jewish person, *or* a black from any other nation. And third class, lowest in the group, the native American Indian and the American-born black."

"Doctor, you were testifying to the inherent fears, residues of three hundred years of slavery."

"Yes," Randolph resumed, "a fear so deeply ingrained that there is in this country no such thing as a secure black man— no matter how educated, wealthy, or accepted by the public he may be. Thus, every lower-class black is a constant reminder and a threat that the middle-class black could easily be forced back into the ghetto by a repressive society which avenges itself on the lower-class black man. So the middle-class black avoids him, slanders him, and when called to serve on a jury, is quick to vote against him."

"In your expert opinion, Doctor, a middle-class black person—with a steady job, a house of his own, children in a good school—might look upon someone like Midgely Grove as a threat to all that he had worked so hard to achieve in this country?"

"Object!" Carroll called out, though he was resigned to Judge Beecher's quick ruling against him.

"Doctor?" Winkler resumed.

"It is my belief that a middle-class black juror would be voting according to his fears instead of expressing his honest conclusion about the facts. In effect, he would be saying to whites, 'Don't fault me. I hate all black criminals just like you do. See, I voted against my brother.' Trying this defendant before a jury of middle-class blacks would be like trying Jesus Christ before the Sanhedrin whose very existence he threatened."

Winkler liked the image of that last statement, so he rested his examination there.

Carroll had a brief last-minute exchange with his own psychiatric expert, before he took up his notes and advanced to the attorneys' lectern.

"Dr. Randolph, I was both enlightened and touched by your recitation of the events of your early education. And also by several comments that you made. You said that you were born and brought up in Harlem in New York City."

"Yes."

"Yet your speech is the speech of the islands. Your accents and intonations . . ."

"Yes," Randolph responded gingerly.

"Would you explain to us how that phenomenon came about?" Carroll asked.

"Quite simple, Mr. Carroll. It is one of the scars of my childhood. When in class with other children, white and middle-class black, I began to realize that because of my ghetto speech, I was an object of ridicule and pity. I determined that I would learn to speak well, well enough to be clearly understood. And respected."

"And possibly by taking on the accent of a non-native-born American black, move up from third class to second class?"

182

"Objection!" Winkler called out. "Such derogatory aspersions on the deprived childhood of the witness are not only in bad taste but are immaterial to the motion presently under consideration."

Carroll turned on Winkler. "If Counsel will be patient I will make the connection eventually."

Judge Beecher said gruffly, "Objection overruled."

"Exception!" Winkler said, to make the point for the press.

Carroll continued his line of questioning. "Dr. Randolph, it was a deliberate decision on your part to learn to speak in the manner in which you do now, and thus take on the protective coloration, if we may use the word, of a non-native-born black. You must have been a deeply hurt and quite determined boy."

"Am I required to answer that?" Randolph asked Judge Beecher.

Beecher turned to Carroll. "The Prosecutor will confine himself to questions rather than remarks or conclusions."

Carroll paused for a moment, then asked, sharply, "Dr. Randolph, in the economic scale of things, how would you classify yourself?"

"I am not given to sitting around classifying myself!" Randolph retorted sharply.

"Only to sitting around classifying others, is that it?"

"Your Honor, the Prosecutor is harassing the witness," Winkler interjected.

"Mr. Carroll . . ." the judge cautioned.

"Let's take the slow road then, Dr. Randolph. How much do you earn? Annually?"

"Thirty-six thousand dollars."

"Do you own your own home?"

"I do," Randolph admitted.

"Are you married and do you have any children?"

"Married. And we have two children."

"Your children attend the public schools of the District?"

183

Randolph hesitated before answering. "One is too young to attend school. The other is enrolled in the Montessori School."

"A private institution?"

"Yes," Randolph admitted.

"Dr. Randolph, subject to being corrected by the court stenographer, I believe you defined the middle-class black as being a person with a steady job, a home of his own, children in a good school."

"Roughly, yes," Randolph conceded.

"Then, Doctor, according to your own testimony, you belong to that group, don't you?"

"By that test, yes."

"Would you consider *yourself* incompetent to sit in that jury box, hear the testimony in this case, and render a fair and impartial verdict?"

"I would not consider myself an average middle-class black."

"Could you or could you not render a fair verdict in this case?" Carroll pursued.

Winkler rose swiftly, interjecting, "I submit this is a patently unfair and irrelevant question. Since the witness has examined the Defendant professionally and knows him, if he were called for jury duty in this case, Dr. Randolph would be excluded on the ground of previous knowledge. So Mr. Carroll's question becomes not only hypothetical, but immaterial."

"So ruled, Mr. Carroll," the Judge agreed.

Carroll turned to Randolph. "Doctor, suppose we were dealing with another black man, a poor black man, an accused black man, whom you had never seen before in your life. Could you sit on such a jury without prejudice?"

Randolph hesitated, then said softly in his pleasant polished Jamaican accent, "Yes, I believe I could."

"So it is not necessarily true that *all* middle-class blacks are prejudiced against their poor brothers, or fear them, or would be quick to convict them?"

"The vast preponderance of those I studied did react in that way!"

Convinced he had properly discredited Randolph's study, Carroll closed by saying, "Thank you, Doctor. Your testimony has been most enlightening."

Winkler rose to the lectern. "Doctor, is it your expert opinion that the vast majority of middle-class blacks would be too prejudiced against the Defendant in this case to serve impartially on this jury?"

"That is my considered opinion."

"Thank you."

Winkler turned back to the table expecting that Randolph's testimony was concluded. But Carroll rose to ask, "Doctor, is there a phenomenon your profession calls projection?"

"Yes . . ."

"Precisely what is this phenomenon?"

"It occurs where the patient, unable to face his own shortcomings, projects them onto or ascribes them to another person," Randolph explained.

"Is it only patients who engage in projection?"

"Everyone does, in one form or another, at one time or another," Randolph said.

"Even psychiatrists?" Carroll asked, smiling.

"Even psychiatrists," Randolph answered, unamused.

"So that a psychiatrist who had suffered from a deprived, poverty-stricken childhood, who had been cruelly hurt by middle-class Negroes might harbor strong animosities, and might 'project' those animosities onto middle-class blacks and thus answer questions not with his expert opinion but in light of his own personal hurts and prejudices?"

"Object!" Winkler called out.

"Doctor, is it possible that, feeling as you do, your opin-

185

ions might tend to favor the Defendant because of a similarity in your backgrounds?"

"Object!" This time, Winkler rose from his seat to emphasize his objection.

Since there were no jurors present, Carroll let Winkler's objection go unchallenged.

Randolph was excused.

Judge Beecher summoned all counsel to the bench. "Gentlemen, I will rule in the morning, unless either of you wishes to submit further memoranda on the subject." None of the attorneys protested.

"Then we will adjourn for the day," Beecher said. The attorneys had already turned away when he began to speak again, "Oh, by the way, gentlemen . . ." They returned to the bench. Beecher looked down directly at Winkler.

"Mr. Winkler, it is my earnest hope and desire to conduct a fair trial here, to give the Defendant every advantage the law allows. But I detect that your purpose is to turn this into a show trial to put the crime the Defendant is charged with in a position secondary to the political and social ideology of his counsel. If that is your plan, I warn you again that this Court will not lend itself to such tactics, and I reiterate my previous injunction. You will make no public comment on this case in any medium. Or I shall deem your conduct a deliberate attempt to taint every potential juror in this District!"

"And if I am so rash and injudicious as to make any further public statement?" Winkler asked.

"Then I will have to use those remedies already pointed out to you," Beecher declared.

"Contempt?"

"Contempt!" Beecher said, though he disliked using the word.

"I would like the record to show that His Honor threatened Counsel with contempt proceedings," Winkler said.

The next morning at ten o'clock, before any jurors were admitted to the courtroom, Judge Beecher ruled on Winkler's motion. Middle-class black persons who met all the other qualifications would not be barred from jury service solely by virtue of income, residence, or other class characteristics.

Winkler took formal exception to the ruling, though he had no need to. To Scott he observed, quietly and with a note of concern in his voice, "Our Mr. Carroll may not be as easy as I thought. But at least we stalled for time, got some space in the press, and established a record for appeal if it should come to that."

Marlene observed to Scott that the judge's latest warning to Winkler had been effective. Linc had not granted a single TV interview during the remaining days of jury selection.

"We'll see," Scott answered simply.

"Meaning?"

"Meaning that until a jury has been chosen and sworn, Linc is not going to risk contempt. But after that, watch him! It's reversible error for a judge to hold or threaten a lawyer with contempt in the presence of the jury."

Scott and Marlene exchanged such thoughts and observations in those moments when they were alone at the Rosenstone house and whenever he drove her home. Each time Scott attempted to embrace her, Marlene put him off.

"I told you. Never again!"

So he would pull the car up to her doorway, watch her run across the walk, open the outer door and disappear. He would wait for an additional few minutes to be certain that she was safely inside, and then he would put the Mustang into gear and drive home. Alone.

XV

It was Friday. Three weeks, fourteen courtroom sessions and twenty-eight bomb searches had gone by.

Outside the courthouse, young demonstrators had changed their tactics as well as their placards. Instead of SAVE MIDGE GROVE! they demanded FREE MIDGE GROVE! and instead of violence their demonstrations now depended on ingenuity. Rock groups gave street concerts, and a mock slave auction was held in which young black men dressed only in loincloths and young, topless black girls were auctioned off by a white man attired in the traditional white suit and holding a blacksnake whip. These won wide coverage on nationwide TV news on all three networks, amid protests about showing the auction's bare-breasted black girls.

Inside the courtroom, the selection of jurors droned on. Three hundred and forty-seven potential jurors had been examined, while only nine had been seated on the jury. Despite the list of Winkler's questions, which Judge Beecher had put to the prospective jurors, the defense had had to use its twenty peremptory challenges. Carroll had found most jurors acceptable, using only six of his ten.

Seated at the defense table were Linc, Scott, Marlene, Midgely Grove and today, with special permission of the court, Al Dixon, who had been one of the eleven Black Pan-

188

thers who had been tried for killing one of their own dissident brothers. Three of the defendants had been found guilty, but Dixon and seven others had gone free to become celebrities. Dixon was to sit in on the Grove case for a few days, as had Bobby Strong and several other well-known black militants, to show solidarity with Grove as well as to instruct him in revolutionary courtroom tactics.

Their presence created an air of tension in the courtroom and provided an obvious headline for those reporters who had run dry writing about the tedious and seemingly endless *voir dire*. These news stories and the many photographs of Winkler entering and leaving the courtroom with the black militants served an important purpose for Winkler. They guaranteed him the continuous attention in the press and on TV which he needed in order to build up an elaborate history of wide press coverage, proving that the entire atmosphere surrounding the case had been poisoned by overwhelming publicity. This documentation would be invaluable if an appeal became necessary. And considering Judge Beecher's order that Winkler avoid all comment to the press, this unorthodox means of staying in the news was not only ingenious but startlingly effective. So Winkler was willing to forego all direct statements to the press, at least until the jury was impaneled.

At the moment, a small, wiry black woman with graying hair had just been seated in the jury box. She admitted that she was aware of the case only through television. She maintained that she had no previous opinion as to the guilt or innocence of the Defendant. She was still open-minded. But despite her seemingly unbiased answers, Winkler was disturbed by her age, her neatness, and her well-dressed appearance.

"Don't like her," he whispered to Scott. "Watch." Slowly Winkler advanced toward the jury box, looking down at the jury board he carried to find the woman's name.

"Mrs. Ida Willamot?" he said finally. "Are you employed, Mrs. Willamot?"

"Yes, sir."

"At what kind of work, may I ask?"

"Domestic service. I have worked for the same family for nineteen years!" the woman declared proudly.

"A white family?"

"Yes, sir." In her voice, Winkler detected a defensiveness, as if his question had made some reflection on her work.

"Tell me, Mrs. Willamot, do you clean, cook, and serve meals in the household of your employers?"

"Yes, sir. I am a very good cook, they say."

"I don't doubt it, my dear. When you are serving the family, do they sit quietly awaiting your food or do they talk?"

"They're pretty good talkers, all of them," Mrs. Willamot said.

"What do they talk about?" Winkler asked, as casually as he could.

"Oh, things."

"Do they talk about this case?" Winkler asked more sharply.

Mrs. Willamot hesitated, then answered, "Yes . . . they do . . . sometimes . . ."

"And what do they say about . . ."

Before Winkler could finish his question, Carroll was out of his chair. "Your Honor!"

"You will not answer that question," Beecher ruled. Then he turned to Winkler and said, "I will ask the next few questions, Counselor." Little Mrs. Willamot stared up at Beecher, obviously awed and tense almost to the point of tears for having been the cause of such an outburst.

"Mrs. Willamot, there is nothing to be afraid of. Just answer my questions. Without telling us *what* they say, tell us if the family ever express any opinions about the innocence or guilt of this Defendant."

"They expresses."

"Have you formed any conclusion about guilt or innocence in this case?"

"No, sir."

"Despite what you have heard them say?"

"Yes, sir."

Beecher turned back to Winkler. "Does that satisfy you, Counselor?"

"Not fully, Your Honor," Winkler answered.

"You may proceed, then, but carefully," Beecher warned.

Winkler turned to the little black woman. "Ida . . . that is your name, isn't it? The name your family calls you by?"

"Yes, sir." She sounded tense and she sat bolt upright in her seat, her hands clasped tightly together in her lap.

"Ida, that is a very lovely coat. Did you make it yourself?" Winkler reached into the jury box, saying, "Forgive me." He felt the collar of her navy blue coat. "Very fine. *Did* you make it yourself?"

"No, sir . . . I . . ."

"Yes?" he coaxed.

"I remade it."

"Remade?" Winkler asked, pretending to be puzzled.

"Mrs. Gorham give it to me. She gives me lots of her old clothes," the little black woman confessed.

"They're so fond of you that Mrs. Gorham gives you her clothes when she's through with them?"

"Yes, sir. We're close. Fact, Mr. Gorham is always joking that if they ever get a divorce he will insist on custody of me." She smiled, proud that they regarded her so highly.

Winkler's next question wiped out the smile that had so tenuously settled on her face. "Tell me, Ida, did Mr. Gorham ever express any opinion about Mr. Grove's guilt or innocence?"

"Yes or no, that's all!" Judge Beecher interjected.

"He . . . yes, sir, he did . . ."

"And being so close to him, so close to the family, Ida, can you tell me now that you have not been influenced by his opinion?"

Without waiting for her response, Winkler turned toward the bench. "I strike this witness for cause!"

Beecher hesitated a moment. "The witness is excused," he finally announced.

Back at the Defense table, Winkler whispered to Scott, "Thank God, we're rid of her! She was too goddamned anxious to serve, to go back and be a hero with her 'family' by voting for conviction!"

The rest of the day Winkler examined each prospective juror, settling only for a young black man who wore a gold pendant and a modified afro. So by the end of the third week, there were now only ten jurors seated in the box, two white, eight black, all under the age of forty.

Before recessing court for the weekend, Judge Beecher called counsel to the bench. "Gentlemen, I would like your agreement now, that some time before the end of court on Monday we will have finished selecting a jury so that we can move along to the presentation of the Government's case."

"It's not the Government's intent to make use of its remaining peremptory challenges, Your Honor," Carroll volunteered.

Beecher turned toward Winkler who announced, much to Scott's surprise, "If Your Honor wishes to continue for another hour or two, I believe we could seat and swear in a jury before we recess for the day."

"If you think so, Mr. Winkler." Beecher then asked Carroll, "Is it agreeable to the Government, in the interest of expediting matters?"

Suspicious though he was, Carroll agreed. They all went back to their places and two new jurors were seated in the box. The judge asked the agreed-upon list of questions. The answers seemed to satisfy Carroll, and Winkler, who judged them mostly on their appearance, assented to both of them.

One was white, the other black. Both were under the age of thirty-five, and neither worked for the Federal Government.

If Scott had been puzzled by Winkler's sudden unannounced change in tactics, he was even more surprised when Winkler addressed the bench once again.

"Your Honor, since we've done so well in the last half hour, may I suggest that we try to seat the four alternates before the day is out?"

Four alternate candidates were seated in the jury box. They answered satisfactorily to the list of questions. Two pleaded inability to serve on such a lengthy case and were excused by Judge Beecher. The other two were judged acceptable by both Carroll and Winkler. A third was found after examining four more prospects, and the fourth and final alternate was a plain-looking white girl, aged twenty-three, unmarried, whom both sides accepted.

When all sixteen jurors and alternates were approved by counsel, Beecher repeated what he had said each day since the selection of the first juror, "Remember that you are not to read anything in the newspapers having to do with this case. You are not to listen to anything concerning it on radio or television. Being sequestered you will have no opportunity to talk to outsiders, but remember: You are not to discuss the case even among yourselves."

Beecher paused to give the matter the precise degree of gravity it warranted, and then he ordered, "You will all rise!"

Stiffly and somberly the sixteen men and women rose, eleven blacks, five whites. The assistant to the clerk passed up and down the double row of jurors distributing a Bible to each.

"Hold the Bible in your left hand, please. And raise your right," Judge Beecher intoned.

The clerk addressed them now: "Does each of you swear to well and truly decide the case now pending before this Court, so help you God?"

Some answered with an audible yes, some nodded, all

193

agreed. The oath had been taken by the sixteen men and women who would decide the fate of Midgely Grove.

Linc Winkler was waiting for Scott on the front steps of the Rosenstone mansion. The limousine was ready and waiting there, too, although Scott could not imagine why. It had been his understanding that they were going to plan their strategy for Monday, the first day of the Prosecution's case.

As Scott approached, Linc called out, "We don't want to be late, Scott. Come on, we can talk on the way." He opened the back door of the Rosenstone Rolls and ushered Scott in.

"Late for what?" Scott asked.

"You'll see," Linc disposed of the question quickly, launching into a discussion of tactics instead. "We won't make an opening statement. Let Carroll open and present his entire case. We'll make the usual motions, get turned down, and only after he's finished will we give him even a whiff of what our defense is going to be."

"Good!" Scott said. "I'm for that. What about Grove's confession? Do you think it was a mistake to let it go unattacked until now?"

"We can make much more of it in the middle of the trial. It's the one big thing I'd like to overcome in the public's mind. So that's where I want to sow a big fat reasonable doubt."

"And the police testimony?" Scott asked.

"We'll simply attack it along the usual lines, looking for signs of sloppy police work and then use that as a lever to break them down."

As Dulles International Airport came into sight, Scott asked, "Are we meeting someone at Dulles?"

"Two groups, one from New York and another from Chicago."

"Groups?" Scott asked, puzzled.

"Black solidarity groups. They've come to observe the trial."

"More Panthers?"

"A few. Also a group from the black bar association, including a Congressman from Illinois. And Willis Cane will be in the New York delegation."

He didn't have to explain further. Cane was a well-known black author who periodically predicted the downfall of the United States due to its repressive character. Cane resorted continually to a cliché he had originated: "There's no black problem. Only a white problem," as if that would solve everything.

"What are they going to do? Picket the courthouse?" Scott asked.

"I wouldn't know," Winkler answered evasively. "But if they fill the streets it'll help."

"Not Midge," Scott said flatly, "and not us."

Winkler's face expanded into his most indulgent, fatherly smile. "Scotty, Scotty, when are you going to listen to me? All the law isn't in the law books. If you want to be a civil rights lawyer, you've got to break new ground—legally, tactically. In every way. Conservative radicals who think they can change the past by revering the past get nowhere. You have to keep the Establishment off balance! Keep them shook up!"

They had arrived at the outskirts of the airport complex. Ahead, Scott could see that a CBS remote truck was already waiting. "Christ, Linc! You're not going to make a TV appearance! Not after what Beecher said?"

Winkler tried to seem surprised. "I wonder who could have tipped them off?" he asked.

They were pulling up at the American Airlines terminal. Since the Rosenstone limousine had now become a familiar target for the press, it was surrounded by newsmen as soon as it came to a stop. Before Winkler could reach for the handle, the door was pulled open. Reporters, microphones and handheld cameras rushed toward them like a tidal wave.

"Is it true that Willis Cane is coming?"

"Are all the defendants in the Chicago Panther trial due here? We got a tip they were."

"What about Judge Beecher? How do you think he'll react? Will he let them into the courtroom?"

"Boys, boys," Winkler protested amiably, "give me a chance."

He eased out of the limousine and waited until Scott was beside him. Then he raised his hands, asking for quiet. He spoke softly, slowly, as a man who had great regret.

"Gentlemen, and ladies, we are at a delicate stage in the course of this trial. I cannot answer your questions—not without prejudicing my client's case. I am under severe injunction by the Court. And although most fair-minded people would consider such restrictions unconstitutional and tyrannical, I am not in a position to question those practices at this time.

"Were I to speak for myself alone"—and here Winkler turned to acknowledge the sudden arrival of the NBC cameraman—"were I to speak for myself alone, were I to risk only my own freedom, I would gladly go to jail for the right to speak out. But another man's freedom is at stake, so I'm sorry, but I can make no statement today."

Since the TV cameras already had all the footage they could use, and the arrival of the plane from New York was just being announced, they gave way to allow the two lawyers to make their way into the terminal building and to the proper gate.

But, in fact, the plane had arrived a few minutes early, and all the passengers had debarked, except the contingent from New York which was still aboard, awaiting the arrival of Linc Winkler and the press before they would show themselves.

The newsmen and the cameras preceded Winkler out to the hatchway. They were met by several extremely attractive girls, black and white, all with Afros or wearing turbans

196

draped from cotton scarves, long, loose dresses of African print design and silver or gold chain necklaces, large primitive pendants of metal and rough stone. Several young men in Panther uniforms hovered in the background, raising clenched fists and calling out, "Linc! Linc! Right on, brother!"

After he had embraced them all individually, Winkler asked, "Where's Will?"

Then, as if on signal, Willis Cane appeared. He came from inside the plane, a tan British cashmere coat thrown over his shoulders. The only article he wore in common with his Panther colleagues was dark glasses. No Afro crowned his face, and he gave no clenched fist. He chanted no slogans, but instead, with some reserve, he lent himself to Winkler's embrace, looking past Winkler to Scott and then to the media men crowding around them. His eyes, reptilian and sharp even behind his dark glasses, searched out the TV cameras. Once he found them, he removed his glasses and seemed to surrender to the insistence of the press with the bored, reserved air of a female movie star.

Cane answered all questions crisply and with disdain. No, white men in a white court could not fairly convict a black man of anything. No, a black jury chosen by a white judge and a white prosecutor could not be considered black at all. Yes, murder was an American specialty, and assassination was an American sport—proof of the final decadence of white America.

Cane was asked if he had any qualms about having Midge Grove defended by two white lawyers. He turned to Winkler, embraced him and said, "Linc Winkler is the blackest white man I've ever known. And the blackest Jew!"

The other blacks chimed in, "Right on! Right on, Brother Linc!" Winkler, with his right arm around Cane, raised his left fist high over his head in a salute. And the entire New York contingent responded in kind. The photographers had

197

Cane and Winkler stage that pose several times. It appeared in the afternoon editions of the Washington papers and on the front page of all three major New York papers.

Inside the Rosenstone limousine, Cane sat between Winkler and Scott in the back seat. Through his dark glasses, he stared intently at Scott all the way back from the airport.

When court resumed on Monday morning, Winkler, Scott, and Marlene submitted themselves to the usual personal search, but when they approached the counsel table, they found the Judge's secretary waiting for them. They were to be escorted to Judge Beecher's chambers.

The Judge was standing with his back to the door, staring out the window, hands clasped tightly behind him. At the sound of the door closing, he asked, "Winkler?"

"Yes . . ." Linc answered.

"Join me?" Beecher invited grimly.

Winkler started forward to stand side by side with the judge.

Below them, on the street in front of the courthouse, a crowd had gathered to watch the delegations from New York and Chicago conduct their courthouse vigil. Reinforced by groups of students from local colleges and universities, they all carried placards and long canvas signs which they brandished at the photographers. Most signs demanded FREE MIDGE GROVE, but others reflected on Beecher, his fairness, his whiteness, his genealogy.

"Quite a spectacle," Beecher observed gruffly. "Winkler, did you have anything to do with this?"

"I had no knowledge of it at all."

"What about *that?*" Beecher asked, jerking his head back toward his desk. Winkler spied the Sunday *New York Times* and the *Washington Post* lying spread out on the desk, both featuring almost identical pictures of Winkler and Willis Cane, with Winkler's hand upthrust in a revolutionary fist. "No knowledge, eh?"

"We're friends."

"*Old* friends, I assume," Beecher said gruffly.

" 'Old' friends," Winkler agreed. "When I heard he was coming to town, naturally I went to greet him at the airport. But this," indicating the demonstration below them, "I had no idea."

"Winkler, let me warn you that the time will come when these 'spontaneous' but highly organized and well-planned demonstrations may be deemed contempt of this Court. But when that time does come, you will not trap me into holding you in contempt in the presence of the jury in order to hand you a reversible error. If that's your game, I can play it, too!"

·◦❧ XVI ❧◦·

U.S. Attorney Carroll was in the midst of his opening statement to the jury. Linc Winkler sat quietly between Scott Ingram and Midge Grove, a yellow pad on his lap and a pencil in hand. Instead of making notes, he was idly doodling unflattering sketches of the lean, craggy face of Judge Beecher. Scott, however, was jotting down notes on Carroll's statement, seeking possible holes in the presentation of the Government's basic case.

"And not only will the Prosecution prove the charges made by the grand jury in the first count of premeditated murder on or about October 14, 1973, but will introduce into evidence a confession to that effect given freely by this defendant, Midgely Grove, after all legal warnings and safeguards were stringently exercised on his behalf."

Scott printed the word "confession" on his pad and began to surround it with continuous circles, while Carroll went through all the other counts of the indictment and indicated who the Prosecution's witnesses would be and what they would prove.

"Finally," Carroll concluded, "much has been said, and much more will be said in this courtroom about the emotional aspects of this case. As soon as the word 'assassin' is spoken, it conjures up all sorts of emotions. For that reason, as United States Attorney I feel it is my duty to present this

200

case without appealing to emotion, to present it only in light of the facts involved and through the testimony of reliable witnesses. For we are dealing here not with the identity of the victim, not with his station, but with the crime of murder in the first degree, which we shall prove beyond not only a reasonable doubt, but beyond all doubt."

Fully realizing the futility of any motion after Carroll's comprehensive opening statement, Winkler rose nevertheless and requested that the jury be excused. Once they were out of hearing, Winkler proceeded, "Your Honor, we move to have this indictment dismissed on all counts due to failure to spell out a *prima facie* case."

Without drawing breath, Beecher ruled, "Motion denied."

"Exception," Winkler called out to underscore his point with the press. Then he continued, "Since in its opening statement the Government has failed to spell out premeditation, we move to have the charge reduced to murder in the second degree."

"Denied!" Beecher ruled promptly. "Any further motions?" When Winkler did not respond, Beecher asked, "Will the Defense make its opening statement now?"

"We have decided to wait until the State has presented its case in full," Winkler said, slipping back into his chair and taking up his pad to scribble some hasty but inconsequential notes on it, only to add to the Judge's curiosity and annoyance.

The jury was called in and seated.

"Mr. Carroll?" the judge said, inviting the Prosecutor to call his first witness.

But before Carroll could reply, there was a stir at the door. Beecher looked up, now quite openly irritated. "Will the attendants see to it that spectators enter and leave without disruption. This is a Federal courtroom, not a vaudeville theater or a television studio, as some people have come to believe!"

Winkler made another note on his yellow pad, to Beecher's obvious annoyance. Then reading the sudden look of distaste

201

that transformed Beecher's face, Winkler turned toward the door. Willis Cane had entered, impatiently straightening his elegant light-tan gabardine suit and matching topcoat, while glaring with disdain and resentment at the court attendant who had had the effrontery to search him. Cane started down the aisle, seeking an empty seat. Rising, Winkler invited him past the bulletproof barrier and into the well to sit at the defense table.

"Additional associate counsel, Mr. Winkler?" Judge Beecher leaned forward and asked acidly.

"Just a close friend. I'm sure the Court will not mind if he sits with us to give the Defendant moral support."

" 'Moral' support?" Beecher echoed without expanding upon his personal reaction to Cane's notorious homosexuality. And though it was irregular, Judge Beecher did grant Cane the right to sit at counsel table.

U.S. Attorney Carroll had already questioned the FBI ballistics expert and the fingerprint expert who identified the lethal weapon and attested to Midge Grove's prints on it. Now he was guiding Medical Examiner Hecker through the final phases of his testimony.

"Tell the jury, Doctor, precisely what you determined to be the cause of Justice Miller's death."

Hecker turned to the easel which displayed an artist's sketch of a man's face, not intending to be an exact likeness of the late Justice Miller. Just under the eye was an entry wound with an arrow indicating its direction.

"This shot was fatal. It entered the deceased's head at this point just below the eye and traveled in this direction, slightly upward . . . and then . . ." Hecker removed the first illustration and uncovered a second, showing how the bullet, on exiting, had ripped away a large part of the dead man's skull.

"Doctor, in your opinion do these artist's renderings correctly and precisely reflect your finding on autopsy?"

202

"They do. But in addition I would like to present actual front and back photographs of the head of the deceased as made by the official photographer of the District Homicide Squad."

"Object!" Winkler said, but did not rise.

"On what ground, Mr. Winkler?"

Linc unwound his legs, taking much time in order to give his statement great weight. "As the U.S. Attorney himself said in his opening statement, we are dealing here with a case fraught with enormous emotion. Photographs as gruesome as those intended to be introduced here are shocking enough to create in the mind of any juror a reaction which calls not for justice but for revenge, so that the question of guilt or innocence becomes secondary to the need for retribution."

Beecher summoned both counsel to the bench. In a whisper, out of hearing of the jury, he asked Carroll, "How essential are those photos to your case?"

Carroll thought a moment, debating how much emotional advantage he might be surrendering. Knowing what the case would mean to his political future, Carroll had promised himself not only Grove's conviction but an irreducible life sentence as well. But realizing that Winkler was fishing for a reversible ruling, Carroll finally decided moderation was the wisest course.

"We can make our case without them," he conceded.

"Good!" Beecher said, disposing of the question.

Carroll returned to the lectern and faced the medical examiner again. "Doctor, in addition to the extensive autopsy, did you make any other tests in relation to the victim?"

"Yes, sir," Hecker said, turning back to the artist's sketch of the rear of Miller's shattered head. "When the missile passed through the head of the deceased, it emerged in this manner, taking with it considerable fragments of skull bone and brain tissue. Due to the force and direction of the bullet, those fragments were imbedded in the drapery behind the chair."

"And precisely what did you do?"

"Using sterile forceps I collected those fragments of bone and tissue and deposited them in sterile plastic containers so that I could remove them to the laboratory for examination there."

"And why was it necessary to use such sterile instruments and containers?" Carroll pursued.

"So that putrefaction would not set in, and the specimens would be in perfect condition to yield the best results."

"And precisely what were those results, sir?"

"Beyond any doubt the bone and the tissue were from the skull and the brain of Justice Miller and had resulted from the fatal shot."

Certain he had advanced his case one more step toward being airtight and invincible, Carroll was content to turn the witness over to Winkler.

"Doctor," Winkler began as he made his way to the lectern, "would you say this case was handled in all respects like any other homicide in this district?"

"We try to handle all cases with the highest degree of professionalism and accuracy."

"Have you ever before been called in to examine the body of a victim in the Supreme Court of the United States?"

"Of course not. There has never been a homicide in the Supreme Court before."

"And certainly not a homicide involving a Justice of that high court, right?"

"Yes. Right," Hecker agreed.

"So that we are dealing here with a case of unprecedented importance in American history. Surely the most important case during your term as medical examiner."

"You might say that."

"Therefore when Mr. Carroll just referred to your 'extensive' autopsy, he meant that this autopsy was not only extensive, but the *most* concentrated, the *most* extensive you've ever seen or been part of. Is that correct?"

"Yes," the puzzled doctor replied.

"In fact, not only the autopsy but this entire case has been handled in this way. To make sure, to make absolutely sure, to accomplish one thing: *Get this Defendant!*"

"We were doing our job, that's all," Hecker answered.

"Did you ever hear others you worked with in this case using such phrases as 'Get Grove,' or 'Get that black bastard?' "

"No, sir, I did not."

"Well, how *did* they talk about him? 'He's a nice, shy, quiet kid, let's help him get off.' Did you hear them say that?"

"No, sir."

"I didn't think so. Now, Doctor, isn't it a fact that due to the importance of the victim in this case, due to the national and international publicity given to this case, every step in your autopsy was checked and rechecked to make sure that there were absolutely no loopholes of any kind?"

"We wanted to be as scientifically thorough as it was possible to be."

"In order to get a conviction and make it stick!" Winkler accused.

"Yes, of course."

"Then why didn't you say so at the outset, Doctor, instead of making me dig and probe and force it out of you?"

Winkler turned from the witness in disdain and started back to his seat. When he slid into it, Scott whispered to him: "Well, you certainly succeeded in making thoroughness look like a criminal conspiracy!" Which was exactly what Winkler hoped.

The two Court policemen who had pursued and cornered Grove after the murder of Justice Miller had both testified to the events of that afternoon, including how Grove had fired at them and missed, then hurled the weapon down the well of the elegant marble staircase. They told how they had apprehended him and brought him to the office of the Chief of

Court Police. And they testified dutifully that they had been warned by their chief to make no statements in Grove's presence, in order not to prejudice his rights.

Then Chief of Court Police Edwards was called to the stand to corroborate what the two officers had said, and also to establish the fact that the Metropolitan Police had been called, and that the prisoner was turned over to them in strict accordance with the District laws and procedures.

When Carroll had finished with Edwards, Winkler rose to cross-examine.

"Tell me, sir, during the time when the arresting officers were in your office and in the presence of the Defendant did you make any statement such as, 'We're going to handle this nigger right'?"

"I did not!" Edwards protested indignantly. "There are four black men on my staff, and I've got too much respect for them to use that kind of language."

"Did you say anything at all about the Defendant?"

"Just that we wanted to handle this all very legal. It was important, and we didn't want any mistakes or accidents."

"Accidents? Such as?" Winkler pressed.

"Well, the way in which other assassinations had been botched up," the Chief explained. "I didn't want to prejudice his rights, so I didn't want any statements made in front of him."

"Not even statements that might help him?"

"I didn't want *any* statements, period," the Chief said.

"Are you always that meticulous, Mr. Edwards?" Winkler asked a bit sarcastically.

"We don't have such cases as a general rule, but we're fully aware of what's happened in other places. And, as I told my men, the one thing we didn't want was another Dallas. 'This isn't Dallas. We don't want any Lee Harvey Oswalds here,' I said."

"You thought the Oswald case was handled badly, did you?" Winkler asked.

"It was sloppy police work, sloppy security. There was no excuse for it."

"And so you were determined, or *over*determined, that the same thing wouldn't happen in your command?" Winkler asked.

"Just determined, Counselor. And it didn't happen, did it?" Edwards asked smugly.

"No, it did not," Winkler had to agree. Then, to recoup his position, Winkler asked, "Sir, if the police were deliberately setting out to frame a man wouldn't they tend to be careful or overdetermined about how they handled him?"

"Object!" Carroll interrupted.

"Sustained!" Beecher ruled. "Counselor, you know better than to ask such questions!"

Winkler smiled at the glaring judge and said, "Perhaps *I* was being overdetermined in my client's behalf."

Most jurors and spectators laughed, successfully diminishing the impact of Edwards' damaging testimony.

"Sir, after placing the wax impressions of the Defendant's hands in separate plastic bags, what did you do then?" Carroll was interrogating blond Henry Callison, the FBI technician.

"I took them back to the FBI laboratory where we ran a neutron activation analysis on them."

"For the benefit of the jury, Mr. Callison, will you explain what a neutron activation analysis is, and why it is deemed the very best method of detection in such a circumstance?"

"Yes, sir." Angling toward the jury somewhat, Callison continued, "An important fact in a crime such as the one we're concerned with here is whether or not the suspect fired the weapon in question.

"We used to use a diphenylamine test. When that chemical was applied to the wax impression, it would usually react to the presence of gunpowder elements lifted from the hand of the suspect if he had fired the weapon. But diphenylamine or phenylbenzidine, the reagents used at that time, weren't conclusive since they were found to react positively to other oxidizing agents as well as gunpowder."

"But now?" Carroll coaxed.

"Now, with the neutron activation analysis, the elements antimony and barium, which are found in most primer mixtures for ammunition, are discovered almost invariably to contaminate the hand of a shooter after firing a weapon."

"Would you explain how a weapon firing straight ahead can contaminate the hand of the shooter which is behind the explosion and the bullet?" Carroll asked.

"Yes, sir. At the instant of the explosion, gases form that back up and deposit antimony and barium from the primer onto the hand of the person firing the weapon. Normally those amounts are so small they were once difficult to detect. But using the neutron activation analysis, now we can positively identify these elements and measure their amounts."

"And such tests were made on both the right and left wax lifts from the hands of this Defendant?"

"They were."

"And what was the result of those tests?"

Callison reached into his bag and pulled out a sheet of paper from which he read, "Examination 10/14/73 of paraffin lifts, right and left hand, Midgely Grove. Left hand negative. Right hand, definite residue on lift, typical and characteristic of residue which generally contaminates a shooter's hand subsequent to the discharge of firearm of type submitted with these lifts."

Carroll took the paraffin lifts and the report, asking, "Mr. Callison, are these the lifts taken from the hands of Midgely Grove on that day?"

"They are."

"And is this a certified copy of the FBI lab report based on those lifts?"

"It is."

"We offer them for identification," Carroll said, handing them to the clerk.

The clerk marked them, offered them to the judge who declined to inspect them. The clerk offered them to Winkler and Scott. Linc examined them very carefully, as did Scott, although Scott had actually examined them thoroughly once before, during the discovery proceedings ordered by Judge Beecher. Instead of agreeing to have them received in evidence, Scott handed them back to the clerk. He rose, "Before we agree to have these accepted and marked in evidence, we would like to question the witness."

Judge Beecher looked to Carroll who said, "We are finished with our direct examination of the witness."

Since Scott had more firsthand contact with the ballistics evidence in the case, it had been agreed that he would examine Callison. He advanced to the lawyer's lectern, adjusted the microphone and placed his yellow pad before him.

"Mr. Callison, a moment ago you mentioned a certain test. I believe you called it a 'diphenylamine test' for detecting certain gunpowder elements."

"Yes, sir," Callison responded respectfully.

"And you said that test had been discarded because it also reacted positively to oxidizing agents other than those in gunpowder."

"We replaced it with the highly reliable test we use now . . ."

"The jury will have to decide on the degree of reliability of that test, I think," Scott said. "But my question is this: In the days before the neutron activation analysis, was the diphenylamine test used frequently?"

"Yes, it was the only test . . ."

"The answer is, yes, it was used frequently. Right?" Scott interrupted.

"Yes."

"And in the same way? Paraffin lifts of both hands were

209

taken meticulously, with clean brushes for each hand, fresh paraffin, sterile bag for each hand, all of it. Then it was subjected to this diphenylamine test. And after that, FBI agents and lab experts would appear in court and testify as to their findings. Is that correct?"

"Yes, yes, it is," Callison said.

"Yet now, after years of that practice, in which countless defendants ·were identified as having fired shots, you tell us that the diphenylamine test was not very good because it reacted positively to elements other than gunpowder . . ."

"Yes, but . . ."

"I haven't asked my question yet, Mr. Callison!" Scott said sharply. "Now if that is true, what assurance do we have that next year or five years from now another FBI expert might not appear in this very same courtroom, sit in that very same seat and tell another jury, 'Oh, that neutron activation analysis, we discovered that really wasn't such an accurate test after all'?"

"Well, the tests are quite different . . ."

"Mr. Callison," Scott interrupted, "are you predicting that no one will ever discover a new test that will replace the neutron activation analysis, a test that may be even more accurate?"

"New tests will always be discovered, and will keep improving. The point is that the accuracy of the neutron activation analysis test is of such high degree that . . ."

"Of such high degree that you can't even say now, in your own report, this man fired this gun! Your report has to say, 'residue on lift *typical* and *characteristic* of residue which *generally* contaminates a shooter's hand subsequent to the discharge of firearm of type submitted with these lifts.' "

"That's a legal way of saying . . ."

"Let's not get into a semantic discussion! Let's try not to confuse the jury!" Scott turned to the clerk to secure the copy of the report. He scanned it, glanced at his own notes, then looked at Callison.

210

"Mr. Callison, isn't it true that the FBI lab report contains an error?"

"No, sir!"

"But the conclusion states, 'characteristic of residue which generally contaminates a shooter's hand.' Precisely what is meant by 'generally contaminates'? What is 'generally'?"

"In the vast majority of cases when a man fires a hand gun there will be traces of such contamination on the firing hand," Callison explained.

"Which means it doesn't *always* happen, right?"

"Right," Callison conceded.

"So you could run this test on a guilty man and not find *any* gunpowder traces, right?"

"That could conceivably happen," Callison agreed.

"And isn't it also possible that an innocent man might be subjected to such a test and you could find traces?" Scott asked.

"No, sir!"

"Impossible?"

"Yes, sir!"

"Suppose you had made a paraffin lift of the hand of the officer who retrieved what the Government alleges is the murder weapon in this case. If the officer had picked up that gun with his bare hand, would your neutron activation test have revealed traces of antimony and barium on the officer's hand?" Scott asked.

"Well, if he handled the weapon or the cartridge case, then yes, his hand might be contaminated with primer residue."

"So that in the one instance of a guilty man you concede your test might *not* pick up traces, while in the case of an innocent man, it well *might* pick up traces. That's one hell of a test on which to determine guilt or innocence in a crime of this serious nature, isn't it? Isn't it, Mr. Callison?"

Callison did not answer.

"Thank you, Mr. Callison," Scott said and started back to the table.

Carroll rose. "Only one question, Mr. Callison. Based on your years of experience in the field of ballistics, identification of weapons, expended bullets and contamination tests, in your opinion do the results of this test support the conclusion that this defendant *did* fire the lethal weapon on October 14, 1973?"

"In my opinion, *yes!*"

"Thank you," Carroll said, bringing the examination to a close. Or so he thought.

But Scott rose and, mimicking Carroll, said, "Only one question, Mr. Callison. Do you have any way of knowing whether before you arrived on the scene that pistol was placed in the hand of the Defendant?"

"I never had reason to inquire . . ."

Scott interrupted, "Do you or do you not know if that pistol was placed in the hand of the Defendant?"

"No, I don't know."

"Thank you, Mr. Callison," Scott concluded, seating himself at Winkler's side.

Linc nudged him under the table and whispered, "I never suspected, Scotty. You're a killer when you're turned on. That was a total wipe-out."

Scott leaned back in his chair. The collar of his oxford shirt had grown damp against his sweaty neck. At his right side, Marlene was staring at him with new admiration.

"Your Honor," Winkler said, rising, "in view of the testimony elicited by my young colleague, I must ask that the Court refuse to accept these exhibits into evidence."

Judge Beecher looked expectantly at Carroll who countered, "Your Honor, Counsel may differ with the conclusions of the expert, but that does not invalidate his findings. These paraffin lifts and this report constitute valid evidence, and we insist they be accepted and marked."

"The clerk will so mark them, Peoples' Exhibits A, B, and C."

"Exception!" Winkler pronounced.

"Noted, though unnecessary," Judge Beecher called back.

The press, after its initial exposure to Scott Ingram's courtroom ability, was quite favorable that evening and next morning.

Even Fred Anthony, who had attended the first day of testimony, had a column in the *New York Times* and on the NANA syndicate, which was headed, "No Generation Gap." It began:

> Those who labor in the cause of hard-won civil rights for oppressed minorities can take heart this morning. For between the grizzled veterans in that war and the generation coming up immediately behind them there is no gap in either dedication or talent. Yesterday, in a courtroom bristling more like a totalitarian court martial than an open trial in a democratic society, a young David in the war against oppression arose to challenge the Goliath of Government and came off handsomely!

213

·◦❦ XVII ❦◦·

Plump and extremely nervous, Mrs. Evalyn Huffman sat in the witness chair. She was dressed in a dark, maroon suit and a small hat, which sat atop her head like a seagull tentatively perched on a dock piling. Her rimless glasses had steamed up again, so she removed them for the fifth time and wiped them off. U.S. Attorney Carroll was questioning her while one of his black assistants set up a tape recorder, threading into it the reel which had been carefully guarded since the day of the assassination of Justice Harvey Miller.

"Now, Mrs. Huffman, will you tell us what happened to you immediately after the shooting?"

"I guess I screamed. Then I began to tremble. Someone led me to First Aid where they tried to calm me down. They took off my shoes and made me lie down on the bed and pretty soon the pounding stopped."

"Pounding?"

"Yes, I have high blood pressure and when I get excited I get this pounding in the back of my head."

"And then what happened?"

"Well, in a while a man, a captain of the Metropolitan Police . . ."

"Do you know his name?" Carroll asked.

"Kaska. Captain Kaska. He said they had caught the perpetrator, and he asked the doctor if I could identify him. The doctor said Yes. I said I'd rather talk to my husband first, but the captain said, 'We have to do this right away, as soon as possible.' "

"Did he say why?" Carroll coaxed.

"We had to do it as soon as possible or else it might not be legal," Mrs. Huffman said.

"And did you agree to go with Chief Kaska at that time?"

"Yes, sir."

"And what happened after that?"

"When we got to the door of the office, Captain Kaska asked me to wait outside. He went in himself and had some conversation."

"Did you hear what was said?" Carroll urged her on.

"No, but I could guess . . ."

"Only what you actually saw and heard, Mrs. Huffman," Carroll was careful to caution, seeking to have the proper effect on the jury.

"I was asked to come into the room. And I did."

"Could you tell us what you saw in there?"

"Yes, sir. There was that man," she pointed to Grove, who sat immobile behind his dark glasses, wearing the black beret, black turtleneck, and leather jacket into which Winkler made him change every morning. "Of course, he was dressed differently . . ."

"Mrs. Huffman, please, just what you saw and what was said on that particular day," Carroll cautioned.

"Yes, sir. I started to say, 'That's him' but the Chief or else Captain Kaska said, 'Wait for the tape recorder because in a serious case like this one we don't want any mistakes.' "

"You're sure he said that?" Carroll asked.

"Yes. Then one of the men brought in a tape recorder. When it was turned on, Captain Kaska asked me, 'Are you Mrs. Evalyn Huffman of Camden, New Jersey?' "

"Thank you, Mrs. Huffman," Carroll interrupted. He signaled to his black assistant. "Mrs. Huffman, I am about to play a tape recording. I want you to listen to it and tell me if

215

it is an exact and true recording of what transpired in that office from that moment on."

Carroll's assistant switched on the machine.

Are you Evalyn Huffman of 138 Converse Street, Camden, New Jersey?

Carroll motioned to his assistant to interrupt the tape. "Mrs. Huffman, do you recognize that voice?"

"Yes, sir. That was Captain Kaska."

Carroll permitted the tape to continue.

" 'Yes.' "

Again Carroll signaled to stop the tape.

"And that voice, Mrs. Huffman?"

"That's my voice, sir."

"Fine. Now let's continue," Carroll said, nodding to his assistant. The tape began again.

I want you to look at this suspect unnamed. I ask if you ever saw him before.

Yes. I sat next to him in the courtroom when he fired the shots and killed that judge.

You are sure this is the man who sat beside you whom you saw stand up, draw a pistol, and fire those shots?

I'm sure. If you want me to be positive, let me see the side of his face. After all, it was the side of his face I saw mostly.

Stand erect . . . turn your head.

That's the man. No question. The Afro hair . . . but not so bushy. The profile . . . the same color gray suit. I'd know him anywhere.

Thank you, Mrs. Huffman.

"Now, Mrs. Huffman, is that a full and complete tape recording of what transpired that day, unedited, uncut?"

"Yes, sir," the nervous, plump little woman said. Her hat had begun to tremble atop her head, evidence that the mounting tension was affecting her.

"Only a few moments more, Mrs. Huffman. The man referred to on that tape, the man about whom you said, 'That's the man, no question' and 'I sat next to him in the courtroom when he fired the shots,' do you see that man in the court-room today?"

"Yes, sir," she answered firmly.

"Can you point him out, I mean actually go to him and put your hand on his shoulder?"

Timidly, Mrs. Huffman nodded. She rose from the witness chair, stepped down to the defense table, and hesitated before placing her hand momentarily on Midgely Grove's shoulder making only the barest contact with his leather jacket. Hastily, and visibly shaken, she returned to her seat.

"Mrs. Huffman, only one more question. Testifying under oath now, in this courtroom where a man is on trial for the crime of murder, can you say that this is the same man who sat next to you in the Supreme Court, drew the pistol, stood up and fired the shots that killed Justice Harvey Miller?"

"Yes, sir. There is no doubt in my mind!"

"Thank you."

Carroll turned toward the bench. "Your Honor, in view of the fact that the witness suffers from high blood pressure as has been testified to, I ask a brief recess before cross-examination is allowed to begin."

"Counselor?" Judge Beecher turned to Winkler.

Winkler unwound himself slowly and rose, his placid demeanor belying the challenge he was about to hurl.

"If it please the Court, we would like to suggest that Mrs. Huffman be free to leave right now. There will be no cross-examination, since we are asking that the Court throw out this entire faulty and defective identification. And on behalf of my colleague and myself, I wish to say that we are outraged and appalled at the obvious breaches of the civil rights of the victimized Defendant in this case."

Judge Beecher glared at Winkler, glanced briefly at Carroll, then said sternly, "Counsel will please come to the bench!"

As he spoke, Beecher's gruff whisper made no secret of his anger. "Mr. Winkler, you and your associate had considerable advance warning of this identification, and of the tape recording . . ."

"Mr. Ingram heard this tape three times in my own offices!" Carroll interjected.

"And yet," the judge continued, "you gave no indication that you objected to it, or to the identification—a right you could have exercised long before this trial commenced, at a time when this entire matter could have been argued out in private, pursuant to proper motion."

Undismayed, Winkler's fingers combed through his hair as he said, "I hope Your Honor is not suggesting that by refusing to avail ourselves of the right to challenge the identification earlier we have lost the right to challenge it now."

"I am commenting on the manner in which this defense seems to be handled. If indeed you have a sound basis from which to challenge this identification, your client's interests might have been much better served had the jury never heard it."

"I will determine what is in the best interest of my client, if you don't mind!" Winkler shot back harshly. Scott tensed.

"I will caution you again, Mr. Winkler. Your function here is, or should be, the protection of your client's rights, not the advancement of yourself or any cause through exploitation of the press."

"It is in the protection of my client's rights that I ask now that this identification be stricken, and the jury be enjoined to disregard it in its entirety!"

"On what ground?" Beecher asked impatiently.

"On the ground that an identification in which only the accused is presented to a witness who is not also the victim is faulty and defective. On the ground that more than thirty minutes had elapsed between the alleged crime and the time of the identification, taking this out of the category of an immediate face-to-face identification. And on the additional ground that it took place without the presence of an attorney to protect the Defendant's rights."

218

Judge Beecher considered Winkler's notion for a moment. "Counsel may submit a memorandum on the points raised," he said. "In the meantime, the trial will continue and the identification will be allowed to stand, subject to a further ruling."

"I wish the record to show our objection and our exception to the ruling!" Winkler said.

"It will so state. Mr. Carroll, is the witness ready to be cross-examined?"

"I believe so, Your Honor."

"Good!"

As Winkler and Scott started back toward the defense table, Fred Anthony of *The New York Times* advanced to the bulletproof plastic shield, his eyes urgently trying to meet Winkler's. When Linc approached, there was a brief but intensive exchange. Then Winkler beckoned Scott to join them. At that point, Judge Beecher called out, "Gentlemen, can you interrupt pandering to the press long enough to resume this trial?

Winkler turned. "Your Honor, a matter of the greatest urgency has arisen. May we confer at the bench?"

Suspecting yet another of Winkler's stratagems, the judge looked to the prosecution table. "Mr. Carroll?"

"Anything that will help facilitate this trial, Your Honor."

They converged on the bench, Carroll, Winkler, Scott and Fred Anthony. Bristling, Judge Beecher demanded, "Who appointed you a member of the Defense in this case, Mr. Anthony?"

"Mr. Anthony's presence is highly essential to this conference, Your Honor," Winkler interposed.

"Mr. Winkler, if this is another of your attention-getting antics . . ."

"Your Honor, I don't think this can be categorized as an antic," Winkler said gravely. "And I wish the record to state that I resent bitterly the use of such a word in this extremely serious and dangerous situation."

Ignoring Winkler's protest, his curiosity now beginning to exceed his annoyance, Beecher asked, "Mr. Anthony, will you explain your interruption of this proceeding?"

"Yes, Your Honor. A messenger has just arrived from my office with an urgent news bulletin. There has been a prison riot in Gainesville, Georgia. Three guards have already been killed this morning. Twenty-eight hostages have been taken and their lives are in extreme danger."

"And exactly what does that have to do with this trial?" Beecher demanded, his voice becoming loud enough to be heard in most of the courtroom.

"The rebellious prisoners demand that a committee they have named be allowed to meet with them and hear their grievances or all hostages will be dead before nightfall! Two of the people they request are myself and Mr. Winkler."

"Indeed?" the judge exploded. "Are you suggesting, Mr. Anthony and Mr. Winkler, that we delay this trial so that you may go off on this . . . this quixotic expedition?"

"There are twenty-eight lives at stake," Anthony said. But Winkler stopped him from arguing further.

"Your Honor," he said, "it will not be necessary for this trial to recess in order for me to assume this grave burden. I am perfectly confident that my able co-counsel will carry on admirably in my absence, which won't be for longer than a day or two, I'm sure."

Beecher turned to Scott. "Mr. Ingram, are you as confident of your ability to carry on alone as your colleague seems to be?"

Scott answered simply, "Yes, sir, I am."

"Mr. Carroll?" Judge Beecher asked.

"If we can stipulate now that there will be no claim later that the Defendant's rights were violated or damaged by this action."

"We stipulate now that no such question will be raised," Winkler replied.

"The trial will continue!" Beecher ruled.

Winkler and Scott conferred hastily, exchanging notes made during Mrs. Huffman's testimony. Then seizing his trenchcoat and his worn briefcase, Winkler joined Fred Anthony and they left the courtroom.

In sole command of the case for the first time since that afternoon when he had been called in, Scott Ingram felt tense. He wished that Linc had followed his own advice and challenged the identification earlier, when they could have requested a line-up with both himself and Linc present. Now Winkler had left, and Scott had no choice but to try to break down this woman, if he could.

Standing at the lawyers' lectern, his notes before him, Scott Ingram faced Mrs. Evalyn Huffman. He could see the flush on her cheeks and the throbbing of the vein in her neck, both evidences of her high blood pressure. Giving his notes a final, brief perusal, he asked his first question.

"Mrs. Huffman, you have already told us how you had come to Washington that day to accompany your husband who had business here. Since he was an attorney, naturally you had great interest in seeing the Supreme Court in session."

"Yes, sir."

"And naturally you went to the Court without any suspicion or premonition of what was going to happen?" Scott asked, giving her a chance to fall into the habit of responding to his questions with assenting answers.

"You're quite right. I had no idea," she agreed.

"What did you do in the courtroom before that terrible event took place? Can you remember?"

"Well, I was looking around. It's a beautiful courtroom. The marble pillars and all that carved wood."

"And were you looking around when the Defendant sat down next to you?"

"Yes."

"When the Defendant sat down, do you remember what he said?"

"What he said?" Mrs. Huffman asked, puzzled.

"Yes, what he said when he sat down? Did he say, 'Excuse me, Ma'am'? Or 'I beg your pardon.' Or 'Would you mind moving over?' Precisely what did he say to you?"

"I don't remember his saying anything."

"So you don't remember what he said," Scott commented. "Well, let's get on to those things you *do* remember, Mrs. Huffman. For instance, can you tell us what discussion took place between you and Chief Kaska *before* he brought you into the office to confront the prisoner?"

"There was no discussion. He asked me could I recognize the man if I saw him. And I said I thought I could."

"That's all?" Scott pursued.

"That's all."

Scott turned to Carroll's assistant, "Mr. Washington, would you be good enough to play for Mrs. Huffman and the jury the very first line of that tape?"

Washington snapped on the machine, rewound it to the opening of the tape and played: *Are you Evalyn Huffman of 138 Converse Street, Camden, New Jersey?*

"Thank you!" Scott interrupted, cutting off the tape. "Now that's a very revealing opening line, Mrs. Huffman, isn't it? Here is this police officer, who had never met you before, and who, you testified, asked you only if you could identify the Defendant, and yet he knew your full name, your correct number and street address, and the city and state where you live. How did that happen?"

"Well, he asked me that, saying he had to have it for the record," Mrs. Huffman answered.

"So there *was* more conversation beforehand?"

"Well, he had to know my name and where I lived," Mrs. Huffman protested. Scott could see the flush on her cheeks

222

deepening, and the throbbing growing more visible in her throat.

"Mrs. Huffman, you can be honest with us now, how much more conversation *was* there?"

"That's all there was," she said stiffly.

"Nothing about the circumstances and details of the crime? Nothing about how your testimony might aid your husband's legal career?"

"No!"

"Nothing about how important it was to convict this 'black assassin'?"

"Absolutely not!" Mrs. Huffman's face was becoming a deep red now. Across her upper lip a glistening streak of perspiration had formed.

Scott ignored her protest, moving on to a new, quite different question. "Mrs. Huffman, as soon as they brought you into that room you recognized the Defendant as the man who sat next to you in the courtroom?"

"Yes, sir," she said with determination.

"You had no doubts?"

"No, sir. After all, I'd seen him only minutes before."

"I see," Scott said, turning back to Washington. "Would you play for us again that part of the tape starting with 'You are sure this is the man . . .' "

Washington found the spot and started the tape.

You are sure this is the man who sat beside you whom you saw stand up, draw a pistol, and fire those shots?

I'm sure. If you want me to be positive, let me see the side of his face. After all, it was the side of his face I saw mostly.

Stand erect . . . turn your head.

That's the man. No question. The Afro hair . . . but not so bushy. The profile . . . the same color gray suit. I'd know him anywhere.

Scott turned to the witness who was wiping her damp face with a small, lacy handkerchief. "Mrs. Huffman, weren't you being coached during that time?"

223

"No, sir."

"When Captain Kaska said 'You are sure this is the man who sat beside you, whom you saw stand up, draw a pistol, and fire those shots,' wasn't he actually telling you what happened in that courtroom? And telling you what to say?"

"No, sir. Because I did see all that."

"If you really saw all that why did he have to tell you?"

"He wasn't telling me, he was merely getting it straight for the taping."

"Do you know that or are you guessing?" Scott shot back.

"Well, he had said that he would ask the questions in a very legal way and for me not to be surprised by that."

"Then there was *extensive* conversation between you two before you went into that room? How extensive? Did he say to you, 'I am going to show you the killer, all you have to do is say that's the man who sat beside you'?"

"No!" she responded defensively. "He never said anything like that!"

"A moment ago you said you were sure of your identification as soon as you saw the Defendant. But on the tape it seems you had doubts, that you had to have him face this way and that, that you only knew his profile and not his face. Yet when you first identified him you were looking at him full face, weren't you?" Not giving her time to answer any of his questions, Scott had caused her tension to increase until she was perspiring heavily, her face now deeply flushed.

"Mrs. Huffman, what color suit was the Defendant wearing that day?"

"It was a gray."

"Light gray or dark gray?"

"Just gray. Medium gray."

"You're sure of that?" Scott persisted in a way that hinted he had evidence to the contrary.

"Well, I . . . as nearly as I remember, it was medium gray," she said, for by now she was quite unsure of herself.

"Mrs. Huffman, I don't want you to think that I have no

224

sympathy for your plight. There you were, a woman in the midst of a terrible situation, seeing a man shot and killed, suddenly confronted by those officers who were telling you that you had to make an identification because you were closest to the killer. Naturally, like a good citizen you wanted to do your duty. But at the same time, may I suggest, Mrs. Huffman, that a woman subjected to the tensions and strains you were under, who couldn't remember what the Defendant said when he sat down next to you, what color suit he wore, or what he really looked like because you had only seen part of his face, may I suggest that you really couldn't make a firm identification, now, could you, Mrs. Huffman?"

"I . . . yes, yes, I could," she said, but her voice trembled.

"Now, right after the part that we heard on tape, was anything else said to you or by you in that room? Try to remember."

Mrs. Huffman knitted her brow as people do when they wish to give the impression of thinking.

"Or can't you *remember?*" he reiterated, strengthening those doubts he had already set in her mind about her own memory.

"Well, he said . . . he said, something like, 'Take Mrs. Huffman back to the infirmary.' "

"Why? Why the infirmary?"

"So they could give me another sedative."

"*Another* sedative, Mrs. Huffman?"

"Well, I'd had one before . . ."

"So that when you made your supposed identification you were actually under the influence of a drug of some kind?"

"Not a drug!"

"Isn't a sedative a drug? What would you call it?"

"Yes, I suppose in that sense it's a drug."

"So you were given a drug, coached in what to say, and brought into a room where there was only one suspect and asked to identify him?"

"No, it wasn't that way at all," she responded, but her per-

225

spiring forehead, the tears in her eyes, and the hat askew on her head betrayed her shaken confidence and the fact that her credibility and the credibility of her eyewitness identification had been destroyed.

"And now finally we can understand why the Captain had the machine turned off when he did. So that he could hide from the record, and from this jury, the witness's sedation and the whole frame-up that took place inside that room!"

"Object!" Carroll called out.

"I withdraw that last," Scott said, as he started back to his place, leaving Mrs. Huffman still sitting in the witness chair and now beginning to weep.

·◦❦ XVIII ❦◦·

Carroll had introduced Harley Bevans. The tall black courtroom attendant testified that he had talked with Midge Grove before the shooting, having asked him to check his coat and get in line, and that later he had rushed into the courtroom, grappling momentarily with the killer without actually apprehending him. Then Carroll played the tape recording of Bevans' identification of Grove.

Carroll waited until the machine was turned off. "And after the taping, Mr. Bevans?" he asked.

"I left the room and went back to my usual duties. Though, of course, there was no more court session that day."

"Thank you, Mr. Bevans."

Scott Ingram rose slowly, glancing down at his notes. There wasn't much there to go on, not even a full page.

"Mr. Bevans, we heard the tape of your identification, and you told us what you did after the tape. But we didn't hear much about what happened *before*."

"Nothing happened before," Bevans replied.

"You just went in. They switched on the tape, asked your name, and you started talking? That doesn't sound reasonable. Unless, of course, it was a staged identification. Unless you knew exactly what they wanted you to do and say before you walked into the room."

"It was not staged!" Bevans protested.

"Okay, then. There must have been something said before that tape started rolling. For example, did Captain Kaska ask you anything or suggest anything for you to say?"

"No, sir!"

"You seem quite sure about that."

"I am sure!" Bevans fought back. "I'm sure because soon as I got in the doorway and saw him I said, 'That's him. I'd know him anywhere!'"

"'That's him, I'd know him anywhere.' That's all you said?" Scott asked, fishing, because he still had not found a loophole.

"Well, I . . . I might have added a few words . . ."

"Such as?"

"I think I said . . . 'That's the sonofabitch. I'd know him anywhere!'"

"That's all? You're sure now?" Scott stared down at the page of vague notes on the lectern, hoping to pressure Bevans into believing he possessed contradictory evidence, although he did not.

In a low, embarrassed voice, Bevans stated, "Well, I think the complete statement was something like, 'I'd know that black sonofabitch anywhere.'"

"'That *black* sonofabitch,'" Scott repeated very slowly, as if expressing great personal regret that he had heard such words from a black man. Actually Scott was thinking that this was the kind of opportunity Linc Winkler would have seized upon with eagerness. Scott was debating with himself whether to exploit it to the full. For the sake of the case and Grove he felt he had to.

"Mr. Bevans, did it matter to you what color the suspect was?"

"No, sir," Bevans responded, already becoming uneasy. "I'd have been just as quick to identify him, white or black."

"Yet it was necessary for you, a black man, to label the suspect a 'black sonofabitch.'"

"It kind of slipped out."

"Slipped out," Scott reprised. "Don't you like the word black?"

"I don't mind it."

"But you don't like it as well as the word Negro, do you?"

"I don't see anything wrong with Negro. They mean the same. Black is black. And Negro is black in Portuguese."

"But isn't it true that to people of your generation the word 'black' is indicative of a young militant generation which is threatening the security that you've worked so long and so hard to attain?"

Carroll rose. "Your Honor, I don't see the relevance of this discussion. The witness admits using the word 'black.' That is no longer in dispute!"

"Counsel will confine himself to questions having to do with the identification!" the judge ruled sharply.

But Scott had begun to sense a rapport with the majority of the young blacks on the jury and he was not about to lose that advantage. So, while he seemed to adhere to the judge's instruction, he actually pursued his original strategy.

"Getting back to your identification, Mr. Bevans, when one man comes into a room, takes a look at another man and says, 'I'd know that black sonofabitch anywhere,' that's indicative of a state of mind. Isn't it?" When Bevans hesitated, Scott continued: "A phrase like 'black sonofabitch' indicates hostility, anger, disapproval, doesn't it?"

Not knowing what Scott was driving at, Bevans answered with a low, "Yes . . . would seem so."

"Now, what were you *angry* about? *Hostile* about? *Disapproving* about?

"Well, he'd just shot and killed Mr. Justice Miller! That was a damn good reason to be angry and hostile!"

"Then if that were the reason, why didn't you say, 'I'd know that assassin anywhere'? Or possibly, 'That's the sonofabitch who shot Justice Miller. I'd know him anywhere'? But you didn't say that. You said, 'I'd know that black sonofabitch anywhere.' Not a word about shooting, or killing Justice Miller. There were two things in your mind. He was a sonofabitch. But, first and foremost, he was black!"

"That's a lie!"

"Is it, Mr. Bevans? Listen to your own words: 'I'd know that black sonofabitch anywhere.' The very first word you applied to the Defendant was 'black,' not 'murderer' or 'assassin.' So that it seems his blackness was your first concern. Now, I suggest what was going on in your mind was the following: There had indeed been a young black man in that courtroom that day, he had shot Justice Miller, and when he was trying to escape you had actually grappled with him in the aisle. And you knew one thing about him and only one thing—that he was a young black. And that fact disturbed you greatly, so that no matter who they would have shown you in the Chief's office that day, if he was young and black, you'd have proved which side you were on by saying the same thing, 'I'd know that black sonofabitch anywhere!'"

"That's not true! I did see him! I did recognize him!" Bevans protested.

"Then why didn't you just say so? Why was it uppermost in your mind to establish your credentials as full-fledged Judas by pointing the finger at him and labeling him a black sonofabitch?"

Pretending to great distaste, Scott turned away from Bevans, and as he did, he made sure to observe the faces of the nine young blacks in the jury box. Then he knew he had scored. Although he hadn't made Bevans retreat from his identification, he had managed to turn the jury emotionally against Bevans or any middle-aged black who might sit in that witness seat during this trial. And he felt elated as he slid into his seat.

"Wouldn't Linc Winkler be proud of his brilliant co-counsel now!" Marlene whispered to him. The sarcasm in her voice made him turn to look at her, but her eyes were averted from him, and the strong set of her pretty face made no secret of the fact that she strongly disapproved of what he'd done.

Behind him, in the three rows reserved for the press corps, low sibilant comments indicated that the media felt justly rewarded for their day's vigil. Several men on afternoon papers were already leaving the courtroom to phone in new leads for the later editions.

But the sight that impressed Scott most, and depressed him as well, was Harley Bevans, who answered a few reaffirming questions put to him by Carroll, and then left the stand a hurt, whipped man who avoided his fellow blacks in the jury box as he skulked by them.

The rest of the day was devoted to the testimony of the checkroom attendant who asserted that he had checked Grove's coat, that it was the only one left unclaimed after the spectators were released, and that it had no labels in it when he examined it, even though it was a new coat.

Perhaps because of the residue of guilt he felt about Bevans, Scott did not question the coatroom attendant very vigorously.

"Mr. Fairlie, you testified that you examined the coat when you found it was the last one left in your cloakroom?"

"Yes, sir. The coat was there. I saw it. I examined it. I turned it over to the Chief of Court Police," Fairlie stated, leaving no openings for Scott to exploit.

"Mr. Fairlie, on direct examination, you testified that you examined the coat and found that the labels had been newly taken out of it. How did you determine that?"

"I could see the stitchmarks where the labels had once been. So obviously someone had sat down, picked the threads out and removed the labels."

"You say labels. How many were there?"

"Two. One in back just below the collar, one on the lining where the pocket was on the left hand side."

231

Fairlie was that kind of witness, precise and sure, hence thorny for an attorney. So Scott shot at him the important question he wanted to ask.

"Mr. Fairlie, did you see the Defendant remove those labels?"

"Of course not. It was done before he checked the coat," Fairlie answered directly.

"So, actually, you have no way of knowing if he did remove those labels, do you?"

"No, not really," Fairlie admitted.

"In fact, what you said before was closer to the truth. *Someone* picked the threads out—not necessarily this Defendant. *Someone.* It could have been a tailor or a dry cleaner. *Someone.* So I ask you again, did you see this Defendant sit down, pick those threads out and remove those labels?"

"No, sir."

"Thank you!" Scott said, returning to the table and to Marlene, who was just as tense and angry as before.

The day's session was finally over. The usual battery of newsmen and cameras awaited them at the top of the courtroom steps, but contrary to Winkler's practice, Scott limited himself to a formal, "No comment" in answer to all questions. And although they pursued him and Marlene to the little red Mustang, he refused to break his silence.

As soon as they had driven away from the courthouse, Scott apologized. "I had to do it, Marlene. You know that." Although he had made no specific reference to his cross-examination of Bevans, he knew she would know what he meant.

"Unless you have to dictate some motion papers or some notes, I wish you'd drop me near my place," she said.

"Why not *at* your place?"

"Near will be good enough," Marlene insisted quietly.

Angrily he exploded, "Do you have any doubt in your own

232

mind that Bevans was laying it on Grove because he was black? *You* tell *me!*"

"I will tell you that that man was testifying to the truth! And the emotional part of it, his choice of words, had nothing to do with that truth. You were lynching him because he was a *decent* black man. And you had nine young hangmen in the jury box helping you, rooting for you!" Marlene said, suddenly on the verge of angry tears.

"If he has a Tom mentality, I had a duty to point that out! It prejudices his identification."

"Look, Mr. Ingram, don't use words like 'Tom.' You have no right to our feelings and our language. Even the honorable A. Lincoln Winkler does not qualify. It's an agreement they have—Winkler and a certain type of black—they use each other, like homosexuals. But there's no real love there. And I don't want to see you get into the same bag!"

She had begun to cry. Scott pulled the car to a stop in the first open space he could find. Embracing her, he let her cry. She groped to open her purse. Scott offered his own handkerchief, which she accepted, using it not only to dry her tears but to hide from his gaze.

"I'm sorry," he said. "I didn't know you were that sensitive."

"You don't understand, do you?" she said without looking at him. "When Linc Winkler does something like that, I don't approve, but I don't cry either." Her voice was filled with emotion, not just anger, but a kind of concern.

"Marlene?" Scott said softly, wanting her to go on.

She turned to look at him. "But don't get any ideas. We're exactly where we've always been. It's over with, and the fact that I love you doesn't change it. There, I said it. Yes, I love you. But it doesn't change anything."

He reached to embrace her, but she drew back and opened the door. "I can walk from here."

"Marlene!"

But she slipped out of the car and raced swiftly down the street toward her house.

For more than an hour after she arrived at her flat and had securely bolted the door, Marlene debated with herself. Finally, she lifted the phone and called person-to-person to Dr. Lee Morrison, Executive Director of the NAACP. She had never met Morrison personally, but she knew his chief assistant, and she was sure that would be introduction enough.

XIX

Justice Ben Robertson was just coming to the close of his annual Charles Evans Hughes lectures at the university law school. Robertson was one of the most popular speakers, drawing crowds that filled the auditorium to capacity with students from all colleges of the university.

"To you who will be the next generation of lawyers, I say, suspect precedent. Put aside ancient concepts. Free your minds. Make the law a living thing!

"After all, what is a precedent, but the prejudices of the past made permanent? We are disloyal to our own genesis as a nation whenever we enshrine the status quo and treat change as if it were subversion!"

They cheered him as usual, pressed forward to shake his hand, to touch him. One particularly attractive girl kissed him delightedly, and he smiled, asking a bit sadly, "Ah, my dear, and where were you fifty years ago?" And when they had finally all drifted away, only Dean Crowell remained, holding Robertson's coat in his arms.

"What I wouldn't give for your job," Robertson said, as they walked through the empty hall. "To be able to work with the young all the time . . ."

"I've lost most of them, Ben, to Winkler. The ones who can't get into his courtroom are demonstrating outside it.

What do you make of the Grove case, the way it's being handled?"

"Charlie, I never read newspaper accounts of law cases, and as for television, I am not impressed by what I see there. I have a grandniece whose dog will sit and watch television by the hour, and when the set is off that animal points at it like a hunter. Never could understand his motivation."

When Robertson reached the outer door, he found the Rosenstone Rolls waiting for him. He was delighted to see that Honey was inside. As he slipped into the car, Honey said, "You were great, Ben. I heard the last half hour. How can someone two generations removed from the students create such rapport?"

"The strictures they're too young to accept, I'm old enough to discard. Revolutions should be planned by very old men and carried out by very young ones. The ones in the middle are defending what they have." Then he said gently, "And now my dear . . . ?" For he knew the need for some urgent favor had brought Honey here.

"I got a call from Linc Winkler," Honey began apologetically. "They need money for the Gainesville Twelve. Linc is taking the first plane back."

"The Gainesville Twelve. So they've given them a number already?" Robertson interjected, smiling. "They run a regular Sears Roebuck of civil rights—each cause with its own catalog number."

Honey broke in on his musing. "The twelve are the men who started the riot. Linc wasn't able to get amnesty for them, so they'll be tried for murder. I've got up an emergency cocktail party this afternoon to raise a defense fund. Would you speak, Ben? As a special favor?"

"I never can say No to you, Honey," Robertson said, smiling. Then he turned more sober. "But I don't wish any meeting with Winkler. Not that he'd discuss the Grove case, or that I'd be influenced if he did, but it does lead to unfortunate public impressions."

"Of course, Ben. I understand."

The fund-raising party at the Rosenstones had been highly successful. By seven o'clock when most of the guests had begun to depart for other parties, the amount of the pledges peaked at seventy-four thousand dollars. Checks for nineteen thousand had already been received, and the others were due within the week. The Gainesville Twelve had found their supporters.

After Robertson had left, Linc Winkler entered the library where Scott and Marlene were hard at work on a memorandum of law for the morning session when the crucial matter of Grove's confession would surely come up. Marlene had typed up a rough draft, which Scott was now editing. As he revised each page, she sat down at once to type it up fresh, working silently, the attitude between them distinctly and uncharacteristically businesslike.

Linc was aware of the changed atmosphere, but he was too full of his own exuberance about the entire Gainesville adventure to be concerned with the feelings of others.

"Well, Scotty?" Linc began warmly.

Scott held up his hand. He was in the midst of an intricate paragraph, the crux of his argument for ruling out Grove's confession as being defectively obtained and hence inadmissible, and he didn't want to lose his train of thought. Linc turned his attention to Marlene, kissed her faintly on the cheek in greeting, and could not forego the chance to pass his hand lightly over her breast.

When Scott finished, he passed the last two pages to Marlene for final typing. Then he turned to Winkler.

"I heard you gave them hell, Scotty!" Linc started. "Faked them out, and then laid them low. On both identifications."

"Who told you that?"

"The boys at the airport, when they came down to greet me and Fred Anthony. They said if I didn't watch out I'd lose my job." Linc chuckled as he went to the bar to mix

237

himself a drink. "You should have been there, Scott. What a setting! Dawn in that desolate, gray, misty place. We went in, Anthony and me, the two ministers and the other newsmen the rebels had asked for. We carried a flag like a truce team on a battlefield. The place was a shambles. They showed us the hostages, all tied and gagged. Some had wounds, but we were surprised how many were in good condition, considering what those guards have been doing to prisoners for years now."

Linc held up his own drink as an invitation to Scott to join him, but Scott declined.

"We sat down to talk. It was something to see. Those men, deprived of education, some of them inmates of prisons since their teens. But they were self-educated and strong—John the Baptist, every one, saying his last piece before they beheaded him. That's what it was like.

"It was twelve black men facing eight white men. And those black men were full of hatred, justified hatred. Even though we were there to befriend them, to plead their cause, our lives were in danger, and I think some of the others with me were afraid.

"That's when I took charge, formalizing their demands, laying out a course of protest for them so that they could fight for what they wanted. By the time I was done they were as sure and strong in their support of me as the kids on any campus. It was truly exciting, inspiring. A religious experience, that's what it was, a religious experience!"

Winkler dropped onto the tufted leather couch, unbuttoned his collar, pulled down his tie, and taking several long sips of his scotch and soda, he asked, "So it went real well the last two days?"

"Smoke screen," Scott said.

"Judges are like Indians," Linc laughed. "Send up enough smoke signals and they're sure there's a message in there somewhere."

"All I did was cloud the issue. In the end, both witnesses still made firm identifications," Scott said soberly.

"That's as good as can be expected under the circumstances," Winkler consoled him. "What's that?" he said, pointing to the pages Marlene was typing. "The confession memo?"

"It's due to come up tomorrow. Kaska takes the stand."

"You feel up to handling him?"

"I think so."

"Good, because frankly, I'm beat! I can't get my head together. And with all the reporters and TV cameras that'll be out there tomorrow, I'll be lucky if I make it into the courtroom at all."

Marlene brought Scott the last two pages. "If they're okay, I'd like to leave now," she asked as he looked them over.

"They're fine. I'll drop you off," Scott said.

"No, I . . . I want to do some shopping on the way. The stores are open late tonight." And she left before he could insist.

Linc smiled up at him. "You're losing her, Scott. Or didn't you ever have her?"

"I think you misunderstand our relationship," Scott protested, trying to appear nonchalant by applying himself diligently to the pages of his memo.

"Scotty, when it comes to the way of a man with a maid, there's not much I misunderstand." Winkler laughed, and drained the rest of his drink.

"Let an old lover give you some advice. If you can't fight the war, don't start. And if it's going to affect your work on this case, don't get involved!"

Linc Winkler was absolutely correct about what awaited him at the courthouse the next morning. Despite the ban that Judge Beecher had placed on all demonstrations, three hundred pickets, mostly young students, had appeared. They

239

marched in a long, ragged oval pattern just outside the police barricades, hoisting high signs that demanded, "Amnesty for the Gainesville Twelve," "Free the Gainesville Twelve," and "Gainesville, America's Auschwitz." There were several signs reading "Free Midge Grove," but in the main, their protest today was devoted to the Gainesville Twelve.

Winkler moved among the demonstrators, shaking hands, patting them, kissing girls, while hungry newsmen called to him from all sides, asking questions about Gainesville.

Scott glanced again at his wristwatch. The hour for court to reconvene was coming close. He nudged Winkler. "Almost ten, Linc." When Winkler didn't respond, so intoxicated was he by his new cause, Scott slipped through the crowd, past the pickets, and made his way into the courthouse alone.

Scott submitted to the usual morning security search and entered the courtroom where he found Marlene already waiting at the counsel table. If her attitude of late had been reserved, today she was irritated as well. Placing the transcripts of yesterday's testimony before Scott, she asked, "Is he out there doing his turn?"

"Gainesville is the biggest story in the news this morning."

"And far be it from him . . ." Marlene began resentfully, not troubling to finish.

"Look," Scott suddenly exploded, "you know what you really don't like about him?"

"What?" Marlene shot back.

"You said it yourself once. He does more for your race than any black lawyer has ever been able to do, and you resent it—because he's white. Maybe *you're* the racist!"

When her eyes grew misty and her chin quivered, he changed the subject by taking out all four copies of his memorandum on the admissibility of Grove's confession and placing them prominently on the table. No matter where Captain Kaska's testimony started, it would end up here,

240

with this question. Scott would see to that. Actually, he had hoped to have a stronger basis for challenging the confession. But for all the legal language and cases cited, his memorandum was, and had to be, a rather mild document in view of the facts, which were strongly against him.

"Will I see you tonight?" he suddenly asked Marlene, unable to truly focus his thoughts on the case. Besides, he wanted to apologize.

"No," she said, simply, adamantly.

Scott was about to insist when Carroll arrived with his assistants, each of whom carried two heavy briefcases. As he passed Scott, Carroll observed dryly, "You think there's any chance that Winkler'll call off this trial because it's beginning to bore him?" Scott looked up sharply. Carroll's face was placid, benign, in no way reflecting what he had just said.

Winkler had still not appeared in the courtroom when Judge Beecher mounted the bench. With obvious annoyance Beecher ignored Midge Grove's fisted salute, stared down at the counsel table, and asked, "Are you ready to continue, Mr. Ingram?"

"Yes, Your Honor," Scott answered.

"Good! Because based on what I observed from my window, we'll have to forego Mr. Winkler's presence for most of the morning. Mr. Carroll?"

"Ready to continue!" Carroll answered.

Then the jury entered, and Midge Grove once again thrust his clenched fist upward, this time calling, "Right on, brothers!"

Next the members of the press came drifting into the courtroom. Once they were seated, Linc Winkler finally entered. Judge Beecher watched with impatient indulgence as Winkler made his way slowly down the aisle, smiling at personal acquaintances who sat among the spectators. It had become the radical vogue for many politically oriented celebrities visiting Washington to drop in on the Grove trial, entertainers, actors promoting their films, authors on tour to

241

promote new books. Today, with the conflict at Gainesville to bask in, Winkler took more time than usual greeting his friends and supporters. He even stopped to shake hands and chat briefly with Marty Wildberg, the noted symphonic conductor and jazz composer, who in his mid-fifties was still being hailed as a boy genius.

Judge Beecher called out in an irritated tone, "Mr. Carroll, are you ready to present your next witness?"

Only then did Winkler seem to become aware that he was in a courtroom. He managed to reach the counsel table just as Captain Kaska in the uniform of the Metropolitan Police was being sworn in.

Carroll led Kaska through his participation in the events of that fateful afternoon. Scott made notes on a fresh legal pad, seeking in the main two things: points at which sloppy police work might be betrayed, and any hint that any recent Supreme Court decision, especially the Miranda decision, had been violated when it came to protecting the rights of the accused.

From Kaska's story, elicited with slow and painstaking care by Carroll, it seemed that if anything, Kaska had overdone the precautions usually observed. He had even asked the Defendant to sign a statement admitting that his legal rights had been read to him, so there could be no question later.

Grove's voluntary confession was one of the most damaging pieces of evidence in the case. Brief and unwritten, it was nevertheless very strong, for it was made by the defendant after due warning, and there were three witnesses to it, Kaska and two assistants.

Carroll finished with Kaska and turned him over for cross-examination. Scott rose, taking his notes with him. He crossed the floor to the lawyer's lectern, which he had come to hate, for it restricted his mobility and thus increased his inner tension. Operating on sheer instinct, he played the clock as he once did during his basketball days in college. If

242

Scott could stall until the lunch break, perhaps a conference with Winkler and Midge might provide an attack against the confession. Meanwhile he began slowly and laboriously to take Kaska over exactly the same ground to which he had already testified.

This method had its advantages. Scott knew from trial experience that no witness ever tells his story precisely the same way twice. So if you were really stuck, the most effective tactic was to get the witness to tell his story over again. The worst you could suffer was that the jury heard the same incriminating story twice. The best that could happen was that under pressure the witness would deviate from what he said before. Or give you a clue to some weakness.

Kaska seemed to luxuriate in the opportunity to recite again the correct and legal manner in which the prisoner had been handled from the first moment he had passed into the hands of the Metropolitan Police.

Scott probed at that a bit, hoping to elicit from Kaska an admission that, like many police officers, he resented those Supreme Court decisions which tied the hands of the police. But no, Kaska endorsed the Miranda decision. It put the police officer on his mettle to make his case strictly according to the Constitution, and that was good, Kaska maintained. Scott realized that Carroll must have prepared the captain very well. And that was logical, for in a case replete with solid witnesses, Carroll knew that Kaska was one of the strongest.

Scott was leading Kaska through the events following his request that Grove sign an admission that the warning statement had been read to him, when the clock showed twenty minutes to one. Surely, Scott thought, there must be a recess soon. He delved again into the testimony that the accused had refused to sign the statement and he asked Kaska to explain again exactly what had happened when his assistant had suggested that Grove be tested to detect drug use.

Kaska repeated that he had refused to do that, because, as

he had said at the time, "We don't want to take any chances on defective self-incrimination. Not with this one. Everything has to be airtight. We don't want another Dallas here."

That phrase stuck in Scott's mind like a splinter. He had heard it before. Most recently, Kaska had used it this morning when Carroll had questioned him. But this time the phrase had new and hopeful significance for Scott. If only he could remember. Dallas, Dallas, Dallas. Someone else had said it before. But who?

Now Scott really did need time. To pursue his hunch he would have to study the transcripts of previous testimony. So he began to question Kaska about the form that he had insisted Grove sign. All the while, he watched the clock hands moving slowly toward one.

"Tell me, Captain Kaska, isn't it possible that an overzealous police officer might present such a form to an arrested man *without* first having read the protections to him?"

"No, sir!" Kaska responded sharply.

"That couldn't possibly happen?"

"Not under my command. And not in this district. We are very careful about how we handle any accused."

"Meticulous?"

"Yes, you could use that word."

At that point Carroll arose and addressed the bench, for he suspected Scott's tactics. "Your Honor, it seems that the Defense is engaged in speculative ventures into what might or might not happen in a hypothetical circumstance. These have no relevance here. Captain Kaska has testified as to what did happen, and cross-examination should be limited to his testimony, not to time-wasting speculation."

Judge Beecher turned to Scott. "The U.S. Attorney's objection is well taken, Mr. Ingram. We will recess for lunch. And if after lunch you have questions of relevance to ask this witness we will continue with him. If not, I trust you won't waste the time of the Court and the jury."

Scott was relieved. He had stalled long enough. When he

returned to the counsel table, he asked in a sharp whisper, "Dallas! Who mentioned Dallas before?" Although he had addressed his question to Winkler, it was Marlene who answered it.

"Edwards, I think," she said.

"The Chief of Supreme Court Police?"

"I'm pretty sure."

They both turned to find the volume of the transcripts in which Edward's testimony was recorded. It confirmed Marlene's recollection. Edwards had mentioned Dallas twice. First in the direct examination, then in Winkler's cross. Marlene ran her finger under the lines in the trancript.

And as I told my men, the one thing we didn't want was another Dallas. This isn't Dallas. We don't want any Lee Harvey Oswalds here.

Suddenly Scott remembered when he had heard those words for the very first time. In their earliest meeting in the private conference room, Midge Grove had spoken them.

Scott's hunch began to crystallize, and he awaited the end of the lunch recess with growing anticipation.

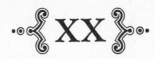

XX

It was Judge Beecher's habit to have a light lunch in chambers each day during the progress of any trial. This practice made him more accessible to attorneys in other cases who wished to present motions or make requests for postponements, examinations or private consultations with their imprisoned clients.

The daily picketing, jeering, and epithets which had been aimed at him throughout the trial came through the window as he ate. Usually his ears shut them out automatically, as if they were the normal sounds of traffic, but on this day the outburst was so marked and intrusive that Judge Beecher rose from his desk to look out.

There, outside the police barricades, a dozen young men, black and white, most bearded and with very long hair or large Afros, were marching in single file. Some wore makeshift costumes that were supposed to simulate traditional striped prison garb, and all twelve were bound together by leg chains. Moving in unison, they cried out the slogans to which the Gainesville crisis had already given rise, shouted obscenities and epithets against the law, the courts and against Judge Beecher himself. Hundreds of comrades cheered them on while mounted television cameras photographed the entire scene. Thousands of spectators out on the streets during the lunch hour had gathered to swell the crowd.

After only some minutes of impatient watching, Beecher lifted his phone angrily.

"Miss Grady! See that the police get rid of that outrageous demonstration at once!"

"But they're outside the barricades," she said, hoping to forestall any precipitous action.

"Those barricades are set up to provide room for people who want to express their opinions about *this* trial. I will not allow this courthouse and my trial to become the rallying point for every goddamn radical cause in the country! Tell the police to get rid of them!"

Within minutes a group of police moved in on the chain gang and the demonstrators, attempting to disperse them. Soon rocks were hurled by the picketers, and the police retaliated, using their night sticks as weapons. In moments, what had been only noisy irreverent picketing turned into a vicious street battle between police and demonstrators.

Sirens began sounding to announce the arrival of police reinforcements. Then of ambulances. Within twenty minutes the riot was quelled, but not before a number of demonstrators had been bloodied and one police officer was taken to the hospital with a possible fracture of the skull.

Beecher, following doctor's orders, took a tranquilizer before returning to court for the afternoon session.

Captain Kaska had taken the stand. Scott Ingram, armed with his notes and with the transcript of Edward's testimony, advanced to the lectern.

"Now, Captain, if I remember correctly, before the lunch recess you testified that, 'We don't want to take any chances on defective self-incrimination. Not with this one.' Did you say that?"

"Yes, I did."

"Was that all you said at that time, or was there more? My

memory is faulty on that part." Scott had used the latter phrase deliberately, introducing the concept of erratic recall to set Kaska on edge, to make him worry whether he might be trapped in such an exhibition himself.

"Your memory may be faulty on that, Counselor, but not mine," Kaska said, accepting the challenge. "I said, 'We don't want to take any chances on defective self-incrimination. Not with this one. Everything has to be airtight. We don't want another Dallas here.'"

"Yes," Scott seized on it, "I believe you did testify to that this morning. But are you sure you said that second part?"

"About airtight, and about Dallas? 'We don't want another Dallas here.' That part?" Kaska asked, cautiously.

"Yes."

"I'm quite sure I said it. In fact two of my assistants can testify to it!"

Scott smiled. "Captain, are there many cases on record in which policemen testify in contradiction to their superiors?"

The judge leaned out of his chair. "Mr. Ingram, if you have evidence that that's what happened, produce it! If not, this Court will not sanction speculative accusations!"

"Sorry, Your Honor," Scott said, satisfied that he had already made a big enough issue of it for his purposes. He turned back to Kaska.

"Captain, that phrase about Dallas, do you use it often?"

"It doesn't apply often, thank God. But in this case, we were dealing with the same kind of situation. And we didn't want the same kind of sloppy police work here that led to the fiasco down there."

"So you were holding up Dallas as an example of what *not* to do in a case involving an assassination?"

"Yes, sir. That's why I'm sure of what I said, because it was the only time in my twenty-six-year police career that I used that expression," Kaska declared righteously.

Scott glanced at his notes, then at the transcript that lay

before him. "Captain Kaska, did you have any previous agreement with Chief Edwards of the Court Police?"

"Previous agreement?"

"Conversation previous to the time when you said in the presence of the Defendant, 'This is not Dallas,' etcetera? "Did Edwards say anything to you about Dallas?" Scott asked sharply.

"No. Why should he?"

"The question isn't why he should or shouldn't. But we have his testimony in which he said . . ." Scott pretended he didn't have the lines marked but had to hunt for them. "Question by Mr. Winkler: 'Are you always that meticulous, Mr. Edwards?' Answer by Chief of Court Police Edwards: 'We don't have such cases as a general rule. But we're fully aware of what happens in other places. And, as I told my men, the one thing we didn't want was another Dallas. 'This isn't Dallas. We don't want any Lee Harvey Oswalds here.' "

"If that's what Chief Edwards testified to, I would take his word. I wasn't there," Kaska said.

"As I read you that statement now and recall to you your own statement about Dallas, do you still maintain there was no connection between the two statements, and no previous discussion between you?"

"Absolutely none!"

"Then it was a coincidence?"

"Yes. But that's not hard to understand."

"Why not?" Scott asked.

"Because the Kennedy case is probably the most famous event of our time," Kaska replied. "I think any police officer confronted with an assassination, that's the first thing he would think of: Let's not have a repetition of Dallas!"

"Captain, you said that the Kennedy case is the most famous event of our time. Then would you say that the events in Dallas are well known to people other than police officials?"

249

"Of course!"

"So that any member of the public might be aware of those events?"

"Any member who can read, look or listen, yes."

"The members of this jury perhaps?" Scott pursued.

"I would think they'd know all about Dallas."

"Just what would they know?"

"Well, the facts. What they heard and saw."

"Such as?"

"The assassination. The President's car speeding away. The scene outside the hospital. Oswald, once they caught him. And of course, the most famous one of all, the way he was shot right on television."

"Can we also assume then that this Defendant would be familiar with those events?"

"I would assume so," Kaska replied.

"To get back to what Chief Edwards said, specifically, 'This isn't Dallas. We don't want any Lee Harvey Oswalds here . . .'"

"That's what you read me," Kaska replied cautiously for he had begun to suspect Scott.

"I haven't finished the question yet, Captain. Edwards made his statement in the presence of the Defendant. We have Edwards' testimony on that. And then later, within half an hour, you said, again in the presence of the Defendant, 'Everything has to be airtight. We don't want another Dallas here.' Captain, what did happen in Dallas? Especially to Lee Harvey Oswald?"

"I think everybody knows that. He was captured, questioned, held in pretty tight security. Though when he was being taken to court to be arraigned, the security was loose, very bad, and at that time he was shot by Jack Ruby."

"Isn't it possible that you left out something 'that everybody knows,' Captain?"

"Oswald died later that same day," Kaska amended. "Everybody knows that, too."

250

"Did you leave out something else?" Scott repeated.

"I don't think so," Kaska said, puzzled and alert to a possible trap.

"You're sure?"

"Quite sure!"

"Then tell me, Captain, did Lee Harvey Oswald ever confess to the murder of President Kennedy?"

"No, he didn't confess," Kaska conceded. "But I think in time he would have."

"Don't *you* speculate now, Captain. Only what we *do* know. Oswald did not confess. And he was killed. Right?"

"Not the way you say it, it's not."

"Why not? He did not confess. And he was shot. In that order. Right?"

"Yes, but one didn't necessarily have to do with the other!" Kaska fought back.

"How can you be sure of that?" Scott demanded.

"I don't see what difference it makes!" Kaska said.

"Put yourself in the place of this Defendant. He's been arrested on a charge of assassinating a high official of the United States Government. He is processed by two police officers in uniform with gold badges and lots of braid. One says, 'This isn't Dallas. We don't want any Lee Harvey Oswalds here.' And the second one says, 'We don't want another Dallas here.' So that twice he has the words and the memories of Dallas held over his head like a threat. And he knows, as does everyone else in this country, that Lee Harvey Oswald did *not* admit his guilt, did *not* confess and was shot to death! Then, after those two threats about Dallas, from two different police officers, this Defendant confesses voluntarily. Is it so strange that he confessed in order to avoid the same fate as Lee Harvey Oswald?"

Before Kaska or Carroll could answer or object, Scott turned toward the bench. "Your Honor, I ask that this verbal confession reported to us in Captain Kaska's testimony be thrown out and that the jury be instructed to disregard it!"

251

"Your Honor, Your Honor . . ." Carroll was protesting, trying to be heard over the outburst that had erupted among both press and spectators. Beecher gaveled for quiet.

"Counselor," Beecher said to Scott after a few moments, "if you wish to make a proper motion the Court will entertain it."

"Your Honor, we ask you to consider all the events and circumstances which the Government itself admits surround this so-called voluntary confession. Defendant had not yet spoken to a lawyer . . ."

"Though he had been properly instructed and had been offered a lawyer!" Carroll interjected.

Beecher warned gravely, "Mr. Carroll, please!"

Scott continued. "In addition to being bereft of legal advice, he was twice, within less than an hour, threatened by two different police officers. And what was he threatened with? The same fate as another prisoner, in another assassination case, with whom he had one other important thing in common—that man had not confessed either. And that man had been killed *while in the custody of the police!* Yes, the pressure was very subtle. Far less crude than the usual police pressure. It left no visible marks of torture, no evidence of physical coercion. But the threat was in the words of those officers, which said in effect to this defenseless accused, Confess or die!

"I ask this Court to take into account the fact that *all* of this testimony came from the mouths of two prosecution witnesses, the two police officers involved!"

Beecher pondered for a moment before he turned to Carroll, who rose quite slowly. He was visibly shaken, for he had not expected an attack on the confession.

"Your Honor, what we are confronted with here is not evidence of any pressure or violation of rights but a twisted hypothesis seeking to place the stamp of abuse of power on highly professional police work. There is absolutely nothing in the testimony of either Chief Edwards or Captain Kaska

252

to indicate that they intended to threaten or coerce the Defendant. In fact, when they mentioned Dallas, they were cautioning their subordinates to be especially careful and solicitous of the rights of the accused. It is clear every step of the way.

"The unfortunate image of Dallas was the best guarantee of the Defendant's rights and his safety. And I submit that in the months which have elapsed this Defendant has been protected and *is* here safe, sound and in good health at this trial. Proof of what those officers meant by their words is in this courtroom in the person of the Defendant himself!"

With a curt nod of his head, Beecher conceded Scott the opportunity of reply.

"Your Honor, we cannot enter the minds of those two police officers at the time they made those statements and read what intention was there. But then, neither can Mr. Carroll. Nor is that important. The important thing to understand is the *Defendant*'s state of mind when he made that confession. If *he* felt threatened with being shot like Lee Harvey Oswald unless he confessed, then that pressure, that threat, even if it existed only in the Defendant's mind, is enough to severely taint this confession and make it inadmissible. I ask this Court to act now to strike it out and instruct the jury to disregard it completely!"

Having finished, Scott stood his ground, staring up at Beecher, whose face wore a troubled look. It had been a daring argument, Scott knew, but evidently it had started some wheels turning in old Beecher's head.

He started back to the defense table, but instead of moving to the right of it as he usually did, Scott veered to the left, passing between both counsel tables and directly behind Carroll. As he reached Carroll, he raised his hand suddenly just over the prosecutor's shoulder. Carroll's reaction was swift. In one movement he rose, turned, and seized Scott's arm, so that for a brief instant they were grappling.

"Gentlemen, gentlemen!" Beecher intervened quickly and

angrily, turning his fierce gaze on Scott as soon as the men had separated. "Mr. Ingram, what was the meaning of such conduct in my courtroom? Another outbreak of physical violence and I shall have to take proper steps in the privacy of my chambers!"

"I'm sorry, Your Honor," Scott said. "I apologize to the Court. I was only trying to brush some dandruff off Mr. Carroll's collar. But it is interesting to note that to Mr. Carroll it constituted a threat. And he reacted to it immediately. So I suggest, Your Honor, that the degree of a threat is in the mind of the man who feels he is threatened, and not in the intentions behind it."

Scott continued to the end of the table, passed behind Winkler and slipped into his seat.

"My, my," Linc whispered, "you're a real barracuda when you get going, Scott. A real barracuda."

Beecher sat pensively for a few moments. Then, leaning slightly forward, he pronounced, "Taking into account all the arguments which Defense Counsel has presented, the Court nevertheless rules that the confession made by this Defendant is both voluntary and admissible."

When the first surge of emotion had passed, Scott half-rose to announce, "We take exception to that ruling."

He had learned from Linc Winkler that even though it was not required, taking exception served to make points with the jury and the press.

"Unless there is objection from Counsel, we will adjourn until tomorrow morning," Beecher announced. Then he brought down his gavel and the session was over.

Linc, Scott, and Marlene gathered up their papers and turned from the table. Waiting at the rail just behind them was a tall, lean, careworn, gray-haired Negro whose saintlike face had been famous for a generation. His photograph had appeared in connection with any newspaper story having to do with black people's rights and grievances. He was Dr. Lee

Morrison. And Winkler knew that Morrison had come to see him. It was a meeting that could not be avoided.

Since they had met a number of times in the past, Winkler smiled and held out his hand. "Dr. Morrison."

As they shook hands, Morrison asked, "Do you have some time, Winkler? An hour or so?"

"I want you to meet my associate, Scott Ingram," Linc said, evading the question.

"Mr. Ingram," Morrison acknowledged, shaking hands with Scott.

"And our assistant, Miss Hutch."

Morrison nodded in Marlene's direction. A knowing look passed between them that went unnoticed by Linc but not by Scott.

"We could go back to my hotel," Morrison suggested.

Winkler agreed quickly, not because he welcomed the meeting, but because having it at Morrison's place left him free to depart whenever he wished.

Morrison had a simple room at the Shoreham, which gave him the prestige of the address and still allowed him to remain within the stringencies of the NAACP budget. In that way he set an example of frugality for the younger men on his staff. There were enough chairs for all, but after inviting his three guests to sit down, Morrison himself remained standing and then began to pace the length of the long, narrow room as he spoke in a moderate tone.

"Winkler, we don't have to fence with each other. We each know what our objectives are. And our means. I don't yield to you or anyone in the battle of human rights for black people, or any minority, but our voices are raised to different pitches. What we seek is often very much the same. We have often been on the same side of the same fight. But there have been exceptions."

Morrison put great stress on that last phrase. By Winkler's standards, Morrison and the NAACP were not only less than radical, they were conservatives, apologists, and Toms.

Winkler's supporters spent as much of their time denouncing the NAACP as they did the Establishment.

Morrison continued, "Unlike the militants, I am not interested in avenging the past, only securing the future. We can't do both. So at other times we have been on *different* sides of the same issue. And where we part company sharply and very seriously is on the matter before the court now."

"Are you saying Grove isn't entitled to a defense?" Winkler demanded.

"I didn't mean that, and I didn't say that," Morrison responded. "I don't even object when the cases that you start on page one we have to take up later and win on page fifty-one. It may even do some good to have our cases publicized in the flamboyant way you do. So that's *not* what I mean."

Winkler interposed, "Did you see the brilliant way that Ingram handled the matter of the confession today? Surely you didn't find fault with that."

"I fully appreciate his legal brilliance in the situation. I am not talking about what goes on in the courtroom, but outside. I am talking about your ultimate objectives. Are you trying to win this case for Grove's benefit and protection, or are you using Grove to aid your own cause? And in aiding your cause, are you doing all of us, all black people, a tremendous disservice and great harm in the long run?"

"Harm!" Winkler said, making no secret of his skepticism.

"Yes, harm! To the young!"

"What we're doing is in the true tradition of the American system of adversary law. The most guilty man is entitled to a defense—the best defense it is possible to make. That's our system!"

"I'm not asking you to deviate from that by a single iota," Morrison countered. "What I *am* asking is this: Why is it necessary to make an assassin into a hero to the young? Why are you asking them to ennoble murder? Because he is *black?* Because it is *black* murder? You are asking our young to take to the streets on behalf of a man who is guilty, and for whom

256

we might all well feel sorry. But that does *not* make him a hero! That's the crime, Winkler!

"We *need* the law, we need *order* to achieve our gains. And in the past thirty years there have been gains. So we need our black young to believe in the law, to study it, use it, find their way into it, into our courts and onto the benches of the nation so that we can be insured of orderly change. Without it we have no enduring chance."

Morrison turned away, as if making a confession he hated to make, even to himself.

"I have a terrible fear, Winkler, that unless we make the most of the opportunity we have now it may be another hundred years or more before we can make any substantial gains again."

Scott glanced at Winkler, but didn't dare look at Marlene because he knew now how Morrison came to be here.

"You started them off demanding a fair trial for Midge Grove. Then it became Save Midge Grove! Now, it is Free Midge Grove.

"Well, Free Midge Grove is not a fit slogan for young black people to be shouting in the streets of this and other cities. Defend Midge Grove? Yes! But sanctify him? I don't think so, Winkler, I don't think so."

Morrison had turned to confront Winkler, who stared up at him. "Winkler, if you really have the great love and sympathy for black people that you claim, then don't abuse them with false ideals and false gods. Winkler, let my people go! My young people!"

It was a demand and a plea.

"Let them go? To what?" Winkler demanded. "A minority does not achieve power by the slow, easy, patient path that you've chosen, Morrison."

"A minority which is only one of ten does not win it in a bloody war either!" Morrison answered angrily. "Stop leading them in that direction!"

"There is a way, Morrison. But you don't want to see it. A

257

minority can win, can control a whole nation through the courts! Courts can legislate where Congresses fail! Courts can even go against the will and prejudices of the majority. And it's the only branch of government that can! That's why I chose this way!

"We must make the courts amenable to the demands of the minority. If it calls for demonstrations, then we will demonstrate. If it calls on occasion for violence, then we will become violent. If it calls for sabotage of the legal system then we will sabotage it. And if it calls for us to sanctify a man you judge to be guilty and unworthy, we will defend him and raise such a hullabaloo that the courts will listen to us either because they think we are right, or else because they fear us. But the courts are our only chance."

Morrison knew that he had failed and admitted it when he said, "So it will go on. When the police try to arrest a pusher who seeks to infect our young, your people will rise up to battle the police, not the pusher. When thieves who prey on us are arrested, your people will riot in the streets to protect the thieves. Where are you taking us, Winkler? Do you even know that?"

"All change demands some destruction. What's left is what you build on," Winkler said grimly.

"So that's your answer," Morrison said sadly.

"What's yours, Morrison? Time and patience? Suffer until you become the majority, is that what you have to offer? Well, your young have no patience for it!"

"Obviously," Morrison said, "and just as obviously you mean to exploit that."

"Right now," Winkler said, "Grove needs all the support he can get. And I intend to get it for him. Meantime, they'll know they've been in a fight."

"You'll never free him," Morrison warned.

"Don't be too sure," Winkler said, smiling enigmatically, puzzling even Scott with his smug self-assurance.

258

Linc Winkler was silent all the way from the Shoreham. When the Rolls drew up at the Rosenstone house, he said wearily, "I've got a meeting tonight on the Gainesville situation. So you'll have to excuse me, Scotty."

"Linc, Carroll can't have more than two or three witnesses left," Scott protested. "We'll have to open our case tomorrow, Wednesday at the latest."

"I'll be ready," Winkler said, but he sounded tired and dejected. He slapped Scott on the thigh, kissed Marlene on the cheek and eased himself out of the car, dragging his inevitable bulging briefcase as if it were the ball and chain of his professional life.

Following the butler's information that Mrs. Rosenstone was in the library, Winkler walked to the open door. Honey was at the bar mixing a tall frosty silver pitcher of martinis when he entered. She greeted him with a kiss on the lips. Then she seized his briefcase, set it down alongside the huge old desk, and turned back to him to loosen his tie and unbutton his shirt. She made him lie down on the leather couch, and when he reached automatically for the remote TV control, she took it from his hand and placed it out of reach.

"Tonight we just relax," she said firmly.

"I've got four people coming to confer about Gainesville," he reminded her.

"I canceled that."

"You canceled . . ."

"Bob is spending two days in New York. And you're exhausted. So Honey is going to be good to both of us. A few drinks to relax you, then a very special dinner that I had Aurelia prepare. And one whole night when we don't have to watch the damned TV news—or discuss the case—or raise funds. Just Honey and Linc, at home."

"You shouldn't have canceled that meeting . . ." Linc protested, though he was glad she had.

Honey smiled as she handed him a frosted martini glass. "I wanted you to discover what it would be like being married

259

to me—in case you want to withdraw your offer. I can be a tyrant."

"Some tyrant!" he joked back, taking her hand and pressing it to his cheek. "So you're thinking about it," he said, encouraged.

"Thinking," Honey answered noncommittally.

"You're what I need, darling. A woman to take care of me, really take care of me."

"Wouldn't Rose do the same, if you let her?" Honey challenged.

"That's the difference. Rose needs permission. You just take charge. I'm at a stage in my life when I need a woman like you—all woman, satisfying and complete in all ways." He tried to kiss her, but she eluded him.

"And what about *my* stage in life? And what *I* need?" she countered.

"Darling, what you need is a husband you'll be glad to see come home. A husband you'll miss when he's away. A husband who's so busy accomplishing something that you'll have to vie for his attention, instead of hiding yourself in activities that only help you escape from the fact that you are bored with your marriage, bored with Bob, bored with your whole life. *I* will change all that."

He pulled her down beside him on the couch, and he kissed her, pressing the length of her body against his own.

"You know what I wonder, Linc?"

He was too busy exploring her perfumed neck to answer.

"I wonder how much of the heat between us is because we're *not* married? What we have is clandestine, so it's exciting. What if we had to face each other night after night? What if I didn't have to scheme and plot to find time and opportunity to seize little snatches of love with you? Would you begin to pall on me, too?"

"No woman has ever said that about me!" he replied angrily, his attention captured. "Not even Rose!"

"Linc," she asked softly, "did it ever occur to you that

maybe Rose permits you to go your merry way because *she's* the one who's bored? That instead of waiting anxiously for you to return home she's actually relieved when you don't?"

"Bitch!" he said, half joking, but half resenting her analysis of his wife and his marriage.

Honey laughed. "You know the one thing that may keep me from ever saying Yes to you? You have absolutely no sense of humor about A. Lincoln Winkler."

He held her closer. But when she felt his weariness being replaced by desire, she drew back.

"We really should have dinner, you know. Aurelia went to such trouble."

"Aurelia can wait!" he answered testily.

"If we were married and you had that attitude, we'd never be able to keep help," she joked. "Besides, if I'm going to take you seriously from now on, I want to be wooed. Really pursued. I'm not going to be easy or taken for granted anymore." Although she was joking, she did disengage herself from him.

"*You* are a bitch," he grumbled, but not seriously.

The Rosenstone chauffeur rolled to a stop in front of Marlene's house. Hastily she opened the door. "See you in the morning," she said as she climbed out of the car.

Scott seized her free hand, "I'm getting out with you."

"I've told you . . ." But she said no more, reluctant to have the chauffeur overhear.

"That's not why!" he answered cryptically, as intent as she was on keeping the facts of their relationship private.

"Why then?" she demanded.

"I have to talk to you."

They watched until the car pulled away and drove out of sight. She said simply, "Okay, talk."

"Not out here."

"If we go in there, we both know what will happen. And I told you, that's over," she said very firmly.

261

"There's something we have to talk about," he repeated.

"What?" she demanded.

"Morrison!"

"Did I send for him? Is that what you want to know? Yes, I did!" She turned away and started toward the steps. Scott caught up with her.

"I promise I won't touch you. But let's talk, Marlene. Please."

She finally nodded and they started up the stairs together. Marlene was digging into her purse for her keys, when she was suddenly confronted by the building superintendent at the outer door. A tall, aged black man, he opened the door for them, but made no secret of his disapproval that Marlene's visitor was young, male, and white.

Once they were inside her apartment, Marlene avoided Scott by busying herself making coffee. Scott tried to talk as she bustled about.

"You had no right to interfere in the case, Marlene. No matter how you feel about Winkler, or about the defense."

"Somebody had to!" she retorted.

"I don't approve of some of Winkler's stunts any more than you do. That phony Panther getup he makes Midge wear. Making him stand up and give that salute every day. I don't like a lot of what he says to the press. But you have to understand, legally we have no defense. No defense at all!"

"There *was* a defense," she countered.

"Insanity?"

"Yes! But Winkler deliberately threw that out."

"We've been through that!" he answered. The anger in his voice betrayed his own sensitivity to the subject.

"*We* haven't been through that. Winkler has. The eminent Dr. Randolph has. But *we* haven't. Specifically, *you* haven't."

"Marlene, darling, at best insanity is a very questionable defense with the evidence as it stands."

"It's still better than what's going on now!"

"We're proceeding on the Doctrine of Social Inevitability

262

and that's that!" he said, uneasily, trying to close off the discussion.

"Lawyers can plead conflicting defenses, can't they, without one defeating the other?"

"You didn't call Morrison to discuss the defenses in the case!"

"If you must know, I called Morrison because of *you*," she declared finally. Her eyes misted up as she continued. "Linc Winkler can take a case like this, use it to his personal advantage, lose it and never miss a night's sleep. For all his humanitarian protests, he's like a general in a war. Win the battle and count the casualties later—if there's time. Well, thank God, you're not made that way." She faltered and her lip quivered.

Scott reached out, lifting her face so she had to look at him.

"And no amount of saying that it became Winkler's case, that he had to run it his way, would make it easier for you."

He nodded. She was right. Gently he put his arms around her, and spoke softly. "In the beginning, I admired that man. I thought, Here's a lawyer with feelings as well as principles. He cares about people. He takes hopeless cases, jousts at windmills, because he cares. And then he pulls off miracles in the courtroom, despite his hopeless cases. Maybe he *is* a medicine man, but I try to convince myself we need men like him to create defenses where none exist, to make the society take a good, long, revealing look at itself. I've told myself all that. Some nights I go to bed believing it. But other nights . . ."

He didn't finish. They were too close. He kissed her, and she kissed him back. Then, what they had promised would not happen, did.

Somewhere in the distance, a church bell tolled eleven times. Scott drew back from her warm body in a way that meant he had to leave now. He dressed slowly, reluctantly.

263

Marlene did not turn to watch him, but lay on her side, facing away from him, her body covered only with the sheet, wrinkled from their lovemaking.

When he was dressed, he leaned over to kiss her cheek, and to whisper into her ear, as if he were making a promise, "We only open our case tomorrow. We have enough time to plead insanity if we want to. There's still time."

XXI

On the morning that A. Lincoln Winkler was to make his opening statement for the defense, there appeared for sale in Washington and in other major cities throughout the nation a thin paperback book written by Midgely Grove. It purported to set forth the thoughts, feelings, and philosophy of Grove as experienced by him during his lonely days in prison since the protest killing of Justice Harvey Miller.

The book was bound in glossy red paper and carried a page-size close-up of Midge Grove's thin, ascetic, black face on its back. The front bore a sketch of a black man being consumed by fire. Superimposed over the sketch was the title *Soul Aflame!* and in smaller print, "Foreword by Willis Cane." The style of the foreword and of the book were not too dissimilar.

Huge placard-size blowups of the cover and the back of the book were carried by pickets outside the Federal courthouse that morning. In defiance of Judge Beecher's orders and despite periodic police roundups, there had been at least two hundred pickets at the wooden barricades every morning.

Finally police and demonstrators reached an understanding. There would be no police interference if the pickets remained outside the proscribed area.

265

Occasionally, whenever a falling-off in TV coverage dictated it, the pickets found pretexts to invade the area behind the barricades. Then the police would move in and take action. Somehow the TV cameras were always there to cover it, as if by divine coincidence.

The morning of the opening of the defense case was one of those occasions. Brandishing their SOUL AFLAME! placards, the pickets burst through the barricades.

The police used clubs, and the pickets fought them with the shafts of their signs. At the end of the free-for-all, four policemen and nine youths had been beaten severely enough to require hospital care. Sixty-two arrests had been made. Over seventeen hundred feet of film had been exposed. And interviews were given by those demonstrators who had not been arrested.

They claimed that the trial had become a travesty of justice, a clear violation of the Constitutional right to public trial, since the number of people granted admission to the courtroom was limited to fifty members of the press and less than a hundred spectators. And until TV cameras were admitted into the courtroom so that Midge Grove's defense could be witnessed by the entire nation, this could not be considered a public, or a fair, trial.

That night on the CBS Evening News, one commentator agreed with them editorially, despite the fact that his credentials as a Constitutional lawyer had never been clearly established.

"Mr. Winkler, are you ready to open the Defense case?"

"We are, Your Honor," Winkler said, rising and taking with him the notes that Scott Ingram pushed across the table.

"Ladies and gentlemen of the jury. First, I wish to remind you, as His Honor surely will during his charge, that you are to presume this man innocent until he is proven guilty beyond a reasonable doubt.

266

"That the Government has *not* proved him so guilty is our main defense. Oh, they have gone to great lengths in their effort to do so, superseding anything I have ever seen before in my experience in the law. Why? Because there is far more at stake in this trial than the guilt or innocence of this man.

"What is at stake here is an entire system, whether we are going to take the final plunge from a supposedly free society into a dictatorship. Into a new era of American fascism—white American fascism, which seems at this time to be directed only against blacks. But if it is allowed to plow under the blacks, then, as in other countries where fascism came to power, it will start flaking off one white minority after another until all that will be allowed to survive will be that spineless, maneuverable, gelatinous mass called by some 'the silent majority.'

"Now that phrase, 'the silent majority,' is extremely significant. The word 'silent' is the operative word. As long as any group remains content to accept in silence the repression which this Government practices, they are allowed to exist."

At that point, Carroll stood up angrily, "Your Honor, the prosecution demands to know if this is an opening in the course of a criminal trial or a political harangue!"

Even before Judge Beecher could intervene, Winkler turned. "Mr. Carroll, whether you like it or not, this *is* a political trial! And we mean to make our defense along those lines. Nor is there any legal restriction on our right to do so!" Winkler turned, glaring up at Judge Beecher.

Beecher hesitated a moment. An adverse ruling from him at this point could easily create a questionable situation, one that might lead to a dismissal and new trial. So he said, simply, "Continue, Mr. Winkler."

Carroll sank back into his seat. Winkler turned to the jury.

"The United States Attorney has brought me to the substance of my opening statement a bit faster than I had planned. Yes, ladies and gentlemen of the jury, this *is* a political trial. Exactly what is a political trial? Whenever you have a poor black man on trial for any crime in a case in which neither the judge, the prosecutor, the police, nor the penal system are attuned to the life style of the Defendant, you have a political trial! A political trial is a trial in which the charge and the evidence relate to a crime, but whose real purpose is to strangle the protest of the oppressed by locking away for years or for life those who dare raise their voices against the society."

Winkler paused to take a sip of water from the glass that was close at hand. He shuffled his notes but did not glance at them. Then he resumed.

"The Prosecution has tried to make it seem that they were being zealous in their concern for this Defendant's rights. Everything had been nicely taped and documented, so that you could actually be there at those important moments when the Defendant was warned and when witnesses identified him. At the same time, through the diligent cross-examination by my brilliant young associate, we have been able to point out, from the mouths of Mr. Carroll's own witnesses, that the threats they made against this Defendant were *not* recorded. That the hatred, the anger that cloud these events and identifications were *not* on those tapes.

"Was that really accidental, or was it planned? I ask you to look around you, to believe only what your own eyes tell you. Look at the shatterproof glass shield that cuts us off from the rest of this courtroom. Look at the very few rows of seats left for spectators, at the large number of uniformed guards present. Consider the individual search made every day on every person who enters this courtroom. Look at the barricades outside this courtroom. Why? Is this Adolph Eich-

268

mann we are trying here? A man who has murdered millions? No. Then ask yourselves this: Are we getting ready for a police state? Or is it already here?"

Rising, Carroll called out, "Defense Counsel knows full well the reasons these precautions are made necessary!" But he refrained from ascribing them to Winkler's political allies, for to do so in the presence of the jury might be judged grounds for an immediate mistrial or constitute reversible error on appeal.

Fearful of the same dangers, Judge Beecher silenced him. "Mr. Carroll! Please!" Then he turned to Winkler. "Matters better left to summation should not be the subject of an opening statement."

Winkler continued. "Ladies and gentlemen of the jury, the process of shutting up those who would speak the truth is evidently not limited to defendants. However, I shall do my best within the limitations imposed on me."

Even though he was faced away from Beecher, Winkler could feel the judge's glare.

"We shall prove a number of things during our defense. We shall prove that this Defendant was treated from the very first instant as what he is, a political prisoner of enormous importance. That the police systematically denied him his Constitutional rights and kept him away from the news media because they did not want the people of this nation exposed to his ideas.

"We shall also prove that despite police-state tactics, his ideas have been made public in the form of this booklet."

Whereupon Winkler produced from his pocket the little soft-cover book, entitled *Soul Aflame!*

Carroll was up from his chair again. "Unless Counsel intends to introduce that into evidence in the proper way I ask the Court to exclude it!"

Beecher leaned forward. "Mr. Winkler, *do* you intend to introduce it into evidence?"

269

"I do, sir, at the proper time."

"Proceed," Beecher said, some reluctance evident in his tone.

Winkler turned back to the jurors. "Ladies and gentlemen, this is a small book, but evidently highly significant, so significant that the United States Attorney is quite anxious to censor it and its contents."

"Object!"

"Mr. Winkler, let's not attribute evil motives to the United States Attorney. His objection was quite proper," the judge cautioned.

Winkler nodded, an appropriate expression of respect and regret on his face. But inwardly Winkler triumphed. The more Carroll objected to the book and the more frequently the judge remonstrated with him over his methods, the more convinced the jury and the press would be that his freedom of speech was actually in jeopardy.

"In the presentation of our case we shall prove that we are dealing here with a situation that virtually defies description. An Alice-in-Wonderland kind of judicial proceeding in which the victim is being tried. Yes, the state, the Establishment was the perpetrator of the crime! This Defendant was its victim! And we shall introduce witnesses, men of high reputation and standing in the community and the nation to prove that!"

Early on, Winkler had decided to avoid specifics in his opening. Vague as it was, the statement had presented their defense without betraying it.

Breathing a deep sigh, as if his opening statement had exhausted him, Winkler started back toward the counsel table. At that moment, Midgely Grove rose from his chair, thrust his closed fist upward and cried out, "Power to the people!" Then he turned toward the glass shield that separated him from the press and repeated the gesture, crying out more loudly, "Power to the people!" A few spectators answered, echoing his words and calling out some vulgarities as well.

270

Taken by complete surprise, Scott did not react until Grove's second outburst, and then he seized him by his leather jacket and pulled him down into his chair. Beecher was already gaveling the court to order but without much success. The press section in particular was still in turmoil. "Unless order is restored at once, it will be necessary to clear this courtroom! Even of members of the press!" Judge Beecher declared.

The excitement ebbed rapidly. Beecher conferred with the clerk, pointing out two black spectators who had shouted obscenities. Accompanied by the court attendants, the clerk approached the men. Amid violent scuffling and an exchange of angry words, mainly about white pigs, the two men were ejected from the room.

Beecher addressed the spectators: "The right of the public to witness a trial is dependent on the exercise of proper conduct. Those who came to express their political opinions are no longer spectators but participants. And there is no Constitutional right to participate in this trial except by those engaged in the prosecution and the defense. Anyone else seeking to do so will be dealt with summarily. Is that understood?"

Beecher glared down at the defense table. "Mr. Winkler, you will caution your client that if there are any further outbursts, he will be removed from the courtroom." Before Winkler could object, Beecher continued, "Proper provisions have been made so that he may witness the progress of this trial on closed-circuit television. This Court will brook no further outbursts!"

Winkler rose. "Your Honor, my client's outburst was totally unexpected. However, when a man feels that he stands to be deprived of his freedom forever because of his beliefs, strong emotions are to be expected."

"Mr. Winkler, are you ready to proceed with your first witness?" Beecher asked abruptly.

"We are, Your Honor."

But outside the courtroom a stir caused by supporters of the two ejected spectators grew louder, until it threatened to interrupt the proceedings again. Judge Beecher declared a brief recess until calm could be restored.

As the courtroom emptied out, Grove leaned across Scott to whisper to Winkler, "Did I do good, Linc?"

"Fine," Winkler said. "Fine, Midge."

Apparently Grove's outbreak had been specifically orchestrated by Linc for this moment. Scott glanced at Linc, who was ostensibly scanning his notes, a tactic clearly designed to avoid a confrontation. And when he turned from Winkler, Scott found Marlene staring at him.

During the recess, Honey Rosenstone arrived in the courtroom. Winkler met her halfway up the aisle and prevailed on his friends in the press section to make room for her in the first row. The reporters were quite willing to oblige Winkler, for they knew that the presence of a close friend guaranteed that exciting news was about to break.

Their anticipation grew more intense when Fred Anthony arrived. He always seemed to be privy to Winkler's strategy and only appeared on those days when a particularly dramatic move was planned.

Adding to the intrigue was the fact that Winkler's first witness was someone completely unknown to the press. The man sat just inside the railing, a mature person of fairly undistinguished appearance, with whom Winkler had exchanged only very brief, whispered conversation.

Like the intuitive actor he was, Winkler not only sensed the excitement building in his audience, he reveled in it. There was one possible danger, but Winkler had to admit to himself that it added the perfect gambler's thrill of uncertainty to the situation, and only excited him more. It could happen, yes, there did exist the technical legal possibility that Beecher would rule out their entire defense. Once Grove had been certified as sane, Beecher might feel justified in holding that Grove's history, physical and mental, was immaterial

272

and did not constitute a legal defense to the crime of murder.

But this was the kind of risk a lawyer took when he proposed a new and revolutionary theory of law. Winkler knew the trick was to get his entire premise in before risking such a ruling by Beecher. And he thought he had a good chance.

To allay any immediate adverse ruling, Scott had drafted an intensive memorandum of law to support their argument that Grove's medical history was an essential part of the defendant's case. The memorandum relied heavily on the theory that since motive and intent were part of proving any crime, it was necessary to probe the psychological motives and the intentions of the accused. To do so, his medical history, being so intertwined with his mental history, was relevant—in fact, imperative. All together, it spelled out the Doctrine of Social Inevitability.

Since the memorandum probed new and unexplored areas of the law, there were painfully few cases Scott could cite with any pertinence. So he depended for support to a great degree on sociological and philosophical articles and speeches that had appeared during the weeks since Fred Anthony's first column in the Sunday *Times.* On the whole, Scott's argument was tenable, if somewhat tenuous.

Linc Winkler rose to call his first witness. He knew that even before he could complete the name of Dr. Otto Langer, Carroll would be on his feet to object. So instead of using Langer's professional title, Winkler merely announced, "I call to the stand Otto Langer."

The man whom the reporters had already dubbed a "mystery witness" started toward the raised witness box, creating great speculation in the press section, except with Fred Anthony, who remained calm.

Langer placed his hand on the Bible, took the oath, and was seated, ready for Winkler's first question.

"Could you tell us, sir, your profession?"

"I am a physician. An internist and specialist in forensic medicine," Langer replied.

Before he had completed his answer, Carroll was crying out his objection, almost obliterating Langer's response.

"Your Honor, before this doctor, or any doctor, is permitted to testify, we wish to point out that the defense of insanity has been waived. If it is to be reintroduced now, the Government is entitled to prior notice. If, on the other hand, this testimony is being introduced as to the Defendant's physical condition, it has no bearing either on the crime charged or the Defendant's ability to stand trial. Hence it is immaterial and inadmissible!"

Beecher looked at Winkler, offering him a chance to reply.

"Your Honor, there is no attempt here to plead insanity on behalf of this Defendant, so no prior notice to the Prosecution was necessary. As for the Prosecutor's argument that the physical condition of the Defendant has no bearing on this case, I say that we will eventually establish that connection to the complete satisfaction of the Court. But to do so we must first introduce our expert testimony. If in the end we fail to make such connection, of course, the Court in its discretion can and should rule out all such testimony. But . . ."

Winkler paused here for emphasis and, more specifically, to influence Beecher. "But I suggest, and very strongly, that it might constitute reversible error if this entire line of testimony were ruled out without the Court having the remotest idea what that testimony consists of."

There was just enough substance in Winkler's bluff to force Beecher to consider it seriously; and to give it further weight, Winkler turned to Scott, who was ready with the Memorandum of Law. Even from the bench, Beecher was impressed by its sheer size.

"Your Honor, I would like to submit this memorandum for your consideration. At the same time, since Dr. Langer is a busy man and is already here, as are several other physicians, I ask leave to continue with the witness until a determination on the motion is made in the future."

274

"I demand to see a copy of that memorandum!" Carroll called out.

"By all means!" Winkler said. Scott was ready with not one but two copies for Carroll.

Winkler glanced up at Beecher for a ruling. Finally Beecher conceded, "The defense may continue, subject to a ruling by this Court tomorrow morning on this entire line of testimony."

With a limited number of hours now available to him, Winkler was determined to get as much as possible of the doctors' testimony before the jury. He had a deep, instinctive hunch that once that was done and once the press had their chance at it, Beecher would realize that he could no longer rule out their defense without seeming to be highly prejudiced. So with speed as his top priority, Winkler asked his questions simply, and in a manner that would encounter the fewest time-consuming objections from the Prosecutor.

Winkler used Langer to establish the fact that he had assembled a team of reputable and capable specialists in order to prepare a comprehensive case history of Midgely Grove from his birth onward.

Winkler then introduced Dr. Barsky, the pediatrician. With the aid of a view box, X-rays and a darkened courtroom, Barsky traced for the jury the tortured early life of Midge Grove, pointing up the growth arrest lines that resulted from his insufficient diet, the healed fractures, and other evidences of severe physical punishment at an early age and the skull fracture incurred at the same time.

Barsky's own personal indignation grew with each shocking revelation, so that he proved to be a highly effective witness, although he had a greater impact on the press than on the jury. The only unexpected moments in Barsky's testimony came when Winkler led him from the physical to the mental traumas inflicted on Midge as a child.

At once Carroll was half out of his chair calling, "Objec-

275

tion! The good doctor has not been qualified as an expert in the field of mental trauma!"

Winkler turned to Barsky. "Doctor, in the field of pediatrics is there an attempt to separate the physical from the mental difficulties of infants?"

"It would be virtually impossible to do so, Mr. Winkler."

"Can you tell us why?"

"Because the physical and the mental so impinge one upon the other that sometimes the physical leads to mental problems and sometimes the mental leads to physical problems. We even find that the mental condition of the mother can have prenatal and postnatal effects on the child. Unlike Solomon, we do not divide the child. We treat the entire infant."

"Since we have satisfied the United States Attorney on this matter," Winkler said, "may we proceed with the effects of the vicious brutality the Defendant suffered in his early life . . ."

Again Carroll was on his feet. "Counsel is leading the witness. 'Vicious brutality' is Counsel's phrase, not the witness's."

Winkler could barely keep from smiling, for Carroll had gone for the bait, as he had hoped he would. "Dr. Barsky, the phrase 'vicious brutality'—have you heard it before?"

"Not only heard it, I used it."

"Under what circumstances, may I ask?"

"In my meeting with you only last evening when I told you what I was prepared to testify to."

"Will you enlighten the jury as to exactly how you came to use that phrase in our conversation?"

"I'll be glad to," Barsky said. "I had shown Mr. Winkler a copy of the death certificate of another child . . ."

"Object!" Carroll called out. "Certificates of birth or death relating to other children are immaterial to this case!"

"Sustained!" Beecher ruled swiftly.

Winkler turned to him. "Your Honor, if we can prove that

276

this particular certificate *does* have a bearing on this Defendant, will the question be allowed?"

"Only if it has a direct bearing on this Defendant!" Beecher ruled, feeling he had disposed of the matter.

"Doctor, whose death certificate were you referring to?"

"The death certificate of a girl aged three and a half, named Vanessa Grove, sister of the Defendant," Barsky said.

At the sound of that name, Midge Grove leaped up from his chair. "NO!" he cried out as Scott seized him by the leather jacket to pull him down. But Midge struggled and flailed about so violently that both marshals interceded, forcing him to his seat. Midge continued to mumble, "No, no, no, no, no," until eventually his words were lost in his sobbing.

Winkler persisted with Barsky, asking more swiftly now, "Doctor, how did that girl die, according to her death certificate?"

"Through an accident."

"Details?"

"There were none. The certificate read 'accidental fall.' "

"Doctor, based on your experience with childhood accidents and beaten, abused children, is it unusual in a family in which one child shows evidence of having been maltreated, such as Midgely Grove, for there to be another child in that same family who suffers from the same kind of maltreatment, even resulting in death?

"On the contrary. Where you have one battered child you generally have others. Unfortunately, death is not a rare consequence."

"Doctor, how did you happen to discover this death certificate?

"I tracked it down. I had talked with the Defendant and heard him refer to a sister, but he could give me no details about her."

"Do you know why he could give you no details?"

277

"It is not uncommon for a child, frightened, terrified for his life to blot out an entire episode. And to find himself unable to talk about or even complain about it."

"Even the death of an only sister?"

"Especially the death of an only sister."

Winkler hesitated, as if in doubt about his next question. His silence permitted the sobs of Midge Grove to be heard in the darkened courtroom. They added to the sympathy for Grove that he could feel building. Eventually Winkler asked, "Doctor, you used an expression last night I would like to discuss. I believe you said, 'Every human being is a composite, a human computer card with his life history punched out.'"

"Yes, I did make that statement last evening."

"This Defendant, based on what you've seen in his X-rays, in examining his body, and on what you've learned about his emotional traumas, fears and terrors, would you say he is such a human computer card?"

"I would, indeed," Barsky said.

"Thank you, Doctor," Winkler said. "You may turn the lights up, if you wish," he called to the court clerk.

The lights went on to reveal Marlene administering to Midge Grove, wiping his eyes and replacing his dark glasses.

Realizing the effectiveness of Winkler's performance, Carroll knew that his cross-examination would have to be brief and to the point. Barsky was too emotionally committed to be easily dislodged from his testimony, so Carroll chose to limit his questions to those that could be answered simply.

"Tell me, Doctor, in your intensive study of this Defendant's physical and mental condition, did you discover anything that indicated that the late Justice Harvey Miller had in any way caused or contributed to the evils he endured?"

"No, of course not," Barsky said.

"Do you see any causal connection, then, between the maltreatment to which Defendant was subjected and the late Justice Miller?"

278

"No causal connection, no."

"Tell me this, Doctor, in your mind is an early life of deprivation a justification for murdering someone not even remotely connected with such deprivation?"

"I'm sorry, sir, I can't answer that."

"Surely you must have an opinion on it, a layman's opinion," Carroll persisted.

"I must confess that I don't know any justification for murder."

"Thank you, Doctor," Carroll said.

Winkler's next witness was Dr. Claire, who testified to Grove's traumatically punctured left eardrum, his vestigial deafness in that ear, and to the healed fracture of Grove's nose.

Two more physicians testified to damage inflicted on Grove by unknown abusers in his early childhood. Carp, the endocrinologist, testified to Grove's stunted sexuality.

Carroll's cross-examination never varied. He made no attempt to attack the doctors' testimony, only its relevance to the issue of murder. But the atmosphere in the courtroom had grown heavy with a sense of public guilt and pity.

The last medical expert Winkler summoned to the stand was Dr. Lionel Catchings. Linc knew that this dignified, white-haired man would achieve the perfect climax to this phase of the case, especially if he displayed the same degree of outrage he had exhibited in the initial briefing.

Catchings offered evidence of the traumatic cataracts he had discovered in Midge Grove, described how they affected his vision and what efforts had been made to correct the condition.

"Was there surgery in the case of the Defendant, Midgely Grove?" Winkler asked.

"It was attempted. But not very successfully," Catchings explained.

"What would explain that, in your opinion?"

"Lack of proper skill. Lack of experience. For example, if,

279

due to poverty, the patient was thrown on the mercies of a hospital free clinic and was used as a practice ground for some aspiring young surgeon, such a man might not have the skill required to carry out the operation successfully," Catchings explained.

"Do you, in fact, know if the operation carried out on this Defendant was done in such a free clinic?"

"So he told me."

"Doctor, from your experience in dealing with children with defective eyesight, will it affect them in areas other than merely their ability to see?"

"Of course. In fact most children are brought to us *because* of these other difficulties."

"Such as?"

"For example, a child with defective vision will not do well in school, and when investigating why, eventually they may discover it is his eyesight. Then he will be brought to us. Or a child who seems fairly well coordinated will do poorly in athletics. He will begin to suffer emotionally, perhaps in his overall adjustment to his peers, and we will discover his problem is due to his eyes. After all, there are no Willie Mays or Hank Aarons with bad eyesight."

"So that bad eyesight, if left uncorrected, or if unsuccessfully treated, can affect a child in all phases of his youthful development?"

"It can indeed. And it is most regrettable in such a case as this."

"Object!" Carroll half-rose to call out.

But Beecher had become quite intrigued with Catchings' testimony and he overruled the objection. Then leaning a bit closer to Catchings, he asked, "Doctor, precisely what did you mean by calling it most regrettable in *this* case?"

"Here was a case where repair could easily have been achieved. Yet due to the failure of our profession, it was not. In my opinion, regardless of the intention of the surgeon or the clinic, this is tantamount to criminal negligence."

As Beecher nodded his head sadly, Winkler took the moment to ask, "Doctor, I assume your feeling is even stronger when a child has been born with perfect vision which is later impaired by a blow or a number of blows to the head?"

"Whoever diminishes or destroys the human body, his own or anyone else's, is a criminal in my view!"

"It would follow, therefore, that whoever's body is diminished is, in your opinion, the victim of a crime?"

"Object!" Carroll called out, already displeased with the judge's lenience during Catchings' testimony. "The good doctor has been eminently qualified as an expert on the human eye, but not in the fields of law or philosophy. Therefore when he states his opinion as to matters philosophical or legal he has overstepped the bounds of his expertise."

Beecher hesitated, then finally ruled, "Strike the last question. The jury will disregard it."

Since the jury already had heard precisely what Winkler had wanted them to hear, he made no protest but gracefully terminated his examination of Catchings. "Doctor, we thank you for taking time out of your busy schedule to share your expertise and your findings with us." Then nodding respectfully to Catchings, Winkler returned to the defense table.

Carroll's cross-examination consisted of the same questions that he had asked of Barsky and the other doctors. Did Catchings discover any connection between Grove's eye condition and Justice Miller? Was Miller in any way involved in those eye injuries? Did Catchings think there was any ground that justified murder? The old man answered no to all of them.

Then Carroll paused a moment to make sure that he had the complete attention of the entire courtroom.

"Doctor, if it were possible to discover who had performed that unsuccessful operation on Grove's eyes, would you say that the Defendant would be justified in tracking down that surgeon and murdering him?"

"Object!" Winkler called out.

But Beecher said, "I think after the latitude the doctor has been allowed in his testimony, it would be interesting to hear his answer."

"No, I do not think he would be justified in committing murder," Catchings answered.

"Thank you, Doctor." And Carroll started back to his table.

XXII

Dr. Paul Randolph had just taken the stand. There had been a brief recess and now Winkler was anxious to get Randolph's testimony into the record before the end of the day. For, impressed as Judge Beecher seemed to be by Winkler's medical experts, he might still rule out the entire line of testimony. Certainly Carroll's last question and Catchings' answer would influence Beecher.

So Winkler knew he had to catapult Randolph into the guts of his testimony as expeditiously as possible. Once he had qualified the handsome black man as an expert, Winkler asked, "Dr. Randolph, are you familiar with the findings of Doctors Langer, Barsky, Carp, Catchings, and Claire?"

Neatly dressed in a light-gray flannel suit, Randolph fingered the heavy-framed glasses that highlighted his lean, muscular face, then spoke softly in a strong, resonant voice. "I have been in consultation with those doctors together and singly over the past weeks."

"Is it true that you had treated the accused previously?"

"Yes."

"Can you tell us the circumstances, Doctor?"

"Yes, more than a year ago, sixteen months to be exact, the patient came to see me at St. Elizabeth's Hospital."

"What did he complain of at that time?"

"General psychogenic symptoms," Randolph replied. "He

was so deeply disturbed that he could not recognize and articulate his real underlying difficulties."

"How did you go about relieving that condition?" Winkler asked.

"I used sodium amytal interviews."

"Would you explain that for the benefit of the jury, sir?" Winkler asked with great deference, conscious of the impression Randolph would make on the black members of the jury. Winkler had already sensed that they were open to Randolph, proud of him, a black man of obvious distinction. They respected his expert status, his educated manner of speaking.

Randolph shifted in his chair to establish direct contact with the jurors. "Whenever a patient is so deeply troubled that he cannot bring himself to talk about it, we resort to an injection of sodium amytal. This is a drug which relaxes the patient to a semiconscious state. His inhibitions subside and he is able to speak much more freely about himself. You might call it a truth serum.

"It was under sodium amytal," Randolph continued, "that the Defendant was finally able to tell me about his time in the reformatory and about the things that were done to him there."

Winkler knew well exactly what would happen behind his back the instant he uttered his next question, but he proceeded nevertheless. "Specifically what things?"

Midge Grove leaped from his chair. "No. No! You keep your mouth shut! No! No!!" he shouted.

When Scott and Marlene's efforts to calm Grove failed, both United States Marshals seized him, pulled him back, forced him down into his chair.

"Counselor, do you wish a recess at this time?" Beecher asked Winkler.

Fearing that a recess might also lead to an early adjournment, Winkler turned to Beecher. "Your Honor, painful as this line of questioning may be to the Defendant, it is vital to his defense. For his sake, I wish to continue."

Since Grove's protest had subsided into low, hostile, indistinguishable muttering, Beecher permitted Winkler to continue.

"Doctor, exactly what were you referring to when you said, 'the things that were done to him there'?"

"What happened to the accused was, unfortunately, not unusual for youngsters who are forced into our destructive correctional system. Being younger, weaker, less experienced, he was chosen as an object of the homosexual lust of older, tougher inmates."

"Were you able to discover if he engaged in such activities willingly?"

"He resisted as effectively as he could. Unfortunately, he was overcome and was made the victim of a gang rape after he had been there only two days."

"And his reaction?"

"What his reactive pattern has been all his life. He withdrew within himself, became compliant, submissive, almost a nonperson."

"Were you able to trace the genesis of this type of behavior in the accused?" Winkler asked.

Randolph seemed suddenly to become angry and resentful. "Frankly, Mr. Winkler, it would be easier for me to answer your questions if you called him 'the patient' instead of 'the accused.'"

"I'm sure the Court would have no objection to that," Winkler said, turning to Beecher.

"Whatever phraseology gets us to the heart of the doctor's testimony is quite satisfactory to the Court," Beecher ruled dryly.

Winkler turned to the court stenographer. "Would you be good enough to read my question to the doctor?"

The stenographer flipped back a fold in his stenotype tape.

"Were you able to trace the genesis of this type of behavior in the accused?"

Winkler said quickly, "Let us change that to 'the patient.' Now, Doctor?"

"The root of this patient's difficulty lies in the early formative period of his life, between the first month and the fourth year. It has been proven that some children who are not shown normal maternal affection, such as nursing, fondling, kissing, and being held tightly by another human being, grow up deprived in a way which they never overcome. They never achieve security or the ability to love or respond to love. This phenomenon has been observed and reported on by Dr. Spitz in this country, Dr. Bowlby in England, and others.

"In view of the testimony of the eminent specialists who preceded me on the stand, we must assume that from birth this patient was thus deprived. In addition, even under the sodium amytal the patient could not recall any father, any male figure. Hence, we must assume that he was illegitimate and unwanted. He was, from the moment of his birth, a threat, a danger, a nuisance. And he must have been treated that way."

Carroll rose to interrupt. "Your Honor, we must insist that this entire line of testimony is completely immaterial to the issue in this case."

Beecher turned to Winkler. "Mr. Winkler?"

"Your Honor, we contend that Dr. Randolph's testimony and the testimony of all the worthy doctors who have appeared on the stand thus far is extremely relevant and vital to the Defense in this case. And we will make that connection quite clear before Dr. Randolph leaves the stand."

"You may continue, Mr. Winkler, with full knowledge that the Court may yet rule out all this testimony."

"We understand that, Your Honor," Winkler said. If he needed proof that he was beginning to succeed he had it now. Winkler was quite sure in his mind that Carroll would not have objected if he hadn't detected a subtle but definite change in the attitude in the courtroom. He turned back to Randolph.

"Doctor, from the point where you were testifying about the miserable and deprived conditions of the Defendant's . . . I mean, the patient's early life."

"Having studied his case history more intensively than anyone else has, I believe that this patient suffered severe deprivation even while under the care of his own mother. After such a deprived infancy, including the evidence of malnutrition which is clear in the patient's X-rays, the crime was compounded by the situation in the household. I must confess that Dr. Barsky's discovery came as a great surprise to me. I had suspected that there was some secret so deep-rooted that even under sodium amytal the patient could not bring it up. Some horrible trauma had made him into a nonperson.

"Dr. Barsky's discovery of his sister's tragic death certificate supplied the answer. The entire episode, horrible as it was, had to be blotted out by this patient if he was to survive even as a nonperson. Since that discovery, I had occasion to see the patient again, and he is still not able to recall that episode fully. All he could ever tell me is that there was a man who used a stick of some kind on his sister Vanessa, while he ran and hid in the other room. He could hear the blows and Vanessa's crying, but he remembers no more than that."

"Doctor, in your long and extensive experience with patients who have undergone terrible traumas, is it unusual for the patient to forget, or try to forget?"

"Laymen expect that the worse the trauma the more it would be remembered. But we doctors find that the reverse is true. As observers of such traumatic experiences, we do not suffer guilt, but the patient does. For example, even though he could not have been more than three or three and a half at the time, this patient felt enormous guilt. He felt he should have defended his sister. Or perhaps he should have been killed along with her, rather than let her die alone while he

287

hid. So we have here great danger, compounded by great guilt. There was one other thing. Despite the danger and the guilt, despite the horror of hearing his own sister beaten to death, there was the undeniable fact that if you hid, if you were quiet, you stayed alive! Yes, you survived! That is an important discovery to make when you are three years old. And you never forget it!"

Randolph turned to look sympathetically at Midge Grove. "This episode shaped the patient's entire life. In the wretched rat-infested, roach-infested home in which he lived, in the vile streets frequented by thieves, junkies, and perverts of all kinds, the patient moved as if he were not part of this world. No friends, no attachment to any girl, no family, nothing. By not being part of life he managed to stay alive. However, there is a price one pays for such an existence.

"After a time, as a juvenile, he fell into trouble with the law. Perhaps it was the only way he knew to finally make the world take notice of him. It is my own personal conviction that most blacks who commit crimes do so not for gain but to make the white world recognize their existence."

Once Randolph had inserted that bit of personal ideology into the record, Winkler cautioned, "Doctor, only what applies to the case at hand, if you will."

"Yes, the patient," Randolph seemed to be reminding himself. "The next most decisive event in his life was the unfortunate term he served in the correctional institution. The crime itself was minor. He stole something of very little value, a cheap tin toy called a Black Sambo, from a five-and-dime store.

"You wound it up and it danced on its tin platform. If you will recall, the toy's face was painted jet black, and it wore a checked black and yellow suit, had long legs and jigged and turned like a trained animal. It was a highly revealing toy for a black boy to steal. The most significant thing about the whole event was that the patient was caught, for he admitted to me that he might have escaped if he had run faster.

"Obviously, he wanted to be caught. He wanted to be put into a reformatory. Why? Perhaps to do penance for his perpetual guilt over letting Vanessa die. Perhaps to be noticed by the white world.

"Now in the reformatory, a white institution, run by white men in order to incarcerate black boys—I am giving you this from the patient's point of view—of course there were some white boys there, but they were the minority, and they were segregated. So that what the patient was confronted with was a black world, ruled by whites, in which the blacks were the criminals and the whites were the law, the authority. And then, of course . . ."

Here, Randolph paused. "What I must say now would be better said without the patient present."

Judge Beecher sat erect in his high-backed swivel chair. "Doctor, in a court of law, it is the judge who determines when, or if, it is desirable to exclude either spectators or participants in a trial." Then Beecher fell silent.

Finally, he ruled, "The spectators will be cleared from the courtroom. The press will be allowed to remain. However, the Court strongly urges the exercise of extreme care and discretion in relation to the material about to be divulged. As for the Defendant, if his counsel wishes to remove him, and if the Defendant agrees, the Court will so rule."

Winkler moved to the defense table, leaned close to Midge. Scott joined them. Winkler spoke softly in a way that reminded Scott of a priest in a confessional.

"Midge . . . I think it would be better if you waited outside. I tried to avoid this coming out, but it has to. If we want to save you."

"You promised . . ." Midge said, his lips quivering, his whole body beginning to tremble. "You promised . . . that day, you promised . . ."

This was the first Scott learned of any promise to Midge restricting a witness's testimony. It was another of Winkler's unrevealed strategies which only came to light in moments when Scott was powerless to affect them. He stared hard at Winkler, but Winkler evaded his questioning stare, concentrating instead on Grove.

"I did the best I could, Midge. Now, I want you to agree to go outside and wait."

Grove refused to answer, except to mumble again, "You promised . . ."

"Shall I tell the judge you want to go outside?"

Grove sat perfectly still, then quite unexpectedly, he shook his head. No. He wished to remain. It was the first time that Scott had seen Midge Grove assert himself about anything. Winkler was not only surprised, he became suddenly apprehensive. But he was forced to rise and face the judge.

"Your Honor, the Defendant elects to remain."

Even Randolph appeared visibly startled by that. Winkler had the court stenographer refresh Randolph on the point at which his testimony had been interrupted.

"Oh, yes," Randolph said warily, as if he would rather not go on. "And then, of course . . . there was the quite terrible episode in the first few days of his incarceration in that terrible place, when he was gang-raped by older, bigger, black boys."

"The episode you referred to before, Doctor?"

"It went a good deal deeper than that, I'm afraid. The victim always feels a sense of guilt that in some way he exposed himself to the crime or actually invited it. In this case the fear was even stronger. Since the patient has a history of noninvolvement with members of the opposite sex, he might have considered himself a homosexual. Not that he was, but because he did not know otherwise.

"You see, here we must go back again to the little sister, the dead Vanessa. We do not know why she was beaten to death. Was it perhaps that she had been caught in some kind of infantile sex play with the patient? We shall never know. But if the patient *thought* that was the reason, then we can understand his guilt. And also that he might come to believe that he must never touch a person of the opposite sex with any sexual intent. It is not surprising that eventually he began to fear that he might be homosexual. The assault in the reformatory confirmed it in his mind. Though I can say that this patient is not, nor was he ever, truly a homosexual."

Randolph paused and then said suddenly, "There was within a matter of several days another episode, even more horrifying to this patient."

At that moment, Scott felt Grove begin to tremble at his side. He reached out to grip Grove's arm and support him, but found his hand instead. It was damp and cold. The fingers were agitated in nervous, uncontrolled activity.

Meantime, Winkler was urging Randolph, "Please, Doctor, continue. This horrifying episode . . ."

"It may have been due to the fact that the patient was still in great pain from the original rape. But whatever the reason, his attackers decided on a different form of homosexual activity.

"I would like to say at the outset that the patient resisted this most vehemently. In fact, it was not until the fourth session under sodium amytal that he found it possible to talk about it. After the rape his tormentors decided to use this patient as a sex object, by forcing him to perform fellatio on them.

"He was held with his arms pinned painfully behind his back by two of the bigger boys. Then he was forced to his knees before the leader of the gang. His arms were jacked up more and more until the pain became unbearable. If at that point he had refused to join in the activity it was his belief, and mine, that his arms would have been broken or his shoulders dislocated."

"And what were the guards doing all this time, if you know?"

"According to the patient . . ."

"Object!" Carroll called out. "The patient is here and can testify to that himself!"

But Beecher suspected that Grove would never take the stand, "We will allow the answer. Doctor?"

"The guards were aware of it, but they did absolutely nothing to protect him. As long as the aggressive gangs made no trouble for them, the guards were not concerned with the fate of black inmates," Randolph said. "In fact, it is my professional opinion that they received some form of vicarious sexual enjoyment out of it."

"Now, Doctor," Winkler continued, "How did these various acts affect the Defendant . . . I mean, the patient?"

"He adjusted to them as he did to all the other horrors and deprivations of life in this grossly repressive society—by acquiescence. He did what was forced upon him while at the same time pretending not to exist."

"For fear that to assert himself was to court death?" Winkler asked.

"Exactly!" Randolph said. "Because at the very time that he faced an inability to speak out or protest on his own behalf, there were a number of ways that fine, young, black people were expressing themselves. In protest marches, sit-ins, and in the Panther movement, which many people disapprove of, but which may be the finest expression of young black manhood that we have in our time . . ."

"Object!" Carroll called out. "We are not here to elicit the political opinions of Dr. Randolph!"

"Your Honor!" Winkler interrupted, for he was reaching the heart of his case now.

"Mr. Carroll raises a very valid point," Judge Beecher declared.

"What Mr. Carroll calls a political opinion goes directly to the heart of this case. The Prosecution has deliberately refrained from introducing any evidence as to the motive or intent of the accused. Why? So the jury will not be able to fairly judge his guilt or innocence? Well, the Defense aims to supply that motive. We contend that the accused acted out of frustration—political frustration caused by a lifetime of dep-

292

rivation. Hence it is unavoidable that some of the testimony dealing with his motives will be of a political nature."

Beecher looked to Carroll, who answered, "If motive or intent are of any value in this case, they should be introduced in determining sentence."

Winkler shot back, "If the Prosecutor concedes that length of sentence is related to the degree of guilt, then he must also concede that determination of guilt in the first instance must be based on those same factors."

Turning slightly so that his words were addressed at least in part to the press, Winkler continued, "Society's willingness to 'forgive,' cannot be a yardstick to be used only after a conviction but before."

"Counsel introduces a totally new concept," Carroll objected.

"We are living in a time of new concepts, Mr. Carroll, when the nation and the laws it embraces must measure up to the guarantees in the Constitution or stand revealed to the world as total hypocrisy!"

Beecher sat back in his chair, pondering what Winkler had just said, for it was indeed a new and revolutionary theory of law on which the Defense was proceeding. But a ruling was demanded. Finally, the judge leaned forward to ask, "Does Counsel's brief submitted this morning support his ingenious theory of law?"

"It does!" Winkler declared.

"Then the Court will rule on it before this case goes to the jury. In the meantime, subject to a final ruling, the Defense will be allowed to continue."

"Thank you, Your Honor," Winkler said, relief evident in his voice. He had free rein now for as long as he needed, and a good chance to get the major portion of his case into the record before Beecher ruled.

Winkler turned back to the counsel table as if to find some further notes, but his primary intention was to make eye contact with Fred Anthony. He had promised *The New York*

Times columnist that he would let him know when he was about to begin the presentation of the real issue, one that might well take him to the Supreme Court.

"Dr. Randolph, would you continue, please?"

"I was explaining that the remarkable thing about this patient was that in a time when many black young people were fighting for education and equality of opportunity, when a movement like the Black Panthers was becoming active and effective, he could not take part. The reason for this quite obviously was the strategy of murder that the local police, the Federal Government and the FBI have adopted to deal with militant blacks. We already know about the many Panthers who have been killed in their own beds, murdered by white police officers in the name of law and order.

"Knowing what we know of this patient's background, and with newspapers and television daily confirming his fear that anyone who protested would die, he was completely frustrated, paralyzed, unable to live with injustice and unable to do anything about it. The wonder is that he was able to retain his sanity at all."

Randolph pulled out a white pocket handkerchief and mopped his ebony brow, now glistening with sweat.

"Doctor, are you saying that this patient despaired of ever having his wrongs righted by the society around him?"

"I am saying that he began to realize that his entire life was a crime perpetrated on him by a society that forced him to endure a terrifying early childhood, that deprived him of an education, that forced him into his first crime, sentenced him to a reformatory, and permitted those horrible homosexual acts to be committed against him. Every wrong that this patient has experienced was instigated, permitted or carried out by the society around him, even while it spoke of law and order. In a society that is mad, eventually sane men must question their own sanity. I think that is what happened to this patient, and that is why he came to see me."

294

"Did you think it was possible to cure him when you first undertook his treatment?" Winkler asked.

"Cure is an absolute word. I would prefer to say help. I hoped that I could help him. Because I feared that if I did not then the consequences might be terrible," Randolph said.

"What led you to that conclusion, Doctor?"

"Once I had assembled his history, I realized that the entire life experience of this patient was such that he had to express his justified hostility or else he would resort to suicide. Or even to murder."

"Doctor, if I may refer to the testimony of Dr. Barsky, he used an expression which went something like, 'Every human being is a composite of all the events that have happened to him during his lifetime. He is a human computer card with his life history punched out.' Would you agree with that?"

"I could not have said it better myself. That was exactly what led me to have such fears in relation to this patient. Just as he was a human computer card with his past punched out clearly, so he was, by virtue of those same experiences, programed to do what the Prosecution claims he eventually did do."

"Can you explain that more precisely, Doctor?"

"Based on what the society had done to him, it was inevitable that he would react as he did. It is what we might call, to borrow a term of enormous relevance to our times, the Doctrine of Social Inevitability in action."

Winkler found a pretext to turn slightly to exchange glances with Anthony, then he asked, "Doctor, would you explain that rather formal term in laymen's language?"

"I'll try. The wrongs that the society commits against any group of individuals set in motion a series of feelings, anxieties, hatreds, justified dissent that make it inevitable that certain crimes will result. In other words, the crimes of the society inevitably evoke crimes from the repressed and enslaved. And the repressed and enslaved have no choice in the

295

matter. Just as when you pull a trigger it will fire a bullet. You don't blame the bullet, it is the inevitable result of the action. What the patient is accused of doing was not an action, only a reaction. If there were true justice in this oppressive society of ours, society would be sitting at that defense table and the so-called Defendant would be sitting at the other table acting as Prosecutor!"

"Are you saying, sir, that the patient had no will of his own?"

"I am saying that what he did was the inevitable consequence of the society's actions against him. That is precisely what is meant by the Doctrine of Social Inevitability," Randolph declared.

At that point, Winkler left the lawyer's lectern to return to the counsel table where Scott held out to him the bulky, impressive folder containing all the clippings on the Doctrine of Social Inevitability. Having marked and arranged them in advance, Winkler now read certain paragraphs and sentences from various publications, popular and pseudoscientific. Randolph commented on each, using each to endow the Doctrine of Social Inevitability with the enormous weight of sociological and psychiatric support.

The file, which had originated from Winkler's disclosure of the theory to Fred Anthony, was serving its purpose well. For Carroll had risen to state, "If the question is, Does this doctrine have support in certain quarters, the Government will concur in that. But that is a far cry from admitting its legal validity as a defense."

It was an important admission to have wrung from Carroll, even with his reservation; and Winkler felt that he could now afford to close his examination.

"Just a few more questions, Doctor, if you will. You said that you detected a potential for violence in the patient. Yet you did nothing about it?"

"If you mean did I commit him, no. There wasn't sufficient evidence. After all, I couldn't have him committed only on a suspicion of a possibility that he might do something violent. The patient was apprehensive, but not insane."

"What *did* you do to help him?"

"I prescribed tranquilizers. I suggested games such as tennis or handball, where he could project his hostility onto an object. But because of his impaired vision he didn't take readily to sports. So I looked for other ways to provide outlets for his hostility. I knew that until he learned to speak out or act out in some modified form, he would always have this terrible conflict. Evidently, I failed. The pressures of his past were stronger than any therapeutic measures psychiatry could supply. It is regrettable, because in many respects he is a most admirable human being. It is not his fault that he was born black and deprived, that he was forced to live in silent terror. Under other circumstances, given a measure of pride, a decent chance at health and education, he might be sitting here now testifying on someone else's behalf."

"Thank you very much, Doctor," Winkler said with great respect, which he knew would appeal to the black majority on the jury.

·•❧ XXIII ❧•·

As U.S. Attorney Carroll approached the lectern to begin his cross-examination of Dr. Paul Randolph, he shared with Linc Winkler the same need to treat the black psychiatrist with great respect. Carroll knew that a sharp and slashing attack on Randolph would seem too personal and, considering the composition of the jury, too racist. So he entered upon the cross-examination with an outward air of honest, grave concern and with great deference toward the handsome black man.

"Doctor, during your rather lengthy examination I have had a chance to look over your credentials and they are extremely impressive. Certainly your record, as presented to the jury today, proves that you have achieved a remarkable degree of success in your chosen field. And to judge from the look of it, in life altogether."

"It would seem so," Randolph agreed cautiously.

Then Carroll reviewed the facts of Randolph's early deprived life in Harlem, his schooling, the scholarships he'd won to Ethical Culture School, the university and medical school, his professional appointments up to and including his position at St. Elizabeth's Mental Hospital, and his present comfortable economic and professional circumstances.

"Now, Doctor, considering the facts of your background,

298

would you say that being born poor, living in the slums, going to second-rate grade schools made *you* a human computer card, punched out to inevitably achieve success as an eminent specialist in the field of psychiatry?"

"There are other factors," Randolph said.

"Are you saying now that this Doctrine of Social Inevitability isn't always so inevitable?"

"Human beings with sufficiently strong determination can, on occasion, overcome the oppressive facts of their backgrounds. And, of course, intervening circumstances may alter the course of development of any single individual, making him an exception."

"So there are exceptions." Carroll sounded relieved to hear it, but he continued with his oblique attack. "Tell me, Doctor, if you will, in your own case in which deprivation seemed to have acted as a spur, not a deterrent, did it leave any traumatic scars?"

"Object!" Winkler interceded. "The Doctor is not on trial here. The facts of his background and his reaction to them are not relevant to the issue!"

"Mr. Carroll?" the judge challenged.

"Your Honor, since we are now treading upon somewhat innovative ground, we contend the thinking and the motivation of the innovator is germane and material."

"You may proceed, Counselor, but cautiously," Beecher ruled.

"Doctor, is it possible that the events of your early life caused some traumatic scars that you have not been able to resolve for yourself despite your success?"

Beads of sweat now visible on his brow, Randolph shifted in his chair and crossed his legs. "If you could be more specific . . ."

"Let me try," Carroll obliged in an exaggerated tone. "As I sat listening to your fascinating testimony—some of it quite horrible, I agree—I kept asking myself, Why does the man continue to say one thing and then inevitably draw a quite opposite conclusion? So now I ask you the same thing, Doctor. Why?"

Winkler and Scott both sat up a bit higher in their chairs. Even Marlene, who had no love and very little regard for Randolph, sensed he was about to be confronted with a trap, and she sympathized with his dilemma.

"Precisely what do you mean?" Randolph parried.

"Well, my notes taken during your testimony reveal that the infancy and childhood of this Defendant were indeed blighted. And I do not quarrel with the testimony of those doctors who introduced evidence such as X-rays and their own clinical observation of the Defendant's . . . excuse me, Doctor, the patient's . . . condition, including fractures and other cruel injuries imposed on him when he was a defenseless child.

"But as I understood it, those injuries and deprivations were inflicted on him by a black mother, and by presumably black men who lived with her from time to time. Is that so?"

"Yes, from what we know, that is so," Randolph conceded cautiously.

"And when the patient as a boy, in his formative years, was so brutally treated in the reformatory—raped and made to do quite terrible things against his will—that too was inflicted on him by blacks. Was it not?"

"Yes, but I fail to see . . ."

Carroll interrupted quite sharply now. "I am coming to my question, Doctor! Since all these injuries, indignities and outrages were inflicted on him by blacks, how can you say that his early life disposed him, or 'programmed' him to kill whites?" Randolph did not answer immediately, so Carroll pressed him, "Doctor?"

Randolph had lost his easy volubility, now speaking more slowly, reflectively, as if feeling his way over foreign terrain.

"As I was quite careful to point out before, the evils visited on him, though delivered by the hands of blacks, were actually the result of the repressive white society."

"So you've said. But I find myself puzzled by the logic of it, Doctor. Not being scientifically trained or gifted with the imagination of my distinguished colleague for the Defense, I need some clarification. Why, if blacks did what you claim they did, why is the white society to blame for that? Can you give us a single example in the Defendant's life when he was abused or denigrated by a white?"

"He was exploited by every white man he worked for," Randolph said. "When he first came to see me, he complained that he was working for a white tailor as a delivery boy and was being underpaid, but he did not know how to ask for a decent wage."

"Any other illustrations? Doctor?"

"He subsequently left that job and began work at a gas station, again under a white boss, and again he was underpaid. Unable to ask for an increase, he eventually left that job too. His whole history is a series of such incidents, always involving white bosses."

"Is it significant to you, Doctor, that the episodes you refer to have all involved whites giving him jobs? Paying him? Enabling him to support himself as a constructive member of the society?" Carroll pressed.

"That is a euphemistic statement for what was actually going on. They were exploiting him!" Randolph answered briskly.

"Did any whites ever rape him? Did they, Doctor?"

"No, but . . ."

"Did any whites ever force him to his knees and make him do those terrible things he hated to do, Doctor?" Carroll demanded.

"No, but as I explained . . ."

"Your answer is No, is that correct, Doctor?"

"My answer is No, with an explanation!" Randolph replied angrily.

301

"We will get to your explanation later! In the meantime, just answer the questions as they are asked."

"Your Honor," Winkler interrupted, hoping to ease the pressure on Randolph.

But Beecher leaned toward Winkler and said, "Counselor, I think the Prosecutor is within the bounds of appropriate cross-examination. You introduced the subject of Social Inevitability; the Prosecutor is permitted to explore it."

Given great latitude now, Carroll referred to his notes before continuing. When he resumed, his tone was much more moderate.

"Doctor, would you say that the Defendant, or the patient, could have been motivated by revenge in perpetrating the action for which he is now on trial?"

"It was an act of self-expression, a way of making overt the hostility that he had been forced to repress during all his life," Randolph answered.

"But you wouldn't call that revenge?"

"Words like 'revenge' are not part of our professional vocabulary. No human being can contain within himself such giant hostilities and conflicts forever without paying a fearful price!"

"And the only way to free himself of this problem was to go out and commit a murder? An assassination?" Carroll asked.

"Of course not!" Randolph answered swiftly. "In fact, as I testified before I tried to provide some release for him from his tension."

"Did you stress to him the need to obtain such release?"

"Naturally!" Randolph said. "We went into it quite at length."

"Several times?" Carroll asked.

"A number of times."

"Doctor, what did you tell him, or prescribe for him?"

"Tranquilizers, physical activity. Anything that would diminish his pent-up hostility."

302

"Doctor," Carroll asked, glancing through his notes to suggest that his question was less than important, "In the course of your sessions with the patient, did he ever mention the judge who sentenced him to the reformatory long ago?"

"He might have. Yes, I believe he did."

"Do you remember his name?"

"Not offhand, but I'm sure it is in my notes," Randolph responded. "If it's important I can look it up."

"Did the patient ever discuss that judge with you? At length, I mean."

"Several times," Randolph said, wondering now what Carroll was leading up to.

"If I told you his name, would you recognize it?"

"I might."

But instead of mentioning the name, Carroll asked, "Tell me, Doctor, did the patient ever tell you what color that judge was?"

"I believe he said he was white."

"You 'believe?' Or you know?" Carroll persisted.

"He was white," Randolph conceded.

"And did you point out to the patient that that fact had certain significance?"

"I'm afraid I don't understand the question," Randolph said.

"Did you point out to the patient that the terrible indignities inflicted on him were not the fault of the blacks in the reformatory, but of the white judge who had sentenced him in the first place?"

"It was an inevitable fact of his background. We . . . we had to discuss it."

"Discuss it, or dwell on it?" Carroll asked sharply.

"We discussed it—more than once. If you want to say we 'dwelled' on it, you may say whatever you please."

"Did the patient express any hostility toward that judge?"

"Naturally."

"Doctor, is it a fact that once a patient is able to recognize

303

his hostilities and discuss them with his doctor that those hostilities tend to diminish? In fact, isn't that one of the benefits the patient derives from the treatment?"

"In most cases. But not all cases."

"Am I to understand that in this case there was no such diminution of hostilities?"

"There was an increase."

"Can you explain why, Doctor?"

"His hostilities had been so enormous and so long repressed due to his fear of death, as we said, that once they began to come out they grew rather than diminished. It does happen."

"Is it possible, Doctor, that feeling as you do, based on what we have heard you testify to, that instead of helping to diminish his hostilities you actually served to increase them?"

"I object!" Winkler called out, rising.

"On what ground?" Beecher asked.

"The question is obviously ridiculous and highly insulting to a professional man of Dr. Randolph's stature and accomplishments!"

"The Court does not find the question ridiculous. And as to its being insulting, no expert takes the stand without running some risk, as we all know, Mr. Winkler. The witness will answer the question."

Carroll asked, "Doctor, is it possible that by specific direction, subtle suggestion or attitude, you communicated to the patient your own feelings about whites and that those feelings served to increase his hostilities against that white judge?"

"No!" Randolph said flatly, seeking to close that entire avenue of questioning.

"Did you discuss his feelings philosophically?"

"I discussed them professionally," Randolph evaded.

"Without reference to your own feelings, your own attitudes, your own philosophy of the relation of the races?"

304

"I discussed them as doctor to patient!" Randolph insisted.

"And naturally you discussed how the white judge was to blame for everything that has happened to this Defendant?"

"We did not make any attempt to blame the judge for everything that happened to the patient!"

"But you did blame the white society!"

"When dealing with black patients it is necessary to take into account the political and sociological facts of their situation."

"Meaning the repressions by white society?"

"When necessary," Randolph conceded.

"And to blame the society for everything!" Carroll demanded.

"To blame it for those crimes it has inflicted on the black race. And which are now finally being acknowledged!" Randolph said.

"The white society in general? Or specific individuals?"

"The society is the criminal. Individuals only act as extensions of it. Whenever the patient tried to blame Judge Miller for his predicament, I was quick to point out that it was wrong to blame any single individual, since the society as a whole was responsible."

Carroll paused briefly, then asked, "Doctor, are you aware that you have just volunteered the name of the judge who sentenced Midge Grove to the reformatory?"

"Did I?"

Carroll asked the stenotypist to read back Randolph's answer.

"Judge Miller, you said," Carroll reminded him. "That was the name of the judge who sent Midgely Grove to the reformatory, wasn't it?"

"Yes, it was," Randolph admitted.

"So you knew it all along, without referring to your records."

305

"Unconsciously I must have known it."

"Doctor, does that name strike you as having special significance in this case?"

"If you mean that the name of the deceased was also Miller, that is sheer coincidence. Miller is a common name. The Judge Miller who sentenced the patient has been dead for more than ten years now."

"Yes, I know. I took the trouble to investigate that," Carroll said somewhat disturbingly. "And now, Doctor, would you listen to this hypothetical question, then think carefully and answer it?"

"I will do my best."

As Carroll turned to pick up a sheet of handwritten questions, Winkler and Scott leaned closer together. "The sonofabitch is a little shrewder than we gave him credit for," Scott whispered.

"We're not done yet, not yet," Winkler answered.

Carroll cleared his throat and began to read, "Doctor, let us suppose that a patient suffering from deep-seated hostilities resulting from a life of danger, deprivation, degradation, and enormous fears found himself unable to express those hostilities and consulted with a psychiatrist who was able to uncover those problems for him. Is it possible that the doctor involved might so influence and direct the patient as to convince him that unless he was able to express his hostilities through some overt act he would not be able to make an adjustment to life?"

Randolph considered the question and finally answered, "That is not what happened in this case."

"Is it possible?" Carroll pursued.

"Possible?" Randolph weighed. "Yes."

"Is it possible," Carroll continued to read, "that such a patient, being influenced by the doctor, could misinterpret the doctor's advice?"

"We do not advise, we discuss," Randolph corrected.

"Forgive me, Doctor," Carroll said. "Let me rephrase that.

306

Is it possible that a patient, being dependent on the doctor, having what is called a transference relationship with him, would tend to please the doctor in the same way he might try to please a father figure?"

"Yes, that is possible."

"Then is it possible that a patient, striving to please a father figure, namely the doctor, might misinterpret what the doctor wished him to do, and might commit some crime as a result of that misinterpretation?"

"Absolutely not!" Randolph shot back.

"Absolutely not, what? That a patient might misunderstand what the doctor said?" Carroll asked, attempting to seem ingenuous. "Is that what you meant?"

"Of course, patients may sometimes misunderstand," Randolph said, perspiring profusely now, but too alert to be trapped in any sweeping generalizations that would leave him open to further attack. "But such a misunderstanding as you suggest would be quite outside the realm of possibility."

"Even a patient who had been 'programed' to commit such a crime, as you testified this patient had been?"

"That was used in a different context!" Randolph replied angrily.

"Are you now disavowing the Doctrine of Social Inevitability, Doctor?"

"I am not!"

"Then if this patient was a human computer card, as you doctors so colorfully phrased it, punched out by society to commit an inevitable crime, is it also possible that his psychiatrist could, shall we say, insert that card into the computer and set those inevitable events in motion?"

"I . . ." Randolph hesitated.

"Is it, Doctor?" Carroll demanded, staring hard into the glistening black face of Randolph.

"It is possible that the doctor might not be able to prevent it," Randolph conceded.

"Is that all, Doctor? Merely 'not be able to prevent'? What

307

about set it in motion? What about that, Doctor?" Carroll persisted. "May I suggest to you that if there was any inevitability about this entire sad crime, it was that the doctor suggested to the patient what act might purge him of his hatreds and hostilities. And that the patient, like an irreversible force set in motion, did not rest until he had carried out an act that he thought would please his doctor, his father figure!"

"I reject that suggestion! I reject it completely!" Randolph exploded, at the same time rising out of his chair. His lips trembled and his face was wet. And somehow his precise Jamaican accent deserted him, as he shouted, "It's a lie. A goddamn lie!"

Carroll did not pursue his cross-examination. Instead, he took off his glasses and wiped away the mist which had spread across them. Then, only after he had replaced his glasses and put his handkerchief back into his pocket did he say, "Thank you, Doctor, that will be all."

As Carroll crossed to his counsel table, Linc Winkler arose, a bit more swiftly than usual.

"Doctor, did you ever counsel the patient to take hostile or aggressive action against any human being?"

"I did not!" Randolph answered strongly, having regained his composure and his Jamaican accent.

"Did the patient ever indicate to you that he intended to take hostile action against anyone, such as the action he is now charged with?" Winkler continued.

"He did not!"

"And if he had?" Winkler asked.

"Naturally, I would have done everything in my power to stop him!" Randolph declared.

"Would your efforts in that cause have been successful?"

"In my opinion, no," Randolph said. "Knowing the patient's background, his inner stresses, his need to express hostility or else disintegrate completely, I am not sure that anyone could have stopped him. He was reacting to the inevitability of his total life experience, and it was outside his

308

power to control. And outside mine. His action was simply inevitable. Society had made it so."

"Thank you, Doctor," Winkler concluded.

Carroll rose and, from his place, asked only one question: "Doctor, how is it possible for a psychiatrist to know so much about the background, inner stresses and inevitable forces within a human being and not detect that he might be contemplating a serious crime such as an assassination?"

"Sometimes the patient keeps secret, even from the psychiatrist, the most important of his subconscious thoughts. In view of this patient's terror of expressing his hostility, it is only natural that he would hide any plan to vent his hostility in this way." Randolph's manner had become completely calm and professional once again.

Carroll's purpose had been merely to ask the question and implant that thought in the jury's mind, so he did not pursue Randolph any further. "Thank you, Doctor," he said. "It's been most enlightening." And he stepped down.

Linc Winkler had not intended to question Randolph again, but he couldn't let Carroll's heavy score go unchallenged.

"Doctor, can you enlarge for us on the phrase which the Prosecutor elicited from you, namely, 'intervening circumstance?' "

"Used in this context 'intervening circumstance' means that even when a pattern of conduct seems inevitably set, it is always possible that something from the outside might enter and alter the course of events."

"Such as?" Winkler prodded.

"Since the Prosecutor made such an issue of my background and my life, I shall use myself as an example. I am not at all sure that my development would have been the same if I had not been singled out and given a scholarship to the Fieldston School. Once I had that glimpse of another world, my chain of inevitability seemed to have been broken. I dread to think of what might have happened to me if I had not been taken out of the hopeless, wretched condition I was born into. I might be sitting there, in that defendant's chair today myself."

"Thank you, Doctor."

It had been a long, grueling day, not only because of the intensive, high-pressured examination of the doctors, but because of the emotions that had erupted within Midge when he realized that his terrible secret was about to be revealed in the courtroom. Linc and Scott had had to spend more than an hour with him before he was in condition to change back into his convict garb and return to the District jail for the night.

Exhausted, Linc now leaned back in the soft, comfortable leather seat of the Rolls, with Scott on one side and Honey on the other. The few times when Honey came to sit in on the trial, Marlene always insisted on sitting in front with the black chauffeur, despite the fact that Scott tried to take that seat. Today, as usual, Marlene had asserted her right to sit, as she put it, "in the front of the bus."

"Well, Linc, what did *you* think?" Honey asked.

"Carroll is tough. Tougher on cross than he was in presenting his own case."

"He's no fool!" Scott said, shaking his head.

"But what does that do to the theory?" Honey persisted.

"Makes it mighty interesting," Linc said, smiling wearily.

"Besides making it interesting?" Honey wanted to know. "After all, a jury is not going to be moved by what's interesting."

"*This* jury is!" Linc insisted. "There isn't a black man or woman on that jury who isn't saying right now, 'Now, we never have to feel guilty for what any other black man does. We can simply say, it was inevitable.' "

"Will it get Grove acquitted?"

"*I* think it will," Linc stated flatly. But then he tempered

310

his conviction slightly, "But if in the end it doesn't, that theory will win us an appeal."

"There's another way!" Scott declared.

"Another way?" Linc asked, resentful that his strategy was being questioned and that his attention had been shifted away from Honey.

"Something in Randolph's testimony struck me. If we never had the opportunity before, after Randolph's testimony we have it now—the basis on which to plead insanity."

"Not a chance!"

Scott persisted, undeterred by Linc's opposition. "If we made a motion to reopen that aspect of the case, submitted all our new medical and psychiatric testimony to a fresh group of independent experts, they might just find that Midge *was* legally incapacitated at the time of the crime. In fact, when you think about it, it's almost a natural corollary to the Doctrine of Social Inevitability."

"Not a chance!" Linc insisted, this time more strongly.

"At worst, if we lose our motion, the jury would never know we made it."

"Not a chance!"

"Because of Beecher?" Scott demanded. "I think his attitude has changed. I don't know whether he's afraid of a reversal or whether he's been influenced by all the testimony he heard today, but I think he'd give us leave to reopen!"

"Scott, when I say not a chance, I mean there's not a chance in the world that *I* am going to follow that line. You're damn right we've got Beecher boxed in. Every newspaper in this country will have the Doctrine of Social Inevitability on its front page by tomorrow morning. And no respectable law school in this country will dare not to have a lead article on it in their next law review. Beecher knows that. So it must have an influence on him. I'm betting that when the chips are down, he's going to allow our defense. And if he does, we've got a fair chance for an acquittal!"

311

"And if we don't get an acquittal, there's always an appeal," Scott conceded.

"Right," Linc agreed.

"Linc," Scott asked suddenly, "what did Midge mean today when he said you 'promised'?"

"That I would do my best to keep out that material about the reformatory. But for his own sake, I had to use it. You agree with that, don't you?"

"I agree you had to use it. But I never agree with making a promise to a client and not keeping it," Scott said sharply, "not any more than I agree with keeping important facts in a case from a colleague."

"I told you about that, didn't I? It was the day of our first private meeting with Grove . . . oh, now, I remember, that was the day you went off to handle the discovery proceeding. I'm sorry, Scott, of course, I should have told you. My fault. I'm sorry."

Despite Linc's apology, Scott felt sick and shaken, the same feeling he had experienced as he watched Midge Grove grow cold and frightened in the moment when he confronted the shocking memory of his own past.

Winkler, meantime, had his mind on another concern and another important decision. Carroll's attack on Randolph had been fiercer and more effective than he had anticipated. Something must be done to overshadow it and diminish its impact on the press and the public. Linc debated whether to make Scott privy to the tactic he was contemplating. "Scotty," he said, breaking what had become a lengthy silence. "We have to ask for another private consultation with Midge!"

"I know," Scott agreed. Linc was apprehensive suddenly, wondering if Scott had anticipated him.

But Scott continued, "We've got to decide whether to let Midge take the stand. Personally, I'm against it. He can't refute any prosecution testimony. He can't deny the crime. He

312

can't even explain it. So what can he accomplish? Evoke sympathy? The doctors have done that better than he ever could. So I'd say, make our case without him."

"What if he *could* evoke sympathy, torrents of it?" Linc asked.

"By testifying?"

"By *not* testifying!" Linc was smiling enigmatically. "I'll call Fred Anthony as soon as we get back to the house, and then we'll ask for a private consultation with Midge."

"Beecher won't like it. And we've got him leaning our way at the moment. Any interviews, and leaks to the press can hurt us, Linc, badly," Scott warned.

"We've got Beecher over a barrel now. I want to keep him there, so he wouldn't dare rule against us in the showdown. Tomorrow we ask for a private session and for permission to bring two men with us."

"Doctors?"

Linc smiled paternally. "Scotty, remember I told you once, when it came to anything questionable, let *me* be the fall guy? This is one of those times. If a contempt citation comes out of this, let *me* take the rap. Okay?"

"Okay," Scott said, for he had suddenly become more concerned with a question he considered more important, one which he chose not to discuss with Linc at this time.

When the car dropped Marlene at her house, Scott insisted on getting out, too, even though she would not invite him inside, not even to talk. So they walked the black neighborhood where children played noisily in the streets in the last remaining hour before sunset.

"You were there," Scott began. "Was there something about Randolph's testimony that struck you? Something strange? Different from what you expected?"

After a few moments of puzzled thought, she said, "No. He did his job well. And he only got rattled once on cross."

"Exactly! And what rattled him?"

"Carroll asked if Midge might have killed Miller because of some suggestion by him," Marlene recalled.

Scott stopped abruptly, taking her hand and turning her to face him. "Marlene, when that happened, did you get the feeling that suddenly a moment of real truth exploded in that courtroom? Did you feel, in that instant, that it could actually have happened that way?"

Marlene nodded once, a strong affirmative nod.

Relieved, Scott said, "Okay. I needed someone to corroborate my feeling. For me, that moment brought this whole case into focus."

"Do you think that Randolph actually . . ." But Marlene didn't finish.

"I don't know, but it fits with something Midge once said. The important thing is, we have a whole new basis for his defense. If there's even the slightest substance to it, it *does* give us a chance to plead insanity."

"Without expert testimony on our side?"

"If *we* had initiated that argument, the court might hold it far-fetched or ridiculous. But we didn't propose it. Carroll did! That's what's so terrific about this defense. Carroll can't refute it! We say, Yes, the Prosecutor has finally come up with the motive. And we agree. Midge Grove acted like a robot, under the strong influence of the only father figure he's ever known. By design or accidental misunderstanding, he only did what he thought his psychiatrist was telling him to do. Under that delusion he went out and committed a murder. He was *not* a free agent, had no will of his own, and no real intent to kill—only the intention to carry out what he thought was therapy prescribed by his doctor. Any man who would do that must be legally insane."

"Would it stand up in court?" Marlene asked.

"After Randolph showed his naked resentment of everything white, I think so. He betrayed more hatred in his brief

314

time on the stand than Midge Grove was ever able to show in a whole lifetime."

Marlene nodded thoughtfully.

"I'll talk to Linc about it first thing in the morning," Scott said, confident now that Linc would have to agree. Without a doubt, this was Midge's best chance.

In front of Marlene's house once again, Scott suggested dinner.

"No, thanks," Marlene demurred. She seemed preoccupied.

"How about a drink in the bar down the block?"

"No. And I . . . I can't talk anymore, Scott. I'm in a hurry. I have to shower and change and get downtown to the stores before they close."

Reluctantly, he acquiesced. "Okay," he said, about to kiss her.

"I don't think that's a good idea—not out here." She turned from him and ran up the stairs to the front door.

Scott arrived at his apartment with Marlene still on his mind. He considered calling her. Perhaps she was out of the shower, just getting dressed, and he could still change her mind about tonight. Although he did understand that between day-long involvement in court and dictation and typing at night, her few free evenings were the only times she had for personal chores, he called anyway. Her line was busy. When he called again she was out. He had a cold dinner, thought and rethought the way in which he would present his defense to Linc in the morning.

It was nine-thirty and most stores had been closed for a half hour when Scott called Marlene again. There was still no answer. He called every fifteen minutes thereafter.

Just before eleven he called again, promising himself it would be for the last time. She answered.

"Marlene?"

"Yes. Oh, hi . . ." she said, in that intentionally casual yet guarded way that let him know she was not alone.

"I called and called, long past the time when the stores are closed. You were out. On a date?"

"Yes."

"And he's there now . . ." Scott half stated, half inquired.

"Yes," she said coldly, decisively.

"Sorry I intruded," he said acerbically. When he hung up, it was with a mingled sense of defiance, jealousy, and hurt—old feelings, and unwelcome.

·❦ XXIV ❧·

On the way to court the next morning, Linc Winkler listened gravely as Scott Ingram expounded his new theory for
basing their defense on the possible truth of Carroll's attack
on Randolph. When Scott had finished, Winkler remarked
thoughtfully, "So you got that impression, did you? Interesting." He mused for a moment. "Extremely interesting. Got to
think about that."

But he would not pursue it further.

When court reconvened Scott Ingram asked that the jury
be excluded while he presented a request. Then he moved for
permission for another private-room consultation with the
Defendant, explaining that they needed to discuss certain urgent matters vital to the presentation of the defense case.

Judge Beecher interpreted his request exactly as Carroll
and the press did—that Defense Counsel, in the normal
course of events, found itself facing a crucial decision,
whether or not to put the Defendant on the stand. Considering the gravity of the issue, the usual client-attorney meeting in the noisy jail rotunda was far from satisfactory. With
that in mind, Beecher postponed the following morning's session until afternoon and granted permission for Grove to be
brought to the courthouse detention area.

As agreed, Scott made one other request. Would it be per-
missible for at least two persons, not attorneys, to be present

317

at that meeting? Since there would be tight security, Beecher allowed the request.

Winkler had learned one thing during the weeks of pre-trial and trial argument. Whenever he needed a favorable ruling from Beecher on any marginal discretionary matter, it was best for Scott to make the request. It had worked again, and when Scott returned to his seat at the defense table, Linc remarked on a job well done.

Now all Winkler had to do was get through the rest of to-day's session and perhaps a day or two more, to give his new strategy time to evolve. So, though he had little faith in the effect on the jury, he played for time by devoting the entire day's proceedings to several character witnesses Scott had uncovered in the weeks of pre-trial investigation.

The first was an elderly black woman, frail and white-haired. Leitha Williams had lived in the same tenement as Midge Grove's grandmother at the time of his birth and for a year thereafter. With great patience, Winkler elicited from Mrs. Williams descriptions of Midge's closest relatives. She painted his grandmother as an angel, and his mother as a jezebel and a harlot. Finally, she offered a detailed, loving, and lengthy description of little Midge himself—a fine, decent child, often shy, but always a good boy.

Mrs. Williams' testimony was of such little value that Carroll did not even take the trouble to cross-examine her. But from Winkler's point of view, Leitha had served her purpose admirably. His own slow, indulgent questioning and her rambling answers had enabled him to use up the entire morning.

During the afternoon session Winkler presented the Reverend Jairus Drew, minister of the little Baptist church on the same block where Midge Grove lived when he was seven years old. Drew contributed his vivid memory of little Midge playing the part of the Child Jesus in the Christmas pageant.

"There was such a Christlike look about that boy that I be-

318

lieved he was actually touched by God. Yes, touched by God!"

Even Winkler cringed a little, inwardly, at the reverend's characterization, but he urged Jairus Drew on gently. "Reverend, did you ever imagine that one day you would be called upon to testify on that boy's behalf in a trial such as this?"

The look that passed between Prosecutor Carroll and his two black associates was as expressive as if he had groaned aloud.

"Sir," the Reverend addressed Winkler, "we must remember that Jesus, too, was put on trial, convicted, and even sentenced to die! In my humble view, this young man is facing just such a trial now. Like the Christ child he portrayed so beautifully, he may be on this earth to redeem his black brothers through his own suffering."

There was a bit of a stir in the press section after that, for even if his testimony had little legal weight, the good reverend had at least provided them with a colorful lead for the evening edition.

Carroll rose, and from his place proceeded to cross-examine. "Reverend Drew, I do not recall anywhere in the Gospels that Jesus Christ took a human life. Do you?"

"The gentle Jesus was not always as gentle as he is pictured. He whipped the moneychangers from the Temple. He said, 'I come not to bring peace but a sword.' He was, to use today's terminology, an activist Christ. 'By their deeds ye shall know them,' he said. Not words, but deeds, sir!"

Carroll persisted. "Yet, in the Garden at Gethsemane, did he not say to Peter, 'Put up thy sword, for all those who take the sword, will perish by the sword'? He was against the use of force, against killing, was he not?"

Judge Beecher interceded. "Mr. Carroll, if your examination takes this turn now, I can envision that within a half hour we may well be debating how many angels can stand on

319

the head of a pin. Unless you have more incisive questions, may I suggest that we terminate this examination and today's session?"

"The Prosecution is amenable to the suggestion of the Court," Carroll acquiesced, glad to have a boring, tiresome day over with. But as he gathered up his papers, Carroll wondered what lay behind Winkler's time-consuming strategy. Why had he produced a senile woman and a pompous clergyman as his only two witnesses of the day?

For Scott, the day had been long and difficult. He had little interest in the testimony, spending most of his concentration puzzling over Winkler's plan for meeting with Grove in the morning. And worst of all, he had been unable to arrange a minute alone with Marlene, and that kept him unsettled and distracted.

She had arrived later than usual, seeming not only distant from him, but extremely tense as well. She had avoided his eyes whenever he sought to make contact with her. And during each recess, she had managed to be completely involved with some detail of the case.

Scott started the day ascribing her attitude to a sense of guilt, but gradually he had begun to feel that he had to make contact in order to make his own apology. He was finally able to corner her just before they left the courthouse.

"I must talk to you!" he said urgently.

"Okay, talk!" she said, briskly.

"About last night. I'm sorry. I had no right to pry. But you know how I feel about you." She was unyielding.

"Marlene, I have to know. Who was it?"

She hesitated, then looked away as she said, "The eminent Dr. Paul Randolph!"

Scott was not only surprised, he was enormously resentful. "Did he call once too often for you to resist?"

"He didn't call. I did," she said. She broke away, but Scott seized her hand.

"I have to see you tonight!"

"I can't," she evaded.

Linc was coming down the courthouse corridor toward them.

"I have to!" Scott persisted.

Because Linc was already close enough to hear, Marlene said hastily, "Okay."

"I'll meet you at home."

"No!" she protested.

"I'll meet you at home!" Scott said with finality.

She nodded. He released her, and she was gone by the time Linc caught up with him.

As soon as she opened her door to him, he embraced her without a word of reproach or apology. She seemed uncomfortable, distant, different even in the manner in which she resisted him.

"I said I was sorry about last night!" Scott apologized again.

"That was all you could think of. I had a date. And I went to bed with him. That's it, isn't it?"

He couldn't answer.

"When I said it was Randolph, then you were absolutely sure. After all, he's the black stud of all time, isn't he?"

"Marlene . . . darling . . ." He tried to interrupt.

"Well, I *did* call him," she went on. "But not for the reason you think. I had to find out for myself if what you and I noticed in the courtroom was true. I knew if I called him, being the vain bastard he is, he'd think I was interested in only one thing."

"And *you* let him believe that . . ." Scott accused.

"Because I also knew, being the vain bastard he is, if I let him talk long enough he'd tell me what I wanted to know. Well, it worked," she said. Then she added, "Not quite the way I expected, but it worked."

"You found out?"

"He didn't come right out and say it, but I'm sure now that

321

Carroll came a lot closer to the truth than anyone knows. In some way, intentional or not, Randolph *did* motivate Midge to assassinate Miller."

"And all I could think was . . ." Scott didn't finish, but said regretfully, "Well, you could have saved yourself the trouble."

Her eyes stared back at him, questioning.

"I discussed it with Linc this morning, and he said he'd think about it. That's his way of letting it die."

Tears suddenly welled up in her eyes.

"Marlene . . ." he asked, "what's wrong?"

He reached out. She drew back.

"Marlene!"

"Dr. Randolph is not an easy man to say no to."

"What does that mean?" he demanded.

"Vanity, which makes him so easy to catch, also makes him very tough to get rid of."

Scott reached for her, but Marlene turned away. He managed to catch her blouse, her swift move revealing her bare shoulder—and a large red welt marring her skin.

"Is this what you meant . . . 'It worked. Not quite the way I expected, but it worked'?" Scott asked in an angry, hoarse whisper.

She nodded and began to weep. Scott held her face gently in his hands as she wept.

"He's a sadistic bastard!" Scott said bitterly.

"I think he was spaced out," she said in her teary voice.

"High? On what?"

"I don't know," Marlene said. "Doctors have access to all kinds of things. But he kept talking about having to relax after his tough time on the stand."

Gently, Scott took her into his arms, and she lent herself to him, seeking comfort.

"This does it," he said with quiet resolution. "I'd just about made up my mind anyway, but this does it."

322

"What?" she asked looking up at him.

"I'm withdrawing from the case," he said, staring straight ahead. "I've had enough of Linc Winkler and his secret strategies, his promises to Grove that he never meant to keep and his secret alliance with Randolph. He cares more about giving news breaks to Fred Anthony than about defending Grove. In fact, he's not defending him at all. He's using him to score political points. And I helped him with my damn theory! Well, not any more!"

Marlene slipped from his embrace. "What do you mean?" she asked, her eyes searching his.

"I mean that I'm going to do what I should have done the first time I caught him being devious. I'm going to quit the case!"

"But you can't!"

"Why not? Because it will mean not having the rare and distinguished privilege of working with the great A. Lincoln Winkler? Well, I don't have any illusions about that anymore. I'm a damn good lawyer on my own. He might be better at manipulating the press, but, in the end, cases are won in the courts," Scott declared angrily.

"But what about Midge?" Marlene's voice sounded urgent with concern.

"Precisely why I have to quit. I can't use or sacrifice him just to prove a point or establish a doctrine. If your client and his fate aren't the most important thing in the world to you, then you're the wrong lawyer for him, and you have only one honorable course—get out of the case!"

"That would apply to Winkler," Marlene said firmly, "not to you."

"What do you mean?"

"You say you'll leave the case because Midge Grove is too important to you, and yet if you do quit, Scott, you hand him over completely and without protection to the one man who is doing what you condemn."

323

Scott didn't answer.

"Imagine what Midge's chances will be if you're not there to protect him? If Winkler has it all his own way?"

"If that poor little man goes to jail for life, with his history, he'll go insane. Hopelessly insane," Scott said, more to himself than to Marlene.

"Exactly. And you can't let that happen to him, even if it means sacrificing your own pride from time to time. Midge needs you. He hasn't got anybody else in this world to depend on."

Scott looked away, troubled.

"I want you to promise me you won't quit. You won't throw him to the wolves, white or black," Marlene demanded.

Scott thought for a long time, then nodded grimly.

By eight o'clock the next morning, Midge Grove had been transported to the private conference room in the courthouse. Linc Winkler, Scott Ingram, Fred Anthony and William Clive, an NBC producer, were admitted to the cell block and searched carefully. The tape recorder that was found in Winkler's bulging briefcase was opened gingerly and thoroughly inspected for possible weapons or explosives. The George Jackson case would always be a sober reminder to all prison authorities that even lawyers are to be deemed suspect. In addition, William Clive's tiny Minox camera was investigated and found to be completely harmless; however, it aroused the curiosity and the suspicions of the officer in charge of the search.

"We want to record Grove and photograph him, to prove to people that he is not being abused or manhandled," Winkler explained. "There's been a lot of adverse talk." Then he flashed his permission from Judge Beecher, and all four were admitted to the conference room.

Once the door was locked from the outside, they acted swiftly. Winkler set up the tape recorder which actually be-

324

longed to Fred Anthony, and Clive began to take candid shots of Grove and Anthony, separately and together, while Anthony conducted the interview.

Anthony's questions were aimed at eliciting Grove's early background which would substantiate the concept of Social Inevitability. And they also insinuated a subtle political bias that could be brought to the fore by a careful editing of the tape so Anthony could gloss over doctrinaire matters which eluded Grove, knowing full well that Grove's militancy would be added later in the studio lab.

By the end of an hour and twenty minutes, Anthony had taped three cassettes of Grove's voice. Clive had several hundred shots of Grove in every mood imaginable, abject, pensive, soulful, fearful, hopeful and despairing. When Anthony had enough material, Winkler signaled the guard. The door was unlocked, and Grove was led away to the cell he would occupy until the afternoon court session.

Left alone once again, Winkler used the opportunity to ask Clive, "How long will it take?"

"If Fred can work through the night on his narration, I have enough stock footage and other stuff back in the cutting room to make air by, say, nine tomorrow night."

"About those still shots?" Winkler asked. "How is that going to work?"

"We've got enough footage of Grove's old neighborhood, of the Supreme Court, and the reform school to give us background and movement. All we have to do with the stills of Grove is keep our cameras moving. We'll dolly in, do slow zooms, pans. With Grove's voice over, the whole effect will be like a piece of motion picture film. It'll work."

"Good!" Winkler said. "And I hope you boys won't forget this little favor."

"For an exclusive like this," Clive said, "anything, anytime, Linc. Just ask." Then he and Fred Anthony hurried off to begin work.

Winkler relaxed, exhaling with great relief, only to find

325

Scott staring at him accusingly. "And when that special hits the air?"

"What judge is going to take on both NBC and *The New York Times*?" Winkler challenged.

Winkler dispensed with that afternoon's court session by introducing two more witnesses from Grove's past, his teacher in second grade, and the former superintendent of the reformatory into which Midge Grove had been placed as a boy and where he suffered the scarring indignities to which Randolph had testified.

By early evening, NBC was already doing network promos about an important exclusive titled, "Who Makes Assassins? A Study in Social Inevitability." At least once every hour, the entire network carried the announcements, highlighting the fact that Fred Anthony of *The New York Times* would do the narration himself.

The next morning on the NBC Today Show, preview clips of the special were used as part of the day's news. By afternoon, Fred Anthony's voice was urging the audience to look in on what he called, "perhaps the only time that Midge Grove will have a chance to state his own case to the people of this nation. I consider it one of the great journalistic events of my entire career."

By nine o'clock that night, in an hour of preempted time, NBC fed the documentary to the entire network. The special opened with shots of the street where Midge Grove was born, a garbage-laden block in a black slum of Washington, looking even worse now than it had thirty-one years ago. Over the noise of the street itself, one could hear the voice of Fred Anthony.

"Somewhere along these mean and filthy streets thirty-one years ago a son was born to an unwed black woman. He was to be named Midgely Grove, but he was to be called assassin! Who makes an assassin? It is a question we must ask ourselves if we are to prevent future assassinations. For assassins are not born but made. Experts, sociologists, psychiatrists, great legal minds have studied this phenomenon and termed it the Doctrine of Social Inevitability.

"For those of us who are less expert, simpler terms may suffice, but the bitter lesson is the same. There is no better proof than the mild-mannered, timid, yet courageous little man, whom I had the privilege of interviewing in the film you are about to see."

Then followed fifty-one minutes of integrated film. Midge's voice on tape answered Anthony's questions while his face was kept alive and moving by a variety of camera techniques. Clive delivered exactly what he had promised Winkler, a smooth, flowing documentary about Midge Grove, carefully edited to depict him as a peaceful, victimized young man, devoted to a political philosophy for which he was now being persecuted.

Most importantly, the documentary introduced to the mass audience the phrase "Doctrine of Social Inevitability." In a single night the phrase was transferred from intellectual circles to the average American home. It was no longer possible for *anyone* to discuss the Grove case without reference to it.

The documentary concluded with a shot of Fred Anthony leaving the courthouse where the exclusive interview had taken place. As the door closed behind him, Anthony's voice could be heard to say, "When that door closed on me, I could remember only one thing, could feel only one thing. The same door that was returning me to freedom was shutting Midge Grove in, perhaps forever. Or at least for as long as that mild-mannered little man lives.

"As I walked away, I asked myself again, 'Who makes assassins?' And I knew. *I* do. *Society* does. By its actions, its deprivations, it makes crime and criminals inevitable. Until that day when the only thing that is inevitable in this nation is a chance at a good life for every child born on every street, *we* are the criminals. *We* are the assassins!"

327

Linc Winkler sat in the library of the Rosenstone house. The images on the TV screen reflected on his beaming face and on the more sober faces of Honey, Scott, Marlene and Randolph.

"That's what I call a good night's work!" Winkler said with great satisfaction as Scott flipped off the set.

"And tomorrow?" he asked Winkler.

"So tomorrow it hits the fan!" They were interrupted by the telephone, which Winkler rose to answer, his delight spread serenely across his face. It was Bill Clive from NBC.

"Linc?" Clive called out. "How did you like it?"

"Beautiful, kid! Bea-u-ti-ful!" he reiterated in exaggerated Brooklynese.

"The switchboard here at the station is lit up like a Christmas tree!" Clive continued. "I already got a call from upstairs. They would like Anthony and me to team up to do a whole series of sociologically oriented specials!"

"Good! Great! Glad to hear it!" Winkler said.

"Did we do right by you?"

"Better than right!"

"Then don't forget the next time you've got another hot exclusive!" Clive said.

The conversation could have been between two businessmen who had just concluded a mutually profitable transaction. And so it was. Their voices rose and fell in repeated congratulations for a few minutes more. Then Winkler hung up. Beaming, he turned to them and said, "Let's see Carroll cross-examine that!"

Scott and Marlene exchanged silent stares. For now they realized that Winkler too had been aware of how telling Carroll's cross-examination of Randolph had been, and that he had chosen this way to obliterate its impact with public and press.

Early the next morning, before Linc and Scott left for court, Judge Beecher's law secretary called, summoning them

328

to a meeting in chambers half an hour prior to the regular starting time.

When they arrived, Carroll and one of his two black assistants were already waiting. Beecher stood behind his high-backed leather swivel chair, glaring at the door as it opened to admit Linc and Scott. Stiff, perfunctory good mornings were being exchanged between Carroll and Winkler when the judge cut in sharply.

"We have no time for courtesies this morning, gentlemen!" the irate Beecher exploded. Signaling the court stenographer to commence taking notes, the judge turned on Scott, "Young man, two days ago when you asked for that private lawyer-client interview, did you know what the real purpose of it was?"

Winkler interceded, "I take full responsibility for what happened."

"I'll get to you later, Mr. Winkler!" Beecher turned back to Scott. "You were aware, were you not, of the ban on all interviews that bound the attorneys for both sides in this case?"

"Yes, sir."

"Still you proceeded to arrange . . ."

Winkler interrupted now. "He arranged nothing. *I* did the arranging! All of it!"

"That, Mr. Winkler, was quite obvious!" Beecher replied. "As has been every one of your tricky moves in this case thus far. This Court has tried in every way it could to give this Defendant a fair trial, and to keep the public temper at a low level. In the courtroom we have tried to maintain an air of judicial propriety and calm, despite the unusual precautions made necessary by your people, Mr. Winkler!"

"Just what do you mean by that?" Winkler asked angrily.

"By what?" Beecher demanded, outraged that Winkler should go on the attack against him.

" 'Your people!' What did that mean? Jews?"

"Don't be ridiculous!" Beecher shot back.

"Well, then precisely what did you mean by that phrase? It

329

was yours. You used it. You're the only one who knows precisely what you meant."

"See here, I don't intend to be cross-examined by you or any other lawyer!"

"And I don't propose to take your abuse or to grovel abjectly or apologize for what happened on TV last night. We have nothing to talk about—not before you explain that phrase 'your people,' " Winkler said, appearing extremely indignant.

"You know damn well what I mean! I mean those people whom you have stirred up to keep a constant vigil outside this courtroom while we are trying to conduct a fair and decent trial inside. I mean the highly organized effort to harass, intimidate and frustrate this Court in its attempt to carry out a fair trial. I mean the vicious mail I get every morning at my home, the constant attempt in the news media to give the people of this nation and the world a highly false impression of what goes on in my courtroom, and the continuous effort to poison this nation with deliberately misleading information.

"I mean, Mr. Winkler, that disgraceful spectacle that I witnessed last night on television."

"I didn't find it disgraceful," Winkler said in a low voice, for now that Beecher had become angered, Linc could afford to be calm.

"Mr. Winkler, it is the considered judgment of this Court that by arranging that interview with Mr. Anthony, by smuggling a television producer into a confidential meeting between lawyer and client . . ."

"We didn't 'smuggle' anyone in. We had Court permission," Winkler argued.

Beecher ignored him. "That by so doing, you stand in violation of the order of this Court against giving any interviews during the course of this trial."

"You will find nothing in that TV special to indicate that I

330

voiced any opinion or answered any question. And the same goes for my associate," Winkler said firmly.

"In my view, your actions are a breach of the restrictions placed on all counsel in this case. I hold you in contempt of court! Sentence will be passed at another time," Beecher said with finality.

Carroll and his associate started to move, as did Scott, but Linc stood his ground. "May I have a clarification on one question, Your Honor?"

"Yes!" Beecher spoke with gruff intolerance.

"Does your ruling this morning mean that the Defendant, too, is under restrictions not to talk to the press?"

"It means that all participants in this case, *all participants,* Mr. Winkler, are henceforth prohibited from talking to the press about this case!"

"Meaning, that in effect, even before conviction, my client is deprived of his Constitutional right to free speech?" Winkler pursued.

"You may phrase it any way you like, Mr. Winkler. There will be no more interviews, no more television appearances, no more articles, no more exclusive bribes to the press!"

"I wish to inform the Court that as soon as we receive our transcript of this meeting and your order, we intend to appeal."

"Of course!" Beecher snapped back. He was silent for a brief moment before he turned back to Scott. "Young man, because of your youth and the promise I see in your future career in the law, I shall refrain from holding you in contempt. But I am strongly critical of your actions and your part in this . . . this conspiracy to frustrate the Court!"

Linc and Scott walked down the corridor of the courthouse, with Carroll and Washington trailing behind by some ten feet.

"So far so good," Winkler whispered. Scott looked at him

intently, wondering how he could say that after such a bitter confrontation. Winkler said, "This morning he blows!"

The usual crowd thronged the door of the courtroom, and the frisking and searching proceeded slowly. When Winkler and Scott approached, the crowd broke to allow them through and many of the newsmen commented on the impact of the TV special and on Winkler's shrewdness in arranging it.

Winkler did not smile at them or banter with them as would have been his custom. Instead, he wore an air of such sobriety that the media people immediately became suspicious.

Those most friendly with him asked, "What's up, Linc?"

"Something go wrong?"

"What happened, Linc?"

But Winkler only followed Scott through the crowd to the door. There they paused for the perfunctory search and then entered the courtroom. They walked together down the aisle, past the bulletproof barrier, and took their places at counsel table. Midge, attired in his Panther outfit, was escorted in by two U.S. Marshals. The clerk announced Judge Beecher, and Midge, as he had done each time court convened, rose and directed a clenched fist salute to the bench. This morning, instead of ignoring it, Beecher glared at him.

"The Defendant will be seated!" he ordered. Once the jury was seated, Beecher turned to Winkler. "Is the Defense ready to resume?"

"Yes, Your Honor. But before we do," Winkler rose slowly as he spoke, "we would like the help of the Court in relieving us of the burden of communicating with the press."

"Exactly what do you mean, Mr. Winkler?" Beecher demanded suspiciously.

"Minutes ago when I approached this courtroom, I was besieged by the press, and I was forced to remain absolutely silent in the face of their questions. I would like to enlighten them as to the cause of my silence. I have never been one to deny the press free access to whatever information I had, but since I am under strict prohibition by this Court and, in fact, I am at this moment under a finding of contempt . . ."

"Mr. Winkler!" Beecher interrupted.

But Linc continued, ". . . you can see that I cannot enlighten the press. So I wonder if the Court would do so, particularly concerning those events that took place in your chambers this morning!"

"Mr. Winkler, you are to remain silent about this entire matter!" Beecher exploded, and turned to the clerk. "Remove the jury!"

Once the jury was locked out, Beecher stared at Winkler.

"Mr. Winkler, you are an attorney of many years' standing. You know very well that matters handled in confidence in chambers are not public property. Your gross and blatant attempt to inform the press was a severe breach of professional conduct. It constitutes a second and more grave charge of contempt of court. And this Court so rules."

"We take exception, of course."

"Of course," Beecher grumbled angrily, looking to the press rows behind Winkler.

"Ladies and gentlemen, this Court does not intend to be, nor has it ever intended to be a censor of the news media. On the other hand, a free and responsible press is not without obligations in such a situation. You shall have to evaluate whether what you do serves to insure a fair trial both for the Defendant and the people. Will you be responsible members of a responsible press, or will you be the whores and handmaidens of anyone who can wave an exclusive under your noses?

"*I* am wondering what the reaction would have been if last night's TV special had been one put on with the cooperation of the Prosecution in an attempt to prejudice the public *against* the Defendant. You might ponder that, ladies and gentlemen."

Beecher glared at Winkler. "Mr. Winkler, you will cease

trying to provoke this Court into a ruling of contempt while the jury is in the courtroom. For you will only succeed in drawing further sentences while the jury is *not* in the courtroom. I trust you understand that! The clerk will return the jury!"

Winkler eased down into his chair, as the clerk went to summon the jury. Scott was grave and red-faced, in sharp contrast with Linc's easy and relaxed attitude. He slapped Scott encouragingly on the leg. "Cheer up, Scotty," he whispered. "It couldn't have gone better. See this afternoon's papers."

Winkler proved right. The first editions of afternoon papers the country over carried huge headlines announcing that Linc Winkler had been found guilty on two counts of contempt. Since the first finding was made in the privacy of chambers, the whole episode took on an air of intriguing secrecy. One syndicated columnist referred to that first finding as a star chamber proceeding and hailed Winkler for his courage in bringing it to light.

During the lunch break, Winkler received invitations from both "Meet the Press" and "Face the Nation" to make appearances the following Sunday, but he declined with appropriate modesty and chagrin, explaining that he feared another charge of contempt for merely exercising his Constitutional rights. But he took the opportunity to suggest that Dr. Randolph, the nation's leading expert on the Doctrine of Social Inevitability, might make an excellent replacement. Randolph chose "Meet the Press." It was significant that no panel member on that show remembered Carroll's revealing cross-examination of the black psychiatrist, or else thought it of sufficient value to question him on it.

It was late evening. Linc and Scott were finishing their supper in the Rosenstone library. Winkler ate and drank with an air of relief, almost as if victory were firmly in his hands. Scott, grim, said little until Winkler took to chiding him.

334

"Scotty, don't worry about it. Beecher'll never find you in contempt—although it might help your standing in civil rights work if he did."

"I'm thinking about Midge. All this shadowboxing has tremendous effect outside the courtroom, but the jury's sequestered. They don't get the impact of it."

"They get it, they get it," Winkler was quick to assure him. "When they were excluded this morning, they got that. If anything, Beecher antagonized them by shutting them out of something they were damned curious about. But the important thing is he blew his cool *before* the jury was excluded, and the record will show it. Should the time come, it'll work for us on appeal."

"Before there can be an appeal, there has to be a conviction. I say it isn't fair to Midge to take that chance. Late as it is, I think we should get leave to introduce the defense of insanity," Scott said firmly.

"On the ground that Randolph influenced him? I told you, it would never hold up!" Winkler declared, coming close to anger now.

"We don't accuse Randolph. We proceed on the basis that Midge misunderstood him, that he was so detached from reality that he took all of Randolph's talk about expressing hostility as orders, commands," Scott urged.

"And how do we prove that? By putting Midge on the stand? I wouldn't take that chance!"

"What chance?" Scott demanded. "So what if he's disoriented, confused, detached! The worse he sounds the better for us. Because he can only seem more and more like a man who would misunderstand his psychiatrist and act out a delusion, which is all we're trying to prove!"

"And in the course of proving that, all he does is impeach and destroy our own best witness!" Winkler argued back.

"Randolph!" The way Scott spoke the name left his anger and contempt undisguised.

"I know you don't like him. I also know why."

335

Scott stared at Winkler, wondering if Linc knew about Randolph's attack on Marlene. Would Randolph have told him? Impossible.

"Well, you don't have to worry, Scotty. I gave him strict orders not to hassle her. Frankly, I don't blame you for being jealous, but you can't let personal feelings get in the way of your judgment." Winkler patted him on the shoulder, an older man advising a younger. "No matter how you figure it, we'd wind up impeaching our own best witness. We can't do that, Scotty, we just can't do that."

Obviously Winkler did not know about Randolph.

There was little more of the defense case to introduce. The Prosecutor received the Court's permission to present a rebuttal witness whose name was not on the capital list.

He was Dr. Arne Andresen, the distinguished white-haired chief of the psychiatric service at the largest medical center in New York City.

Carroll led him through a presentation of his credentials and his long and distinguished standing as an expert. When that had been accomplished to the satisfaction of the Court, Carroll elicited Andresen's opinion on the Doctrine of Social Inevitability.

"It has absolutely no scientific support. It has never been studied under laboratory or clinical conditions. At best, one might call it the unsupported opinion of one man, Dr. Paul Randolph."

"So that from a purely scientific point of view there is actually no proof to support such a doctrine?"

"None whatsoever!" Andresen declared. "It is not to be found anywhere in the medical literature."

Like most good cross-examiners, Linc Winkler proceeded on the basis that each witness carried within him the seeds of his own destruction. If a lawyer attacked along enough lines, eventually he would reveal the seams and cracks in the witness' personality.

336

"Dr. Andresen," Winkler began, as he advanced to the lectern, "do you find it easy to make such a categorical statement about any doctrine in a field as inexact as psychiatry?"

"After you have devoted a lifetime to it, as I have, you know all the methods of diagnosis and treatment," Andresen answered.

"And all the doctrines?"

"Doctrines, theories, any newfangled idea that comes along. We have to be aware of them all, until they are either proved or disproved."

Andresen's use of the word "newfangled" alerted Winkler. He made a mental note of it, then continued.

"Doctor, within your own lifetime have you seen theories come along which seemed improbable at the outset, but which later proved out?"

"Yes, and I have also seen methods of treatment come on the scene, be used for a time, and then discarded," Andresen countered.

"Could you give us any examples?"

"The lobotomy is one example, the surgical removal of the trouble centers of the brain," Andresen explained.

"This lobotomy procedure, did you ever use it?"

Andresen smiled. "I never prescribed a lobotomy, although some of the younger men on my service urged it very strongly. But then young men are always more adventurous with new therapies."

This was a second indication, and now Winkler knew of what—age. Age was the fissure along which Andresen would crack, especially with a jury so young.

"Doctor, would you say that the quality of young men and women coming into the field of psychiatry today is as high as it was in your time?"

"In brain power, yes. In attitude, no."

"Would you explain that, Doctor?"

"These days, unfortunately, our young doctors seem to give medicine second place to political activism. It is not helpful either to the hospital or the patient," Andresen said sadly. "Young men in sloppy uniforms, with long hair and scraggly beards. It's not a situation in which the patient can have confidence—and confidence is essential in our work."

"Tell me Doctor, if a young man 'in a sloppy uniform with long hair and a scraggly beard' were to come to you with a new theory, would you be less inclined to take him seriously than if he were clean-shaven and neatly dressed?"

"My personal reaction to the man would have nothing to do with my professional evaluation of his work," Andresen maintained.

"Doctor, do you have any black men or women on your service?"

"Yes, two," Andresen replied at once.

"Do you find their work suitable?"

Andresen answered softly. "I find one of them adequate. The other . . . less than adequate."

"Yet you retain them on your staff?" Winkler pressed.

"These days . . . one has to."

"What does that mean . . . 'one has to?' "

"Pressure—from the community, from the board of trustees—enormous pressure."

"Do you resent that pressure, Doctor?"

"I prefer to choose my staff solely on the basis of proven ability."

"Do you know Dr. Paul Randolph?"

"He is the man who first proposed this Doctrine of Social Inevitability, I know that," Andresen replied.

"Does the fact that he is black and young play any part in your reaction to his theory?"

"Of course not! I am evaluating a theory, not a man," Andresen insisted.

"Isn't it possible that someone like yourself, who by his own admission is resistant to things 'newfangled,' to young interns who won't dress as you want them to, or get their hair cut when you think they should, isn't it possible that you

338

have a prejudice against the ideas of these young people? And that your reaction to the Doctrine of Social Inevitability may be an exercise in prejudice rather than a scientific evaluation of a highly significant idea?"

"When I examine a new idea, I do not consider the color of the proponent's skin, his age, or his appearance."

"I wonder about that . . ." Winkler said slowly as he started back to the counsel table to take the sheaf of papers that Scott held out to him. Then, confronting the doctor, he said, "I present to you this file of material, clippings from *Time* magazine, a transcript of an NBC documentary, plus several articles from reputable publications including *The New York Times* magazine and *Harper's*. Each is a sober, cogent appraisal of the Doctrine of Social Inevitability. The majority of them support and endorse it."

"I am familiar with these articles," Andresen stated.

"Then I ask you, in face of this evidence, Doctor, how do you defend your opinion as anything more than a prejudice against a new idea from a young person?"

"I am not in the habit of defending my professional opinions against the amateur opinions of popular publications. I am still one of that dwindling minority who believes that not all of human wisdom is contained in *Time* magazine or the *Ladies' Home Journal*," Andresen declared indignantly.

"All these highly intelligent people," Winkler pursued, "and all these reputable publications find merit in the Doctrine of Social Inevitability. You alone, Doctor—a man who obviously has a prejudice against new ideas, especially if they come from young men, and most especially from black young men—you alone dismiss it as unworthy!"

"That's a complete distortion of what I said! A complete distortion!" Andresen fought back.

But Winkler was not even listening. Instead, he flipped through the articles, clippings and transcripts as if to emphasize the preponderance of material that refuted Andresen. Then he returned to the table.

339

Unexpectedly, Andresen turned to the judge. "May I make a personal statement at this time?"

Beecher nodded, "If you wish, Doctor."

"Despite the impression Counsel tried to create, I have never discriminated against any human being, black, white, or of any color, either as a patient or as a member of my staff. My record will bear that out. And as for the young, I welcome them, provided they are dedicated people of science. The doctor, like the disease he treats, is above politics, or should be."

With that, the tall, white-haired man rose and left the stand. The Prosecution rested its rebuttal case. Winkler could see no advantage in presenting any further testimony, so Judge Beecher adjourned the court, ordering both sides to prepare their summations for the next court session, Monday morning.

·◦⧉ XXV ⧉◦·

In the fourth row on the aisle in the smaller of the Kennedy Center theaters, Justice Ben Robertson and Honey were occupying the two Rosenstone subscription seats.

Ben Robertson loved the theater. Watching a deeply engrossing play or an outstanding actor was like reliving the past, his college days, his work in the dramatics society. After all these years, he still believed he could have succeeded on the stage if he had tried, and he would often catch himself imagining that he had replaced one of the stars in the play, as the leading man. As he grew older, Ben Robertson's heroes changed. First he was another Lou Tellegen or Ian Keith. Then he vied with John Barrymore. In more recent times, he had fancied himself in the place of Edmund Gwenn; they both had the same elderly charm, warmth and geniality. After Gwenn died, only an occasional performance by Edward G. Robinson could give the Justice that same thrill. Now with Robinson so recently gone, the old Justice knew his fantasy game was coming to an end.

And how he needed some relief from his professional life, which was bounded on all sides by his stiff, dry colleagues. There were times when Ben Robertson would sit at the weekly conferences, staring at his colleagues and addressing them silently, "Boys, boys, boys, stop being so goddamned

341

conscious of being judges of the High Court. You're forgetting you're human beings, too."

Today had been one of those days. All through the meeting, he had anticipated this evening and his appointment with Honey. And she had not disappointed him. She appeared on time, looking beautiful and provocative, as if she were having a rendezvous with a lover. It flattered him, and he loved it.

Robertson made sure they arrived at the theater early, to avoid the crowds that Honey detested and to allow himself plenty of time to read the program from beginning to end. He liked to follow the careers of actors that way, picking up bits of gossip and also the intimate thoughts of the playwrights and stars who wrote pieces for the program.

He had just begun the last piece when his sensitive hunter's ears caught a barely perceptible sound from outside the theater. He was sure it was the sound of a gunshot. With a soft, "Pardon me," to Honey, he slipped out of his seat and hastened up the aisle, reaching the lobby and the doors as quickly as he could.

Through the glass he could see a struggle on the steps between uniformed policemen and a crowd of youthful demonstrators. The demonstrators were being pushed down the steps of the center, leaving behind their placards, which carried slogans aimed against Judge Beecher and his conduct of the Grove trial. Just as Ben Robertson began to wonder why the Kennedy Center had been chosen as the location for the demonstration, he glimpsed two old people being escorted across the lobby by a police lieutenant and two other officers. The woman, nicely dressed but now disheveled and distraught from her contact with the mob, was tending her dazed husband, who held a handkerchief to his face. When the man momentarily took the handkerchief from his cheek, Ben Robertson was shocked to discover that the injured man was Judge Alfred Beecher. Since Beecher was in the capable hands of the police, Robertson made no effort to reach him. Instead he approached the police lieutenant.

"What happened?" Robertson asked.

"They knew the judge would be here tonight, so they set up a demonstration out there. When he and Mrs. Beecher stepped out of the car, they surrounded them. Mrs. Beecher was knocked down in the scuffle, and the judge suffered a face wound," the lieutenant explained.

"But there was a shot," Robertson pressed.

"One of my men lost his head," the Lieutenant admitted. "He attempted to fire over the crowd."

"Attempted?"

"He hit one of the girls in the mob. But it was only a surface wound."

"You're sure?" Robertson persisted, his distress clear in his voice.

"Yes, Mr. Justice," the lieutenant said. Then, as if to justify his man's action he continued, "You should have heard them. 'Fascist pig,' 'Killer,' 'Hangman,' 'Up against the wall, Beecher.' "

Robertson nodded sadly. He wondered who was to blame more, the young for their impatience in an unchanging world? Or the world which adamantly pursued its old course, despite the obvious proof that sameness and old courses had failed? But the most disturbing thing of all was the violence that seemed the inevitable result of their confrontation.

How he wished it could be otherwise. His lifetime of legal and judicial experience demanded peaceful change through the law and the courts. He hoped the process would not prove too slow, and more was the worry now, with the new conservative Court.

Regretfully, Robertson started back across the lobby and down the long aisle. It was dark, and the curtain had already gone up. He found his aisle seat, slipped into it.

"Something wrong, Ben?" Honey whispered.

"No, nothing, my dear. Nothing."

343

Robertson was relieved when the evening was over and Honey dropped him at his house. He did not even engage in their usual banter, or make his usual playful attempt to seduce her up to his bedroom. Instead, he kissed her on the cheek and said goodnight.

Honey leaned back in the seat after he had gone. She was concerned about Ben's health. He had never appeared quite so aged or so tired as he had tonight. It wasn't until later, at home, when she turned on the late news that she learned about the demonstration, the shot fired, and the reason Ben had hurried up the aisle. And perhaps the reason for his weariness.

On Monday morning, Linc Winkler's defense motions were heard and disposed of.

Beecher, a small white bandage covering his facial wound, seemed more composed and judicial than ever. He had not even frowned when Midge gave his usual morning closed-fist salute. And each time he rejected one of Winkler's various motions to dismiss, to instruct the jury to acquit, to lessen the charges, to declare a mistrial, he did so without emotion. When Winkler took unnecessary exceptions to his rulings, Beecher did not react, but seemed anxious to make sure that the stenographer had carefully noted each one.

Now United States Attorney Carroll was in the midst of his first summation, the Prosecution having the right to sum up again after the Defense had done so. The courtroom was tense and quiet.

"As the Prosecutor in this case it is my duty now to reassemble the facts we have introduced and to assist you in reaching your decision. The State set out to prove, and we believe did prove, that this Defendant planned to kill a Justice of the Supreme Court, that he prepared himself with a weapon, that he attempted to conceal his identity by removing the labels from his coat, that he went into that Courthouse with the intent to kill, that he did indeed fire the shots

344

that killed Justice Harvey Miller. He was identified by the woman who sat beside him at the moment that he committed the crime. He was also identified by the man who wrestled with him, face to face, when he made his abortive escape.

"The Prosecution has also proved that his was the hand that pulled the trigger, that his was the gun that fired the fatal bullets. In all respects we have proved, and we believe beyond *any* doubt, that this Defendant committed these crimes. So we ask that when you assemble in that jury room, you consider only the facts. I agree it is not easy to overlook the sad, outrageous life history of this Defendant. But although this history may explain his actions, it does not absolve him of the consequences of his deed, which was a planned, premeditated murder, requiring of you a verdict of murder in the first degree."

Carroll contented himself with that, knowing that he must save any further ammunition for rebuttal against Winkler.

Court was recessed for lunch.

Before it reconvened, Scott Ingram and Linc Winkler were summoned to the judge's chambers, where Carroll and the stenographer already waited.

Beecher began rather dryly, "Mr. Winkler, I assume that you will sum up for the Defense?"

Winkler nodded.

"Considering the nature of this case and its worldwide notoriety, the Court is prepared to grant you considerable latitude in your summation."

"Thank you," Winkler said, unable to stifle a touch of sarcasm.

"However," Beecher continued, "I must inform you that it is the considered ruling of this Court that during your summation the use of the phrase 'Doctrine of Social Inevitability' will not be permitted."

"But it's part of the evidence! We have a right to refer to it!" Winkler protested.

"I've heard all that evidence and studied your extensive

345

memorandum with great care. I find that at best that theory is the opinion of one physician and does not constitute any professionally accepted theory of medicine or psychiatry. Even if it were substantiated, it does not constitute a legal defense to the crime charged here. Therefore I am ruling that none of the testimony on the subject of the doctrine itself may be referred to in your summation."

"We take strong exception to this!" Winkler declared. "This may well turn out to be significant and reversible error!"

"Nevertheless, I feel compelled to rule as I have. And for the purpose of this trial my ruling is final!"

"I understand, Your Honor," Winkler said, as if accepting the ruling. But as he started to leave he added, "It is shocking that this Defendant must pay for what happened to you and Mrs. Beecher Friday night—something for which the Defendant was not responsible!"

"Mr. Winkler!" Beecher called out. Winkler turned back slowly in obvious impertinence. "That entire event was shameful. A travesty on the exercise of rights in a free society," Beecher said grimly. "But it has nothing to do with this ruling. Nothing!"

"I'm sure of that," Winkler said, his tone belying his words. "Nevertheless I would like to introduce into the record the issue of the *Washington Post* which carries a full account of that confrontation on its front page!"

"It will be so received and entered. One word of warning, Mr. Winkler. I know your reputation and your capacity for being a legal pyromaniac. I warn against using your summation for that purpose."

When Winkler rose to begin his summation the courtroom was not only filled to capacity but a reinforced contingent of uniformed guards surrounded the rear door and lined the aisles. Despite his many warnings, Judge Beecher obviously did not trust Winkler to keep his summation within bounds.

346

Winkler himself was tense, as he usually was in the moments before any important speech. "Feel my hands," he said to Scott. They were ice cold. Scott's look of concern was met with a confident smile from Winkler. "Don't worry, Scotty. If my hands were warm and I was relaxed then we'd be in trouble." With that and one last glance at his notes, Linc Winkler rose to begin his summation.

First, he stood behind Midge Grove, resting his hands on Grove's shoulders, and gently angling him to face the jury. Then he patted Grove comfortingly.

"Ladies and gentlemen, I wish to thank you for the attention and the consideration you have granted us during the long weeks of jury selection and trial. It was not easy for you to sit here day after day and listen to lawyers argue and the judge rule, most times about matters that are, or seem to be, inconsequential to the question in hand. Sometimes we lawyers argue in front of the jury, sometimes only after excluding the jury, as you have been excluded from time to time. If you have been wondering what we discussed in your absence, it has been the rules that govern trials and the application of those rules. For example, sometimes the attorneys and the judge know the truth, and the only question is whether the jury should be allowed to hear that truth. That's the kind of question we discuss when you are not present.

"Now, you good men and women must be asking yourselves, if it's our duty to decide on the fate of a human being on trial, why are we the only ones to be excluded from hearing the whole truth? Why, for example, are the men and women of the working press allowed to hear it, but not the jury? However the fact remains, that is the way trials are conducted under our rules."

Winkler was going far afield, but Beecher pretended not to take notice of it. Ever since the shocking events on the Kennedy Center steps, he had become scrupulously determined to exercise fairness toward the defendant, almost to the point of being unfair to the Prosecution.

"Nor is suppressing facts from the jury the only obvious puzzle in our system of law. For example, the Prosecution has made much of the very careful preparations that led up to the crime, in order to prove premeditation, which is essential to a verdict of first-degree murder.

"But nothing has been made of the Defendant's motive. Why this strange and suspicious absence? The Prosecutor knows the Defendant's motive. It has been present in this courtroom every single day since this trial began. It is present and made abundantly clear by the manner in which this Defendant greets this judge every morning!"

Winkler raised his own clenched fist and vaguely directed it toward the bench, without losing eye contact with the jury. Then he moved back to stand behind Grove.

"This man, this black man, is here because he stands for something! It is evident in the way he dresses. He is a soldier in uniform in a war against hatred, racism, and genocide. And every one of you men and women who have sat in that jury box during these weeks knows that. Only the Prosecutor pretends not to know it.

"Ladies and gentlemen, what we are confronted with here is a plain fact which no one wants to recognize. This is a political trial! This man is on trial because of his beliefs. He is here because of what he believes about this repressive government, this system under which he has suffered injustices beyond the capacity of any man to endure, be he black or white!

"This court, this judge, this prosecutor, our whole system of justice, our police, our penal system are merely instruments for keeping the black man in a new form of slavery. And as long as that is so, this Defendant has not only the right to protest, but the duty!

"Except that if he does, there is the system standing over him with its rules, its judges, its prosecutors, its jailers, all to keep him from protesting. And that is the worst kind of repression!"

348

Winkler paused to take a sip of water from the cup on the prosecution table. He was taking the pause in order to shift gears and to allow the blacks on the jury to assimilate what he had said before he went on.

"And now we come to the reason why the Prosecution has failed or refused to introduce testimony as to motive. This was not a personal crime committed out of hatred for the victim. This was no crime at all, but the only available means of expression for this Defendant under a system that had deprived, tortured, and tried to destroy him virtually from the moment of his birth.

"You heard the testimony from the eminent doctors as to this young man's early life, his physical and psychological problems. I do not intend to repeat it here. But if I had to sum it up in a single sentence I would say that the doctors had discovered this man had to kill or die! There is no system of justice I know of, in any country, which forbids a man to kill in defense of his own life.

"The Prosecutor made some ridiculous attempts to insinuate that this Defendant was motivated to commit this crime by Dr. Randolph. That is a theory spun out of thin air by a prosecutor who is trying to becloud the real issue. What a shameful thing to do to a decent, honest professional man, a doctor of integrity and distinction who lifted himself from the slums to make a constructive, successful life against the toughest odds. And after having achieved all that, this good doctor had to endure the ignominy, the shame, of being accused as an accessory to murder. I wonder if the Prosecutor would have dared go that far with a white doctor!"

"Your Honor!" Carroll cried out.

"Mr. Winkler, please! There is nothing to be gained by such speculative reflections on opposing Counsel."

"Ladies and gentlemen," Winkler continued, "it is obvious that I must try to present our summation of this case under great restrictions and interruptions. I am warned against speculating on the intentions and motives of the Prosecutor.

349

Well, perhaps the Prosecutor, who has yet another chance to sum up after I do, perhaps he will relieve us of the burden of speculating by answering a question or two for us.

"Why the overdetermined proof of every step leading up to and surrounding the commission of the crime? Why did the U.S. Attorney himself choose to prosecute this particular case among all cases? Was it because the system was working at its utmost to apprehend, try, convict and put away forever someone it hates?

"If this young man were white, rich, the son of a well-to-do, well-connected father, do you know what would have happened to him under exactly the same circumstances? He would have been turned over to a group of expensive psychiatrists, hustled off to a very fancy sanitarium, and eventually he would have been declared to be temporarily insane at the time of the crime and released. And the U.S. Attorney would have assisted in that process!

"But this Defendant is not white and not rich. So he must pay for his moment of protest with the rest of his life. Because that's what it was—not an act of murder, but a moment of protest.

"How do I know? The same way the Prosecutor knows. By what is missing from the evidence. We are presented with the most meticulous proof of what happened *before* the crime and *during* the crime. But not a word, not a solitary comment from the Prosecutor on the fact that this Defendant *had not provided himself with a single avenue of escape!* No car, no plane ticket, no confederate, no map—no plan whatsoever. And why? Because he did not intend to escape! That's right, ladies and gentlemen of the jury, he did not intend to escape."

Winkler let that sink in, as if to let the newsmen and women who were writing down his every word catch up.

"What is the significance of that fact? It is the ultimate proof, that this *is* a political trial. This man *wanted* to be caught and tried because it was his only way to let the whole

350

world witness his political protest. That was his real purpose.

"Is it the same means of protest that you or I would have chosen? Probably not. But then have I, or have any of you, been subjected to the same destructive oppression by this society as this poor man? Even those of you who are in this jury box and who are black, who have been discriminated against since the day of your birth, who have had to run twice as hard as any white person merely to stay in place, have any of you been subjected to what this Defendant has been forced to endure?

"Think about that. If you have any conscience you must think about it. A man cannot be expected to be deprived, starved, beaten, thrown into a reform school, forced to commit homosexual acts, a man cannot be expected to endure a lifetime like that and then go to his grave without a whimper, without a single protest."

For the first time, Scott felt that Winkler had truly lost himself in the cause of Midge Grove. This was his moment of genuine concern for Grove and only for Grove.

"The society could not go on saying to him, as it had said for all the years of his life, 'Nigger, why don't you just go 'way and die?' He was ready to die. His absence of any plan for escape proves that.

"But I will not stand here and ask for your respect, your confidence and at the same time lie to you. *He did this thing!* But not as a crime, only a protest. The criminal here in this courtroom is not this man. It is society! The society which made the act of this Defendant inevitable. The Defendant acted in self-defense against a society that was bent on killing him. He acted on behalf of every poor man, every black man, every deprived man who has faced the society's attempts to crush the manhood out of him.

"If he is guilty of any crime, it is of standing up and acting like a man for the first and only time in his life! And if that is a crime, then find him guilty!"

Winkler was wet now, right through to the collar of his

jacket. But his effort was not in vain, for when he finished, several men on the jury also mopped their faces, and the atmosphere of the courtroom was heavy with drama and with sympathy for Midgely Grove.

Winkler started back to his table, satisfied with his accomplishment. Although he had not mentioned the Doctrine of Social Inevitability, he still had preserved his right to appeal on that ground as well as others. And he had scored the same point, perhaps with even greater effect, since he had put it in emotional rather than theoretical terms.

Scott shook Linc's hand vigorously. Even Marlene was willing to accept him without reservations for the first time. Whatever Winkler's motives had been originally or would be ultimately, on this day he had done his very best for Midge Grove.

Beecher had offered the U.S. Attorney the choice of holding over his final summation until the next morning, but Carroll chose to go on at once. He addressed himself to the jury, but also, for the first time, to the press as well.

"Ladies and gentlemen, we are all met in this courtroom not by personal choice but out of a sense of duty. As citizens, when called upon and qualified, you are under legal as well as moral obligation to serve in the process of determining guilt or innocence in criminal cases. And once a grand jury hands down an indictment, it is my duty as United States Attorney for this district, to present the people's case to the best of my ability.

"That I am white and the Defendant black is an accident of circumstance. Regardless of his background, we did not choose this Defendant to prosecute. He elected himself by virtue of the deeds planned and committed by him as the evidence clearly shows.

"Just as it is the professional duty of a United States Attorney to prosecute, without choice or favor, so it is the duty of a jury to decide on the facts without favor. There are no black facts. Or white facts. There are only the facts as presented in the case.

"Even the Defense attorney, in his touching summary, does not deny the facts. He does not deny his client's commission of the crime, but he pleads for understanding, for sympathy. Understanding and sympathy may have some part in determining sentence, but they play no part in deciding guilt or innocence. Only the facts can decide that.

"And the facts remain. The witnesses testified to them. This Defendant is guilty, guilty of the crime of murder. When murder is committed upon the person of one in public life or public office, it is termed assassination. In a way, assassination is the most pernicious form of murder, for it strikes not only at the victim himself but at the entire structure of law, of order, at the entire judgmental process by which we make progress toward that day when all men *will* have all rights justly due them.

"That day will not be speeded by excusing or becoming accessories to assassination."

·◦❦ XXVI ❧◦·

It was a chilly day with low, dark clouds overhead. The car dropped Judge Albert Beecher at the rear entrance of the Federal courthouse. To the sound of a guitar and a single male voice singing "Ballad of a Hanging Judge," Beecher passed through the door that the attendant held open for him. He had no time for guilt or anger now, his charge to the jury rested too uneasily in his inner coat pocket, demanding to be read.

The press was in unusually heavy attendance. Carroll and his assistants were at their table. Winkler, Scott, Marlene and Midge Grove were at theirs. Beecher entered, expecting that Midge would rise and throw him the usual fisted salute. He was not disappointed.

Judge Beecher looked out over the courtroom, his grim gaze exacting silence. Then he glanced down at his notes, faced the jury and began his summation.

Beecher made it clear, as he had at the outset of the trial, that he was the arbiter of all questions of law, and that they, the jury, were charged with deciding all questions of fact. He also spelled out the various degrees of the crimes involved, including, of course, all the degrees of murder.

He pointed out in clear terms that the burden was on the Prosecution to prove its case, and it must do so beyond a reasonable doubt. If the Prosecution had failed to prove the charges made in the indictment, then the jury had to acquit.

But, on the other hand, the phrase "beyond a reasonable doubt" had a precise meaning within the law. It was the doubt that a reasonable person might have after carefully weighing all the testimony. It did not mean that the Government had to prove its case beyond all doubt.

Beecher stressed that the verdict of the jury in a federal case had to be unanimous. Jurors were not to be told how the count stood during voting, and every scrap of paper used to vote or tally votes was to be destroyed and not even the court attendants were permitted to see them.

If at any time the jury needed to have its recollection refreshed about certain parts of the testimony they were to signify that to the attendant. And if the judge agreed, it would be arranged, but only in the presence of the Defendant and Counsel for both sides.

Finally, the judge read the entire indictment, dismissed the alternate jurors from the case, and sent the remaining twelve out to the jury room to commence their deliberations. Then he ordered Midgely Grove removed to District jail.

Winkler embraced Grove. "We'll know soon," he whispered. "We'll know very soon." He pressed Midge's thin arms to comfort him, then he let the two Marshals manacle him and take him away.

Linc turned back to the table where Scott and Marlene were gathering up papers. Linc suddenly seemed years older. Instead of turning to talk to friends among the press or shove papers into his battered briefcase, he simply sank down into his chair, pushed his reading glasses back on his head to nestle in his unruly hair, and buried his face in both his hands.

It was a gesture of such weariness that Honey Rosenstone, who had been sitting in the courtroom every day for the last three days, came forward, brushed by the attendants and past the bulletproof glass barrier to reach his side. She knelt alongside his chair and put her arm around him.

"Linc? Darling? You all right?" she asked softly.

The warmth of her at his side, the scent of her perfume made him turn to her. He pressed his cheek against hers. Her hand slipped around his neck and patted him gently as if he were her child rather than her lover.

"Tired," he said. "Just worn-out tired."

"Let's go for a drive. There's a quiet place out along the river where we could have lunch, away from everyone."

"We have to be available, in case any questions come up. The Judge has to know where to call us. Let's go home," he said. "Home," as if she were already his wife. Honey helped him up, straightened his tie, kissed him on the cheek, and they walked out together.

Scott and Marlene followed immediately behind them. Outside, rain had begun to fall quite steadily. Reporters and TV men waited, and beyond the police barriers, the young crowd waited. The same singer was still playing his guitar and singing underneath a makeshift tent a dozen other young men and girls had built by buttoning together several raincoats and holding them aloft on the poles of their placards.

The rain, the singing, the grayness of the scene combined to lend a mournful sound and appearance to everything beyond the courthouse door.

As Winkler descended the steps, newsmen pressed around him, asking for his speculation on the outcome of the case. He muttered a tired, "No comment," and allowed Honey to shepherd him through the crowd toward the limousine.

Once they were comfortable in the back of the limousine, Honey asked the question that no one else dared, "What do you think they're going to do, Linc?"

He responded wearily, cautiously, "I think we have a pretty fair chance. We definitely have allies on the jury."

"I don't know if you can call them 'allies,' " Scott said, "but there's no desire for vengeance, that's sure. In a strange way what's going to be hammered out in that jury room is not the question of guilt or innocence—only guilt. I think it'll all depend on how much guilt the jury feels toward Midge Grove." Then Scott added as an afterthought, "You know, it just dawned on me, I'd hate to be sitting on that jury myself."

"They have to come in with an acquittal!" Linc said suddenly. Whether that was a firm belief or a hope he never made clear, for he was silent the rest of the way home. And they were all too exhausted to pursue it.

The rain was still falling in the early evening when the call came to the Rosenstone house. The clerk reported that the jury had gone out to dinner with no indication that they were close to reaching a verdict. They would resume after dinner, but if they did not arrive at a verdict by ten o'clock Judge Beecher would retire them until the next morning. It was unlikely that the attorneys would be required for the rest of this night.

Scott had begun to feel exhausted and he welcomed the clerk's news. After a brief drink, he said goodnight to Linc and Honey, and offered to drop Marlene on his way home.

Scott and Marlene stood on the top step of the Rosenstone mansion as Scott contemplated the rain, which was coming down quite heavily now.

"Wait here. I'll run for it, then pick you up," he said. Raising the collar of his coat, he hopped down the stairs two at a time, and raced halfway down the block to where his red Mustang was parked. He started the engine, set the wipers going, and when he could see clearly he pulled out to double park in front of the house. Then he leaned over, opened the passenger door and called out, "Okay!"

Marlene came down the steps so hastily that she slipped on a worn stone on the walk, and fell forward. Scott leaped out of the car, lifted her. Holding her tightly, he asked, "You all right?"

"Uh huh," she said, but her manner betrayed that she was hurt.

357

Once inside the car, Scott turned on the map light. In the glow, Marlene's knee showed a bright red patch. She had scraped it badly.

"That's pretty ugly," he said. "Can you move it?"

She flexed her knee, but with some pain.

"We ought to put something on that right away. Maybe we should have a doctor look at it."

"I'm okay!" she said, laughing, hoping to alleviate his concern.

Instead her laughter seduced him. It dimpled her right cheek and lit up her black eyes in that way which was most provocative to him. He embraced her so swiftly that she had no chance to fend him off. Her lips resisted him at first, but her desire overcame her. In a moment she drew back, breathless, but in control of herself once again.

"That won't help," she whispered softly but quite seriously.

Reprimanded, he retreated to safe territory. "We should have someone look at that." He offered her his clean breast-pocket handkerchief, placing it over the bloody scrape on her knee.

"Let's go get something to eat," he suggested.

"You're zonked. And I have to put something on this," she said.

"Let's go get something to eat," he said firmly. This time she didn't protest.

They had supper at one of the small restaurants that stayed open late to catch the after-theater crowd. Out of consideration for his weariness, Marlene refrained from discussing the case. And out of concern for her injury, Scott was preoccupied with getting her home as quickly as possible. So they ate in silence, having either too little to say to each other, or too much.

"I'd better go in with you tonight," Scott said, as he pulled up in front of her house.

358

He parked the car and assisted her to the doorway. By now her leg was beginning to throb and the knee had become stiff. Opening the front door, he led the way down the hallway to the far end. Then he opened her door, stepped in and looked around to make sure the place was secure. It seemed so. He turned to admit her.

She went to check the windows, then summoned him to look. There were deep marks in the metal grill. A prowler had obviously made an unsuccessful attempt to enter.

"We'd better notify the police," he decided.

"What good would that do? They don't act even after an actual robbery," Marlene answered.

"How do we know if it was robbery that was intended? Don't forget the two Australian girls who were raped and killed. On this same block."

"Two years ago," Marlene said. "The police have forgotten, I can assure you."

"I still think you should call."

"And explain what you're doing here? Scott Ingram. It would be one hell of a story, wouldn't it?"

It had never occurred to him. But she was right. It would make one hell of a story if Scott Ingram called the police from a black girl's apartment. She thought of such things, did Marlene. She must think about them quite a lot, he realized. It was a sort of honesty that warmed him, encouraged him.

He turned to her suddenly, embraced her. They kissed, and then their faces still touching, she said softly, "It is absolutely idiotic for two grown people to stand here kissing in wet raincoats."

Scott agreed very softly, as if to speak loudly would shatter the intimacy of the moment. For without saying it, she had invited him to make love to her.

They shed their coats and clothes quickly. And when they returned to each other's arms, they were naked. She raised his face to hers, holding it with both her hands, as she kissed him passionately.

359

Afterward, he would not remember which of them led the way to the couch, but they were there, exploring each other, with hands, lips, caresses until he was in her and they were one, and their long unsatisfied hunger for each other finally was fulfilled.

They lay together, breathing softly, drowsing, not speaking. There was nothing that needed saying. Then Scott remembered her knee. "Your knee still hurt?" he asked.

Marlene didn't answer, but turned on her side to face him. Her hand found his thigh, and she ran her nails across his flesh until it rose in tiny puckers. He could feel the stirring again. He rose to meet her, pressing against her, letting her know he was ready again as she wanted him to be. She let him find his way to the center of her fragrant body, where she received him easily, tenderly. She began to undulate gently. He joined her, their movement growing together until it reached its final peak, and they relaxed.

As they rested side by side, Scott's fingers toyed gently with her nipples, which were soft and rosy. She moved slightly, and he thought perhaps she did not want him to touch her breasts, but she said, "Go on, have me. And have me! And have me!"

The vindictive way she spoke made him rise up on one arm. He looked down, questioningly.

"I mean it! I've been thinking about it for weeks now. If we have each other enough, the mystery will be over. The hunger will be gone. Then we can go our separate ways."

"Don't joke about it!" Scott said strongly.

"I'm not joking," she said. "It's the only way. Let it burn itself out, and then we won't have to face the future difficulties."

Before he could protest, she turned her body to him and pressed his hands against her breasts.

"It's the only way," she whispered into his ear. "The only way."

"You know it isn't," he started to say, but the phone interrupted him.

On the third ring, Marlene answered. "It's for you," she said, handing the receiver to Scott.

A shocked expression spread across his face. Who could know where he was? "Yes? Hello? Who is this?"

"Scotty? Linc."

"Oh! What's up?"

"Just got a call from Beecher's secretary. He wants us in court first thing in the morning," Winkler said.

"They reached a verdict!"

"No. The jury sent out a note. They want some testimony read back."

"Did he say whose?"

"Randolph's," Winkler announced with great satisfaction.

"Randolph's?" Scott repeated. "That means there's a chance!"

"*Only* a chance," Winkler said before Scott could become too optimistic. He had seen juries make similar requests before, but they could be misleading. Just when you thought they were going one way on a case, they came up with a completely opposite verdict. It didn't pay to speculate.

"So they want to hear Randolph's testimony . . ." Scott mused, after he had hung up the phone.

"How good is that?" Marlene asked.

"It means that the jury bought the theory, even if Beecher didn't. And that's good news—damn good news." Scott took her in his arms with a great sense of relief. When he sought her lips to kiss her, she turned away suddenly.

"Marlene?"

"It just dawned on me. How did he know to call you here?"

"The hardest thing to keep secret is the fact that two people are in love," Scott said matter-of-factly.

·❧ XXVII ❧·

When Linc and Scott arrived at the courthouse the next morning, the young protesters were out in front, warming themselves around fires they had built in trash cans and empty oil drums. Their raincoats, still wet from last night's storm, hung limply on the police barricades.

The young clustered around Linc and Scott as they passed, patting them on the back, shouting their encouragement and an occasional epithet of derision against Beecher. But there was no militancy in their tone. They seemed in a light-hearted, victorious mood.

Word seemed to have spread accurately, for none expected the final verdict. They knew the appearance of counsel had something to do with the jury seeking further information. But to them, that had the scent of victory.

Bareheaded, his trenchcoat over his shoulders, Winkler smiled as he pushed his way through the crowd.

"Don't relax, brothers! It's not over yet! It doesn't even look hopeful."

"They'll never reach a verdict!" One jubilant voice called out. "It'll be a hung jury!"

"I wish I felt that sure!" Winkler called back. "But we have to be realistic. No judge is going to settle for a hung jury in just two days. So Midge is still depending on you! Fight the good fight! Right on!"

362

They pressed closer to him, to touch him or just his rumpled trenchcoat. They needed him, and more than ever, Linc seemed to need them, too. Girls pursued him, hugged him, kissed his lean, deeply wrinkled cheeks. And Winkler's hands went out to them, reaching for the young breasts that provoked and inspired him.

On the other side of the protestors, the press waited for Linc and Scott to arrive. Their greeting was just as warm. They always had great affection for those who provided them with the raw materials of their craft in such everlasting abundance. Winkler, being their hero and able to feed them highly quotable lines, was a special favorite.

"How does it look, Linc?"

"Up to this moment, Midge Grove is innocent. And obviously there's a good part of the jury that feels that way!"

"Is it true they want to hear the doctor's testimony again?"

Smiling knowingly, Linc called back, "I'm not allowed to comment on that at this time."

"Is it true that one publisher has offered seven hundred and fifty thousand dollars for Grove's life story, if he's acquitted?"

"That's only a rumor. Actually the offer is only half a million."

"What would you say the odds are, right this minute?" one newsman called out.

"Two things a smart lawyer doesn't do: Pick horses, and try to guess what a jury will do. That's all for this morning, fellows!" Winkler declared, but he had projected a strong enough feeling of confidence, and the newsmen assumed that he expected a hung jury at the worst.

The courtroom was filling slowly, as usual, hampered by the tight security procedures still in effect. Carroll was already at the prosecution table with one of his black assistants and five copies of what appeared to be a lengthy legal memorandum. Evidently they had been up all night preparing an argument against granting the jury's request to hear Randolph's testimony again.

Winkler and Scott took their places at the defense table. Marlene joined them, and immediately set to work arranging papers and laying out pencils. Most industriously she avoided Scott's eyes.

Fortuitously, Winkler was called to the bulletproof plastic shield by a gesture from one of the *Times*'s legmen. Scott took the opportunity to ask softly, "Marlene . . . what's wrong? Is it Linc's calling me at your place last night?"

She nodded and turned away, as if Linc's knowledge had suddenly soiled their relationship in some way.

At the barrier, Winkler was answering the reporter who had asked if he should phone Fred Anthony yet.

"Don't bother. We'll lend him our copy of Carroll's brief, and I'll call him later to give him our own arguments."

Judge Beecher must have been ready to ascend the bench, for the Defendant was entering, manacled to the two United States Marshals. Though he was dressed in his black uniform, leather jacket, denims, sweater, beret and glasses, on this day Midge Grove looked less imposing than ever. He seemed apart from the trial, apart from the world, apart even from the clothes that surrounded him but which he did not seem to wear.

Scott suspected that Midge had lost weight, pounds of weight, in the two days the jury had been deliberating. And his dark glasses, hiding his eyes, accentuated his forlorn, lost appearance. Unable to resist, Scott gently took the glasses from Midge's face. Midge's eyes startled him. Black and staring, they were rimmed by a red crusty border. He probably hadn't slept at all in the past forty-eight hours, and most likely he had been weeping a good part of that time.

"This isn't it, Midge—not yet. This is just an argument on whether the jury is allowed to hear certain testimony. That's a good sign, Midge, a very good sign." Scott tried to hearten him.

But Midge did not take encouragement from it. He only stared straight ahead until Scott slipped the glasses back on.

Beecher entered the courtroom, took the bench, and addressed both sets of Counsel quite briskly.

"Gentlemen, as you've been informed, there has been a request by the jury to rehear the testimony of Dr. Randolph."

Carroll was on his feet at once, his thick legal memorandum held out toward the bench. "Your Honor, as this memorandum points out clearly and abundantly, the testimony requested by the jury concerns a matter of law, not fact. Since the defense of Social Inevitability has been ruled out, it would be a serious error to allow any part of such testimony to be read back. It would severely prejudice the Government's case."

Beecher looked to Winkler, who rose in his slow and grave way. "True, the Court has already ruled out the defense on legal grounds. However, the Court cannot deny that a great deal of Dr. Randolph's testimony had to do with fact—scientific fact, relevant fact. And since the jurors are the final arbiters of the facts, I think they have an undeniable right to hear that testimony. To deny it to them would, in my opinion, constitute the gravest of reversible error."

Beecher responded, "The Court, too, has had the chance to ponder this question overnight and has anticipated the arguments on both sides. Therefore, the jury will be brought in."

Once the jury was seated, Beecher addressed them. "Ladies and gentlemen, a jury's request that testimony be read again is not automatically granted.

"In this particular instance, it is the decision of this Court that this testimony *not* be read again. I urge you to return to your deliberations and do your best to arrive at a fair and just verdict based on the knowledge you now have."

Once the jury was dismissed, nothing remained but more waiting. Instead of going back to the Rosenstones', Winkler stayed at the courthouse where he granted several television and magazine interviews, using the courthouse lobby as a background. He refused to speculate on the outcome of the case, but gave some hints as to their future course if the jury were to convict. Mainly he dwelt on his deep dissatisfactions with the judicial system.

"Let's face it! Judge Beecher was subjected to a few minutes of discomfort because he was surrounded by a group of fine, eager young people who were only demanding a fair trial for Midge Grove, and since that night he has ruled against us every single time. He is taking out his anger on a poor black man who is defenseless against such judicial lynching. I think our system has to be shook up until it is made clear who is the judge and who is the hangman."

"Linc, when you say shake up the Courts, how do you mean that?" one newsman pressed him.

"I mean shake them up! Shake them right to their roots!"

"How?" the reporter reiterated.

"Right in the highest court in this land!" Winkler said with an air of prophetic significance.

Having made a statement provocative enough to win him at least a minute or more on the nightly TV news, Winkler was content to bring the interview to an end.

At that moment the clerk of the courthouse came to summon Linc and Scott back to the courtroom, and this time the excitement of a verdict was in the air. As they went down the corridor toward the elevators, Scott asked, "Linc, did you mean that before? About shaking up the 'highest court in the land'?"

Smiling, in the enticing but evasive way he had, Winkler said, "You'll see, Scotty. If we don't get an acquittal, you'll see. It'll be a day to remember, I can promise you that."

"But if they do acquit him, then we never have to go to the Supreme Court," Scott said hopefully.

"You can't win 'em all," Winkler replied enigmatically, leaving Scott to wonder suddenly if going to the Supreme

366

Court was more important to Linc Winkler than defending Midge Grove.

"Gentlemen," the judge announced once they had all assembled, "I have in my hand a note which I will read to you. 'Your Honor, we are not able to reach a unanimous verdict as instructed.' That being the case, I intend to call the jury back and instruct them to try again."

Winkler rose quickly. "Your Honor, this jury has tried for more than forty-eight hours to reach a verdict and failed. We insist it be dismissed and a mistrial be declared."

"Denied!" Beecher ruled.

"We shall put our motion in more formal written terms."

"Counsel may do so."

After the jury had entered, Judge Beecher opened the book that every judge had at hand for just such situations, and read, " 'Ladies and gentlemen, we have your note. I'd like to tell you that the mode provided for deciding questions of fact in criminal cases is by a verdict of the jury. In a larger proportion of cases, absolute certainty cannot be attained. So in order to bring the minds of twelve jurors to a unanimous verdict, each juror must examine the question submitted with candor and with proper regard and deference to the opinions of each other. If the larger number of your panel are for conviction, a dissenting juror should consider whether a doubt in his own mind is a reasonable one, which makes no impression upon the minds of so many jurors equally honest, equally intelligent as himself, and who have heard the same evidence. On the other hand, if a majority are for acquittal the minority should question the weight and sufficiency of that evidence which fails to sway the minds of their fairminded fellow jurors.' "

Then Beecher looked up from the book. "This jury at this time is concerned with only one question, guilt or innocence —not the sentence, not any other questions presented in the course of this trial, save that one. Guilt or innocence. You

367

will return to the jury room and take up your deliberations again."

Once the jury was gone, Winkler rose. "Your Honor, we take exception to your last words. We think both by word and attitude it was intended to prejudice this jury against the Defendant and thereby to deprive him of a fair trial. Therefore we again move for a mistrial at this time."

"Motion denied!"

"Exception!"

"Noted!"

Hours passed. The day had become a clean, clear afternoon. The encampment of the young had grown steadily, swelled by students whose classes had let out at the numerous colleges and universities in and around Washington. By early evening they numbered several thousand.

The police multiplied at the same rate as the students. At the mayor's request, trucks full of National Guardsmen were moved into the city, remaining at a safe, though ready, distance from the courthouse. The entire city seemed to feel that some time tonight there would finally be a verdict in the most publicized case ever tried in the District.

Older, mature citizens gathered before their television sets awaiting the verdict.

In the White House, the President had his television set on as he worked through the evening on questions of trade relations with Mainland China and Japan.

Fred Anthony was home having dinner with his family— one of his most paternal duties—but he had left word that the office was to call him as soon as the principals were recalled to the courtroom. And as he ate the well-balanced meal Aggie had prepared, Anthony was trying out in his mind several lead sentences, seeking just the right phrases to frame his own personal feeling in statesmanlike language.

Young as he was, Anthony fancied himself the only logical successor to Arthur Krock and Walter Lippmann. So he always wrote with an eye toward collecting his columns into a book with a title such as *The State of the Nation*. In fact, Fred Anthony had already received several interesting offers. Surely one of the important highlights of such a book would be the piece he would write about this historic trial.

In various embassies, hotel reception rooms and entertainment suites, the usual Washington cocktail parties had begun, parties carefully planned for months and organized for a purpose. But this particular evening saw them all sabotaged by the final dramatic moment in the trial of Midge Grove. Ambassadors, lobbyists for large companies and entire industries, smiling graciously, played host for guests whose only topic of discussion was not the purpose of the party but the Grove verdict. How could a jury be out that long on such a simple case? He had murdered the judge, there was no question about that. Foreigners said only in America would such a clear-cut question take so long to resolve. So while they all drank and ate voraciously, the purpose of the party grew dimmer in their minds.

At the Rosenstone house things were thankfully quiet. By chance and good luck, Honey had arranged no cocktail party or buffet for that evening. There was only a small dinner for two. Honey and Linc Winkler.

Linc wanted to watch the television coverage of the trial, so Honey had the table set before the fireplace in the library. CBS was running a special with Walter Cronkite and Eric Severeid, who had originated their telecasts from the capital ever since the jury had started its deliberations. Linc picked at his roast beef, while he watched the CBS shots of the enormous crowd that was growing outside the courthouse.

Now that darkness had descended on the city, the photographic effects were becoming more interesting. Bonfires accented the scene as it was shot from a high crane atop a CBS remote truck. The camera kept making slow pans of the area, with special reference to the police who moved among the clusters of the young. And telephoto lenses picked up a few army trucks with uniformed National Guardsmen surrounding them a short distance away.

Cronkite's commentary was as impromptu as the random camera shots. At one point, as a camera fixed on the army trucks, Cronkite could not help but be reminded of the tragic events at Kent State and expressed the hope that both the Guard and the students would accept with forbearance the jury's verdict.

For a good part of the time, the network just opened its microphones wide so the singing of the various student groups could be heard. The singing sounded less militant than it had in the earlier phases of the trial. It was filled with either resignation or devout hope, acknowledging that the law had laid down and the jury had taken up the burden. Juries, they seemed to be saying, were more equitable than courts and judges.

When Severeid's turn came, he spoke with the usual pompous modesty and omniscient wisdom of TV commentators.

"One would have to go back to the days of the Civil War to recapture the ominous and pregnant feeling that is at large in the capital tonight. Not even the recent anti-war protests gave the same sense that the fate of the republic was being decided. These are our young. And they are questioning tonight whether our judicial system can survive in fairness and equity. Now it is in the hands of a jury of twelve ordinary men and women, untrained for the decision of destiny they are called upon to make, but make it they must. The effect of that decision upon our young may be as climactic in this nation's affairs as was the Civil War itself."

The cameras were playing over the crowd again. Linc watched, and Honey watched him, watched the changing reflections from the tube play across his lean, intent face. Nothing, not even a woman, could distract him from his most glorious moments when he could see the impact of his work so vividly displayed on television.

Linc was especially pleased when CBS replayed some shots of him taken earlier that day. Smiling like a devoted mother, Honey studied him as he studied himself. She could indulge him in that, in ways that she had never indulged her own husband. For whatever Linc Winkler's shortcomings— his vanity, his effulgent ego—he was a man who moved people. He accomplished the things he set out to do. So Honey could admire him and accept his shortcomings. But whether she could accept a lifetime of them, that she did not know.

In his little flat, Scott Ingram was trying to eat the light snack he had prepared. With the verdict so imminent, he had promised Linc that he would be home so he could be reached on a moment's notice. He had invited Marlene. But she refused, because of Linc's call of the night before, he suspected. So he sat alone, watching the television coverage of the scene outside the courthouse and eating a dry tunafish sandwich he had prepared.

As he watched, the entire mass of young people were singing and swaying in unison for Midge Grove. The TV cameras played across them and the feeling that was reflected on the screens in the nation's homes was that of a giant revival meeting. And so it must have been, for it seemed to involve everyone in the street, even those who had not joined in. There was a reverence about that that was touching, regardless of how one felt about Midge Grove, his crime or the outcome of the case.

Scott became so engrossed that he left his sandwich and let his coffee grow cold. He wondered whether the case would have become so significant if Linc Winkler had not taken it. He thought back to that afternoon when the call first came in to him in his father's office. Important as it seemed then, he had not dreamed it would reach such proportions. In the time he had been watching the news coverage, he had heard Winkler's name mentioned often. A number of times they had even included his own, and he felt the sudden need to share it with someone. For the first time Scott could fully appreciate the feeling of satisfaction Linc always enjoyed when he sat in a roomful of friends and associates and saw himself or heard his name on TV.

Scott's musings continued as the cameras showed other views of the courthouse grounds, until he was almost lulled into a state of infinite patience.

Then the phone rang, breaking his mood. He leaped to answer it. It was Winkler.

"Scott! I just got the call. There's a verdict. Hurry on down!"

As impressive as the scene had appeared on television, it was even more so as Scott approached the courthouse. Either the gathering had grown even larger or the cameras had not done justice to it. He was warned away from the police line that surrounded the outer fringes of the crowd until he identified himself. Then, with a police escort, he penetrated the line and the crowd, making his way among the young, who were now packed in fairly closely. His police escort won him only jeers, but once he was recognized the crowd gave way freely, shouting their encouragement and predicting a favorable verdict.

Scott Ingram was at the courthouse now. Identified, he slipped through. In the courtroom members of the press were already being frisked and admitted. Scott waited his turn. As soon as he entered the courtroom Scott could see that Marlene was already at the counsel table, but Linc had not yet arrived.

He started down the aisle, past spectators and the rows reserved for the press. There was a sudden stir of excitement behind him. He turned, expecting it would be Linc, but it was Fred Anthony, coming to witness the final moment of this drama, like a theater critic at a new play.

When Scott reached the barrier, he had to be frisked again by a uniformed court policeman. On this particular night, extra strict security was enforced. Finally he was allowed to pass the bulletproof plastic shield.

At the counsel table, Marlene tried to smile at him. But the moment was too grave and she failed.

The Marshals were bringing Midge Grove into the courtroom. Spectators stood to see him. Even members of the press, who had seen him every day for weeks now, stood to watch him enter. He wore his uniform and his dark glasses. He moved slowly, a man in a stupor, giving the impression of a blind man bereft of his seeing eye dog or his cane. Marlene went to him, took his hand, led him to the table. Grove's hand was damp, icy, and it trembled. Marlene covered it with both her own warm hands. She had never touched a dying person before, but she knew it must feel like this.

Scott took him gently by the shoulders and eased him into his seat. Winkler and Honey arrived at that moment. After leaving Honey outside the railing, Linc greeted Midge with a pat on the shoulder and took his seat. Once the courtroom was filled and sealed from the outside, word was passed back to Judge Beecher. The judge looked more tired than he had during the most hectic days of the trial. Assuring himself that everyone was in place, that everything was as secure as it could be, he pounded his gavel once.

"Bring in the jury!" he ordered.

The clerk was gone for what seemed like a long time, but anxiety made it only seem so. The door opened. The twelve men and women entered. Sober-faced, trying not to stare to one side or the other, they took their places in the jury box.

Judge Beecher addressed the foreman. "The Court has been informed that you have reached a verdict."

Rising, the black man said, "We have, Your Honor."

"The Defendant will rise," Beecher said solemnly.

Midge did not respond, as if he had not heard or not understood. Gently, Scott helped him to his feet, and then, feeling Midge tremble, Scott remained standing beside him for support.

"What is the jury's verdict?" Beecher demanded.

"We, the jury, find the Defendant guilty on all counts."

Before the outburst could gather strength, Beecher sounded his gavel. Calling out to Winkler, he asked, "Does the Defense wish to poll the jury?"

"We do, Your Honor." Winkler said, rising, unperturbed, cool.

The jurors were each questioned and each responded, affirming that he or she had voted guilty on all counts.

Scott Ingram had allowed Midge Grove to slump quietly into his chair as soon as the verdict was announced. It seemed an unnecessary cruelty to make him stand through the polling. Now Marlene leaned toward him, placing her arms around him, pressing her face against his. In this worst moment of his wretched life, he was at least entitled to the close, consoling touch, the warmth of a woman.

Judge Beecher announced when the jury would be reconvened to determine sentence and Winkler made several motions, asking again that the judge declare a mistrial. But they were formal, empty motions and all were rejected by Beecher.

The two marshals stepped forward to take control of Midge Grove, now convicted of murder in the first degree. But Winkler intervened, asking, "One minute, boys?"

The Marshal in charge nodded, but they did not retreat.

"Midge, listen to me. This isn't as final as it sounds. Do you understand me? It'll be months, maybe years. Linc Winkler is making this promise to you: I'm going to get you off! Keep the faith! *I* am going to get you off!"

Both Scott and Marlene heard Winkler's words, and they wondered if he meant them. Or was he just trying to give Midge courage until he grew used to the fact of his conviction? Neither of them imagined that Linc could be making such a promise seriously.

But he was.

·◦❧ XXVIII ❧◦·

Word of the guilty verdict reached the huge crowd outside the courthouse only seconds after it was announced by the jury's foreman. The protest was instantaneous. It began with the anguished outcry of a single, young, long-haired, bare-footed white girl who cried out, "No! No! No!" She broke down sobbing. It spread through the crowd. Young men expressed their anger in harsh, loud voices. Young women broke into tears. They wept and clung to their young men or to other young women. Black and white, woolly Afros and straight, long, flaxen hair, they clutched at each other and wept.

It was not the presence of the police and the National Guardsmen that kept violence from erupting, but the weeping, a kind of public mourning that greets the death of every national hero.

The networks had brought up a number of huge arc lights to enhance their coverage by allowing the cameras to zoom in and pick up colorful and impressive individuals and groups. When Winkler, Scott, Marlene, and Honey came out of the building all the arcs focused on them so they stood in a light brighter than the sun. They seemed transfixed by it. A microphone attached to several loudspeakers was presented to Winkler.

He moved a step forward from the others and reached out to the crowd with his voice.

"Brothers . . . and tonight, no matter what your color, if you're here, you are a brother!"

He was rewarded, as he knew he would be, by a huge, resounding cheer.

"Brothers and sisters, you have kept the faith and the vigil. And for your time, sacrifice, and trouble you have been rewarded by a first row seat at the final breakdown of the American judicial system.

"When a man is on trial for his life, no judge should have the power to gag the attorneys who are struggling to defend him, as we have been gagged time and again. No accused should be forced to fight for vindication before a jury that is especially chosen to simulate fairness by the color of its skin.

"No accused should be made to fight for his freedom with barricades around the courthouse, armed guards in the courtroom, bulletproof barriers. These are the tools of dictatorships, not democracies! In truth, this trial may finally have revealed to the people of this nation and the world the hard realities of this repressive fascist society. If it has done that, then Midge Grove will not have suffered in vain. And, if he must, he will not pay in vain with the rest of his life!"

Winkler tossed the microphone to whoever was closest to him and plunged into the crowd. He moved among them like a messiah. And they greeted him as one, catching his hand, the edge of his garment, anything. Contact with him would be a cherished memory of a historic night.

Scott and Marlene watched him, not daring to look at each other. But when their eyes met it was with a look of fear. The spectacle, though not unexpected, was frightening. Marlene drew closer to Scott, reached for his hand as if she needed reassurance.

Only Honey stood alone, shaking her head in wonderment. That they could love him did not surprise her. She loved him, too. But that they could accept him so completely and without reservations amazed her and caused her some regret.

In the small but very comfortable den of his quiet home, Justice Ben Robertson was watching the television coverage of the crowd outside the courthouse. He had just heard Winkler's speech and watched him plunge into his crowd of followers.

He was relieved that there had been no violence, but his relief was replaced by disapproval as soon as Winkler delivered his speech on the courthouse steps. True, the trial was over. Still, from a member of the bar and an officer of the court, the speech was ill-advised.

Robertson found himself speculating on what Grove's sentence might be. With the Supreme Court's recent decision and the many confusing opinions that had been written to strike down the death penalty, he knew that life imprisonment was the maximum that Carroll could ask for. But Robertson wondered. A jury that debated guilt or innocence so long, might they not also vote on the side of leniency?

He was to be proven wrong. Within a week, the jury would vote unanimously for a life sentence without mercy for Midge Grove.

Honey, Marlene, and Scott waited until Linc had finished with the crowd, then they started toward Honey's car. Scott declined Honey's invitation for a drink and supper, explaining he preferred to walk home in the cool night air. It was a lovely night and besides, Scott wanted to rid himself of the tension and sense of failure he felt.

Marlene found another pretext to refuse Honey's offer, then hurried after Scott who was already halfway down the block.

"Do you mind?" she asked softly. He shook his head.

Suddenly she said, "It was hopeless from the start. You always knew that."

"My fault! I should have insisted!"

"On what?" Marlene asked.

"Insanity! It was his only chance!" Scott said, angry with himself.

"When it comes to political cases, Winkler's the best there is. You had to accept his judgment," Marlene comforted, though she felt as strongly as Scott did.

"I should have had more faith in my own judgment. I should have insisted!"

They were at her house. Marlene could not bring herself to send him away feeling as he did. "Would you like some coffee? Or something to eat?" she asked.

They had talked. They had had coffee and some frozen cake which Marlene had heated up. They had used up every time-consuming pretext to pretend that making love was not the main purpose of this night. Now they were in bed. She had enticed him actually, and for the first time. She had used her body to dispel his defeat and her warmth to warm him. She had drawn him into herself as though there and there alone he could spend his frustration and anger in a burst of sexual relief. Now, physically and emotionally spent, he lay beside her sleeping.

Marlene was not sleepy. She lay on her side, staring down at Scott's handsome face, even toying with the strands of his longish blond hair. Gently she cradled his head close to her breasts. Marlene knew for the first time in her life how much she yearned to be free of the burden of being black, and all that that meant. For the chance to choose to love a young man like Scott Ingram without all the difficulties and the pain that must go with it.

Soon, she knew, there would have to be a verdict for them, too. She wondered, Was the Grove case the real bond between them? Or was it deeper, stronger?

At the Rosenstone house, Linc Winkler was taking yet another telephone call from another friend, another admirer, another militant civil rights lawyer, another leader of a black activist group. The phones that had been ringing when they arrived home hadn't stopped yet, and it was now past two o'clock in the morning. Through all his conversations, Honey had made Linc's drinks, brought his food, poured his coffee. She had even taken off his shoes and helped him out of his tie and shirt.

Linc talked on, saying essentially the same thing to each caller. He would need the help and assistance of all sympathetic groups—money, of course, but also public support, protests, and meetings. The main thing was Midge Grove. He had to be kept alive in the minds and hearts of young people, especially young black people.

To those who sought to sympathize with Linc on the loss, he protested that the fight was far from over. It had only just begun.

Eventually by three o'clock in the morning, Honey was able to pry the phone away from him. And when it rang again she firmly put her hand on it, preventing him from answering. Linc laughed and gave in. He pulled her down on the couch and kissed her on the lips, the face, the neck, lingering on her breasts, pressing his face against the warm flesh and inhaling its perfume. Weary as he was with the events of the nights, he was quick to become aroused.

Honey laughed. "Linc, you know how you're going to die? In a motel room with some seventeen-year-old coed, from a heart attack. *After!*"

In his solitary cell in the District jail, Midge Grove slept alone as he had all the nights of his life. Exhausted from fear as well as the tension of three days of wakeful waiting, he had finally fallen into deep sleep.

It was the first time that Marlene had ever permitted Scott to spend the night. He awoke to the smell of fresh coffee perking. Feeling battered and bruised at first, Scott realized

379

that these were only the internal hurts of the guilty verdict still with him. He turned over. Marlene, in her robe, was sitting across from him, having her first cup of coffee. She smiled. He felt better instantly.

Scott washed, and was having his coffee when Marlene asked soberly, "What did Linc mean last night when he promised Midge that he was going to get him off?"

"We'll go to the Circuit Court of Appeals, of course. I'd say we have a fair chance of getting a new trial."

"Will you have the right to raise the question of insanity next time?"

"Yes." He was silent for a moment, then, "You know what's strange? I feel so sorry for Grove now that I'm almost willing to overlook the fact that he killed a man. When you become deeply involved in a case you feel that he *has* to go free. The jury *has* to see it your way; and if they don't, you feel like I felt last night." He paused and then he said, "Thanks, Marlene."

"Was it another grandstand play?" she asked.

"What?" Scott looked puzzled.

"Was it just to keep Midge's spirits up? Or does Winkler really believe there's a way to get Midge off?"

Scott shrugged, extremely doubtful. Then he reached out to flip on the television set to see how the morning news shows were handling the conviction. When Marlene smiled, he exclaimed defensively, "I'm not Linc Winkler! And no, I don't expect to see myself!"

Even before the picture appeared, they could hear the familiar voice of Linc Winkler saying, ". . . if Sacco and Vanzetti had been acquitted at their first trial, who would remember them today? It takes many defeats to insure the final victory."

Then the picture flooded the entire tube, and Winkler appeared, being interviewed on the Today Show. The smiling, solicitous woman who was questioning him suggested, "Would you call what happened to Sacco and Vanzetti a final victory? Or are you saying that you've given up hope for Midge Grove?"

"Given up?" Winkler echoed defiantly, "My dear girl, the last word in this case will be spoken by the Supreme Court of the United States. And that word is going to surprise a lot of people. A hell of a lot of people!"

Stunned, Scott turned to face Marlene, "He means it. He really means it."

PART FOUR

THE
SUPREME COURT

XXIX

While Scott Ingram labored at drafting the brief on appeal to the District Circuit Court of Appeals, Linc Winkler divided his time among three other notorious cases, one the murder trial of the Gainesville Twelve. Scott was relieved to have full freedom and responsibility for the appeal brief, though he had to concede that as he worked on the transcripts of the trial his respect for Winkler grew. Linc had provoked a harvest of highly questionable rulings by Judge Beecher, almost as if he had been aiming for an appeal from the outset of the trial.

Scott worked at the brief with great diligence, researching every case and making endless notes which he later dictated to Marlene. Where there were no prior cases to support his arguments, as on the new issue of Social Inevitability, he beefed up his position with impressive quotations from eminent sociologists, psychiatrists and philosophers.

He mailed off each draft to Winkler and awaited his reactions and suggestions. The brief had to fit Winkler's specifications, because his would be the final responsibility for arguing the appeal before all nine Judges. Normally three judges would hear an appeal, but the Grove case was considered so significant that they were sitting *en banc*, all nine of them.

The points Scott stressed in his brief, in addition to the

doctrine, included Beecher's admission of the face-to-face identifications and Midge's confession, the general hostility and prejudice in the community at large, the military atmosphere in the courtroom and Judge Beecher's prejudicial attitude, especially after the attack on him at the Kennedy Center.

Linc's contribution to the brief was to stress two points. He urged building up even more the argument that their new doctrine should constitute a defense in law. And he urged that more emphasis be placed on the argument that Midge Grove had been denied due process of law. When Scott demurred about this last, explaining that it was too vague, Linc insisted that it remain vague, for purposes he never quite fully explained.

Finally the brief was in shape. It was printed, served on Carroll's office, and filed. Scott felt certain that it was strong enough to win them a new trial even without argument.

Linc Winkler was in the midst of another trial in California when their appeal was scheduled. The night before the argument, he packed his bags and flew to Washington. He and Scott went over the brief in detail and then Linc locked himself in a room at Honey's house to prepare himself for the important encounter in the morning.

As always, his presence assured extensive news coverage outside the Federal Courthouse. But on this bright clear morning Linc Winkler had no time for the press. That impressed Scott and heartened him. Midge Grove would get his fair hearing this day before the Court of Appeals.

But once Linc rose to deliver his argument, opening with a brusque rebuke to the bench concerning the fact that eight of the nine men sitting were white, Scott began to realize with sickening impact that Linc was more intent on scoring political points than winning Grove the new trial that the brief easily could have secured for him. As the argument proceeded, and Linc provoked increasingly obvious hostility

386

from the judges by responding to their questions with attacks rather than answers, Scott knew that their appeal was doomed.

Carroll must have known it too, for he limited himself to a brief argument and answered all questions from the bench without any great emotion or personal involvement.

Later, when Linc and Scott were ensconced in the Rosenstone Rolls and Scott's depression had become extremely evident, Linc urged, "Cheer up, Scotty!"

"Linc, I think we blew it," Scott said grimly.

"You mean *I* blew it. Well, say so, kid, say so!" Winkler declared, still smiling.

"Okay! Yes! You're damn right, you blew it! We had a strong case, a good brief. I would have staked my life on a new trial. And yes, *you* blew it by antagonizing the whole bench!"

Winkler leaned back and laughed.

"They're going to turn us down on a new trial!" Scott exploded. "And if you don't know it, Carroll certainly does!"

"Which is why I want you to start drafting a petition for a writ of *certiorari* this afternoon. I told you once before, we are going to the Supreme Court. A new trial wouldn't turn out any differently than the first trial. And I want more!" Winkler declared.

"How much more can you want?"

"The Court of Appeals would probably have given us a reversal. I want dismissal."

"Dismissal?" Scott was astounded.

"Yes, dismissal!" Linc reiterated. "You get that writ granted, and I'll guarantee you a dismissal in the highest court in the land!"

Whether Scott believed Linc Winkler or not, he knew that the burden fell on him to draft a powerful and persuasive petition for a writ of *certiorari*. Midge's life depended on it. If he succeeded, Midge would have his new trial. But if he

387

failed, the poor little man faced a lifetime in jail where he would live in perpetual fear and would eventually, but surely, go insane.

It was a cool September day in Washington. Some twenty hours of drenching rain had not only washed the streets and the stone buildings and monuments until they were bright and clean, it had washed out the last of a humid summer and brought in the first crisp day of fall.

Benjamin Robertson, Senior Justice of the Supreme Court of the United States, was striding along Constitution Avenue on his way toward the Courthouse. It was his custom, weather permitting, to walk to the court each morning. It fulfilled his doctor's orders to get some regular exercise to keep his heart and body in tone, and gave him the best chance to think clearly without interruption about those matters which weighed on his mind. This morning, with fall in the air, Ben Robertson was enjoying his walk. He strode along at a good clip, making sure to breathe deeply and regularly. He felt healthy and invigorated.

No doubt part of his good humor was attributable to the dinner he had had last evening with Charlie Andrews. Charlie had been his law clerk back in 1959 and he was back in Washington to argue his first case before the Supreme Court. He had brought with him his wife, Marie, and their two children. Since Robertson had performed the wedding ceremony, he felt gratified that they all seemed happy, and that Andrews was advancing so well in his career.

Law clerks were like sons to Robertson, who had no children of his own. He adopted them, not only for the short period of their tenure but for all the years thereafter. He kept in contact with them all, which by now meant a long, imposing list of correspondence each year, especially at Christmas and on those dates when his diary reminded him of birthdays and wedding anniversaries. Each Christmas there were more children to buy gifts for, more cards to be sent. In the past four years Honey Rosenstone had assumed his shopping burdens. To judge from the joyous calls and the enthusiastic letters of gratitude, she did the job well.

Perhaps Robertson particularly enjoyed last evening's reunion because it relieved him from having to wrestle with the problem he faced today. This Friday, as every Friday, was conference day at the high court. Having heard cases argued all week, this morning the Justices would discuss each case and vote on its outcome. Robertson already knew from the questions that had been asked during the various arguments that there would be some sharp, even bitter, divisions. Cases growing out of the Vietnam war were still plaguing the Court. Though by agreement the war was over, there were still cases pending in which the use of executive power to wage undeclared war was the key issue. Unlike the majority of the Justices, Robertson felt strongly that the Court was shirking its duty by not ruling on the question. There would be one such question coming up this morning.

Another case sought to defeat by fragmentation *Brown vs. The Board of Education* by delimiting the power of the courts to provide for enforcement of integrated education. With some of the new members on the high bench that question would undoubtedly result in a fierce conflict.

But as Robertson walked along, he knew that the real cause of his concern was not any of the cases that had been heard, but the petitions for writs of *certiorari* that were always the first order of business in the Friday conference. Prime among those applications was the writ requesting permission to appeal to the high court on behalf of Midgely Grove. Robertson's view of that application was affected by many things. For one, his own personal memory of the day of the crime, that sudden confrontation with violence and death from which, he could privately admit, he had not quite recovered. On that ground, he would have liked to be relieved of hearing the appeal.

Yet, there was the question of the admissibility of a de-

389

fense *de novo*, the Doctrine of Social Inevitability. It was an intriguing concept, even though it had shocked many people. Perhaps *because* of the many people it had shocked, it deserved the Court's consideration. But out of necessity, the Supreme Court selected only those cases that raised important and far-reaching questions—an average of only one case out of every twenty among the thousands urged on it—and Robertson suspected that most of the Justices would vote to avoid ruling on the Social Inevitability aspect. So he was prepared for a fight this morning.

The farther he walked, the faster his pace and the stronger his determination. He marshaled his arguments, aiming them at the colleagues he hoped to bring over to his side. Fortunately, he needed only three, since any four Justices voting in favor of granting a writ of *certiorari* assured that the entire Court would hear the case. He would concentrate on Braham, Engle, and Courtwright. Courtwright because he was black, Braham and Engle because they were considered liberals, though by his own yardstick they were moderates at best. But in this war of judicial progress one sought allies where he could. The last few appointments to the Bench had isolated Ben Robertson from the majority, swinging the Court to the conservative side.

The imposing white building loomed through the trees now. Justice Robertson quickened his pace, eager to arrive in time to have a cup of coffee with Engle before the conference started.

Engle was not in his office when Ben Robertson dropped by, so there was no opportunity for prior discussion. He went to his own office, trailed into private chambers by his secretary who read off to him the list of calls of late yesterday and early this morning. All could wait; none were important enough to interrupt his concentration on the impending meeting.

The buzzer sounded, summoning him and all the Justices to the conference room. He glanced at the antique wall clock, a gift from his wife when he was appointed to the Court years ago. It was precisely five minutes to ten. He left his office, went down the quiet hall to the large room and discovered that he was the first to arrive. The black court attendant, traditionally called a messenger, was laying out pads, pencils and papers at the place of each of the nine men.

"Good morning, Elton," Robertson said.

"Morning, Mr. Justice," the attendant said gravely.

"Nice day, extremely nice day. Best season of the year, fall," Robertson said as he looked around the familiar room. In all his years on the Court, he had never entered the conference room without being impressed by the exquisitely carved oak walls, the marble fireplace, the simplicity of the long, green-topped table around which much of the nation's history was made. Everything in the room was precisely symmetrical, except the arrangement of the chairs around the conference table.

The chair of the Chief Justice at one end faced the chair occupied by the Senior Justice at the other. This second chair was Ben Robertson's, as the small bronze plate on its back indicated. On one side of the table were four chairs, on the other side only three, and whereas in the courtroom each Justice chose a chair of a design to his own liking, in this room all the chairs were identical.

The other Justices began to file in, each shaking hands with all the others, as was the custom in this room. Even if two Justices had shared a cup of coffee in chambers a few moments before entering, they still would observe the ritual of shaking hands once they had arrived in this room. It was an old and hallowed tradition going back to the time of Chief Justice Fuller, who had originated it as a symbol that harmony of aims, if not of views, was the guiding principle of the august court.

Robertson took his seat at the end of the table and glanced at the agenda of petitions. He noticed that the matter of Midgely Grove was last on the list, perhaps an indication

391

that the Chief Justice wanted to dispose of all others before confronting this thorny one.

Seventy-two petitions were presented and all were put to a quick vote. Only three were granted leave to appeal. The seventy-third and last came up for discussion now.

As custom dictated, Chief Justice Crane began the discussion on the Grove petition. He spoke with cold reserve and judicial aloofness.

"Gentlemen, I must confess that I am not particularly moved by the arguments in the Grove petition. From my point of view, there is no singular or important question of due process presented here, nor is there a question of equal protection under the law. In truth, were it not for the sad and unfortunate fact that the victim in this case was one of our own number, I would find nothing here worthy of our consideration. To decide to hear this matter on that ground would be to decide on a personal and emotional basis rather than a legal one. I, for one, am against granting the writ."

Crane glanced down at his paper, for to look straight ahead would be to confront Robertson sitting opposite him at the end of the table. Crane had a strong suspicion about how Robertson felt, even though they had never discussed it. Robertson, being the senior member of the Court, took his turn next.

"I wish to make a comment at this time, which I trust will not be misinterpreted either by the Chief or by any of you. I, too, am for a legal determination of this matter, not an emotional one. But I fear that underlying our determination this morning, there may be just such emotional resentment. Even those of you who have little contact with the mass media have become aware of the abusive manner in which the defense in this case has been carried on. I would not for an instant defend the conduct or the actions of Defense Counsel in court or out.

"However . . ." and Robertson paused to give weight to his words, "I would not feel that I had acquitted myself of my duties as a Justice of this Court if I allowed that to sway my opinion. I know there may be a tendency to say, 'Let's close off this overpublicized matter here and now. The District Court of Appeals has already ruled. Let that ruling stand.'

"Whatever you may think of this case until now, the petition before us is a sound document. It poses several important questions. And I think *because* the victim was one of us we must undertake to hear this.

"I admit the question raised, concerning whether the Doctrine of Social Inevitability is a proper defense, is a unique issue of criminal responsibility. But precisely because of its uniqueness, it demands consideration by this Court. If it seeks to break down old boundaries of legal thought and open up new vistas, then it is our duty to examine it. If we fail to do so, then I disagree with the Chief, I say we *have* deprived the Defendant of due process of law."

He had spoken strongly, but not at great length. He would wait until after the others had spoken and if it became necessary, he would elaborate then.

Justice Overton, next in seniority to Robertson, had the choice of speaking or passing. He presented his opinion succinctly.

"The desire to endow this particular case with new and unusual legal aspects may only be in pursuit of more publicity. To give note to it is not only to pander to public clamor but to invite more of it. The Court should always be above that."

Robertson had never had much hope of budging Overton, and now that was confirmed. The discussion went around the table, and as each man spoke, it became more and more clear that Robertson's earlier estimate was correct. Without Braham, Engle, and Courtwright, he had no chance. He was tense when Braham's turn came.

Braham, too, was highly sensitive to the public interest focused on the case, but precisely because of this, he was inclined to hear the case. Skillful propaganda had created doubts in this country and throughout the world. It was important to put these questions to rest, he felt, to prove that Grove had had his full measure of consideration from the American judicial system. Braham did not like to recall the consequences of the Kennedy fiasco, which was still debated and probably destined to be debated as long as men were on this earth.

He believed that refusing to hear this case would only add to such discussions: Why had the Supreme Court refused to hear the Grove case? What were they hiding? Why had they refused to rule upon the concept of Social Inevitability? Sometimes it was the wiser course to confront an issue and defuse it, rather than avoid it because of public clamor and interest.

Yes, Braham was in favor of granting the writ.

So was Courtwright, though he was somewhat self-conscious about it since he was the only black man on the Court.

That left only Engle, youngest in both age and standing in the Court. He had been appointed to fill the vacancy created so abruptly by the shocking murder of Justice Miller. Engle had been considered a conservative at the time of his appointment and confirmation, but if Robertson had any chance at all, Engle would have to vote his way.

Engle began a bit self-consciously, for although he had been a highly regarded judge on the Federal bench of California before his present appointment, he felt, and for a long time would feel, a bit intimidated by those senior members who surrounded him. "Gentlemen, having spent the past eight years of my life presiding in trial courtrooms, I am closer to the hard realities of criminal trials than any of you. Perhaps that will add sufficient weight to my words to balance my youth and the brevity of my service on the Court.

"We are living through a time of great ferment. At the bar, in the courtroom, as well as in our political and social life. Unless new ideas are given a chance to be heard, we shall be

394

building up an irrepressible force that, seeking some form of expression, may well lead to revolution."

Robertson glanced up from his pad where he had been doodling with the name Honey. This young Engle was a bit deeper than he thought—and not as conservative as the President had thought. Perhaps it would benefit all these old buzzards around this table if they were to go back and preside over a few trials, to feel the mood of the people again. Then Robertson smiled, remembering that of all the Justices, including the Chief, he was the eldest.

"If there is no valid defense in the concept of Social Inevitability, we might do better to consider it and lay it to rest once and for all," Justice Engle continued. "But if there is, we might as well face it and admit it. I must say frankly that I for one have no opinion on that yet, but I do feel, as does Mr. Justice Robertson, that the question raised during Grove's trial demands answering, despite the ruling by the Court of Appeals."

The Chief Justice called for a vote, his attitude clearly marking his disapproval of the obvious outcome. By custom, the man most junior in tenure voted first. Engle voted to grant Scott's petition for a writ and hear the Grove appeal. Steinkraus, Wardle, and Fields voted against. Courtwright voted for. Overton against, Braham for. So that when Ben Robertson voted to hear the appeal, the writ was granted, making the vote of the Chief Justice academic, though he insisted on registering a negative vote to indicate his feelings in the matter.

On his way back to his chambers, Ben Robertson considered calling Honey Rosenstone, to have her suggest to young Ingram that he inquire about the fate of his petition. But he decided such conduct would be questionable at the very least. Besides, let it come as a surprise to the young man, it would sweeten his victory.

The first word about the fate of the writ came to the Rosenstone house in the form of a call from an NBC television reporter who urgently asked for Scott Ingram. It had just been announced at the Supreme Court that the Justices would hear Midge Grove's appeal. NBC wanted an exclusive two-minute spot for the six o'clock news.

Scott was at the law library hunting up cases that would be useful if their writ was granted, so he did not learn of his victory until he returned to the Rosenstone house to find Marlene waiting with a stack of messages. From friends, civil rights lawyers, black activists of the highest rank, and finally, from Dr. Paul Randolph, they all offered their congratulations.

And both phones were still ringing. Marlene answered one phone, put it on hold to answer the other, and announced both callers. One was a former colleague in his father's office. The other was Honey Rosenstone, calling on her car telephone en route to a cocktail party to raise funds for Cesar Chavez. Scott took Honey's call first.

"I just heard the news on the radio. Fantastic! We've got to give a dinner to celebrate! Invite all your friends!"

"What about Linc? Where is he?"

"No idea," Honey said, "you know I only hear from him when he needs help." Then she laughed. "Fortunately, he needs help often enough." She paused for a moment, then ended the conversation. "I'm proud of you, Scott, really proud. Yes, Mama is very pleased."

For some reason, that delighted Scott more than any other call he would receive that day. When he hung up, Marlene pointed the second line which was still flashing. He answered it, at the same time drawing Marlene close. With his arm around her and his cheek pressed against hers, he listened to his former associate congratulate him. It was good to hear, but not nearly so good as it was to have Marlene close to him. She was proud of him. He could feel it in her body.

As soon as he could manage to stem the flood of phone

calls, Scott raced over to the District jail, to tell Midge Grove the important news. But the shy, small man seemed unmoved. He just kept nodding his head while Scott explained all the possibilities. The high court would grant a new trial. They could even decide that the first trial was so defective that the case should be dismissed. Or the Court could place such restrictions on a new trial that the Prosecution might decide not to venture into court again.

But even the promise of possible eventual freedom did not stir Midge Grove, who remained totally aloof, his head nodding in an automatic motion.

Through Winkler's lecture bureau, Scott was able to locate Linc early that evening at a small college in the Middle West. He was in his room at the motel and in the company of a young girl, the first female president of the student body, who had issued his invitation and who had driven thirty miles to the airport to meet him. When the phone rang, Winkler had already begun to explore her youthful body.

"Hello," he said with obvious annoyance.

"Linc? Scott!" the exuberant voice assaulted Winkler's ear.

"Oh, Scotty. Yeah, what's up?"

"The writ! It was granted! We have leave to appeal!" Scott shouted on the other end.

"Great! Fantastic!" Winkler responded. Instantly, all thought of anything else deserted him. He withdrew his hand from the young girl's breast and turned his full attention to the phone.

"Scotty, now listen. Begin your rough draft of the brief by emphasizing the question of equal protection under the law and failure to receive due process. Work as much of Randolph's testimony into the draft as you legitimately can—I mean give it room, let it breathe. And refer, at least in the footnotes, to the various publications that have printed articles about Social Inevitability."

397

Scott nodded to himself, only half-listening to Linc's instructions, which were not new.

Then Winkler said something which caused Scott to pause before he answered.

"And, kiddo, at the end of your argument on due process, leave it just a little vague. I might want to insert a paragraph or two of my own at that point."

"Such as?" Scott asked sharply.

"Just a thought I'm fooling around with. If it jells, we'll discuss it. But leave it vague, okay?"

"Okay," Scott said skeptically.

"Great! Let me know how the draft goes. Be in touch," he said, hanging up.

The class president was disappointed but resigned to the fact that Winkler's attention had now been irretrievably diverted from her.

"The Grove case," he announced exuberantly, "we just won the right to appeal to the Supreme Court!"

"Funky!" she said, sarcastically, certain that now he would be too distracted to continue his seduction. But she had yet to discover what many other women already knew about Winkler. Conflict, even the contemplation of conflict, was his most potent aphrodisiac. With a broad, satisfied smile and with his day before the high court burning in his imagination, Linc Winkler reached out for the pretty but unkempt girl. He drew her close.

"Where was I?" he asked, laughing. "Kind of life I live, I need a bookmark."

Surprised and delighted, the young politico placed his hand back on her breast, embraced him, and kissed him with an open mouth. He kissed back, desire growing within him with each caress.

After he hung up, Scott's hand lingered on the phone. He was contemplating not only the words Linc had used but his manner as well. Scott feared that either before the brief was

398

done or during argument, the thought which Linc had labeled "vague" would finally assert itself, and he had learned that the result was usually startling and upsetting.

Tomorrow Scott would assemble all the notes he had made in recent days and begin to formulate his thoughts and his approach to the rough draft of the brief on appeal. It was an exciting prospect. For the first time in his legal career the words "On the brief: Scott Ingram" would appear in a case that had succeeded in going to the highest court in the land.

That evening, after he had done his own dishes, Scott was filling a second yellow pad with notes, phrases he might use, and an outline of the order of his arguments. The phone rang. It was his father, *that* Ingram.

"Scott?" The voice that came to him over the phone had its usual unmistakable power. They had not met or spoken since Scott had quit the firm almost a year ago, and neither one of them felt comfortable with this first gesture of reconciliation.

"Hi, Dad . . ." Scott said, quite gingerly.

"Heard about the granting of your writ, son. Nice work!"

"Thanks, Dad. How's Mom?"

"She's fine. We're both fine. Just came back from a golfing vacation at Sea Island. Great weather!" Then a bit precipitously, Ingram asked, "*He* going to argue the appeal?"

"Of course," Scott said.

"I see. Do you think he might prejudice your case?" his father asked, anxious to give his son advice, yet reluctant to be caught doing so.

"He's a little unconventional, I'll grant you that."

"No chance you might argue it yourself?" his father pressed.

"Not unless something happens to Linc."

"Linc," his father repeated, as if evaluating the closeness of his son to a man he considered a radical maverick, a danger to the bar and to the nation as a whole. "Well, you've got a tremendous job ahead of you, enormous challenge, that brief. By the way, if you need any help, I mean if it would make it easier in any way I could lend you a junior or two for research or an added secretary . . ." His offer hung open and tentative.

"What would the rest of the firm say, Dad?"

"I've already discussed it. All the partners are quite amenable." Scott knew how much it must have demanded of the old man to go to his partners and make such a request after Scott had left the firm because of this very case. The old man must be extremely proud of him.

"Thanks, Dad, but I really don't need any help. In this instance I prefer to do my own research, and I've got an excellent secretary. Thank your partners too. Tell them I appreciate it very much."

"Okay," his father said, noticeably disappointed. The conversation seemed at an end until his father added, quite urgently, "You know, son, I think about that evening often. I wonder what I said to make you quit. That wasn't my intention, so I think maybe you misunderstood."

"I might have . . ." Scott granted, but only because it was the first time he could remember his father being uncomfortable in his presence. Strangely, it troubled him, though most of his life he thought he would have welcomed precisely that.

"When this is over . . . I mean, once the appeal is argued, we ought to get together—just the two of us. Maybe play a round of golf, or just have dinner, and . . . and talk. One case isn't a whole career. You'll have to think about your future. I'd like the chance to discuss it with you. You make up your own mind, of course, but you could at least listen to what an old man has to say."

"Sure, Dad. As soon as the appeal is argued," Scott promised quickly, trying to ease the moment for his father, and also because if he allowed him to continue, Scott knew his father would ask him to come back into the firm. And he wasn't ready to confront that question yet.

400

"Good, good," his father said, sounding like this was all he had hoped to accomplish by making the call. Then he added, "Oh, by the way, son, could you call your mother? She's tried to get you several times at home, but you're never there, it seems."

"Of course, Dad," Scott said, and they hung up.

It was the longest conversation he had had with his father in many months, and the most revealing. The old man missed him, was proud of him, wanted to see him succeed even in a case with which he had no political sympathy. It was no small concession, and no little praise that his father thought him capable of arguing the case in the Supreme Court.

All his young life, he had measured himself against Scott Ingram the Second and wondered if he would ever be as successful a lawyer. Sometimes, in his more solitary moments, Scott wondered if he had leaned toward civil-rights work for the reason he had given Marlene or because it would permit him to practice law without running into inevitable comparisons. The people who always remarked when they discovered who he was, "Oh, your father is *that* Ingram." Here he was, preparing a case for the highest court in the land, and *that* Ingram had just given him his vote of confidence. He felt quite good about that.

However, Scott did not feel so confident when he considered what his father's reaction to Marlene might be. He wondered if he would change his mind about asking him back into the firm. And how would his mother feel? What a meeting that would be! Mr. and Mrs. Scott Ingram the Third— and wondering what Scott Ingram the Fourth would look like. Or how Mrs. Scott Ingram the Second would introduce her daughter-in-law to her friends and to the elegant WASPs with whom the family associated at Sea Island during the spring and fall golfing seasons. For that matter, Scott wondered, what effect would it have on his own career should he decide to return to the more conventional practice of the law?

But the fact that he thought about the problems didn't serve to diminish his feelings about Marlene. It only made clear how deeply he was involved and how much he loved her—more than he had ever realized.

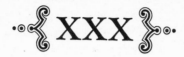

XXX

EQUAL JUSTICE UNDER LAW

The inscription in the white Vermont marble shone in sharp relief in the sun of the bright fall morning.

At the curb before the broad, white steps of the Supreme Court building, several mobile units from television networks and local channels in the capital were lined up awaiting the appearance of A. Lincoln Winkler and his associate Scott Ingram, who were counsel in the first case on the docket of the high court this morning. When the familiar Rosenstone Rolls Royce swept up to the curb, the newsmen converged on it, besieging Linc and Scott as soon as they emerged from the luxurious car. In the frenzy of questioning, Honey and Marlene slipped away and hurried up the steps.

The questions ran the gamut of political views from those who invited Winkler to condemn the system to those who asked if his presence in the high court today did not signify the ultimate fairness of the system. Winkler chose not to respond specifically. He confined himself to a simple statement, which he had obviously been mulling over for several days and which he delivered in a somber manner, as if unaccustomed gravity had been forced on him by his proximity to the highest court of the land.

"Gentlemen, we are entering this hallowed building to place before this Court several challenging questions. They are not matters to be casually discussed out here. The only important discussion can take place in there, where the law of this land is made. If we fail Midge Grove this day, we fail more than one black man. We fail every underprivileged man, woman, and child in these United States! Either the law proves itself worthy of the people it is written to serve, or we must look for answers elsewhere," Winkler concluded.

"Would you care to comment on which new questions are going to be raised, Linc?" a TV newsman asked, shoving forward his pencil microphone.

"That would be arguing my case before the people instead of before the Supreme Court," Winkler evaded.

"Would you expand somewhat on what you mean by 'we must look for answers elsewhere'?" another reporter asked.

"Boys, we are due in the courtroom in minutes."

With that brief evasion serving as his apology he edged his way through the persistent press corps.

When they were atop the first level of steps, Winkler paused to look up at the architrave, to read the words inscribed there. It presented the press photographers with a perfect opportunity to catch his disheveled, bushy-haired silhouette against the courthouse with the words "Equal Justice Under Law" framing the top of the shot. All that was missing to make it a typical Linc Winkler pose was the inevitable trenchcoat, which was absent today as was his bulging briefcase. He had considered it improper to enter the Court so burdened, but he had not thought it necessary to wear the traditional cutaway coat and striped trousers. Instead, he wore a neat, freshly pressed dark blue suit.

Scott, too, was dressed in a dark suit, of banker's gray.

404

Carrying his own brief bag in which were all the papers Linc might need in the course of his argument, Scott felt as tense as if he were going to argue the case himself. Linc, however, seemed calm; and as they stood on the top step, he even found time to remark on the excellent late fall day.

At the doorway, they were greeted by a small group of students who were leaving the building. The students were overwhelmed to run into Linc Winkler, and as they clustered around to wish him luck, he asked, "Aren't you going to stay for the show?"

"No seats!" a pretty blond-haired girl explained.

Her black companion added, "They've got the longest waiting line they've ever had. Most of them will never get into the courtroom. Right on, man!" He raised a big black clenched fist.

"Right on!" Winkler rejoined, raising his own fist. One of the girls kissed him on the cheek. He embraced her and kissed back. All the girls followed her example, so that for a few moments Winkler was at the sport he enjoyed most, being kissed and kissing young girls. It belied his conservative appearance today.

It also made Scott uncomfortable. The one thing Linc Winkler did not need now was his own special form of intoxication, youthful adulation. The high court was the crucible in which not only laws but lawyers were tested, especially their nimbleness of mind and their ability to think and speak extemporaneously. The Justices had already studied his brief and knew it well. So each lawyer was expected to depart from the brief, arguing from only a few notes. At any time during his argument, a Justice could interrupt and ask questions. A lawyer had better know his case well so that he could answer without hesitation, and answer convincingly. If ever a lawyer needed calm control of his emotions and his thoughts, it was when he argued before the Supreme Court.

And, Scott thought apprehensively, these students and

their enthusiasm were precisely what could seduce Linc into blowing his cool by becoming overly daring and possibly even irresponsible. Scott felt compelled to interrupt.

"Linc!"

The urgency in his voice made Winkler look at him with considerable concern. "What's wrong, Scotty? Nerves? Well, I've been here before. Don't worry about it!"

"Not nerves. Just that this is the Supreme Court, Linc. You can't treat these Justices the way you handled Beecher or the men on the Appeals bench."

Winkler smiled, allowed himself a light laugh. "You want to make sure my fly is zipped? Don't worry, kid, I am not going to disgrace you. I might shock them a little. But I guarantee I won't disgrace you."

He began to walk on, but Scott continued, "That's another thing, Linc. . . ."

"Yeah?" Winkler's smile diminished wearily.

"Don't shock them. It's too big a risk. We've got a fairly strong argument in Beecher's reversible errors, and at least an intriguing one on the social inevitability defense. We don't need shock."

"Scotty, there's no telling what questions they're going to ask, but they don't know what answers I'm going to give. So *they* have to be ready for anything, just as I do," Winkler warned.

"Like what?" Scott challenged him directly, more intensely than at any time since they had started working together. Firm in his mind were Linc's previous surprises, particularly Grove's Panther dress and demeanor and the substance of Randolph's testimony.

"You'll see, kiddo, you'll see."

Winkler started for the open doors, but Scott seized him by the arm.

"Linc! Listen to me! We're not here by right. We're here by sufferance, by virtue of a writ of *certiorari*. If you overstep

406

the bounds they can declare that the writ was improvidently granted and throw out our appeal! Right from the bench! If they do, that's the end of the case. Finish! And Midge Grove ends up under a life sentence which is irreversible, except for Presidential intervention, and no President is going to anger millions of people. You know what life in a prison will mean to him. For Midge's sake, please . . ."

"Don't worry about it, Scotty," Winkler assured him. But Scott did not feel reassured. He doubted both Winkler's judgment and his word.

They passed into the Courthouse, up the few steps to where the long line of eager spectators waited. Linc stopped to shake hands with several of the black celebrities who had come from New York and Hollywood for this crucial hearing.

Then they continued to where a group of radical chic devotees clustered around Honey and Marlene, who had somehow moved up to the front of the line. That must be Honey's doing, Scott decided. She was a woman born never to wait in line. In others that characteristic might be considered pushy, but for Honey it was simply a matter of right. Standing beside Honey and smiling graciously as if he were the host at this legal event was Dr. Paul Randolph. Tall, elegantly groomed, he had added a small beard to his already distinguished features. Marlene's discomfort at his presence was quite noticeable.

After much greeting and kissing, Winkler and Scott reached the doorway of the courtroom itself. Suddenly they were face to face with Harley Bevans, the tall, aging black man who had grappled with Midge Grove on that terrible day now many, many months ago. Winkler did not recognize him at once, but Scott did. And Bevans recognized them. But he said nothing as he granted them entrance.

Carroll and his two black assistants were already waiting at the counsel table. Carroll was in the formal dress consid-

407

ered mandatory for Government attorneys appearing before the high court. Winkler, shaking hands with him very perfunctorily, jibed, "Come to give the bride away?"

Carroll didn't smile, only gravely shook Winkler's hand, then Scott's, and continued to refresh his mind from his notes. This could be a fateful and historic day for the United States Attorney. If his position was upheld, his name would go down in the books as having successfully prosecuted to the highest court in the land the assassin of a most important Government official. Great political careers had started with such promising opportunities. Any aspiring prosecutor had only to think back on what the Alger Hiss case had done for Richard Nixon. So there were personal as well as professional motivations driving Carroll today.

The spectators were allowed to file into the courtroom. In the very first row of spectators were Honey and Marlene, and a black male singer who had sold more than five million records in the past year alone. In the second row sat two movie stars, both of whom had flown in from Hollywood the previous evening to represent the Free Midge Grove Committee, Beverly Hills Chapter. And sitting beside them, quite unnoticed, was Dr. Lee Morrison of the NAACP, who had come down that morning on the early Metroliner to observe the argument.

Looking out over the spectators, Scott could see that the majority were young people, and among the young, most were black. For a moment he had the queasy feeling that there might be a demonstration. That would destroy all chance of securing the quiet, judicial hearing they needed if they were to convince the Court that Midge Grove deserved a new trial.

But there was no longer time for speculation, for the Marshal of the Court was summoning everyone to attention. The entire assemblage rose as the eight Justices filed in and took their accustomed places behind the imposing mahogany bench. Last, Chief Justice Crane entered.

While the entire Court, including the nine Justices, remained standing, the Marshal pronounced, "Oyez, oyez, oyez! All persons having business before the Honorable, the Supreme Court of the United States, are admonished to draw near and give their attention, for the Court is now sitting. God save the United States and this Honorable Court!"

The gavel sounded. Justices, attorneys, and spectators took their seats. The Supreme Court of the United States was convened.

First there were some routine matters to dispose of, such as the admission of new candidates to practice before the Court. This morning there were seventeen, and they took the oath together as it was administered by the clerk.

Now the Chief Justice, looking more concerned and severe than usual, turned his attention to the docket as if he were not aware of which would be the first appeal. He announced it quite soberly.

At counsel table, Scott felt a stiff pang of tension—his work was about to be given its ultimate and most rigorous test. Suddenly his mind filled with citations that he had used but which now he felt the Court might question. There were the lengthy quotations from Randolph's testimony which Linc had demanded, but which now gave Scott great regrets. Had it been a mistake to follow Linc's dictates? Perhaps a few more cases in point would have served Midge Grove better than his medical history or Randolph's opinion of it.

Scott felt a strong, sickening urge to flee the courtroom. He vowed to himself that never again would he yield judgment to anyone on anything for which he had the basic responsibility.

It was too late now. Winkler was taking his place at the lectern, facing the nine men who could decide this case finally, for all time. On the lectern, two lights confronted him. A white one to warn Winkler that fifty-five of his allotted sixty minutes had elapsed, and a red one which terminated his right to argue, no matter what questions had been left unanswered or which crucial argument he had not fully developed.

Winkler opened his argument formally.

"Mr. Chief Justice and Honorable Associate Justices, in the brief time allotted to me I shall not attempt to go into all the aspects of this case. They are too numerous and too well covered in the brief prepared by my brilliant young associate.

"The conduct of the trial judge, his numerous rulings, both in court and out, served not only to harass Defense Counsel but to severely limit Defendant's right to a fair trial, and hence to due process of law. Counsel, laboring under the continuous threat of contempt citations, some deviously administered in the privacy of chambers, could not with whole heart and whole mind devote himself to the defense of his client. Nor was the ambiance of the courtroom itself conducive to a fair trial. It has been my privilege to defend young men in courts martial, but I have never experienced such an atmosphere of military presence and pressure as I did in the course of this civilian trial."

Suddenly Chief Justice Crane leaned forward in his huge, high chair and interrupted, "Counselor, do I understand that you refer to the precautions taken inside the courtroom?"

"Inside as well as out!" Winkler rejoined. "The excessive presence of uniformed personnel within the courtroom, the erection of a plastic barrier separating the trial from the spectators, and outside the courtroom the barricades to keep the public away from the trial. To say nothing of the paranoid searches each day of the person of each individual admitted to the courtroom. It was far from the calm judicial atmosphere in which a jury should deliberate the fate of a man. I had not meant to dwell on that aspect of things for it is well covered in our brief."

"One thing is *not* well covered in your brief, on which I would like some clarification," the Chief Justice challenged.

"If I may be of assistance . . ." Winkler offered.

"I find nothing in the brief explaining that the reason for

410

all the precautions of which you now complain were the very inflamatory speeches, news conferences and television appearances to which counsel so willingly and frequently lent himself, which created conditions calling for such security measures."

"Whatever the cause, Mr. Chief Justice, today we are dealing with effects, with the question of whether Midgely Grove received due process of law, full and equal protection of his rights as guaranteed by the Constitution."

The Chief Justice was not mollified, but neither did he press the issue. He settled back in his chair, his face still showing his full opposition.

Winkler glanced down at his notes.

"Not only within the courtroom, but long before the Defendant entered any courtroom, it was obvious that subtle and carefully planned pressures were exerted on him through constant reminders of Dallas and of Lee Harvey Oswald."

At that point Justice Overton, who had a habit of talking without looking directly at counsel, observed in his dry and rasping voice, "A careful examination of the United States Attorney's brief indicates that rather than being *under*protected, the rights of this Defendant were, if anything, *over*protected. The police and the United States Attorney went to such great lengths to guarantee his rights that this Court might well reconsider some of its previous strictures in decisions of recent years."

Scott sat up stiffer on hearing those words. If Overton's attitude reflected the majority, then the appeal was doomed. Perhaps if Linc weren't so belligerent, so obviously eager to engage in head-to-head confrontation with the Justices, it might help. But Scott knew from experience that once Linc Winkler was challenged, he was far more likely to fight back than to resort to diplomacy.

Winkler stared at Overton until the Justice was forced to look down at him. Then he said in a condescending tone, "We hope the Court will take into account that whatever the

411

intent of the Prosecution and the police, the effect on the accused is the only test. If the accused felt threatened to such a degree that he considered his life to be in danger, then his confession was not voluntary.

"The question involved in failure to grant a change of venue is well enough covered in this brief," Winkler continued. "And that refusal was of a piece with the trial judge's persistent, almost belligerent refusal to permit certain areas of comment in Defense Counsel's summation, as well as his instructions given to the jury forbidding them to consider any testimony concerning the question of social inevitability, which is the cornerstone of our defense."

Winkler paused for a moment to take a sip of water.

"For all these reasons, *and one more,* it is our contention that the Defendant was deprived of due process of law and equal protection.

"May I address myself to the question of the legality of the defense of social inevitability. It was not error that caused our brief to be short on legal citations on this point, while replete with quotations and opinions of scientists, philosophers and other students of human behavior.

"There is ample precedent for that in this honorable Court. One of your own number, before he ascended to this bench, introduced just such a brief almost a century ago. The revered Mr. Justice Louis Brandeis, when he argued before this Court in the case of *Oregon vs. Muller* involving an Oregon statute limiting the working hours of women to ten hours a day presented a brief which included only two pages of legal argument. The remainder was devoted to the opinions of doctors, health inspectors and factory inspectors who had had actual experience with overworked women and the sickly children they bore. In those days now past, some men argued that no state had a legal right to limit anyone's hours of work. Today, thanks to this Court, we know better.

"Acting on the precedent so brilliantly established by the

412

revered Mr. Justice Brandeis, we have chosen to break new ground in exactly the same way, by presenting to this Court not legal citations of the past, but the present opinions of those who are forced to deal with the mistakes of today's society.

"As attorneys we use the phrases 'due process of law' and 'equal protection under the law' with an easy carelessness that must come to an end now!

"When does equal protection under the law begin? Only when a man is brought before the bar of justice? Not so in the opinion of many who have had to live with the results of today's repressive society. A child who is born to an unwed mother in a black slum, who lives his life deprived of love and affection, with so little sustenance that his skeleton will forever bear the marks of his deprivation, such a child has *not* received the equal protection of the law! Certainly not equal to children born into better circumstances, children who are adequately fed, housed, cared for, educated, and loved.

"You cannot raise a child outside the protection of the law and then bring the law to bear upon him only when he has transgressed it. As one doctor who is cited in this brief has said, you cannot program a deprived child for a life of hatred and rebellion and then blame the child for his actions, which are not a matter of free choice but of social inevitability. The society, not the Appellant, should be on trial here!"

At that point the Chief Justice interrupted, making no secret of his opposition: "Is Counsel setting forth the proposition that there is no longer individual legal responsibility for crimes?"

"We are setting forth the proposition that when society has been derelict in its duty to a child, it is *society* that is guilty, not the child! And the determination of that matter is a question of fact to be decided by a jury, not a question of law to be determined by a judge. The Doctrine of Social Inevitabil-

413

ity should and must constitute a legal defense against crime, and in ruling otherwise Judge Beecher was guilty of grievous error!"

"Any crime? Including murder? Assassination?" the Chief Justice demanded.

"No court, not even this Court," Winkler continued, "can lightly brush aside a defense so well founded in scientific fact merely because of novelty. There are historic turning points in the course of this nation, most of which have occurred in this hallowed Court. The time comes when old legal concepts must give way to new conditions, when change must become the order of the day, lest the people take change into their own hands. A society that cannot bend with the times is destined to break and shatter under the force of events and the people's reaction to repression.

"It is only fair to point out that this doctrine, novel as it might seem at first, has long been accepted law in several jurisdictions under the 'irresistible impulse.' In essence, what is the difference? We suggest there is none.

"This Defendant, because of a life history replete with suffering, was turned into an instrument of hatred and revenge by the very society that prosecutes him now. It is time the law took cognizance of his situation as well as that of millions of others.

"For this reason we maintain, and we trust the Court will hold with us, that the Doctrine of Social Inevitability is and should be a defense in law. To say otherwise is to condemn future generations of poor black children and all poor underprivileged children to a life of unequal protection under the law. It would make a mockery of the words so proudly blazoned on the architrave of this very building, 'Equal Justice Under Law'!"

Winkler paused to take another sip of water. Scott could feel his own throat parched from the tension, for it was becoming obvious that Linc not only had failed to win over the

414

Chief Justice but had alienated him by the increased power of his attack after questioning. Scott could not read the other faces, which seemed uniformly grave. Even Robertson, upon whose innovative and liberal spirit they had been depending, seemed aloof.

It was Winkler's pause to take a sip of cool water that seemed to stir Robertson into action. He fingered his copy of the brief, eyed some notes he had scribbled and, as Winkler was setting down his glass, the oldest member of the Court asked, "Would distinguished Counsel clarify certain points which I find troublesome?"

"By all means, sir," Winkler answered.

"Are you contending that the society as a whole is responsible for the care, feeding, and education of all children from the instant of birth?" Robertson's attitude indicated that he sought to develop Winkler's argument, not defeat it.

"Equal protection must begin at the moment of birth, just as due process of law must begin at the very first contact with the law. This Court itself has held that when a defendant is denied due process at the outset, the entire proceeding is incurably tainted and any conviction must be reversed. So it should be with equal protection. Either it is granted from the beginning of one's life, or else one should be deemed never to have had its benefits at all. The law cannot stand aloof and disclaim responsibility, only to step in when it feels so inclined. And even when it is finally invoked, the law is never invoked on a basis of equality. I need not burden the Court with the statistics that reveal how sadly our less fortunate brothers fare in the criminal courts of this land, and what immunity our well-to-do citizens seem to enjoy."

Robertson was nodding his head in agreement. He had made the same point endless times in his various lectures to enlist young law students in volunteer work. He felt impelled to comment now. "I have always deemed it significant that it was under the Chief Justiceship of a man who had himself

415

been a prosecutor that this Court established some of its most significant guarantees of due process and equality before the law for those accused of crimes."

"Who would know better how the unfortunates of our society are treated by the law than a man whose work it was to prosecute them?" Winkler remarked, delighted to have finally found some support from the bench.

Scott began to breathe more easily now. Not that Robertson was a majority, but his words would carry impressive weight in the Friday conference. Playing it out in his mind like a bridge hand, Scott felt they must give away three tricks, Chief Justice Crane, and Justices Overton and Steinkraus. Courtwright, Engle, and Braham were possible tricks, and Robertson was the sure one. It hung then between Wardle and Fields to make the ultimate decision. Neither had asked questions or exhibited any outward signs of their inner attitudes. But with Robertson's reputation for being a tough and convincing advocate in the Friday sessions, having him in their corner was worth three other votes for sure and possibly even the fourth to make a majority of five.

If Linc stopped now, he would be far ahead of the game, at least far ahead of what Scott would have estimated their chances to have been forty-five minutes ago.

But the Chief Justice intervened. Anticipating the Friday morning debate, and obviously angered by Robertson's helpful and cooperative attitude toward Winkler, he refused to close off debate. Leaning far out of his chair, he stared down at Winkler to ask, "Would Counsel answer a hypothetical question?"

"If it's within my power," Winkler responded, feigning modesty.

"Assume a situation in which an accused is thoroughly briefed on his rights, is confronted by identifying witnesses immediately after the crime, witnesses whose testimonies are recorded on tape. Assume also an accused who is not even

416

questioned until a lawyer is furnished him, and who is then, in addition, given the one lawyer of his own choice. Assume an accused who is given a trial during which great pains are taken to provide a fair jury after many days of selection, who, after a finding of guilty, is permitted to appeal to the District Court of Appeals, where his conviction is upheld, and who is further granted the right to appeal to the highest court in the land. Would you still maintain that such a Defendant had been deprived in any way of equal protection and due process of law?"

"I would!" Winkler declared without reservation.

"Isn't the fact that you are here now, arguing this appeal, proof of due process and equal protection under the law?" Chief Justice Crane persisted, his voice becoming strained, his face failing to conceal his irritation.

Scott sat up, rigid and tense. Why was Winkler deliberately seeking to provoke a bitter confrontation with the Chief Justice now that he had Robertson working for them? It was a tragic miscalculation brought on by Winkler's cockiness. Or else it was a deliberate plan. Scott decided it was the latter when he saw Winkler take another one of his leisurely drinks of water. Then Winkler paused meaningfully before making a statement that he knew would not only shock the courtroom but would lead off the nightly news of every TV and radio station in the country.

"Mr. Chief Justice, the fact that we are here today arguing this appeal is the ultimate proof of the utter lack of due process involved in this case!" Winkler declared.

All nine Justices became alert and tense in reaction to that statement.

Before any of them could interpose a question, Winkler raced on, "If I may continue to develop that argument! I am sure I need not remind the distinguished Justices that on *voir dire* one of the first questions asked of any potential juror is, do you know any of the parties or counsel involved in this case? Another question always asked is, Were you in any way connected with the crime, or *were you a witness to that crime?* "

The Chief Justice had begun to anticipate Winkler's argument. His look became sullen and angry, his lips tightened. Robertson, who was as quick to perceive it, stared down at Winkler, wondering if the lawyer would dare to follow the argument to its logical conclusion. And if Winkler did, what would his own reaction be?

"I am sure," Winkler continued, "that I need not remind eight of the nine Justices presently sitting in this august Court of certain events which took place in this courtroom on October 14, 1973, which events constitute the crime we are now discussing. *I* was reminded of it when I entered this room and was approached by the very man who was one of the identification witnesses the Chief Justice referred to in his hypothetical question.

"There hangs behind you the same red velvet drape which was spattered with the bone and brain of the victim of that crime. What remains ingrained in the memories of the eight august Justices who witnessed that crime, I cannot say. But I can say, and I *do* say, if a witness to a crime is barred from sitting on a jury, how much more so should such restrictions apply to a judge! Surely none of you can sit in judgment on this case with open minds, since each of you must consider yourselves to have been potential victims of that crime. Surely you have thought of that many times during the long months since that tragic event took place.

"If you search your minds and your hearts you must come to the conclusion that you, above all men, cannot sit in impartial judgment on this case. Therefore, I ask that those eight of you who were witnesses to the crime disqualify yourselves and declare that the conviction in this case must automatically be reversed. Having so ruled, the Court is forced to confront the fact that our judicial system cannot provide due process of law to this Defendant and must declare that the case of the United States of America against Midgely Grove be forthwith dismissed!"

Even though spectators in the august chamber of the United States Supreme Court are known to sit in reverent silence, there was an outburst at the conclusion of Winkler's bold move. For the first time that Chief Justice Crane could remember the Marshal of the Court had to intervene to ensure silence.

At counsel table Scott Ingram stared at Linc Winkler, who seemed to stand more erect and more combative in posture with each passing minute. So this was Winkler's secret, his final cherished weapon. It is a preposterous argument, Scott thought. No one had ever dared ask the Supreme Court to disqualify itself—but then, no one had ever had an opportunity to do so. From Winkler's attitude, Scott knew he would be unrelenting. He almost wished the Justices would allow the challenge to pass without debate.

"Would Counsel care to elaborate on what we must consider at best a highly novel if not specious argument?" Chief Justice Crane asked.

"It need not take great elaboration, sir. If a defendant in a criminal case, regardless of how else his rights may be protected, is, from the outset, deprived of his Constitutional right to appeal to the Supreme Court of the land then he can never be deemed to have had the full advantage of due process or equal protection under the law. And since this Defendant is so deprived, by virtue of the prejudice of the Justices who constitute the majority of this Court, he simply cannot be tried."

"Are you saying," Justice Overton took up the questioning, "that there are crimes which are beyond the law?"

"I am saying that, if we are to ensure due process and equal protection to this Defendant, *this* crime, because of the circumstances involved, cannot be tried in our courts!"

Since they were on sticky ground from a substantive point of view, Justice Steinkraus sought to move the argument to procedural grounds where there was promise of an escape.

"Will Counsel take the position that this argument is as impromptu to him as it is to the Court? I would doubt it, since he seems to have it quite carefully worked out in his mind."

Scott could feel the burning in his cheeks now, for he knew precisely what Steinkraus was getting at. If Winkler had this argument in mind all along and had failed to include it in their written brief, then the Court might exclude it now and shut off any further discussion of it. Or even worse, the Court might rule from the bench that the writ of *certiorari* had been improvidently granted and that the appeal would not be heard.

Ingenious as Winkler's concept was, it could lead to disaster. If they lost their right of appeal, then Grove's sentence would be allowed to stand. So the manner in which Winkler answered Justice Steinkraus's question became of utmost importance.

"I would be less than frank with this Court," Winkler admitted, "if I pretended that this argument burst upon me with the suddenness of divine revelation."

"Then is there any valid reason why it was not briefed by Counsel in this document?" Steinkraus demanded, holding up the copy of the Appellant's brief.

"There is!" Winkler declared. "If that argument had been included in the brief, then this Court might have invoked the very action it is contemplating at this very moment—to declare that the writ of *certiorari* was improvidently granted and thus to stifle all argument on this case forever!"

None of the nine men could deny that the thought occupied a large part of their attention at this moment. It would be a way out, a way to wipe the entire matter from the record. With that intention the Chief Justice swung his huge chair around until its imposing back faced the courtroom. He signaled to Overton, who turned toward him, and without in-

420

vitation, Robertson swung his chair about so that the Chief Justice and the two Senior Justices could confer.

Overton was furious. "He admits that he meant to make the argument all along. He was obligated to brief it. Obligated! He cannot be permitted to play fast and loose with the Court in this outrageous manner!" he contended.

The Chief Justice nodded gravely, but without the outward fury that Overton displayed. But his opinion was strong and firm. "He did have the obligation to present the argument in brief, if only to give the United States Attorney the opportunity to rebut it. Our granting of this writ might well have been an improvident move, might well have been . . ."

"Gentlemen," Robertson interrupted, "I don't intend to defend Mr. Winkler's manners or his tactics, but he does pose a serious question. Unless we address ourselves to it now, it may arise again to plague this Court. It would be an evasion to throw it out on a technicality by attacking the brief."

"Are you suggesting that we encourage this sort of conduct?" Overton declared, his tone so harsh with personal animosity that several other Justices turned their chairs around to participate in the discussion.

Meantime, Winkler stood at the attorney's lectern, tall and defiant, awaiting their decision. Whichever way it went, his challenge to the Court would make its mark in history. Even the sudden lighting up of the white five-minute warning light did not disturb him, for now if time was running, it was running against the Court. Linc Winkler had said all he had to say.

Behind him, Scott Ingram sat at counsel table, his eyes focused, unmoving, on the high, black backs of the Justices' chairs. Knowing what they were discussing, wondering how they would decide, he asked himself if this was the end of the case to which he had devoted himself so completely for so many months now. Could it all come down to this—one last,

421

bold, flamboyant and quixotic gesture on the part of Linc Winkler, who thought it more important to challenge the system than to protect the rights of Midge Grove?

Shielded behind the backs of the Justices' chairs, Ben Robertson insisted on the last word.

"Chief, it is wrong for any of us to try to decide this matter now, but we cannot avoid our responsibility by taking the easy way out. I urge, and very strongly, that we take this matter under advisement, and that between now and Friday, each of us search his mind, and ask himself if witnessing the crime *has* influenced him in such a way that he cannot render a fair decision. *We* must decide first. But we cannot avoid our responsibility to rule on this question."

The Chief Justice was silent a moment, then, finally and grudgingly, he acquiesced. He swung his chair about. As he did, the red light on the lectern flashed on.

Addressing Winkler, the Chief Justice asked, "Does Counsel wish additional time in view of that consumed by our conference?"

"No, Mr. Chief Justice. We are content to rest our argument here and now."

Relieved, and inwardly exultant, Linc Winkler returned to the counsel table, slid into his chair beside Scott. Carroll rose to argue the Government side of the appeal. Winkler hardly troubled to listen, for no matter what Carroll said, it would not overcome the effect of Winkler's bold innovative challenge that defied the Court as it had never been defied before in all its history.

They were leaving the Courthouse, Winkler, Scott, Marlene, Honey, Randolph and a host of admirers who patted Winkler on the shoulder, gripped his arms, shook his hand in congratulation for his startling argument to the Court.

Ahead, Scott could see the TV cameras and the newsmen waiting on the broad marble steps. He hoped that Linc would exercise some restraint, for there were still four days

422

until the Justices had to come to their decision. Any unto-ward comments from Linc would only hurt their appeal.

So Scott watched with some apprehension as newsmen, cameras and microphones closed in on Linc. Gathering Scott, Honey, and Marlene and Randolph around him, Linc was in his glory, smiling, waving, shaking hands with friends in the press.

NBC had sent Clint Canfield to cover the event. This was a special honor for Linc because Canfield was a celebrity in his own right and only appeared at occasions of extreme na-tional importance—so Canfield had this moment to himself, as the other newsmen stepped aside and let him ask the ques-tions.

"Linc, you certainly took the Court and everyone by sur-prise today. What do you think your chances are for pre-vailing?" he asked.

Winkler's usual warm smile, his familiar friendly and inti-mate attitude, gave way to a reserved look. He limited him-self to a very proper "No comment."

The press was taken aback; even Scott was surprised, but he also felt a welcome sense of relief.

"If your argument is upheld, do you think it will have im-plications for the entire American judicial system, and not just the Grove case?" the NBC star asked, hoping to provoke a response.

"No comment," Winkler said, his voice even, without emo-tion.

"Would you care to predict what the Court will do?" an-other newsman broke in.

A CBS newsman moved closer and held his microphone up to Winkler. "Wasn't there enormous risk in making such an argument when this is the Court of last resort and has the final say?"

These and all other questions, Linc Winkler answered with a solemn "No comment," and then he descended the steps.

The newsmen, most of them burdened with equipment,

were not swift enough to keep up with him. He made his way to the limousine, which pulled quickly away and out of sight. Left behind and feeling foolish at having come up dry in the midst of this most important news story, Clint Canfield decided to wing a few hundred feet of video tape to salvage something for the nightly news.

Hat off, hair neatly coiffed and slightly long, he faced his own camera crew and began to ad lib:

"It was a new and different Lincoln Winkler we have seen today. Gone the warm, easy, informal, free-talking civil-rights lawyer who has been delighted to take the nation into his confidence. Today, Lincoln Winkler appeared a solemn man, sparing in his words. Is it the austerity of this majestic building that has worked the change? Or is it the awareness that he has raised some questions that may shake this building and this Court to its very foundations? Only time will tell—time and the ultimate decision of this Court. Though the decision may not be publicized immediately, it will be made Friday morning in a secret session in the Justices' conference room in the imposing building you see behind me.

"Never in history has there been a leak from one of these sessions, so we can only speculate about what will go on there this Friday morning. Will the Court vote to disqualify itself from sitting in this case and thereby free Midge Grove? Can it disqualify itself and not free Midge Grove? Will the Court decide to retain jurisdiction and rule on Lincoln Winkler's new and daring legal theory of innocence through social inevitability?

"These questions may sound like the sign-off of a soap opera, but it would be a serious mistake to assume that they are anything less than the most important issues in the most important criminal case to come before the high court in recent years, perhaps in all its years. Whichever way the Court decides, one thing is sure. Linc Winkler's bold challenge has knocked some of the stuffing out of what has become in the last few years a very stuffy Supreme Court. This is Comment by Clint Canfield, NBC News."

Canfield held his pose for a moment until a cue from his director told him that he was no longer being taped. He relaxed and asked, "How many seconds?"

The director glanced at his stop watch. "Fifty-seven."

"Okay, that'll cover the six o'clock news. Maybe I'll do another piece for the eleven o'clock. Call you later." With that, Canfield sauntered down the steps in plenty of time to keep his luncheon date with a Hollywood actress who was currently appearing at Kennedy Center. As he walked briskly along, his thoughts drifted to the affair they had started in Switzerland last winter, and whether she would be in a mood to resume it.

They returned to the Rosenstone house where Honey's staff had prepared a special lunch.

Linc had been silent all the way home, as had Scott, who was painfully concerned about the effect of Linc's argument and particularly anxious to ask questions. But Winkler's state of exhaustion after his hour before the Court, and his adamant refusal to talk to the press had surprised Scott as well as the reporters, and he knew his questions, like theirs, would have to wait until later.

When they entered the library, Honey immediately went to the bar to mix Linc a scotch and soda. With drink in hand, Winkler slipped into the antique cherry leather wing chair and breathed a great sigh of relief. Then he began to chuckle.

"Christ, what's everybody so glum about? This isn't a funeral! Just because once in my life I said, 'No comment'?" He laughed uproariously. "It seems I can affect people more by shutting up than by talking. Maybe that's what I'll do from now on!"

The phone rang. The butler answered in another room and then came to the library. "Fred Anthony of *The New York Times*," he announced.

Winkler leaped up from his chair, no longer exhausted, and seized the phone on the desk. "Fred? Were you there for the argument? Good! I guess you heard, I gave them the no-comment treatment. Not a word, just as I promised."

Winkler was silent for a moment, then he said, "My estimate? I think those old bastards are going to have a few very rough days. It'll be even rougher on them if you run the article we talked about. No one in Washington, not even a Supreme Court Justice, is above being influenced by the *Times*, Fred!"

Anthony must have made some modest disclaimer for Winkler replied, "Listen, among lawyers they say they'd rather have one column from you than two votes on the Court." It was not exactly true, but Anthony was a man who needed flattery, and Winkler knew it.

Whatever Anthony's reply, Winkler said, "Okay, read me!" When Anthony demurred, Winkler urged, "Then parts of it." Winkler listened and sipped at his scotch. His eyes twinkled. He nodded, then chuckled, sipped his drink again. "Boy!" he exclaimed at one point. He covered the mouthpiece with his hand. " 'Not since John Adams dared to defend the British soldiers accused of the Boston Massacre has an American attorney displayed as much courage as A. Lincoln Winkler . . .' And that's only for openers."

When Anthony had finished, Winkler suggested, "Fred, there's one little bit of inside maneuvering you didn't quite take advantage of. It's a tricky business, and I'll bet no one else in that courtroom got it."

Anthony responded, and Winkler could hardly wait for him to finish. "Fred . . . Fred, listen! You might still work it into your piece. I have put their august asses squarely and painfully on the horns of a dilemma. Either question, their right to jurisdiction *or* social inevitability would have been tough enough. But this way, if they insist on their right to jurisdiction, they are forced to rule on social inevitability. How would it look for them to write a long opinion insisting that they have jurisdiction and then say, but we refuse to rule on the main question raised? It makes them seem pompous and useless. On the other hand, if they rule that they can't properly exercise their judicial function because they were witnesses to the crime, we've delivered a body blow to the entire legal system!

"Do you realize the consequences? In this age of television when every citizen is practically a witness to everything! Who can pick a jury? Who can preside as an unbiased judge? The whole system has to grind to a halt! There's got to be a whole new concept of law and justice, trials and evidence, juries and judges!" Winkler exclaimed.

"Right, Fred. So it might be worth rewriting the piece. I guarantee you, no one else will have that angle. That's why I didn't want to spill it on the Courthouse steps. Right! Anytime, Fred!"

Winkler hung up, and downed the last of his drink. "Christ, I'm hungry as a bear!" he exclaimed as he started for the dining room where the buffet was stocked with all of his favorite foods.

Honey followed Linc in, inviting Randolph with her gracious smile. Marlene lingered to wait for Scott, but Scott remained behind for a few moments. Finding a pencil and a blank pad, he wrote himself a note which he tore off, folded and slipped into his pocket. Then, joining Marlene, he followed the others in to lunch.

There, Linc Winkler was raising his wineglass. "To Mr. Justice Ben Robertson!"

"I wouldn't count on that," Honey warned. "He may not vote your way."

"It was his idea in the first place!" Winkler chuckled.

"What?" Scott asked, as he entered the room.

"That night, at Honey's ecology dinner, he suggested the whole strategy."

"*I* didn't hear him," Scott protested.

"Nor *I*," Honey added.

427

Winkler smiled even more broadly, the creases cutting deeper into his lean cheeks.

"Remember when he said, 'If the shock of witnessing the crime didn't prejudice me, surely I can retain my judicial impartiality in face of something as corrupting as a little flattery'? 'The shock of witnessing the crime.' Those words stayed with me. If he admitted it was a shock, how could he take the position that he was impartial, fair and sufficiently removed to sit in judgment? So I was determined that somehow we had to get to the Supreme Court, to challenge their right to sit on this case! And to establish the precedent that there *are* crimes that cannot be tried by our courts! Can you imagine what that will mean in a time of such mass communication!"

"So the Doctrine of Social Inevitability was only the legal question that would get us to the Court," Scott said, half to himself.

"And it worked, Scotty!" Smiling, Winkler raised his glass again, "To Mr. Justice Robertson!"

But only Winkler and Randolph drank.

Lunch at Honey's was followed by what seemed like hundreds of phone calls which Linc answered as if he were celebrating a victory rather than still having to await the determination of the Court. During all those conversations the name Midge Grove was mentioned only a few times. The effect of the Court's decision on Grove's life seemed a matter of far less consequence than the blow which Linc Winkler had struck at the Establishment.

Scott was relieved when they dropped Linc at the airport to return to the case he was trying in Los Angeles.

Still exuberant, Linc embraced Scott, and said, "Scotty, a masterful brief! I'm proud of you! Proud! When I get back we've got to talk seriously about you joining Winkler and Pottish!" He punched Scott playfully on the chin the way the fellows on the basketball squad used to when Scott was the high point man in an Ivy League win.

Linc had words of praise for Randolph, too. Then they embraced like brothers. Finally Linc turned to Honey, his voice growing softer, more intense.

"Now?" he asked, *"now* will you think seriously about what I said?"

Honey smiled a small but knowing smile. "I've been thinking, Linc," she said. "Believe me, I've been thinking."

He embraced her and kissed her long and hard. Then he waved to the rest and disappeared through the gate.

The limousine dropped Marlene at her place. Scott got out, too, inviting her to have dinner. But she refused. Lunch had been lavish and late, she explained. Scott did not insist, for he knew she wanted to be alone. And so did he. Something about the day, about Linc's argument and his connivance with Anthony had cast a pall over both of them.

Marlene summed it all up when she said, "Midge deserved better."

She turned away. Scott caught her hand, but she whispered softly, "Please?" and he released it.

He watched her disappear into the house. Then he turned and started down the block, relieved to be alone with his own self-recriminations.

·◦❧ XXXI ❧◦·

Friday started off wrong for Justice Benjamin Robertson. He awoke earlier than usual, troubled about the Grove case that would be decided at the day's conference. To ruin his breakfast, the third column this week by Fred Anthony in the *Times* elaborated on the dilemma Winkler had presented the Court. This one was stronger than all the others, obviously written specifically for the morning of the conference.

And, making matters worse, the day itself was gray and threatening. If Robertson walked at all this morning, he would have to keep a hurried pace in order to reach the Courthouse before the rain began. And such haste would rule out his usual contemplation, leaving his words, if not his thoughts, insufficiently developed to make the most effective presentation of his view on the Grove case.

Several times since Monday other members of the Court had tried to ask his views, but Robertson had always discouraged them. These were questions each man had to answer for himself. So when the younger Justices had dropped by his office to drink a cup from his perpetually hot coffee pot, he had kept the conversation a shade too stiff or too informal for them to comfortably bring up the Grove case. Robertson had not even expressed an opinion to his law clerk, who had lingered at his desk several times hoping to pick up some clue to the Justice's thinking while Robertson scanned his memoranda without saying a word.

Now, on this Friday morning at quarter to nine, Ben Robertson started down the stairs to the first floor of his quaint old house. Oliver waited at the door, ready with coat, hat, and umbrella. Robertson slipped into the coat and took his hat, but when Oliver held out the umbrella, he declined. "No, I don't think so, Oliver."

On most days of the week, when it threatened to rain, Oliver would have insisted. But not on a Friday. And certainly not on this particular Friday when the Justice seemed too aware of the weight of office to be concerned about anything else.

Oliver opened the door and watched as Robertson went down the steps. He kept watching until the old man had turned the corner and disappeared from view.

Poor Mr. Justice, as Oliver preferred to call him secretly. He made no jokes today, had no time for small talk. Not a mention of the world news, or even a bit of gossip from a recent cocktail party or dinner. Only the tough and lonely job of making decisions of vast importance. Although he had never articulated it to the Justice, Oliver felt deeply that the fate of one unfortunate black man, who had undeniably committed a murder, was not worth the trouble it caused the Court or the rest of the nation. The time and money spent on the trial would be better spent on black children who needed help and could still benefit from it. Besides, the longer the case dragged on, the more dramatic Grove's defense became and the more heroic his image.

Oliver could never understand why those same blacks who kept insisting on being called black instead of Negro, who chanted slogans like "black is beautiful," who wanted to upgrade the image of the black man, why were they the very ones who made a hero out of Midge Grove? Grove was not the kind of man black children should emulate. It had never

431

made sense to Oliver. And if Mr. Justice had asked for his opinion, Oliver would have told him just that.

Suddenly Oliver found that he was still holding the Justice's umbrella in his hand. He returned it to the stand, then to check on things, he opened the front door again. Yes, it seemed very much like rain.

Justice Ben Robertson hurried along Constitution Avenue. He thought about Fred Anthony's column in the morning *Times.* Anthony wrote with an obvious appreciation of Lincoln Winkler's shrewd strategy, although his ostensible purpose was to urge the Court's consideration of the Doctrine of Social Inevitability. Robertson was irritated. At first he blamed Anthony, who should refrain from commenting on matters currently before the Court. Then he realized Anthony was not the real source of his pique. A rebel himself, Robertson was not one to resist any new thought, theory, or doctrine. What irritated him this morning was that Fred Anthony was typical of the new liberal faction who claimed to assert their freedom of thought and their independent spirit but had actually surrendered both.

How so many of the most intelligent people of the nation could confine themselves to such limited subjects and speak in precisely the same vocabulary always baffled and amused him. Often he speculated that somewhere there was one little gnome of a man who sat in a library making up new words and phrases for his subscribers, the self-proclaimed intelligentsia of the country. And on the same given morning, there arrived in the mail for each of them a set of new words and phrases for the week so they could go forth as well-armed as all other intellectuals.

What had happened to that old-fashioned thing called personal style, Robertson asked himself, where a man spoke in his very own way, using his very own phrases, and God forbid, his very own ideas as well?

Someday, when individual thought and expression had dis-

432

appeared altogether, perhaps one of those tax-free foundations would set up a fund to discover or create individual style all over again.

Yes, this new breed talked a great deal about communicating, yet they only seemed capable of communicating with each other. They had produced a world of instant doctrines, instant heroes, with no room left for sober thought or discriminating selection. It was a dangerous time for the republic.

That Doctrine of Social Inevitability, Robertson reminded himself with some distaste, that was a case in point. Although it was a completely new theory, it had become so common that it was discussed at every cocktail party in Georgetown and dinner party in Washington. It seemed to have become a political issue as well. Liberal Democrats were for it. Conservative Democrats and Republicans were against it. The thought that the doctrine had not even existed some months ago was enough to make a man wonder—and worry.

The temperature had dropped, and it had begun to rain lightly. Ben Robertson turned up his collar, crossing the lapels of his coat to protect his chest from the wet wind. In recent years he had suffered a weakness in the chest, and his doctor warned him against inviting pulmonary afflictions. He would have hailed a cab but he could already see the Courthouse beyond the trees. Robertson walked faster and lapsed back into his thoughts.

He knew that it was the method by which the question of Social Inevitability had been raised that offended him. As for the concept itself, it had some merit and clearly presented an interesting question to the Court. He knew, too, that most of his colleagues would either refrain from considering it or else, having considered it, would vote against it. But standing alone had never affected his personal decision. The problem this morning was deciding in his own mind where he stood.

The evidence in the record was shocking. There was no justification for a child in any society to grow up as the

433

Grove boy had been forced to grow up. More shocking was the fact that for millions of youngsters today the outlook was not much brighter. Yet sympathy alone was no ground on which to make legal decisions. The issue came down to the troublesome question of intent. To what degree was Midgely Grove able to control his own actions? Young Ingram's brief had made a good point. The doctrine it urged was not far removed from that of irresistible impulse, and while irresistible impulse was not accepted in all American jurisdictions, it had standing in some. The brief aimed to extend that doctrine from the sudden compulsive action of a man experiencing some extreme emotional crisis to an impulse ingrained in him since his earliest days. If one thought about it, there was more to be said for the long-term attitude than the sudden impulsive one. What was it that doctor had testified to? Oh, yes, that the Defendant had been programed as if he were a computer card punched out to commit the assassination.

That word caused a sudden change in the direction of Robertson's thoughts. Assassination. It raised the other challenge that Winkler had raised.

In the four days that had elapsed since Winkler's presentation, Ben Robertson had thought about his argument. From a strictly legal point of view, it was a strong one. If a case came before Robertson in which a juror had witnessed a crime and also had been permitted to serve in judgment, he would have ruled it reversible error. Potential jurors who were witnesses to an act were excluded from jury service because their involvement might hinder them from returning a fair and unprejudiced verdict.

It was a rule that Robertson had never questioned before. But he had never had the problem of applying it to a case such as this one. The question was, Could he himself honestly arrive at an unbiased decision despite his witness to the crime? He knew one thing. He could never forget the shocking event—that moment when the majestic quiet of the Court had been shattered by those shots. He could not forget the effect on his heart, which had suddenly exploded into an arhythmic panic, nor could he forget the sight of the slain Justice Miller sprawled awkwardly in his huge leather chair, eyes still open, the maroon velvet drape behind him stained with red blood and grayish specks of brain matter and bone.

A man could not be expected to erase such a memory. And if he could not, then he must examine his right to sit in final judgment on the person who had been the cause of that scarring event.

The rain was coming down harder. It felt sharp and icy against his face. Robertson yanked his hat down tighter on his brow, pulled his collar closer around his throat, and began to walk even faster, conscious now that despite the cold he had worked up a sweat, and the wind had started to chill him. Fortunately he was less than a few minutes from the Courthouse. Unfortunately, he was also that close to the time when he would have to make his decision.

He had to admit that he liked to favor rebels in the Court. They gave life to the law and kept the Court on its toes. To Robertson, the glorious years of the Court had been the Warren years. If some argued that the Court had gone too far in liberalization, still that was much better than if it had not gone far enough. Democracies needed shaking up if they were to remain viable. If the law was allowed to settle like old wine so that the sediment went to the bottom, so would the divisions between the classes settle and become immutable.

This nation was the one nation on earth which could not exist without the promise of change, without the hope in each man's breast that he could rise above what he was to something better. And if not he, then his son or daughter. And the basis of it all was a viable system of law and a court that was open to influence as much by a vision of the future as it was by the precedents of the past.

Contentious radical lawyers did serve their purpose. Despite his impertinence, Winkler had served a purpose. If only he were less a rabble-rouser. But perhaps it took that kind of grating personality to pose such challenges. But Ben Robertson had to divorce the issues from his personal feelings about Winkler and decide both questions on the basis of law and law alone, making the well-being of the nation his primary concern.

He was at the Courthouse now and relieved to be there, for the rain was pelting down. Robertson was damp, inside and out. He needed some hot coffee and a few minutes of privacy to make his final decision.

Justice Robertson sat alone in his inner chamber, which had been his second home for twenty-seven years. On the day that his wife had died, he had come from the hospital to this room to sit alone and mourn her. It was the room in which he had written, in his own hand, decisions that had caused consternation in some quarters of the nation and great joy in others. In the true sense of the word, this was a historic room, and he had made it so. Today was a day when another small bit of history would be made, signifying a change in the nation and in the nation's laws.

Ben Robertson was sipping the hot broth his secretary had prepared to help him overcome his chill. She had volunteered to call Dr. Blaine, but Robertson refused, and quite irritably too. The hot broth would do it.

So he sipped and continued thinking until he was interrupted by the buzzer. Five minutes to ten. Ben Robertson drained the cup and rose, feeling refreshed and warm. He passed through the outer office, glancing at his secretary and his law clerk without saying a word and started down the corridor toward the conference room.

Robertson shook hands with Engle, Braham, Steinkraus and Wardle who had already entered the imposing room. Courtwright and Fields arrived within moments and they exchanged the time-honored handshakes. Overton was last, coming just before Chief Justice Crane. Overton seemed more tight-lipped than ever this morning. When he extended his hand to Robertson, it felt cold, an instrument of personal opinion.

They seated themselves around the conference table, the Chief Justice and Robertson facing each other from the ends of the table. Courtwright, Wardle and Braham on one side of the table; Overton, Steinkraus, Fields and Engle on the other. The Chief Justice had before him a list of the matters to be decided this morning. Anticipating the fierce struggle that the Grove appeal would create, he had placed it last on the list.

Under the guidance of the Chief Justice, and with his expression of opinion first each time, they disposed of the other cases heard during the week. There were no sharp conflicts, but few unanimous decisions either. Robertson was in the minority each time, a situation he had grown accustomed to. But this fact served to heighten the tension, for it did not augur well for the final decision they would have to make this morning.

It was with considerable gravity that Crane said, "And now, finally, the appeal in the matter of *The United States versus Midgely Grove.*"

Then he paused briefly before presenting his own opinion.

"Gentlemen, I refuse to admit the concept that this Court is barred from taking jurisdiction of any case that may arise in any court in this land. Under the Constitution, it is solely within the province of this Court to determine such a question. And no litigant, not even another branch of this Government, can challenge that right. So much for the matter of disqualification of the Justices by virtue of having witnessed the crime."

With an abrupt self-conscious glare at Robertson, Crane continued, "Now as to the other basic question raised in the Appellant's brief, the Doctrine of Social Inevitability. I find that it is just that, a doctrine, a theory, and though it might

437

have some medical or psychiatric foundation, it does not have sufficient legal basis for me to give it credence. It is my conclusion that the conviction be allowed to stand."

Crane glanced at Robertson at the far end of the table. He had spoken gruffly, expecting disagreement. But Robertson's face betrayed no emotion. He was sitting back in his chair rubbing his hands, as if still trying to overcome the effects of his chilling walk in the rain.

"Gentlemen, I would like to announce my conclusion but reserve my reasons for the time being." Robertson had addressed them all, but he looked to Crane for approval. Although the Chief Justice disliked any tampering with the traditional practice of the Court, he did nod his permission.

"I am for granting Defendant Grove a new trial," Robertson said, very softly.

Crane was not surprised. Neither did any of the others react outwardly.

The expression of opinions and reasons went round the table. When they had finished, it was obvious that a vote taken now would stand six against a new trial, three for. Only Courtwright and Braham would vote with Robertson.

The Chief Justice looked to Robertson to grant him the right to make his argument last. Robertson paused, pushed his chair back from the table and said, "Gentlemen, this is a moment of great personal anguish for me. And I think I will be able to speak more freely if you would indulge me to the degree that I be allowed to stand and move about freely."

He rose and stood behind his chair, resting his arms on it. Then he began to speak in a soft, low voice, as if making a personal confession rather than expressing an argument to fellow Justices.

"This case has been a matter of deep concern to me, deep personal concern—perhaps because my years of service on this Court have been longer than any man in this room, or perhaps because I have been of that school which has been characterized by some, and stigmatized by others, as liberal.

I am not unaware of the fact that in some areas of the press I am lauded as the leader of informed liberal dissent, while in others I am called names as extreme as the leader of the disloyal opposition. Frankly, I have never given a damn!

"The older I become, the more I am concerned with one thing only. I would like to leave behind, insofar as it is within the power of any one man, a living, expanding system of democratic law, justice, and government, because it is my earnest belief that without it, the concept of human freedom as it has been known on this earth for five thousand years will wither and die."

The old man turned away from the table, away from the eight faces that sought contact with him. He moved to the fireplace, caressing its cool smooth stone.

"I am afraid, gentlemen. Afraid that liberty has fallen into disrepute, as the pressures against it are now more formidable than ever. I am afraid of bigness, the tyranny of bigness against which individual man seems to grow smaller and smaller—big business, big labor, big government.

"The time when a man could seize the musket from his mantel and run out to fight for his freedom is gone. Technology has made that man obsolete, and put power on the side of size. Thus, individual freedom has gone out of style in many nations, and mere survival has taken its place.

"Only here, in the United States, does individual freedom still have a chance."

He turned from the fireplace to face them again.

"I wish to acknowledge that I owe a great debt to a certain Lincoln Winkler. His argument before the Court made several things clear to me, the main one being the question he raised unintentionally: Is our system of justice archaic and unable to cope with modern conditions and pressures?

"Now I know many of you will say Winkler is purposely seeking to play havoc with our system, that he is shrewd, a skillful, dangerous trickster, that he directs the forces and pressures of our society against our institutions, and that he

439

uses all the tactics afforded to an experienced demagogue by an avaricious press. And he is clever, innovative, and bold, very bold. I would not disagree with you about him.

"But there is more here than that. We are confronted by the disturbing fact that there is a kernel of truth in each argument he makes."

Crane and Overton made no effort to hide their disapproval, but the young men remained stiff and noncommittal.

"Yes, a kernel of truth. There *is* evidence of undue tension in that courtroom and outside it. There *was* enormous public animosity against the Defendant. Most important of all, Midgely Grove *did* have a quite shocking and terrible early life, and there is no denying his medical history, which must also include his psychiatric history. None of us can deny those facts. So Winkler's theory of Social Inevitability does have an underlying rationale.

"We would be wrong to overlook the fact that we, society, in some way help to breed criminals. Still, that is a far cry from saying that all criminals should be set free and society imprisoned. But we must take account of our imperfections. Surely we must strive to repair them, to cure present injustices and prevent future ones.

"To me there is only one fit measure for any society, the degree of individual freedom. But without a viable free society, individual freedom cannot exist. Therefore, the society, even as it experiences change and growth, must also be safeguarded. We undertake that in the oath of office, when we pledge 'to preserve, protect and defend the Constitution against all enemies, foreign and domestic . . .' For if it were not so preserved, then individual liberty would be lost as well. So I have always believed that it is the sacred undertaking of this Court to constantly strike a fair and equitable balance between the individual's rights and society's rights.

"But that balance can only be achieved by the enforcement of societal responsibility for societal actions, on the one hand, and individual responsibility for individual actions on

440

the other. I cannot depart from that concept now, or ever. So I do not accept Winkler's doctrine."

Robertson paused, smiled a bit whimsically. "You will have to forgive me, gentlemen, but I was so curious about it that I set my young clerk to doing a bit of research. Do you know that until this trial the phrase, 'Doctrine of Social Inevitability' does not appear in any periodical, professional or otherwise?"

He chuckled. "Yes, it seems to have been created solely for the purpose of this trial." Then Robertson's manner became grave.

"Then there is Mr. Winkler's attack on the jurisdiction of this Court in this case. At first, I was outraged by the impertinence of the man! That any lawyer should dare to question my calm, dispassionate judicial mind! But on reflection I realized that my indignant reaction meant only that I have become old, pompous, and even vain.

"So I questioned myself. Deeply. What *did* happen to me on that awful day? Did I, perhaps, feel that it might have been me, not Miller, who died from the assassin's bullet? And the answer was Yes, I did. Yes, gentlemen, I felt fear, personal fear. And there was also fear of another kind—fear for the future of the republic. A criminal had dared to invade the high court, the last refuge of justice in the nation. That is something to fear.

"The tendency of a man who is afraid is to strike back, so I was compelled to face the fact that on that day *I* was shaken enough to want to strike back.

"But that was on *that* day. Since Winkler raised his question I have thought about it a great deal. I don't know about any other man. But for myself, having examined my conscience, I say without reservation that I am capable of sitting in this case without prejudice. I *can* separate my personal feelings from my feelings as a judge. I *can* conscientiously render a fair decision in this matter. And I have confidence in this Court that it can do likewise. Therefore I reject coun-

441

sel's argument that this Court is disqualified from ruling in this case by virtue of having witnessed the crime.

"Yes, I would rule against him on his second major premise. And still I find value in his skillful argument, for it opened my eyes to some of the errors of the past, *my errors!*"

The old man returned to his chair, stood behind it. Resting his arms on the back, he stared down the length of the table at the Chief Justice who had also been his chief adversary since his ascension to that post.

"This Court, and I am one of its main offenders, has made a game of Justice!

"We have enshrined the rules and let the basic matter of guilt or innocence slip through our fingers. We have become sociologists and politicians, instead of judges. We have abandoned our standards and found reasons to excuse criminals, to make crime too readily explainable, too understandable. And we have acted as if to understand is to condone. But most of all, in the name of justice, we have allowed ourselves to be manipulated by those who seek to destroy the very system by which justice is achieved.

"To address myself now to the real and basic question which Lincoln Winkler raised, is our system of justice archaic and unable to cope with modern pressures and conditions?

"To that I say No! However, if we permit it, abuses and perversions of the law and its practice will make it seem so.

"It is my feeling that this Court in ruling on this case must make it clear that we do *not* intend to permit that. This Court in this decision must remind lawyers that they cannot create conditions of danger that demand security measures and then plead those security measures as a defense. They cannot use every legal device to stall for time and then plead the passage of time as a defense. They cannot use the media to publicize their cases and then seek protection by claiming overexposure. They cannot try to obscure the issues by claiming a political trial and then complain that the issues were never fairly tried. Justice, not the rules of game, must prevail. Or

442

else the rules and eventually the system itself will disintegrate."

Robertson paused, then in a quiet, tired voice he said, "Because I have been more responsible for this state of things than any other man in this room, I ask leave to write this opinion, Mr. Chief Justice."

"You understand from the look of things that it would be the minority opinion, Ben," the Chief Justice said, using Robertson's first name for the first time in all the months they had served together.

"Gentlemen, for the very reasons I have cited, I would ask those of you who are inclined to reject this appeal to reconsider a new trial for the Appellant."

"After ruling out the main arguments of his counsel?" Overton demanded, his lips pursed in an acid attitude of impatience.

"*Because* we have ruled them out!" Robertson answered sharply. "If we refuse to let Winkler manipulate this Court by his shrewd and wily tricks, then how can we abandon this Defendant to those same practices?"

He turned from Overton to face the other seven. "Gentlemen, the Bible speaks punitively about the sins of the fathers being visited on the children, but I find no doctrine in the law calling on us to cause the sins of counsel to be visited on the client. This young man, no matter what his crime, *has* been deprived of due process and equal protection by his own counsel who, instead of defending him, used him! Abused is the more accurate word, for he did not even plead certain obvious defenses on his client's behalf. I say, under the circumstances, this Court owes the Defendant a new trial and the hope that, whatever the outcome, this time he enjoys all the protections our law intends him to have."

No more argument. The Chief Justice called for the vote, starting with the junior Justice first. When it came Robertson's time to vote, the score stood at four in favor of a new trial, three against. Robertson's vote sealed the decision. The vote of the Chief Justice, while recorded as against, did not affect the outcome. It was decided that two opinions would be written, the majority opinion by Robertson, the other by Overton. Both opinions ruled against Winkler's Doctrine of Social Inevitability as a legal defense, both ruled against Winkler's attack on the Court's right to jurisdiction in the case. Robertson's opinion granting Midgely Grove a new trial was the more cogent argument, yet the more stringent in its tone. For underlying Robertson's decision was the clear indication that Grove had not received a defense adequate to the gravity of his crime.

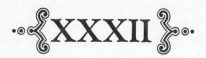

·◦❧ XXXII ❧◦·

It was Saturday morning, two days before the decision on the Grove appeal would be announced by the Supreme Court. On the preceding Thursday, Ben Robertson had sent the final draft of his opinion back to the printer with the approval of all four Justices who concurred with him. It was a lengthy opinion. Writing it and redrafting it had taxed him considerably. Now that he was done with it, he felt ill at ease, at once tired and restless. He decided to call Honey Rosenstone.

"Ben!" she declared, surprised and delighted. "I'm having a small buffet tonight to welcome the first ambassador from Bangladesh. Wouldn't you like to come?"

"No, Honey, but thank you."

Since Robertson's calls meant that he was lonesome, Honey decided to cancel her lunch date with the ambitious liberal mayor of a large eastern city who wanted her to launch him into Washington society.

"Ben, I happen to be free this afternoon. And this may be the last nice weekend of the fall. I know a quiet inn near Dumbarton Oaks that serves an excellent lunch. And the countryside there is delightful for walking."

"Thank you, my dear. But I think I'm a bit too tired today."

Honey was alarmed by that. It could mean his heart action was depressed again but he was refusing to admit it.

"There *is* one thing you might do for me," Robertson suggested.

"Anything, Ben!"

"That young man . . . Ingram . . ."

"Scott? Scott Ingram?"

"Yes. After our decision is announced on Monday, tell him, if he'd like, I wouldn't mind having a chat with him," Robertson suggested. "In fact, he might like to be there when I read my opinion."

"So it'll be out on Monday," Honey remarked, but she refrained from asking which way the decision would go. As much as she would have liked to know, she never imposed on him.

"Monday," was all that Robertson said, until he added, "And if you're free next Saturday, and the weather holds, we'll have that lunch and that walk after all."

"Good! I'll keep next Saturday free. I'll check you on Friday. Or if you'd like some company before then . . ." she volunteered.

"Is that the way I sound?"

"Frankly, Ben . . . yes," Honey said softly.

"I think maybe you're right, my dear."

"I could have Aurelia prepare us a lunch now, and I'll bring it over. We wouldn't have to go out at all," she offered.

"Would you mind?" he asked, sounding delighted.

"Of course not!"

Then, in the seductive voice he reserved for their imaginary affair, he said softly, "I'll find some way to get rid of Oliver after lunch, my darling."

She responded in kind, "If he becomes stubborn, I have a ring that once belonged to Lucrezia Borgia. When it opens, all kinds of things happen. See you about twelve-thirty?"

"Twelve-thirty," he confirmed, relieved that he would not have to spend the long day alone.

446

Word had leaked that the decision in the Grove appeal would be announced on Monday morning. So the press corps desks arranged in front of the bench of the Supreme Court were crowded with the men and women representing the wire services and the networks. On a lower floor, directly below the bench, another battery of newsmen and -women stood by, ready to relay the Court's rulings as soon as they received copies of the decisions and the opinions. Within minutes, the word would be flashed to the public by radio and television, not only in the United States but in countries around the world, where the assassination of Justice Miller and the trial of Midgely Grove had been headline news for many months.

The courtroom was called to order, and all rose as the Justices entered. The clerk opened the session. The Justices took their seats. Then Chief Justice Crane turned to Ben Robertson and, with a slight nod, invited him to open the proceedings.

When Ben Robertson announced the decision of the Court to grant a new trial to Midge Grove, there was an immediate stir of excitement among the press. The decision was not only important in its own right, but it promised more news mileage out of the Grove story. In fact, it might even be better now than ever before. Some of the media people seemed a bit restless and annoyed when they realized that Ben Robertson was going to read his lengthy opinion in full. They were anxious to get the story out, and would rather have done their own embellishing around the decision for a new trial than wait for Robertson to deliver his opinion.

Sitting just inside the rail, at a place reserved for counsel, Scott Ingram felt not exultation but relief. He would savor Robertson's every word.

The courtroom quieted almost immediately as Ben Robertson began to speak. He delivered his opinion in a grave manner, for he felt the words and thoughts were of far

447

greater consequence to the nation than just the fact that Midge Grove would receive a new trial.

At times he aimed his words at the press or directly at Scott Ingram. Occasionally, he projected them beyond the rail to those spectators of both races, who had gathered to make political capital of the decision.

Long as the opinion was, Robertson's voice was so compelling and his conviction so intense that the churchlike silence that descended on the huge room at the outset prevailed throughout. Finally he came to the last page.

"This Court might well have ruled perfunctorily that because of the total absence of precedent, Appellant's contention that this Court be disqualified was specious. And, since there is likewise no sound legal precedent for the concept of social inevitability, this Court would have been justified in making like summary dismissal in regard to that argument also. But this Court would have been derelict in its duty if it had allowed its decision to rest on those grounds, which are by their very nature purely technical. We have had a surfeit of technicalities in this Court in recent times.

"Hence, it felt compelled to treat fully both arguments, for this Court has always been a proponent of peaceful change. Through the judicial process, freedom evolves and is enlarged. If freedom is the life blood of a democracy, then Government and the courts are the arteries through which that life blood flows. The rights of the individual, precious as they are, cannot demand the destruction of the society or the endangerment of its structure. Government, especially free government, cannot be allowed to become an instrument which men use to work their own special political ends at the ultimate cost of the society as a whole."

Scott Ingram sat up a bit higher in his chair at that. Robertson went on.

"The rights of the individual can only be protected within the confines of a free society. To destroy the society is to destroy the rights of the individual as well. Those who would hold that we must destroy society to reform it are either blind men or charlatans. Either way, they constitute a real and present danger to all men who are free or wish to be free."

"In the instant case, Defendant may well have been deprived of due process and equal protection, not by the law, but by his own counsel. It becomes the duty of this Court to protect a Defendant in such circumstances. In the exercise of that duty, a new trial is hereby granted."

The entire courtroom, the Justices, press, attorneys, and spectators remained quiet and motionless after Ben Robertson had finished.

It was not only that the opinion marked a change in Robertson's thinking, but there was about the whole event the feeling that Robertson had just delivered his last notable opinion, his farewell to the life he had lived for more than thirty years, and to some thoughts he had harbored for as long. It gave the feeling of history in the making, and the courtroom was respectful and reverent in acknowledgment.

Robertson leaned back in his tall-backed chair, breathing as deeply as he could, trying to restore his heart to its normal, regular beat. What he had done had demanded an unusual amount of exertion. He knew that he would never read another long opinion in open court again. But he had read this one, and felt that if he had done nothing else, he had justified all his years on the Court this day.

On the steps of the Courthouse the press surrounded Scott Ingram, congratulating him, bombarding him with questions about his reaction to the decision and his plans for the new trial. They wanted to know how he would contact Linc Winkler and what he proposed to tell Midge Grove and when.

"After an opinion like the one you just heard, no comment by any lawyer can be of great consequence. As to the new trial, nothing can be said until I have spoken with my associate."

449

Scott hurried down the steps, pursued by reporters. But he did not stop or answer any of their questions. As he pushed through them and hailed the first taxi, he heard one of the newsmen say, "That kid needs experience! Linc Winkler would have been worth three columns on a day like this!"

Linc Winkler was on trial in San Francisco representing a Black Panther who was charged with the murder of another Black Panther in an organizational dispute. Because of the time difference, Winkler was just starting his court session when it was lunchtime in Washington. His California associate told Scott that he would convey the news to Linc, who would be delighted and no doubt would call back during their lunch recess.

While Scott waited for Linc's call, he was inundated by a flood of congratulatory phone calls and telegrams from civil-rights organizations across the nation. Some were addressed to him, but most were addressed to Linc Winkler. Three celebrated motion picture actors, two of them white, all working together on a film of great social significance, called him by radiophone from their location in Kentucky to salute him and to pledge additional funds for the new trial. Even two of Scott's old law school professors called to add their congratulations.

The day had all the hilarity that generally accompanied the winning of a World Series or the opening of a play that had become an overnight hit. Both telephone lines were continuously busy, Scott talking on one while Marlene held calls on the second. Three different times Scott had to refuse the TV networks, each of whom offered to interview him live at their studio or even to send their portable equipment to his office at the Rosenstone mansion. But Scott would say nothing, not even visit Midge Grove until he had talked to Winkler.

It was almost four o'clock in the afternoon when the call finally came through and he heard Winkler's voice, not laconic and disarming as it was most times, but booming now with the exhilaration of final victory.

"Scotty! I knew it! I felt it in my bones on the day I argued it. They simply couldn't disregard us. They had to take up the challenge, and once they did, they had to find our way! Had to!"

"Linc . . . Linc . . ." Scott tried to break in.

"Tell you what! I am going to fly in tonight . . ."

Scott interrupted, "What about your trial?"

"I'll let my associate carry on for a few days. We've got to make the most of this while it's still hot. I'll fly in on the overnight. I'll be at Dulles at seven-fifteen. It's early, I know, and the boys'll grumble, but for a story like this they should move their butts a little!" Winkler chuckled. "So you line up the press. Call all three networks . . ."

"Linc!" Scott interrupted sharply.

"What?" the older man asked, a bit impatiently.

"I think you should read the entire opinion before you make any statements."

"Judges' opinions are like the contents on the label of a can of soup. Everybody knows they're there, but nobody reads them."

"They'll read this one!" Scott warned.

"So they'll read it!" Winkler disposed of Scott's objection. "Line up the press! Let's have a news conference at the airport. Then from there let's go right to the jail and hold a session with Midge. I'll figure out something appropriate for him to say that we can hand out to the press. See you tomorrow, kid! Early!"

When Scott hung up, Marlene told him that Honey Rosenstone was holding on the other line. She had just left an ADA meeting when she heard the news. Scott was ready to listen to her congratulations and to reply as politely as he had to the endless number of other people. But to Scott's surprise, Honey did not congratulate him.

"Scott? Have you talked to Linc?" she asked instead.

451

"Just hung up."

"Is he coming in?"

"Early plane, at seven-fifteen in the morning."

"Good," she said. "Now, I know you're up to your ears in congratulations. That's not what I'm calling about. I have to give you a message."

"From who?" Scott asked, puzzled.

"Mr. Justice Benjamin Robertson."

"Oh." Scott sounded somewhat tense and expectant.

"I had lunch with him Saturday. He said that after the decision came down, if you wanted to, he'd like to talk to you."

"Sure, I'd like to. I'd love to!"

"Then call him," Honey urged.

"I will. As soon as I take care of some other things first."

"And Scott, if Linc's going to be on the plane all night, he'll want to come right to the house to freshen up and change. So I'll send the car. Gordon'll pick you up at your place at six-fifteen."

"Thanks, Honey. Thanks for everything," he said warmly.

When he hung up Marlene had another call waiting. It was an old law school classmate now practicing in Houston. He was effusive and full of congratulations, and he mentioned that his firm was looking for a new young partner to eventually head up their litigation department. Scott accepted the compliment, but declined the offer. He had other plans of his own.

When Scott hung up, Marlene was holding still another call, but he whispered, "Get me out of it somehow!" She made an excuse and hung up. "Let's get away!" he said, weary from hearing the same things and saying the same things for hours. "Let's go for a walk, or get a drink. Let's do anything but answer that phone. Better still, let's go for a drive."

They said little until he had driven the red Mustang out of Georgetown and onto the highway.

"Well, so you did it!" Marlene finally said. "How does it

452

feel? And don't give me the same canned answer you've been giving everyone else all day." She laughed.

"It feels good," he admitted. "But not as good as it should."

"Because of Robertson's blast at Linc," she concluded.

"He couldn't blast Linc without in some way blasting me. I have to call myself an accessory."

"You only did it for Midge's sake. And now he'll have his new trial," she consoled.

"But this time it will be different," Scott promised.

"From now on a great many things are going to be different." Marlene said it in a way that made him momentarily glance at her. But she was looking away, and he couldn't read her eyes. "Waiting for the decision to come down gave me time to think. I guess you've been thinking, too."

The tenseness in her voice betrayed how extremely important it was for her to say what was on her mind, so Scott didn't answer in words, but just nodded.

"I've thought a lot," she went on, "about us. Sometimes I thought about how wonderful it could be. But other times I thought about how it actually *would* be."

Scott felt impelled to interrupt her, but she didn't give him the chance. "It's one thing when two people are devoted to the same cause, as we've been to Midge. For the moment, what they have in common is stronger than what divides them. But once that's gone, you have a chance to take a good long look at the two people themselves. You have to ask, what do they bring to each other? What do they receive? And what does it cost?"

"Doesn't love play any part in your marital mathematics?" Scott asked sharply, at the same time realizing that it was the first time marriage had come up between them, even though obviously they both had thought about it a great deal.

"Love plays a part," she went on, undeterred, "and sex. And knowing the difference between the two."

"If you're going to call what's between us purely sexual, or

453

put it down as black-white curiosity . . ." Scott said, staring right at her. Then looking back at the road, he continued, "I think you're wrong. I think it could work. We could *make* it work. No matter what happened to your mother, or what your father did, *we could make it work!*"

"Exactly," she agreed in a soft yet disconcerting voice.

"What does that mean?"

"Exactly what you said. Exactly the way you said it. *We could make it work!*" she echoed. "Well, that's precisely what I don't want. I don't want to enter marriage with my teeth clenched and my fists knotted. I don't want to live my whole life on the defensive—trying to prove something. I know too many couples like that. White girl, black boy. White boy, black girl. White Jew, black anything."

"Sometimes it works very well," Scott insisted.

"They concentrate so hard on making it work, they have no time to enjoy it, no time to relax. They're on edge for the rest of their lives—proving they could *make it work*. Marriage is difficult enough when two people make a commitment only to each other. But when they make a commitment to a cause at the same time, they're simply not allowed to fail. Well, lots of marriages fail. People admit it and try to make new lives for themselves.

"But when you marry across the line, you're not free to do that. You've enlisted for the duration—and that's as long as your pride can hold out over every other feeling you have. I can show you a few, if you'd like."

Scott didn't answer.

"When I marry I want my home and my family to be a refuge, a place where I can come after days of fighting for what I believe in and not have to live the cause all over again there. I want a husband and a marriage, not a colleague and a cause. I'll find my causes elsewhere."

Those words made him glance at her.

"Yes," she said, "this case helped me decide what I'm going to do. I'm going to law school. I'll do secretarial work

454

on the night shift in a law firm and go to school during the day. So I . . . I wouldn't even have time for marriage."

The way Marlene said those last words, the strain in her voice, betrayed how difficult it had really been. If she felt so strongly about him, and still had come to this conclusion, then Scott knew there would be no changing her mind. He drove on in silence.

Finally, accepting her decision, he asked, "Will you at least stay on and help me with the new Grove trial?"

Marlene nodded her head yes, turning to look out of the window so he would not see the tears filling her eyes.

Scott dropped Marlene at her place and drove home. Tired, as if he'd played half a dozen games of squash or five sets of tennis, he showered and mixed himself a drink. He flipped on the TV set, wondering how the networks were covering the story of the Supreme Court decision. They wouldn't have much to go on since he had firmly refused to grant interviews. Before the picture came on the screen, he could hear a familiar voice—that of Linc Winkler. And when the picture finally spread across the tube, there he was, glasses up on his forehead, hair wild and unkempt, with many microphones aimed at him—Winkler in his glory.

". . . and I want you boys to know that I have been in contact with my associate in Washington, and he has been in touch with our client. Midge Grove says, 'Much as this new trial means to me, I look on it as a victory for all oppressed peoples everywhere in this nation!' He hopes it is a sign that the time is coming when the power structure as well as the courts will recognize the demands of blacks and other minorities for equal and fair justice."

Scott had contemplated not notifying the press about Linc's arrival in the morning. This display made it definite. No press.

The phone rang. He picked it up and heard his father's voice say, "Scott?"

"Yes, Dad."

"Congratulations!"

"Thanks," Scott said, waiting, for he could always tell when his father had more to say.

"I didn't call earlier because I wanted to read the opinions first. I read both of them, especially Robertson's. I think he made it quite clear, don't you?"

Scott was in no mood to give him any easy tricks. "Made what clear, Dad?"

"He practically said the same thing about Winkler that I did. Remember?" his father asked, as if Scott would ever forget that day he undertook the Grove case.

His father laughed a bit stiffly, "You never thought your square, conservative father and a rebel like Ben Robertson would be on the same side of any question, did you? Well, maybe your old man is right every once in a while."

He laughed again, then turned more serious, "Son, I'm damned proud of your part in this case. It was your brief that did it. All the men around the office feel that way, too. In fact, you might say that's why I'm calling. I've been kidded all afternoon about how I let such a fine piece of legal talent get away from the firm. So I promised to get you back. That's why I'm calling."

Although he pretended his partners had initiated the move, the older man could not disguise his pride in Scott, or his strong personal desire to have him back in the firm.

"There'll be a new trial, Dad. And I'll want to be part of it . . ."

His father interrupted, "We've already discussed that. You continue on the case. We'll make all our facilities available to you. You'll be handling the Grove case as a member of this firm. And we don't give a damn what it costs!"

He'd made his final offer, and now Scott Ingram the Second waited for his son's acceptance.

Scott Ingram the Third weighed his father's words for a

456

long moment, then replied, "Dad, thanks for the offer. But it's going to take a bit of thinking."

"Most of the young lawyers in this country would give their right arms for an offer like this," his father urged.

Scott laughed, "If I run across a one-armed lawyer soon, I'll know the job's been filled."

"Scott," his father pursued urgently.

"Everything's happened so fast, Dad, I need time, time to make plans."

"Okay, son. But promise me you'll think about it."

"I will," Scott agreed.

"And, son, call your mother. Please?"

"Okay, Dad. Sure. I'll call her."

He hung up, feeling the same way he had felt that day in college eight years ago, when he had considered handing in his basketball uniform because it had the number three on the back.

·◦⧉ XXXIII ⧉◦·

The overnight flight from the Coast came out of the dense clouds to make its landing at Dulles. Scott reached the gate just as Linc Winkler appeared. His deeply lined face and his wrinkled shirt gave testimony to a sleepless night spent sitting in the uncomfortable plane seat. His reading glasses were perched high on his head, his open trenchcoat looked even more disheveled and worn than it had ever been. His briefcase bulged.

When he spied Scott, Linc's face lit up. "Scotty!" he called out, rushing toward him. But his eyes kept searching elsewhere. Dropping his briefcase, he shook Scott's hand, embracing him with his free arm.

Then he looked around. "Where are they? What happened?" Linc demanded.

"I decided it was best not to notify the press, Linc."

"Why the hell not? We've got to make the most of this while it's still hot!" Winkler protested. He was reaching for his briefcase, but Scott anticipated him. As they made their way to the baggage area, Winkler again urged contacting the press, but Scott suggested a private meeting of their own first.

Back in the Rosenstone car, they drank hot coffee from the thermos Honey had instructed Aurelia to prepare for the ride back to the city. Winkler erupted in a torrent of plans, strategies, and tactics for exploiting the new trial.

This man is indefatigable, Scott thought, on trial all day in California, giving interviews during his breaks, spending all night on a plane, yet still as ebullient, combative and driving as if he'd just had ten hours of restful sleep.

"Issues, Scotty! We need public issues! So, first thing, you are going to ask for bail for Midge!"

"Bail?" Scott demanded. "In first degree murder?"

"Yes, bail! Since the Angela Davis trial, there's no limitation on bail for *any* defendant!" Winkler insisted.

"You don't really think any judge or court in the District is going to find for us, do you?"

"Of course not! That's how it becomes an issue! Another thing, we are going to move for the right of Midge Grove to hold a full-scale news conference with all the media, including television!"

"Linc . . ." Scott started to interrupt.

"Now that he has been granted a new trial, he's restored to his previous situation. He is a man entitled to the presumption of innocence. And no innocent man should be deprived of his right of free speech."

"That's a little different from a full-scale news conference," Scott argued.

"Access to the news media is as much a part of free speech as the right to give a lecture on a street corner. I've been looking for a case to test that theory. And this is it!"

Scott Ingram did not argue, but leaned back in the comfortable leather seat listening to Linc expound his plans, including the pre-trial publicity and the later courtroom tactics he envisioned.

As they were nearing the house in Georgetown, Winkler said, "Of course, Scotty, you'll have to bear an even greater share of the burden this time. I have the case to finish up in California. That'll take another six or seven weeks. Then I have to appear in Lansing to defend the SDS kid who bombed the physics lab at the university. That judge is getting hot under the collar. He thinks I've put his case too far

459

down on my priority list. So the burden of Midge's new trial will fall on you.

"Of course I'll fly in for any crucial meetings or press appearances. But I'm depending completely on you for the library work and the leg work."

Vaguely, Scott could remember someone saying to Linc Winkler, "You start cases on page one of *The New York Times* and we have to take them up later and win them on page fifty-one." Who said that? He couldn't recall.

When they pulled up in front of the Rosenstone mansion, Honey greeted them, her face fresh and bright with color. She was dressed in a morning coat of Indian sari fabric, reds and golds which complimented her own glowing face and her golden hair. She kissed both Linc and Scott warmly as the butler took their coats and Linc's bulging briefcase. Then with her arm around Linc, she led them toward the library. "I thought a celebration breakfast in this room would be fitting," she said.

Through the open door, Scott could see that the breakfast table arranged before the blazing fireplace had been set for five people.

"I thought on a cold gray morning you'd all enjoy a fire," Honey added.

When they entered the room, Scott realized with a start that Paul Randolph and Marlene were both there. Winkler offered an explanation.

"I called Paul myself last night. I thought he ought to be in on it from the beginning this time. He's been so much a part of the case."

Scott nodded stiffly and shook hands with Randolph. Sensing a sudden tension, Honey quickly rang for the butler, and then began seating everyone around the table.

The butler served Bloody Marys to all, and then offered scrambled eggs, bacon, and croissants and strawberry jam made of tiny *fraises* imported from Paris. The breakfast conversation was limited to casual trivialities. Linc boasted

460

about his successful efforts to entrap the judge in California into reversible errors. And Randolph devoted all his attention to Honey, who seemed cordial but no more encouraging than that. Scott and Marlene said little, and Honey played her usual gracious hostess self.

As soon as breakfast was over, Winkler said, "I think I'd better call Fred Anthony. He'll be steamed if he finds out I came to town and didn't let him know. Then I'll get hold of the networks. We might do better if we actually set up a news conference for Midge *before* we ask for one. When they refuse to allow Midge to meet the news media, then we have them! A denial of Constitutional rights, and the press is right there to cover it! Perfect!" he exulted.

He started toward the desk phone, but Scott blocked his path. "I wouldn't do that, Linc!" he said.

A mixture of shock and anger flooded Winkler's face. It was the first time in their association that the younger man had used so commanding and stringent a tone with him. Honey stopped sipping her coffee, and set her cup down gently, soundlessly. Marlene tensed.

"What do you mean, Scotty, *you* wouldn't do that?" Winkler demanded.

"I wouldn't call in the press. I wouldn't talk to Fred Anthony. I wouldn't go making motions for bail. I wouldn't start arranging interviews with the press. Not until I cleared up one thing."

"And that is?"

"That is, what the hell this trial is all about!"

Winkler glanced at Honey and Randolph, then back to Scott. "Meaning?"

"Meaning ever since you got off that plane, you've spouted a whole series of strategies, plans, and motions. But not one of them has anything to do with defending Midge Grove! You're right back on the old kick of turning this into a political trial. Well, we saw where that got us the last time. A conviction! Murder one!"

461

"What the hell did you expect?" Winkler demanded. "A man assassinates a Justice of the Supreme Court in full sight of witnesses and gets caught. Of course he's going to be convicted. That's why I *entered* this case! Because this man was doomed unless we *did* make a political trial out of it—and it worked. Here we are with a new trial!"

"Which gives us a chance to do what we didn't do the first time," Scott said. "Defend him properly, give him every protection the law allows, and not use him as a political football. Now, if the burden of this new trial *is* going to fall on me, and it will, it's going to be run my way. In the courtroom, where my client's fate is at stake! And not on the courthouse steps.

"I don't intend to meet Fred Anthony for lunch so he can give me publicity. I don't intend to stand out there and showboat for the TV cameras. One other thing I don't intend to do, Linc. *I don't intend to destroy!*"

Without giving Winkler a chance to answer, Scott raced on, "The first time we sat in this room, I didn't realize what you really meant when you explained your approach to the law. My eyes were so blinded by stars that night, dreaming what it would be like to work with the great A. Lincoln Winkler, that I listened but I didn't hear.

"That night I would have said Yes just to get your autograph. So I bought all your theories about how the system had to be shocked into change to ensure justice for all men. Frankfurt! No slums! Remember? And you had to be the gadfly, the radical in order to knock down existing evils. You had to destroy in order to change. And it sounded thrilling.

"But what I didn't hear that night, and didn't miss, was your stand on creating a *new* system. And I haven't heard it yet. Not until I heard your argument before the Supreme Court did I realize that you're only interested in destroying.

"Well, that's where we differ. I'm for changing, but not destroying! And I am for *defending* Midge Grove. Not exploiting him!"

Scott turned on Randolph. "I am for *treating* Midge Grove. Not using him to avenge your personal hatreds! Or as therapy for your own problems. I have my own ideas of what his defense ought to be this time, and while that may *involve* you, Dr. Randolph, it does not *include* you."

Scott challenged Winkler, "Unless you agree with me, we have to part company, Linc. Right here! Right now!"

Winkler stared at Scott, then gave a grudging smile and a bit of a grunt that was part laugh.

"Well, well, well. One victory in the Supreme Court and he's become a big man overnight. He read Robertson's opinion and bought it."

"I've been leaning this way a long time, Linc," Scott said softly. He reached into his pocket and held out a small folded slip of paper. "I wrote this down the day you argued in the Supreme Court."

Winkler unfolded the paper and read aloud: " 'Beware of those who profess to save whole peoples but let individual men die.' " He glared up at Scott.

"A long time, Linc. I just didn't have the guts or the confidence to say it out loud until now."

In an attempt to belittle Scott and assuage his own hurt, Winkler turned to Honey and smiled. "And now he's got the guts!" He turned back to Scott. "Sonny, do you think you're capable enough, experienced enough to carry on a case like this by yourself?"

Defiantly, Scott smiled back and said, "With all the hours I'll save by just making swift entrances and exits from the courthouse I'll have enough time to *become* capable."

Honey stifled her own temptation to smile. Marlene sat up proudly.

"Linc, you can take this case on by yourself and I'll step out. Or I'll continue by myself and you step out. Take your choice."

"You call that a choice?" Winkler said after a moment of consideration. "With my schedule? The cases I have upcoming? I'll be spending most of my time in California. Then months and months in Michigan . . ."

"Whatever you say, Linc," Scott insisted.

"Then I guess I'd better step out."

"Okay," Scott said. "Besides, the cream's off this one as far as the publicity is concerned."

"Not yet," Winkler said, laughing again. "I'll have to hold a press conference to explain why I have to step out and turn this over to my capable young associate."

"Do you want me to be there?" Scott asked.

"It would make it more graceful," Winkler said.

"Okay. Let me know where and when." He started for the door but Winkler stopped him.

"That's all? Just 'Okay, let me know where and when'?" Scott turned back to face him.

"No goodbyes?" Winkler asked. "Nothing to be said to the old man for old times' sake? Is this the way colleagues, comrades, friends part?"

"What do you want me to say, Linc? 'It's been great fun'? Well, it hasn't. You're a user, Linc. You use the young. You use women when they let you, including Honey. And you use men. Midge. Me. Fred Anthony. Randolph. Anyone who crosses your path or serves your purpose.

"And most people *let* themselves be used because you're dynamic, brilliant, a hero. A real folk hero to the kids. You do anything they want you to do, be anything they want you to be, just as long as they give you your fix—their youthful enthusiasm, their young and vibrant bodies to help you forget you're growing old. So you've become the Pied Piper of dissent, and just as irresponsible. As long as they follow you while you're around, you don't give a damn what happens to them when you're gone.

"Linc, I'm not entirely ungrateful. You've taught me a lot —a lot about what I don't ever want to become."

Scott started out of the room, stopping to take his raincoat

464

from the closet. As he opened the door, Honey caught up with him.

"Scott!"

"I'm sorry I brought you into it," Scott said. "But he *does*. He uses your house, your contacts, your guests and friends, but mostly he uses *you*."

"I'm not reproaching you," Honey said. "It's true. He *is* a user. But then there are some of us whose only purpose in life is to be *used*. People like that need each other. I'm not saying it's healthy, but without each other, we're no good."

Scott nodded.

"This doesn't mean that I won't be seeing you again?" she asked.

"No, of course not. I'd miss you, Honey."

"And I'd miss you." She kissed Scott tenderly on the cheek. "You won't forget about Ben Robertson, will you?"

"I had to do this before I could face him," Scott explained.

She nodded, then said, "You will keep in touch, won't you?"

"I'll keep in touch." He kissed her soft, fragrant cheek.

"Did any man ever say to you, 'If only I'd met you at some other point in time, or under different circumstances' . . . ?"

"Practically every nice man I've ever met," Honey said sadly.

Marlene and Randolph left soon after Scott. Randolph offered Marlene a lift, but she declined quite firmly, choosing to take the bus.

Left alone, Winkler said, "I never would have expected that from him. He seemed like such a nice kid."

"Yes," Honey agreed. "And bright, too."

"Bright!" Winkler said disparagingly. "Wait until you see where a routine defense gets him. Grove will get life!"

As he spoke, Winkler reached out to take Honey's hands, to draw her close. She resisted.

465

"He said it all, Linc—for both of us. You are not going to destroy me, reduce me to another Rose. For you, the fountain of youth is youth. I can't play that game, and I'm not even sure I want to."

"What does *that* mean?"

"What you asked me, the answer is no. Because I have to be free to come and go, just as you are. Your vanity wouldn't take that, and mine wouldn't stand for anything else."

Linc seemed to accept her decision. She hoped he did. And now that it was said, Honey felt free to let him kiss her.

The press conference at which Lincoln Winkler publicly turned over the defense of Midge Grove to Scott Ingram was a full-dress session. All three networks were present, as were all the wire services and a score of reporters from the Washington bureaus of important newspapers. Even Fred Anthony put in an appearance.

Despite Scott's harsh words that day at the Rosenstone house, Winkler was more laudatory about his former colleague than he had ever been. Only the pressure of other cases was forcing his unhappy withdrawal from the Grove case at this time, he said. And if he had to withdraw, what a magnificent circumstance that he could entrust Grove's destiny to the hands of so capable a young man. In fact, Winkler joked at his own expense, with young men like Scott Ingram coming into the law, older men like himself might soon be pushed into the shadows.

Scott was only as conciliatory as the situation demanded. When the press pursued him with questions about his future strategy, he simply said that he had not yet had time to consider the possibilities.

Mainly he tried to leave the conference as early as he could, for he had a prior engagement at the home of Justice Ben Robertson, a fact which he did not make known to the press or to anyone else.

When he arrived, Oliver admitted him, taking his hat and

coat and leading him into the library. It was much smaller than the Rosenstone library, but it was a warm room of old leather, glowing antique woods, and the welcoming smell of many finely bound volumes.

The old man was sitting at his desk writing a letter, and he didn't look up until he had finished. Then he lifted his head, smiled at Scott and said, "You wouldn't believe that a Justice of the Supreme Court of the United States has to write letters of complaint about his electric bill, would you?"

He rose, extended his hand in greeting.

"Come," he said, inviting Scott toward the hissing fire. "A cold day. Would you like some tea? Or something a bit stronger? My doctor advises brandy—to stimulate heart action."

"Either one," Scott said.

When they were sitting in comfortable armchairs, holding their brandy snifters, Robertson said, "I am taking this liberty because if this case ever comes up to the Court again, I won't be there."

Scott was about to protest, but Robertson continued, "I don't want false assurances—from you or from my doctor." He set the brandy whirling in his glass, inhaled it, then took a sip.

"Young man, I have read all the papers in the Grove case with considerable care. And I must say it's a rare pleasure to come across legal documents as well drafted, as sound, and as persuasive as those. You're a good brief-man. In a time when most brief-men don't even use proper grammar, you exhibit a flair for language."

"Thank you, sir," Scott said.

"What compels me to have this meeting with you, young man, is that I feel you will make a valuable addition to the bar. And we need that, as desperately as we need able judges, good honest legislators, and executives. The bar has fallen into disrepute, but it is a noble profession if practiced correctly. And without it, free government cannot work. That's especially true in troublesome times—times like these."

467

The old man took another sip of brandy.

"We're under attack. We are being called vile and nasty names. People are mistaking imperfection for repression. But no system is perfect, certainly not a democracy. The job of perfecting it is our daily work—has been mine, and will now be yours. And it is a never-ending job. Each generation makes its contribution, its changes, as does each man, but only if he does so out of decent motives and constructive intentions.

"The slanderers who go round crying 'repression,' 'police state,' who accuse us of not being capable of giving a fair trial to an accused man because his skin is black or his station is low, they are enemies of freedom. Those lawyers—and Winkler is not the only one—who try to turn the courtroom into a Roman circus destroy the sanctity of the law. Every courtroom is a cathedral of justice. What *we* do within it makes the difference. Where would man be today without free courts, judges, lawyers? We have only to look at those nations where courts serve the state instead of the individual to know the answer to that."

Robertson fell silent now. The shadows in the room grew longer and deeper. Oliver came in to see if they wanted more brandy, or if Robertson wanted the lights turned on, but he wanted neither.

When it was almost dark, the old man said suddenly, "You'll be going back to your father's firm, I expect . . ."

"No, sir," Scott said softly but quite firmly. "I've decided to go out on my own. In fact, I've already found space in a small office."

"These days?" Robertson commented, indicating that it might be a questionable move in a time when the trend was to larger and larger firms.

"I've decided to do civil-rights work. It isn't fair to burden any large firm with that. On my own, I can choose the cases I like and handle them the way I think best. I've learned to trust my own judgment, to depend on my own ability in the library and in the courtroom."

468

"And with good reason. I read some of your cross-examination in the record on appeal," Robertson complimented him.

"And one thing more," Scott said, "I no longer want to be known as 'the Third' of anything. I want to be the first of me."

Robertson smiled. Even in the dark his eyes shone brightly. Then he confessed, "You know, when I came East to study law, my chief ambition was to go back home when I was done, open an office, and go into practice for myself. And there was a girl back there I was set on marrying. But I could never raise the fare to come home at year's end. So I had to stay away for all three years, and when I finally went home, she was gone. She had married some other boy and moved away. I think about her often—even now—and I wonder how things would have worked out if I had settled down to practice law in that small town."

Suddenly Robertson put down his brandy glass. He rose slowly and offered his hand to Scott, who rose to shake it. As they stood with hands gripped, Scott spoke.

"I think I know what you expect of me. I'll do my best, sir."

"Good," the old Justice said. "Good."

Scott walked out of the dark room to find Oliver at the door holding his hat and coat. In a quiet voice, the black man said, "It was nice of you to come and visit. We both appreciate it."

Scott nodded, and went down the steps to the quiet street lined with fine old houses.

The rotunda of the Metropolitan jail was alive with the indistinguishable sounds of lawyers and inmates conferring at the numerous small tables. Scott Ingram waited until he spied Midge Grove being led through the door toward him. Then he slipped out of his chair and greeted his small, timid client. They shook hands. Grove looked markedly different now than he had during the trial. Gone the black leather jacket and jeans, gone the black turtleneck sweater and the dark glasses. He had even had the jail barber trim down his Afro. Intentionally or otherwise, Midge Grove was again receding into the state of anonymity that had characterized his entire life.

"Midge . . ." Scott commenced. "You know about the new trial."

Midge nodded.

"It means we start all over again from the beginning, just as if there had been no trial before. But we have a big edge this time. We know their whole case, and we know our own mistakes. They have to repeat what they did before, but we don't have to make the same mistakes . . ."

"Those things come out again?" Midge asked, suddenly tense.

"I want to be honest with you, Midge. It may be necessary. But this time, I'll leave it up to you. If you don't want those things brought up, I'll respect your wishes."

Grove seemed reassured. He nodded thoughtfully.

"Now, there's something else different this time . . ." Scott began. "Linc Winkler is out. What I came to ask you is whether you want me to continue. The final decision is up to you. You can have me, or any other lawyer. Or me *and* another lawyer. You're entitled to a free choice of two lawyers again."

Midge Grove pondered it a time, a long time.

"You make me dress up like a Panther?"

"I'm going to ask you to wear a dark suit in court, with a neat shirt and a tie. I want you to impress the jury favorably. I want them to know what you really looked like before all this happened."

Grove nodded.

"And books?"

"Books?" Scott was puzzled momentarily.

"That newspaperman."

"Anthony? Fred Anthony?"

"He ask me questions about the book I was supposed to

470

write. And I didn't even understand him. Whatever I done, I don't like to be a fool."

"Midge, I want to tell you how I propose to go about it this time. First, you have to understand it's a tough case. On the facts we haven't got a chance. Even on the law, we don't honestly have a strong defense. But I intend to save you," Scott said, "and I think I can. On the ground of your mental condition at the time due to the influence another person had over you. That could mean life in an institution, or maybe a parole a long, long time from now. But that's the best I can honestly promise."

He waited for a response, but Grove only turned away.

"I'll give you every defense the law affords. But you'll have the one thing you always wanted. Dignity. If that's all right with you, I'll represent you."

Midge thought for a while, then nodded his head.

"I have to hear it, Midge."

"I want you to represent me," Midge Grove managed to say.

They shook hands, sealing the understanding between them. Scott got up. One of the guards came toward them to take custody of Midge Grove and lead him back to his cell.

Scott Ingram returned to the small quarters he had sublet close to the Federal Courthouse. Marlene had a desk in the outer office with the secretaries of the other two lawyers in the suite. She was typing furiously when he entered. Scott beckoned her to follow him into his office. She brought her steno pad and a handful of new pencils.

But instead of dictating, Scott picked up his phone and dialed long distance, instructing the operator to make the call person-to-person to Dr. Lee Morrison at the NAACP in New York. They waited silently until the call went through.

"Dr. Morrison? This is Scott Ingram in Washington."

"Yes, the Grove case. I remember you," Morrison replied, sounding a bit impatient.

"I've just assumed sole responsibility for the defense of

471

Midge Grove. Under our practice here, a person accused of murder must have at least two attorneys. So, if you have an attorney whom you would strongly recommend as co-counsel, I would be very happy to consult with him. And if we agree on the theory of the defense, I will urge his appointment by the court," Scott proposed.

"Are you looking for a lawyer or a ringmaster?"

"This isn't going to be another Linc Winkler circus, I can promise you that."

"No, you're probably looking for a nice, impressive black face to sit beside you in the courtroom. Is that it, Mr. Ingram? Some people think our main function here is to operate a casting agency." Morrison was testy and resentful. He did receive many such requests in the course of a week, and he was understandably beyond the point of politeness.

Scott himself grew angry now. "I want someone to take an active part in the defense of Midge Grove!" he insisted, adding sarcastically, "Of course if you have a lawyer who looks like Sidney Poitier, great! Or—why not go all the way—if you have a black *woman* lawyer who looks like Lena Horne, I'll take her!"

Morrison relented and chuckled, "I'll level with you, Ingram. The one lawyer on our staff who happens to be free right now is a white man. So I had to make sure of what you really wanted."

"Well, send him down. What's his name?"

"Pennington. Gil Pennington. You see, I can't even supply you with a Jew. We have days like that here," Morrison said.

"Send him down. We'll do the best we can," Scott Ingram said, chuckling himself by now. He hung up the phone, and turned to look at Marlene.

"Okay?" he asked her.

"Okay," she said. And she went back to her desk and her work.

472